"Let's stay here ᴀ͟ ͟ ͟ ͟ ͟ ͟ ͟ ͟ ͟ ͟ ntly.

She pushed back from his chest and swatted away the open arms he re-offered. "No. I don't want to stay here. I want to walk back." Her door opened and slammed shut before he could protest. The back door flung open.

To get the damn backpack.

He got out of the car. "Leave the backpack," he said sternly.

"I'm not leaving my gear. Anyone can come down this road and break into your car." She tugged the backpack halfway out.

That lit his temper. "No one is going to come down this road. It isn't even on the map. I don't know what possessed Karl to build a summer home in such a God-forsaken place."

Before he could rant further, mostly from embarrassment that he'd run out of gas, he heard the sound of breaking glass.

"Shots! Heads down."

Two more shots pinged the Jeep as he dove to her side of the car. He covered her with his body as three more shots fired. A ping breezed next to his ear.

He flattened her to the ground and jerked his gun from his ankle holster. "Stay low, as low as you can. I want you to run until I tell you to stop," he commanded, then he pointed her westward into the dense field of goldenrod. Wide-eyed she nodded then her sneakers kicked back sand.

He waited until she disappeared between the stalks to fire off a few shots, but stopped, thinking one might ricochet off a rock and hit Cassie. His hand stretched up to the open car door and in one motion, yanked the backpack though the door.

In a dead run, he took off after her.

Praise for Susan St. Thomas...

"Sensual adventures that will satisfy any romantic sweet tooth."

~Nicki Greenwood

Meltdown

by

Susan St. Thomas

Meltdown

Cover Art by *Kim Mendoza*

The Wild Rose Press
PO Box 708
Adams Basin, NY 14410-0706
Visit us at www.thewildrosepress.com

Publishing History
First Crimson Rose Edition, 2008
Print ISBN: 1-60154-523-1

Published in the United States of America

Dedication

For Mom and Dad

Acknowledgement:

There are so many people to thank, starting with the Laptop Dancers: Gwen Bolton, Arlene Wu, and Jennifer Talty. Hugs to all of you for the hours spent making my dream a reality and unforgettable Friday evenings spent brainstorming at the Marx.

And special thanks to my critique partner, Nicki Greenwood, for her start to finish dedication to perfecting Meltdown, and her pep talks when I wanted to trash my manuscript. You're an amazing friend and fellow author.

Thanks to my editors at The Wild Rose Press: Joelle Walker and Ally Robertson for their great suggestions and patience with a newbie, and my publisher, Rhonda Penders, for having faith in me. I'm also indebted to Saturday morning critiques with CNYRW. They always found something positive to say when my writing was atrocious and gently coaxed out the writer in me. I will be forever grateful.

Lastly, I have to thank my kids, Ricky and Erica, for putting up with take-out dinners while I had a moment of inspiration, my mom for encouraging me to dream big, and my sister, Allene, who has always believed in me. Right back at ya, sis!

And one further note, for those of you who believe in karma and magic, on a flight to Reno for an RWA conference to pitch this book, I sat next to a lovely couple who were ringers for Cassie and Evan.

Chapter One

Since kindergarten, Evan Jorgensen pretended to see ghosts, something his friends and family found amusing. Then came the war, and he met the real thing. Actively searching for a ghost meant he'd crossed the line into certifiably insane territory.

Then again, some risks were worth taking.

As he ventured inside Roomer's Night Club, the back of his neck chilled, but he wiped sweat from his brow, a sensation he'd lived with since returning from Iraq ten months earlier. Memories of the last tour clawed at his conscious like an Adirondack black bear defending her young. Anxious to put the war behind him, he resumed his position with the New York State Police specializing in search and rescue training. The current exercise brought him from his home base in Syracuse, New York, to the cool, rugged mountain ranges of Lake Placid, where his trainees practiced weeks of grueling mountain-range rescues. Now with their training completed, his men were ready for a different kind of action and Roomer's was the best place to pick up hot chicks. Having avoided the bar scene since his return from duty, he made tonight an exception and joined his men.

Tonight, he searched for a ghost from his past.

Surveying the crowd, he apologized to the men behind him. "Crowded," he said gruffly, wanting to add, "the unseasonably warm weather brought tons of tourists to view the changing leaves," but his throat constricted.

The trainees shrugged and headed for the bar. After six weeks his men had picked up his habit of minimal talk. Hiding inside four sweltering bombed out stonewalls with the silence broken only by hovering insects made a man talk more to himself. It took him weeks to form sentences in order to discuss his final raid with his commanding officers in Qatar. At least his operation succeeded requiring fewer answers, unlike other groups unfairly scrutinized by superiors or the media.

Hanging behind he slumped into an open chair, his back against the wall with a view of the entire room. Measuring the space he stretched out his legs marking his territory. An overhead speaker cranked music so loud it thumped uncomfortably in his gut—the only part of his insides that could beat—but he held his position. A stream of people entered, their whispering voices mimicking static discharge in the air. A deep breath shuddered out of him. Feigning normalcy he scoped the room.

He began by counting heads of his men until all were accounted for. One of his young trainees made a move on a sexy brunette. She laughed at something he said and tapped his chin, toying with him. After she'd teased him good she wandered away. The guy trailed behind her like an obedient leashed puppy. *Aams knows all about mountain rescues, but is green about women,* he thought. The way they could tie up your insides tighter than a tourniquet or leave you to bleed out until nothing human remained inside.

All but one woman.

The one he thought he'd seen on the summit of Mount Jo this morning.

'Course, it couldn't have been her. She'd made a new life for herself in California. A hallucination probably from heatstroke must have caused him to envision her checking the view from Lake Placid's smallest mountain's summit. Mirage or hallucination, another *habit* leftover from the war but one he never wanted to change. Dreaming about touching her all over kept him sane on those black, bone-chilling desert nights. Imagining her drifting across the hot desert sands saved him from running into a Taliban patrol. While burning with fever on the longest day of his life, the memory of her touch brought him out of his delirium.

If she were in Lake Placid she'd check out her favorite hangout.

"Did you see that?" someone barked from the bar.

A row of guys, mostly his men, swiveled on their barstools to gawk at a petite redhead in a short skirt approaching the pool table. The woman jiggled her breasts to emphasize she was braless. Rolling his eyes Evan turned to talk to his top young trainee, Tony Garibaldi, who held a draft beer to his open mouth and stared slack-jawed. After a slap on the back of the head, Tony unfroze and pointed. "What? The chick's advertising, Ev."

He humored Tony and assessed the action at the pool table.

Tapping a long dark fingernail on the end of the pool stick, she circled the balls on the table, ready to spring into action at her command. Meanwhile guys were adding quarters to the rail stacking a pile higher than Whiteface Mountain. There was a time when he'd have been the first in line to teach her how to play pocket-ball. Nowadays, feeling every one of his thirty-three years multiplied by two, he'd rather be settled in front of a banked cabin-fire finishing Dean Koontz's latest thriller. Deciding her shot and satisfied every guy was watching, she bent over the table.

As he expected, she'd gone commando.

Tony groaned and turned to Evan. "Jeez. Ya know it wouldn't kill ya to smile. We've been dragging hundred-pound dummies across these mountains for weeks. About time we had some fun."

"You don't call rappelling one-hundred feet fun?" Evan paused to tip the waitress for his beer.

"Falling down mountainsides is your kinda fun, not mine. You nearly killed us on Wolf's Head Pass. I can barely lift up my arms after yesterday's final drill."

Tony had no problem lifting his arm and slapping Evan on his sore shoulder. Evan bit back a yelp and fought the urge to rub out the pain.

"I can't wait to get back to Syracuse where insects the size of pinheads aren't trying to eat me to the bone," Tony added, still eyeing the redhead.

Evan slouched further into his chair before answering. "A hundred pounds is nothing. Wait until you get a hundred-and-eighty pound hiker." *Or have to carry a fellow wounded soldier miles for help… that kid was barely out of high school.*

The kid's distorted face still haunted his dreams.

He heard whistles. The horny redhead had leaned over the table for another shot. Moans from the spectators—especially Tony—followed, but Evan ignored them and closed his eyes, yearning to forget the pain of war. The image of another woman appeared, one with green eyes matching the color of Adirondack ferns lining every forest trail and hair as yellow as the delicate mountain butterflies that played tag between them. Recalling her sultry tone and vibrant laugh soothed his soul after a long day eating powdered sand in temperatures hotter than a blast furnace. He'd replayed her voice so many times he imagined conversations with her.

For three years he'd fought for his life, waiting for the day he'd see her again.

Hear her say his name.

Touch her soft skin.

Feel her body shudder beneath his.

One ambush and an IED changed everything.

Easy, he told himself. Bitterness never had been part of his code. He ordered his shoulders to relax, lessening some of the twisting pain. A restless trigger finger absently scratched off his beer label. The other hand twitched, lost without a rifle belly to hold.

Quiet times meant trouble.

The enemy seemed psychic, knowing the exact moment you let down your guard.

Sitting up straighter he rescanned the room. More and more people crammed into the long rectangular room. The barroom chatter amped to a persistent hum.

Some of his men were missing.

Holding his breath, he strained to hear footsteps scuffing over stones.

He dampened the roar of blood rushing in his ears and listened for the sound of commands in Arabic.

He listened.

And waited.

The back of his shirt felt damp and perspiration clung to his forehead. Heat poured off his face and settled around his neck like a noose. He heard the ping of a rifle shot. He fought the urge to throw up as his finger squeezed a phantom trigger. Black and white spots exploded before his eyes. He gulped air until his vision cleared and then glanced around the room. Fortunately no one stared at him. An overturned beer bottle spun on the table. His lips were parched but no beverage would quench this thirst.

Months ago these bouts ceased, at least in public. Alone at night, he lay awake.

Remembering.

He'd been in the mountain too long. He'd feel better once he was back in Syracuse where the city's populated terrain didn't remind him of combat. He righted the beer bottle. Peeled silver pieces from the label floated on a puddle of spilled beer, winking like a cache of diamonds ready to set in an engagement ring. On the bottle, the remaining label resembled a jagged silver heart.

Yeah, he needed to get out of Lake Placid.

Shrill whistles and chuckles all around him brought him back to the present. The redhead retrieved the cue ball from a nearby garbage pail and queerly eyed Tony. Leaning on his pool stick, Tony hunched his shoulders in obvious embarrassment.

"Good shot, man," one of the other trainees shouted to Tony.

Unused muscles tugged the corners of Evan's mouth but a smile never formed. His hands still shook. Restless eyes continued their inspection of the smoke fogged area stuffed with people who were certain of what continent they were on.

No sign of his ghost. Time to call it a night.

He stood, ready to leave until his gaze snagged on a pair of long, tanned legs moving across the dance floor. Shapely with the right amount of muscle tone in the calves and thighs, they were the perfect length to wrap around a man's waist.

He absently scratched the back of his hand.

"Got an itch? This place is filled with beautiful women, Ev. Pick one." Tony returned for his abandoned beer, all smiles for someone who lost a pool game to a girl. "I'm out. Want another brew?"

Evan pulled a bill from his wallet but his gaze never left the legs. They swayed and turned as if she modeled for him.

Other females out prowling tonight wore either high heels or some trendy boot. Not her. Flip-flops. He smiled to himself.

When the legs stopped moving, his eyes traveled up their length to a tiny waist and generous breasts. He paused to look his fill. She uncrossed her arms. Her hands fisted at her sides. Frustrated about something? He'd cataloged other details—the color of her top, length of her skirt, lack of jewelry or watch.

Attention to details kept him and his men alive more than once.

A tingly sensation raced up his arms. His teeth grated together. Metal blades overhead chased after each other and slowly raised the veil of haze, revealing her form.

He knew that lithesome body—memorized it upon first sight.

She looked in his direction.

Another dream? Or was he lying in some Iraqi prison awaiting torture, or strapped to a gurney in hospital left for dead?

When those gorgeous eyes widened in recognition, a fist of lust punched him squarely in the gut.

Cassie.

Sparks from her eyes torched the air between them.

Angry? Because she still cared?

God, he hoped so.

He stood up, feeling a pull stronger than any whitewater current but his feet were immovable like he'd sunk in quicksand. Prickles roamed his arms in warning, partly because four years ago after her divorce, he convinced himself she'd be happier if he kept his distance. The war had started. As an officer in the National Guard he'd be re-commissioned to Iraq.

All that he yearned to tell her no longer mattered. Odds favored he'd return in a flag-draped coffin.

He had nothing to offer her.

But she came to him the night before deployment, full of fears, arguing he'd gone crazy, ordering him to be safe.

Wanting to make love.

For once, he had a reason for living.

After two tours he returned to Syracuse and learned she'd gone to L.A. to sell real estate. Maybe become a movie star. She didn't resemble a starlet in those flip-flops unless the word stretched across her T-shirt, *Juicy,* advertised a movie. His scratchy skin intensified. Hopefully, he still packed Benadryl in the first-aid kit.

So, what brought her to Lake Placid?

Engrossed in a conversation with another woman, Cassie paused to glance his way again.

His skin burned like toast.

Damn. He wiped his brows and cleared the itch from his throat. The walls of the room shrank the longer he stared at her. Soon, the darkness would arrive.

Time to greet his ghost.

Before he could step in Cassie's direction, the horny redhead hit on him. A full-body attack. She pressed her fake breasts up against him, rubbed his forearms, squeezed his biceps like she owned him. Whispered the usual in his ear. She smelled lemony, like furniture polish, but he didn't have the heart to turn her down in front of a bar full of guys, so he put her number in his wallet to toss away later.

Tony charged through the crowd. Evan expected him to ask for the redhead's number. Instead, Tony gawked at Cassie. "Hey, will you look at that? Where'd she come from? I saw her on Mount Jo today. She's hot!" Tony's voice went up an octave.

Evan shrugged, trying to act cool while burning at the stake. The same intense heat he'd experienced this morning on Mount Jo. Reaching the summit, his eyes flitted across a familiar scene—treetops like wads of orange and yellow paper carelessly thrown on a carpet of forest green, purple mountain ranges framing the colors, and that peculiar little lake.

Heart Lake.

Compared to the grandeur of Lake Champlain, the little misshaped puddle of water received more attention. People looked for romance in the oddest places. Cassie's image appeared in a beam of sunlight, more mirage than real.

Tony wolf-whistled. "I got some great pictures of her this morning. Ya think she's a supermodel? Picture *her* in a teddy."

He stepped in front of Tony.

Undaunted, Tony craned his neck. "Here's your brew, Ev. See ya tomorrow."

Biting back a growl, Evan clamped a hand on Tony's shoulder. "Wait."

Tony's head snapped around. With lips pursed to whistle again, Tony's puzzled squint looked comical.

"Listen, I know her." Evan grimaced as he spoke the next words. "She's Jake's ex."

"Great. Gimme an intro, then get lost," Tony replied.

"She's not like that."

Tony's smile read like a Vegas ad. Arguing with Tony never worked.

No matter. Cassie could handle Tony.

****

After finding every stray tree root and slippery stone hiking up Mount Jo this morning, maneuvering through the crowded bar worsened Cassie Hamilton's sore ankle. "I think I'll head back to the motel room," she said to her best friend, Karen Walters.

"Relax. I've been watching three kids and their friends twenty-four seven and I deserve a little fun. I may not go back to the motel until sunup," proclaimed Karen. She flashed a huge, toothy smile while munching on a lime twist.

Pains pinched Cassie's chest. It hurt to hear Karen talk about her three children. She swallowed a groan and forced her voice to sound neutral. "You can stay and have fun. I have to get off this ankle."

Karen tilted her head and studied Cassie over the rim of the glass. "If you'd stop pacing it wouldn't hurt so much. What are you so nervous about?"

Cassie stopped. She'd been jittery all week but purposely neglected to tell Karen. At work, her spine felt tingly, like something possessed it. She couldn't shake the creepy feeling of being watched even while hiking up Mount Jo. Certain someone watched her now, she checked around the room. "I'm not nervous. I don't know how you talked me into climbing a mountain to view turning leaves I can see in my own backyard," she declared while shifting to hide behind Karen.

Karen set her drink on a table. "It's the smallest mountain in Lake Placid, only two-thousand feet. The view at the top was breathtaking today, wasn't it?" As Karen sighed, she eyed a row of guys standing at the bar. One waved to her. She giggled and waved back.

"Remember, you're happily married," she said. An unnecessary warning. Unlike hers, Karen's marriage possessed that rare chemistry that would last forever.

"I'm just having a little fun. You're the one who is free to do more than flirt. Take your pick. A lot of mountain men are here, like my Karl. They make the best husbands."

Karen's wink made Cassie more anxious. "I don't want a mountain man or any man right now."

Karen rolled her eyes, linked their elbows. "There's a bunch of cute guys at the bar claiming they're here for rescue training. We can get them to buy us drinks. You can tell them about your shop and make them drool with talk of your sinfully sweet chocolates."

"No," she said, and dug her flip-flops into the floor, abruptly halting both of them.

Karen's forehead folded with concern. "No harm in talking, sweetie. Call it drumming up business."

Business. Although she'd enjoyed seeing Lake Placid in the fall, Cassie regretted closing her shop for the getaway weekend. If it weren't for the catering contract with the large deposit, she'd never have accepted Karen's offer to escape her troubles for one weekend.

"I'd rather go back to the room, where it's safe." She tried to march around Karen, but her flip-flops found a sticky spot on the floor preventing a quick retreat.

"Safe? What are you afraid of? There may be some worry lines around your eyes, sweetie, but you still look eighteen." Worry lines formed brackets around Karen's mouth. Karen had been the only person she could turn to when she'd returned from L.A.

"I feel eighty after Mount Jo," she joked, trying to ease Karen's alarm. No matter how traditional, she wished she ignored Karen's suggestion of a quick drink at Roomer's after dinner. These days when not experimenting on a new chocolate recipe, her favorite way to spend an evening was soaking in a scented-oil bath. Lord knew her sore ankle needed soaking badly.

Cassie unlinked their arms. "I'm heading back." Rummaging through her purse for her room key, her knuckles scraped the edge of her photo key chain. Fingers hugged the rectangular plastic but offered little comfort. What was Heather doing now? Maybe playing with S'mores, her new calico kitten? Or being read one of the dozens of Eric Carle's books she'd bought her.

"Suit yourself." Karen lifted her hands to shoo her away then stopped mid-wave. "OMG!" Karen's eyes popped out of her head.

Cassie looked over her shoulder. "What? What is it?" Turning too quickly on her bad ankle shot pains up her leg. She bit back a groan.

"Over there. By the pool table. I think I see Evan." Karen pointed to a beacon of light through the smoky haze.

A large figure rose from his chair. "Evan Jorgenson?" She whispered. With that telltale gilded blond hair and height, it could be him.

"You remember Evan!" Karen exclaimed. "I wonder what he's doing here?"

Cassie peeked again. *Evan.* He stared boldly at her. Her traitorous heart skipped a few beats, the way it always did when he stared at her.

He looked great, unmarred by the war.

Thank you, God.

Shamefully after four years she still wanted to run to him. When she'd closed her eyes at night she'd easily summoned his face. Butterflies danced in her stomach every time she thought about him touching her intimately. Imagining dragons swallowing those butterflies helped get her through those long, lonely nights in L.A. and eventually dried her tears.

Without her dragons, she turned away. "I don't see him."

Karen swung her head from side-to-side trying

to see around, then gave up and nudged her gently aside. A huge, satisfied smile formed on her face. "Oh yeah. It's him. Wow. They don't make 'em like that anymore."

"Yeah. It's him," she admitted, peering over her shoulder.

God, he looked so good.

Where are those lizards?

"He's staring at you." Karen still whispered like they were in front of their high school lockers, sharing secrets. "Why don't you go over and say hi?"

Soon as a dragon or two wakes up, she wanted to reply. Like an unquenchable thirst she drank in the sight of him. By now she'd expected to run into him in Syracuse. Jake would've told him she was back. Deciding to make the first move, she took a step in his direction. A barely dressed redhead intercepted him.

Pain stabbed her chest so hard she trembled from the force. Her hands fisted. "He looks busy. Besides, he's a player."

Karen pinched her arm. "So, go play. Don't hate the player."

"Get whatever you're thinking out of your mind," Cassie growled. She rubbed the pinch, although it didn't hurt.

Karen stared at her until she squirmed. "Divorced doesn't mean you're dead, honey."

"Karen—"

"You can't pass up this opportunity. Wasn't he always nice to you?"

This time Karen cuffed her on the backside in Evan's direction. She'd never confided to Karen her momentary lapse of reason. Some secrets were better off not shared with a best friend. Luckily, her flip-flops permanently fused her to the sticky floor.

The bimbo still engaged Evan, smoothing her hands all over his muscular chest as she talked.

Cassie knew how his chest looked under his shirt, muscular and tanned with soft golden hair, a shade darker than on his head. She knew his legs and taut abs, and the feel of those strong arms clutching her as if the world were ending.

A breath hitched and burned in the back of her throat. Her eyes welled with tears she'd never shed.

No word in four years.

Overhead, a ventilation unit roared to life. It sucked up the air surrounding her. She feigned a cough in order to wipe the beads of moisture from above her lip and pathetically continued to watch. Evan's hands stayed in his pockets as he grinned at something the bimbo said. Her fake breasts jiggled across his chest and stubby hands clung to his biceps like she had the right. Then on tiptoes the skank whispered something in his ear and handed him a piece of paper.

Cassie's breath tasted hot, and she felt a bit seasick. "Did you see that? Probably shoving her phone number in his wallet," she remarked to Karen between her heated lips.

To his credit, Evan remained statue-still.

"Oh, what do you care? Once he sees you he'll forget all about that slut," said Karen.

"Evan's the last person I'd encourage. I'm not going to be a number on someone's list."

The lie set her cheeks on fire.

"I'd kill to be on his list if I weren't already married to the greatest husband in the world." Karen looked regretful as she retrieved her purse and jacket.

"Where are you going?"

Karen continued walking. "To the bar to get a drink. I see Aaron and Gayle Lucas waving. You're on your own, sweetie. I'll see you later...much later."

"Wait!" Cassie yelped.

She tried to follow but only one flip-flop snapped

off the floor. The other seemed nailed. She pivoted around on her good foot. Halfway across the room the crowd shifted and Evan disappeared. She sighed, feeling a moment of relief.

Until he broke free.

Dark eyes sharper than any laser-sight found and marked her.

A tingle of excitement neutralized the seasick feeling. Thankfully, Karen encountered him next, buying her time to calm down. He grinned at something Karen said. Not about her. Karen knew how to play it cool. She even made Evan whisper something in her ear. She'd be bragging later.

Cassie glanced at the muck around her feet and remembered what she wore. Why did she let Karen talk her into this horrible outfit? Instead of her comfy shorts and loose cotton top, the *Juicy* purple T-shirt was too tight, and the faded-denim skirt with the tacky sequined belt, too short. Karen insisted she looked great. Hardly. Cassie drew the line at the sexy heels Karen offered. The blue flip-flops stayed.

Evan's gaze never left her as he chatted with Karen. The way he always looked at her. Intense. What she'd mistakenly interpreted as something more than lust.

All my letters returned unopened.

At last the muck turned slippery and she managed to shift from the spot. She tried a few steps. *Ouch!* A nearby barstool took pressure off her throbbing ankle. She wished she had some aspirin in her purse. Behind her someone giggled. It sounded like Heather's laugh. Tears pinched the backs of her eyes. *Have to get out of here.* She tested the ankle, but it ached so much she doubted it would hold her weight. The pain was nothing compared to the perpetual one in her heart.

The young girl laughed again.

When was the last time she'd laughed so boldly

or smiled so easily?

Evan rarely smiled but from the distance she felt the heat of his stare. The first time he gave her a sexy half-smile it felt like she'd spent hours in the sun. She used to pity the poor women who tried to resist his unforced charm.

She shut her eyes to catch her breath. *One step at a time.*

Karen scooted aside. Evan resumed his march. Someone trailed him, a dark-haired man at least a head shorter, deeply tanned, with shoulders almost as wide as Evan's.

Evan's gaze never left his target. At least the chill up her spine disappeared.

Swinging her hair over her shoulder, she exhaled through her nose and then licked her lips. The absence of letters or phone calls from Iraq reminded her the night four years ago meant little more than a hook-up.

He probably never thought of her again.

Schooling her face she thought of frozen chocolate Haagen-Dazs.

She could handle Evan Jorgenson.

****

Evan stopped when close enough to see the ring of amber fire in those unforgettable green eyes. He covered his mouth to hide the breath he sucked in. For so long he imagined her, wearing swimsuits, teddies, even in jeans and T-shirt, but mostly naked. No memory or fantasy matched the flesh and blood woman. He wanted to grab her and kiss her senseless. Instead, he tucked his hands in his pockets.

"What brings you here?" he said, relieved he got the words out before his breath caught. He waited for her to vanish into thin air.

"The Flaming Leaves Festival," she stated flatly.

Chilly welcome, but at least she still looked him

in the eyes. One slender eyebrow lifted, impatient for his reply.

"All the way from L.A.?"

Her arms crossed over her breasts. "No. From Syracuse. I've moved back."

"Why'd you leave L.A.? Too much sun, or stars?"

"Neither." Her eyes blazed like twin green torches.

While he struggled for a charming comment someone bumped into her causing her elbows to poke his chest. The hit ricocheted to the balls of his feet.

Definitely not a ghost. Say something. "Working or taking it easy?" he said, wishing he owned an ounce of charm.

"Working."

"Your old job?"

"No."

"Something new?"

"Yes."

Christ, he sounded like an interrogator. Six weeks barking orders at his recruits hadn't help. Plus, he tiptoed around a minefield of emotions. Sweat trickled down his back as if the situation were reversed.

Some communication expert. Never had this much trouble talking to suspects. Or terrorists.

Why didn't he pump Karen for information? Everything about her, from board-straight posture to clipped speech and fiery gaze said she was angry and with good reason. When he arrived in Baghdad he learned his covert mission prevented contact of any sort including Clay, the only family he had left. Orders prohibited even a message explaining there would be no communication of any sort. But on the worse day of his life, he was allowed to compose a letter to her.

By the frosty reception, she never received it.

Now wasn't the time to go into it.

Switch to a safer topic. "So, how's Heather?"

"Heather's as good as she's always been."

Did she wince? The corners of her mouth trembled like she wanted to add more, but what? And were those sparks in her eyes really tears?

Her reply hung in the room's stagnant air. He wanted to question her further but something warned him not to go there. He searched her face for an answer and came up empty. "Glad to hear that."

She swallowed and swiped the corner of her eye before looking away. He didn't know how to respond. He wanted so badly to hold her, but set his hands on his hips and drank in her profile.

Tony's breath scalded his neck. A well-aimed elbow in his ribs forced Evan to grunt out an intro. "Ahh...Cassie, this is a buddy, Tony Garibaldi."

At the mention of his name, Tony slithered in front of Evan. "Nice to meet you, Cassie. Are you familiar with the MRT program?"

Her head tilted. "I'm not sure. Are you a doctor?"

Yeah right, Evan thought. He couldn't stop another grunt from escaping. Besides sweating profusely his pulse raced like some middle school adolescent in puberty and his skin itched. It was like he caught the "Cassie-flu" whenever she was near.

"No. MRT stands for Mobile Response Team. I finished my training here this week. I work for Ev's Syracuse Unit."

"Oh. Congratulations, then."

He envied the small, shy smile she gave Tony, who danced from foot to foot, explaining something about MRT and trying to "impress to undress." Cassie nodded politely, encouraging Tony to ramble. It was his opportunity to check her out.

She looked twenty, but he knew she was about thirty. Tanned, probably from some California beach, definitely too golden-brown to come from a bottle. It looked real good on her, too. He wondered if she sunbathed naked.

She once wore lots of gold necklaces, bracelets and rings, like some kind of Egyptian princess. No jewelry or rings on her fingers. Her blonde hair still cascaded in a thick waterfall to her waist. He always liked her hair that way best, a silken cape ready to unveil the lady's charms. She looked thinner than he remembered, dropped about twenty pounds on an already great body. *Probably an L.A. requirement. Diet to the point of anorexia.*

She crossed her arms under her *Juicy* breasts, nodding at something Tony said.

He definitely recalled her breasts being larger.

As Tony rambled she raised a hand to push back her bangs and snuck a glance his way. Her vibrant eyes torpedoed him right in the area where his heart used to be, still having the power to paralyze a man. Full-lashed and exotic they were the kind of eyes you could stare at for a lifetime and never grow tired of their beauty.

He wanted to join the conversation but the way his skin itched he was certain he'd sprouted hives. "Good seeing you. I've gotta go," he said and stepped back.

Without waiting for a reply he angled his shoulders through the crowd. Outside, he let out a big *phew* and then took several breaths of the crisp, fall-scented air. After all this time, he still appreciated he no longer breathed air permeated with powdered sand. The first sign he'd made it home. The next sign, hot food and showers and no bullets whizzing by his ears.

One by one his muscles uncoiled but the itchy skin persisted.

Damn. Still condemned to the same old itch.

He looked at the closed door and then at blinking neon signs in the window. A yellow palm tree centered on a green island swayed back and forth advertising Imported beer. A blue mountain range blinked on another sign. There was a time when all he cared about was hiking these mountains and drinking drafts with Clay.

Before the war.

Before the accident.

Before his life changed forever.

The bar door crashed open. A couple came out hand-in-hand, eyes only for each other and brushed past him.

He stood still for a minute listening to the laughter of the girl until it was silenced by her lover's kiss.

He remembered Cassie's last kiss. The best kiss of his life.

Tattooed on his heart.

He had to talk to her. One of the coffee shops in town stayed open all night. Over coffee they could discuss what happened that night. How a kiss goodbye led to more. How one night forever etched in his mind comforted him when all seemed lost. *Tell her about the letter.* If he thanked her face to face for giving him a memory that kept him sane, maybe it would be easier to say goodbye, again.

She deserved more than a shell-shocked soldier.

Relieved to have a plan, he yanked open the door. A woman was trying to exit as he tried entering. Her hands grasped air. Before tumbling backward down the stairs he caught her around the waist. "Didn't see you coming. You okay?"

The face looking up at him was two shades of red, but he'd know those eyes in the darkest cave.

Cassie was in his arms, and looked relieved.

His grasp tightened until he molded to every part of her body. *Still fits like she was made for me.* He bit back a curse.

"Evan? Ah, thanks."

He focused on those kissable lips and squeezed

her closer.

One kiss...to make certain she's real.

She cleared her throat. "You can let go. I've got my footing."

On cue, he looked down her long legs to her perfect toes exposed by the sexiest pair of blue flip-flops. At his downward gaze, she maneuvered away. His arms instantly cooled. "Leaving? I thought you were talking to Tony."

She nodded. "Talked me into canoeing on Mirror Lake tomorrow. I thought I'd turn in early. Get a good night's sleep." She cleared her throat and took an awkward step as if testing her chance at a clean getaway.

"Alone?" She gave him a petulant look, and he expounded. "You can't walk around the streets this time of night by yourself."

Nearly knocked off his feet when she not only smiled, but also let out the sweetest sounding laugh, he barely registered her reply. "I don't have far to walk. My motel is a few blocks away. Goodnight, Evan."

He blocked the sidewalk. "You sure? Think of all the sex offenders running around."

She scowled at him like he was the FBI's Most Wanted.

No time for charm. He decided to be honest. "There's a coffee shop down the street. It's a quiet place to talk."

She held up both hands. "What's there to talk about? I'm glad to see you made it home safely. Truly." She hesitated, biting her lower lip. "But I'm tired."

She pushed past him. His chest tingled where her palms made contact. Swaying as she walked away made other parts of him come to attention.

You're not going anywhere without me, Mrs. Hamilton.

If she didn't want to talk tonight, fine, but he'd escort her to her motel room.

And not go inside, even if it killed him.

Unless invited.

Chapter Two

Cassie turned as gracefully as someone could in flip-flops with an aching ankle and heavy heart, and headed down the pumpkin-colored cobblestone sidewalk, away from Evan.

Two steps brought him to her side. He shoved his hands in his pocket. "I'm walking you to your room." The grim line of his mustached mouth told her there was no other option. She hoped he didn't ask any more questions about Heather or L.A. Or the night she threw herself at him. The last thing she wanted to do was discuss the past. Even worse, cry.

She shrugged. Maybe she needed an escort. His shadow cast from the lamplights was twice hers. Normally she could run if she sensed someone followed. Although the creepy feeling of being watched had disappeared, what if it came back? What if someone were following her? Besides, she could act like nothing happened between them, too.

They walked in silence. She winced as she tried to match his strides. He slowed and allowed her to lead the way. A light breeze stirred the hair around her face. She glanced at him under a swath of hair.

He looked the same. No. Better.

Taller and more muscular than she'd remembered. When his arm rose to scratch the back of his neck, biceps strained against his shirt, muscles packed with power ready to rescue at a moment's notice. Or hold someone tightly like a minute ago. Or tenderly while making love.

Her purse fanned her hot face. Feeling suffocated, she inhaled the clean mountain air. Bad idea. His smell assaulted her...a mixture of something earthy and dark, and dangerously male. Wearing a dark chambray shirt and well-worn jeans, he moved easily, confidently. She knew how quickly his easygoing mood could explode into passion.

If Evan were on a poster for bad boys, he would be a sell-out.

They were such polar opposites.

Quiet or brooding, worried about someone or something happening at work, Sergeant Jorgenson always appeared on duty, ready to save the day. Chatty, carefree and caring only about two other people in the entire world, she'd ignored the trumpets in her head announcing his arrival at her home and the butterflies that danced in her stomach whenever he commented about his day. According to her ex-husband, Evan was the ultimate player. Newly divorced and with her eyes wide open she walked into Evan's apartment the night before his deployment, intending to talk him out of leaving for war. Fear turned to passion, and the most incredible night of her life occurred.

Despite the comfortable Indian-summer night she began to shiver. Hopefully super-cop didn't notice. He might do something stupid, like give her his shirt.

"So how was L.A.?" he asked.

Not expecting the direct question, she stumbled, twisting her flip-flop under her foot. The sidewalk rose to meet her face. Large hands stopped the fall, and then righted her.

"You okay?"

"I'm a little sore from today's hike." Her ankle burned, and she gingerly stepped.

He nodded respectfully. She remembered that about him. Always polite. At the moment, it was nerve wracking.

"About California?" he prodded further.

"You know what they say, it never rains in California, it pours."

She looked at him under her lashes. Did he detect the discomfort in her voice?

Again, he nodded as if he knew what she was talking about.

Of course, he knew. Jake probably filled him in on all the painful facts about L.A. Another bolt of pain shot up her leg when she slipped up and stepped normally. She bit her tongue to keep from yelling with frustration.

Evan stopped and looked at her foot. "Are you hurt?"

The concern on his face softened the granite, emotionless visage she remembered as Evan's normal face. Part scowl, part Rodin's, *The Thinker*. The comma-shaped white scar on his chin added to the enigma. Thankfully, there were no new marks.

"No."

She'd stepped again, and moaned.

He pointed in the opposite direction. "My Jeep's in the parking lot."

Momentarily forgetting her anger with him, she flirted. "Or you can carry me, since you're playing at being galant."

Something hard struck the back of her legs. Were they being mugged? Instead of falling, her body came to rest next to a warm, deliciously scented wall. When her head stopped spinning, she looked up and saw the blond stubble on Evan's cheek.

She sighed. *Back in Evan's arms.*

"You should have told me you were hurt. Your ankle needs tending. Do you have a first aid kit with you?"

Nestled in his arms like a lover's caress registered in every nerve as he took efficient strides down the street. She was joking about his carrying her, then recalled how quickly he'd dumped her with Tony and stiffened in his embrace. "Back at the room."

"Where to?"

He stopped at the end of the street. The faint green glow of the traffic light cast a shadow on half his face, imposing the image of a comic book superhero across his features.

"The Wood Lake Inn," she replied and pointed ahead.

The long strides resumed. Somewhere in the second block, she raised her arms around his neck for safety, she told herself. But it wasn't necessary. Evan carried her as effortlessly as if she were a down pillow. She dropped her arms to his well-rounded shoulders and took a long look.

She never dreamed she'd see him again, and now he carried her. He was so handsome, in a rugged, outdoorsman way. He'd grown a thick blondish-brown mustache suited to his cowboy looks. He dressed casually, like he modeled clothes for J. Crew for a living instead of being a New York State Police Officer. And a decorated soldier. She'd been furious four years ago when Jake phoned and reported Evan was hours away from leaving for Iraq. Always the hero. That terrified her. Evan could die playing the hero.

She'd rushed over to his apartment. Seeing him packed when she went to wish him Godspeed opened some door she never realized existed. Newly divorced, her emotions were all over the place for weeks. She shocked herself by kissing him. She wanted only to comfort him and let him know someone cared. When he kissed her back, something broke inside her. He'd held her so tenderly, supporting her in his hands. Then the kiss changed, and he attacked her lips until they felt permanently altered. Before she knew it, her clothes were slipping off. They spent his last hours making the sweetest love.

When news came he'd made it back in one piece her prayers were answered. This time she'd cried tears of joy.

Now after four years and no communication, not one letter or phone call, she thought she'd forgotten him. Not true. Every nerve in her body remembered his touch.

Only, she'd been the one to change, and for the worse.

She needed a diversion. "Tony mentioned you're the head of his State Police unit, specializing in search and rescue. Are you happy with the job?"

Occasionally light from street lamps pooled, breaking up the darkness in the deserted streets enough to see his tantalizing eyes. A long time ago she decided they were the rich color of Godiva chocolate.

He looked down at her again.

Her mouth watered.

"I'm usually behind a desk, mostly PR." He looked over his shoulder to see if there was any traffic before crossing the street. Even checked twice.

"Sounds like a great job. I'm happy for you."

In answer, he stared at her lips again.

He'd changed, so quiet and serious. Still, a lot could happen in four years. Maybe he'd met someone and settled down. Maybe *that* was why he wanted to talk.

"Are you married, Evan?"

A sterner face turned from the traffic and studied her again. He still wore a grimace, but his lips moved. "I'm not wearing a ring."

"Not all married men wear rings."

He stopped once they were safely across the street. Held her so close his minty breath fanned her face. "When I marry, I'll wear a ring."

She nearly jumped out of his arms when a car full of teenagers blew by and blasted their car horn. He didn't flinch at the noise, rather held her tighter.

Battling good sense and curiosity, she asked one more question. "Then a girlfriend?"

His gaze stole her breath, singed her cheeks. He jostled her a little, and continued walking. "There's been no one steady for a long time."

She hoped he couldn't see her blush in the dark. The comment made her neither happy or sad. So what did he want to talk about? How she humiliated herself when she found out he was hours from leaving for Baghdad? How she thought being in his arms was the beginning, rather than the end? Didn't all her letters come back unopened? It took her months to forget that night and move on with her life in L.A. Then she met Dylan.

Evan's chin tilted upward. "We're almost there."

She looked up the vertical grade. The Inn boasted a beautiful view from the top of a very steep hill. No way could he carry her. She remembered walking down to Main Street with Karen, thinking *that* was a hike.

His arm muscles behind her back bunched. Chest muscles flexed next to her breast. Her heartbeat tripled and her nipple tingled in response.

This was a very bad idea. Thinking she could limp up the hill, she said calmly, "Ah, Evan, you don't have to carry me anymore...."

Black eyes speared hers, ending any vote of doubt. One last jostle, then he turned, military-style and marched up the steep slope to the motel. He wasn't even breathing hard when they arrived at the top.

Amazing. She was winded from being carried.

"What room?" he asked tersely.

"This is far enough...one-oh-five. It's in the back."

For a minute she thought he'd drop her and drag her by the hair, caveman style, he looked so dangerous. When they reached the door he took the key from her hand and cleared the threshold, still trapping her in his arms.

The door slammed shut. In pitch darkness, Evan placed her in the center of the small loveseat. *Humph.* The MRT officer had no need of infrared goggles with his night vision.

The end table light flashed on, momentarily blinding her.

Where'd he go?

Every drape in the room fluttered, as if someone moved in the inky darkness. Then she heard running water.

"Where's the first-aid kit?" Evan's voice boomed from the bathroom.

"In my backpack, in the closet. But I can handle it from here." No way was she going to allow him to continue.

Crash.

What was that? Sounded from outside. She stood up and nearly fell to the carpet from the shock of pain up her leg, but her spine tingled, forcing her to hobble over to the window.

Nothing but cars in the dimly-lit parking lot, but the creepy feeling persisted. The running water shut off in the bathroom, so she drew the curtains closed and hopped back to the couch. No need to let Evan know she was slowly loosing her mind, thinking she was hearing and seeing things.

Evan came out of the bathroom with one dry towel wrapped around his neck and another folded in his hands, dripping. She balanced gingerly on one foot. He frowned. Tempted to laugh at his expression, she thought better of it and bit her lip.

"You better let me tend to your ankle," he said, moving toward her, "otherwise, you won't be able to stand, let alone walk or canoe. Tony will be disappointed."

Tony...? Disappointed...? Canoeing...?

When did she forget about her plans for tomorrow?

When the superhero picked her up and left her brains on the sidewalk. Good thing she'd sworn off *Godiva*-eyed blonds. "I can take care—"

A firm tap on her shoulder toppled her back onto the cushions. "I need to examine your ankle...to make sure it's not broken."

Before she could protest, he'd knelt at her feet. His hands lifted her foot from the floor, removed the blown-out flip-flop and tossed it over his shoulder. His fingers circled her ankle. He looked into her eyes, and squeezed.

"Does it hurt when I do this?"

Hurt? You're killing me, she wanted to shout. Besides the bolt of pain, she felt his toastie touch all the way up her leg to her already moist panties.

He waited for her answer.

"No. Not a bit."

Those hot-poker fingers slid lower. She squinted anticipating the pain. Carefully he flexed her foot, all the while watching her face.

She couldn't hide her wince.

How was she ever going to get out of this one?

"No bruises or swelling. I don't think it's broken. Probably a foot sprain. We can get it X-rayed tomorrow if it swells up tonight. Wrapped and elevated, it should be fine tomorrow."

He rose from the floor, and towered over her. "Do you have a good pair of hiking shoes?"

She pointed to the muddy pair by the door.

A warm, wet towel wrapped around her foot before he elevated it on a pillow on top of the coffee table. "Don't move," he ordered and disappeared into the bathroom, this time with her boots.

She fell back on the couch, gasped for air, and vowed if she got through the next few minutes she'd treat herself to a dozen imported Belgian truffles. She didn't need to get involved with him, no matter how much she'd dreamed of his touch. Although he had warm hands, his heart was frozen. He'd served his country, twice. Probably saved a few lives over there, too. It's what Evan did best, saved lives.

A real hero.

He deserved better. She never wanted anyone to find out about L.A., especially not Evan. He walked out of the bathroom with her boots all clean and shiny.

"You didn't have to do that," she said and fought off a warm, mushy feeling.

He hesitated, looked about to say something, but instead placed her shoes by the door where he'd found them. Then he crossed the room again and was back on one knee.

Eye level.

Inches from her body.

Her tummy fluttered. She pressed her hands against it, but it was pointless.

Calling all dragons.

"I better wrap you up and get you into bed or you'll be too tired for canoeing tomorrow. When are you meeting Tony?"

Did she imagine a mega-watt smile when he said he'd put her to bed?

31

Forget her stomach. The ache beginning between her legs was a bigger problem. "Seven...for breakfast at the M-Mirror Lake Inn, before canoeing." She squeezed her thighs together to stop the throbbing.

He shook some tablets from a bottle and handed her a mug of water. "I found some aspirin in the medical kit. Take two. It will help with the pain and stop the swelling. I don't remember you being allergic, are you?" Without permission again, he lifted her foot and carefully rested it upon his bent knee.

She shook her head, not trusting her voice to remain steady. She swallowed the pills and then lots of water, but they still scraped down her throat. Strong fingers touched her ankle, turning it from side to side. How much longer would he fuss over her foot? Her libido couldn't take much more of his manly scent or tender touches.

As he wrapped her foot, he glanced up at her face.

How was it possible to go to war and come back looking even better? She'd missed him terribly. Where would they be now if he hadn't left for war?

"Did you meet anyone in California?" he said.

She jerked her foot, and he dropped the roll of Ace bandage. He paused and searched her face.

"I'm okay," she said.

He seemed satisfied and bent to pick up the unwound roll, so she answered his original question. "I met someone," she cleared her throat and quickly added, "but I moved back alone."

His broad back faced her as he rewound the roll, and she noticed he stiffened slightly on the word *alone*.

"I'm living in the suburbs, DeWitt." She didn't know why she'd added that information, unless her mouth allied with her hormones.

Evan didn't acknowledge what she said but went back to wrapping her ankle as efficiently as someone who performed it a thousand times. He attached Velcro clips to secure the end.

Still no comment.

She'd forgotten how non-talkative he could be. This was probably their longest conversation. When he'd attend various parties at her home, he'd make polite small talk. Other times when he'd stop by to say hi to Jake, her attempts to talk about something besides his job were unsuccessful. One time she'd asked him about a girlfriend. His eyes narrowed. The temperature of the room had dropped to below freezing.

But now, his stare could melt a glacier.

Neither talked after her initial hysteria that fated night. One minute she was scolding him for reenlisting, insisting he'd lost his mind, begging him to reconsider. But as soon as she touched him and saw the desolate look in his eyes, words didn't matter. He'd needed her.

He seemed to absorb the information, then stood up. "Change into your night clothes, and I'll get the bed ready."

Liquid pooled in her panties at the insinuation. He didn't seem fazed. A man of few words, and he knew how to place them.

She marched as gracefully as she could into the bathroom, rummaged through her backpack for her bag of Hershey's kisses, and ate a few per her usual bedtime routine. The chocolate smell and taste were the only normal part of the evening. She pulled her hair up into a ponytail on the top of her head and brushed her teeth. Before limping into the room in a New York Giants jersey that fell to her knees, she prayed she'd stay strong.

Evan's gaze locked on her. At over six feet, hands planted on his hips, he crowded the room. Did she see a ghost-smile again? No, she was dreaming. This was all a dream. She yawned despite her nervousness. It happened whenever she put on the comfy jersey and ate her kisses.

Seeming to take the yawn as a signal, he lifted her and cradled her in his arms. Not that she minded. He cuddled her next to his chest like he cherished her. The bedroom door flung open from his kick. Then he carried her to the bed, pulled back the covers, and set her gently in the middle. He organized all but one pillow under her leg and foot, and the extra one went behind her head. In a quick move, he snapped the blankets over her legs. "You need to keep the foot elevated. Hope you can sleep on your back."

A drop of sweat rolled between her breasts. "I have no problem sleeping in any position," she replied.

Evan stepped back from the bed so fast, she wondered if he'd experienced whiplash. For a moment he stared with hungry eyes, looking like he wanted to take his clothes off and join her. A burst of excitement made her squirm under the covers. Her nipples tingled and the ache between her legs was so strong it threatened to make her beg for his touch.

Hadn't she learned anything by now?

For several long minutes he stared at her, but made no move to touch her again, except with his eyes. Her jersey stuck to her chest, outlining her breasts. She held her breath, then exhaled softly.

Evan wouldn't touch her. Tonight, she was another victim in need of rescue. As usual, Sergeant Jorgenson excelled at his job. Feeling defeated, she closed her eyes. She heard the bedspread rustle. *He's moved closer.* Relaxed and fearless, she spoke. "This morning on Mount Jo, I saw the strangest thing. A couple got engaged, ring and all, right on the summit."

He didn't answer until she pulled open her eyelids. He'd cocooned the bedcovers around her and leaned so close she could see the golden flecks floating in the chocolate syrup of his irises. "Happens a lot on Mount Jo."

"Why?"

The corners of his eyes crinkled but he didn't smile. "The mountain's named after the wife of a surveyor. He picked that spot to build their dream home. She died before he could build it."

She twisted her hands in the covers. *If I could hold his face one more time, kiss those lips.* "How sad."

Their hands nearly touched as he smoothed the covers. "Then there's that funny-shaped lake. People swear it's heart-shaped, but it looks like a jagged circle to me. Heart Lake's a clever tourist draw."

His husky voice weakened every muscle in her body, like before.

"It all sounds so romantic...a mountain named after a woman someone loved, a heart-shaped lake...people proposing...you know what I mean?" All she had to do was reach her hands up to cup his face, but her arms felt weighted down.

He brushed her wayward bangs off her forehead. His breath fanned her face for several heartbeats, then said, "I do."

She closed her heavy eyelids. It felt so good to be near him again. Too bad he was only doing his job. If she could stay awake a little longer maybe he'd tell her about the war, why he never wrote.

But at last her dragons had arrived to whisk her away.

****

"Fuck. That's what I get for not grabbing her sooner," Stone hissed, watching the girl through the motel window. He rubbed the cramp in his side. The guy flew up the fucking hill like some Olympic strongman. Some trick. When she'd walked out of the bar alone, he'd followed, but brawny guy had it bad for her and was waiting. In the bar she looked like she gave him the brush off, chose the littler guy. Now *that* one he could handle.

Stone grunted. Who could blame him? The blonde was a knockout. Christ, what would his client say about her hooking up? Maybe he'd keep that bit of information to himself. *Bad business to tick-off The Man.*

He dragged on his cigarette butt and scanned the parking lot. Remote and poorly lit. *My kinda place.* No one would see him drag her into those woods.

He crushed the butt on the ground, then bent low and peeked inside again. Was the guy gone? Light spilled on the carpet from another room. He had him by about fifty pounds, but the guy carried himself like a panther, ready to strike. Maybe he was military?

He didn't want to mess with him.

Of all the rotten luck. The job was cake to this point. As instructed, he'd watched her routine for a few days. He loved when they made it easy.

She stood up. *Damn. She was looking right at him.* He plastered his back to the concrete wall. How the fuck did she know he was there? He'd been stealth-like.

No point staying. That guy wasn't leaving.

"Wasted fuckin' trip," he mumbled, wiping spider webs off his sleeve.

Best to head back to Syracuse.

No one was looking out for her there.

Chapter Three

Evan cursed in several languages as he threw the Jeep into gear and nailed the accelerator.

Fool.

He'd carried her when his battered but dependable Wrangler was parked a few feet away, an easy drive to her motel. Picked her up and cuddled her next to his chest, so close he tasted her vanilla scent. The weight of a beautiful breast rubbed against his chest for blocks, like the drip of Chinese torture.

But she felt so good in my arms.

He'd have carried her up that blasted hill a hundred times to hold her longer. At her motel room, he'd expected another protest, but she accepted his medical authority. His hands shook like a rookie's as he taped her ankle. Aching to remove her clothes and taste every inch of her, he kept reminding himself she was injured.

Luckily, I'm well trained.

It didn't feel like a compliment.

The light turned green, and he nearly ripped the shifter out of the gearbox. He'd cleaned her boots like a servant. *Pathetic.* He battled his good sense to get out of Dodge, while his testosterone level demanded he act like a man and bed her and be over with it. When he suggested he put her to bed, another body part had taken over. Like that amazing night. He knew better than to take advantage of her fear. Odds were stacked about ninety-nine to one he wouldn't come back alive. She'd have suffered further if he died. But years of wanting her to look at him with yearning, short-circuited his brain.

The last shreds of his control kept him from grabbing the football jersey hem. The way it outlined her breasts made him want to pull it in one thrust over her head. But he didn't know real torture until she'd obediently laid on the bed and looked up at him with those spellbinding eyes. All he could think about was how much he wanted to lie on top of her and sate his growing need to be inside her. Good thing those pillows magically arranged themselves under her leg.

He'd tucked the covers around her fast, to keep her safe. From him. All the time he'd carried her his mind clocked overtime recalling his fantasies. The kissing part of his "Cassie" fantasy was long and hard, not frenzied like the first time. Then he'd undress her and answer one of the hundred questions about his fascination with her.

Make love to her slowly, thoroughly. The kind of lovemaking that took a week.

When she said she could sleep in any position, it felt like an assault rifle recoiled in his gut. He'd shot up like an idiot before he begged her to show him her "positions." Thankfully, she made the decision easy when her eyelids fluttered shut. He was ready for sex, and she talked romance, and then she'd fallen asleep.

When had he lost his charm with women?

When he met Cassie.

He told himself he stayed and watched her sleep to make sure she was okay. She looked like an angel. Part of him wanted to wake her with a kiss, but she deserved better. Not someone who couldn't sit for five minutes without reliving some aspect of battle. He'd been spinning fantasies about her for so long, he might confuse dreams with reality.

Then again, there was the frostbite of her reception tonight. But lying in bed, her expression warmed and looked the way it did four years ago. Although she'd given him everything he'd ever wanted, the possibility that sympathy guided her actions that night gnawed at his gut.

Good thing he'd kept to the business of fixing her up.

Her foot should be healed for her canoeing trip tomorrow. Tony owed him big time. The image of Tony pawing Cassie in the middle of Mirror Lake came to mind, complete with them pitching into the water. It ended with Cassie drowning.

The steering wheel creaked under his knuckles. Only one thing he could do to prevent that from happening. Without signaling, he swung the Jeep around and headed back to town, to find Tony.

****

Cassie felt so good she nearly jumped out of bed, until she spied the bulky Ace bandage. Her covers were heaped on the floor but her foot rested on the pile of pillows where Evan placed it. She flexed. No pain. She stretched, feeling better than she'd felt in years.

"Where did you get *that* thing? You were sound asleep when I came in last night."

Stars. She wanted to escape to the bathroom before Inspector Karen noticed. "The first aid kit." She swung her legs over the bed, tested her weight on her ankle, and walked gracefully to the bathroom.

She felt Karen's eyes on her. "Where did you

learn to wrap an ankle? And when did you become a neat freak and clean your boots?"

Karen followed her into the bathroom. Cassie stuck her toothbrush in her mouth so she didn't have to answer. Karen watched her with the patience of a mother of three while she brushed and rinsed.

"What aren't you telling me?" Karen demanded, and turning bloodhound, started sniffing around the bathroom. "I thought I smelled something familiar in the bathroom last night. It smelled like the cologne I bought Karl once, but then I thought I missed him and dreamed the scent."

Cassie shrugged her shoulders and feigned boredom. After she pulled the football jersey over her head, then stepped into a steaming shower, she decided to confess. Over the rushing water, she tried to sound nonchalant. "Evan walked me home from the bar last night. Well, he actually carried me. He came inside and wrapped my ankle so I could go canoeing with Tony today. He cleaned my boots before he put me to b—, er, p—put pillows under my foot."

Silence.

Karen must have left the bathroom. She and Karl met Evan several times at her home, and they liked him. Karen often asked if she knew why he wasn't married. Even so boldly commented she'd have his baby in a heartbeat if she weren't happily married to Karl.

A few minutes later, she walked out of the bathroom with one towel wrapped around her and another drying her hair. Karen watched from the couch, arms and legs crossed and mouth open, ready to fire the first question.

"Hottie-Evan, the player you wanted to avoid at Roomer's, carried you home and taped your ankle, then put you to bed? Please tell me it was after mind-blowing sex with him." Karen sounded like she did when interrogating her sons about homework.

"Never in a million years." Darn. Too quickly added, a dead giveaway to someone as wise as Karen.

Karen lept off the couch. "Why not? Have you stopped breathing? If given the chance I'd have locked him in the bedroom myself."

Cassie rolled her eyes. "He may be great looking—in a rustic, outdoorsy way—and it was kind of him to take care of my ankle, it feels great, but *he's not my type.*"

She wanted to believe she'd convinced Karen, but she could hear the excitement in her own voice. *No.* No way was she going to allow herself to think of Evan that way, ever again.

A hero deserved better.

Karen drew up to her full height to stand nearly eye-to-eye with Cassie. "That gorgeous, single, hunk of man was in here, and you let him fix your foot and tuck you in? Did you at least kiss him goodnight?"

Four years ago. After we made love until sunrise. "He was the perfect professional, concerned only with my sore ankle." He didn't try to kiss her, proving he felt nothing for her. She didn't feel like talking anymore, so she sat on the couch and vigorously towel dried her hair.

Karen paced the room and mumbled under her breath. "This is worse than I thought. I know divorcing Jake messed you up, and in L.A. he-that-shall-not-be-named added to your troubles, but I never thought you'd turn frigid. Because you caught some bad breaks doesn't mean you can take yourself out of commission. Oh boy, now I not only have to shape you up, but I have to teach you how to get laid—I mean date again."

"I don't want to date men like Evan, or get laid. They are control freaks. Last night I didn't even ask him to walk me home. He wouldn't take no for an answer." Cassie inhaled a sharp breath and then finished the tirade. "Men like Evan spend so much time making life and death decisions in order to save lives they can't stop. They think they need to make all of your decisions. When I start dating again, I want a nice, quiet guy, one who reads a lot and works a nine-to-five job. A job that doesn't involve saving lives. Maybe a computer programmer. I want him home having dinner with the kids and me, *watching* the news not ending up on it. And I want a man who will *stand by me* when I mess up."

She didn't mean to admit that last part, but now it was out there, no point taking it back. She brushed her hair and dressed in a green Lake Placid T-shirt and khaki slacks. Karen remained silent as Cassie bent over and tied laces on her clean-as-new boots and pushed aside again the thought it was a nice gesture.

Unwilling to see pity on Karen's face, Cassie pretended to recheck her boot laces, but stiffened when she heard the sorrow in Karen's voice. "I know you, honey. That kind of guy would bore you in ten minutes. You crave excitement—"

Cassie held up both hands. "Not anymore. I'd rather be alone than end up in another relationship with a guy like D-Dylan... Oh!"

It doesn't matter, she wanted to shout. Evan would be crazy to want her now.

Her lips trembled. She turned away from Karen and hid behind the veil of her hair. One hot tear popped free and dove to the floor. She pinched her nose to keep others from escaping. A cleansing breath whooshed through her teeth, taking some of the pain and anger with it, leaving behind a dull ache in her chest.

More in control, she faced Karen. Lines marred Karen's fairylike face. "I've got to go. I'm meeting Tony, Evan's friend—for breakfast—and then canoeing. I'll catch up with you at the downtown shops later." She gave Karen a stern look, hoping it ended the discussion. Her childhood friend knew enough to let it go. Besides, wanting to go canoeing with Tony should count for something.

****

Cassie waited patiently for Tony. She glanced around the entrance of the restaurant, certain he'd be there any minute. She decided to thank him for the offer, but no longer wanted to go canoeing. If she left Lake Placid now, she could spend part of the afternoon with Heather, provided Jake didn't have plans to take her to the zoo, or shopping, or riding her favorite carousel horse in Carousel Mall.

What was she thinking when she agreed to spend the day with Tony? Gone was the real estate agent capable of networking with five agents at once, or calculate any percent commission in her head. Seeing Evan again rattled her. To make matters worse, she woke up thinking about his penetrating gaze.

Those dark eyes studied her every move last night. Officer Jorgenson probably had a folder of information on her by now.

Did the folder include information about L.A.?

Weary, she leaned against the porch rail. If Evan cared even a little for her, she'd have reason to hope. Four years to write, email or phone. Last night proved he no longer cared, and she couldn't afford to dwell on her disappointment. She needed to focus her energy on making her business a huge success. According to Karl's calculation of the last few months the shop turned a profit. And when she returned to court she'd impress the judge and be granted more than a few hours supervised visitation each week. No matter how much Evan invaded her dreams and gave her foolish heart hope, best to forget him.

Dreams were all she'd ever have.

She pushed away from the wall and straightened her back. *Live in the present, positive thoughts about the future,* was her new motto. No relationship until she had her precious angel back. With three strikes against her in matters of the heart, it was as wise a decision as a self-preserving one.

The sight of a well-built man striding toward her in a faded green baseball cap and mirrored sunglasses made her regret the pledge. If she could find someone who looked that good who was honest, kind, and forgiving, maybe she'd reconsider her plan. She sighed. A girl could count on those broad shoulders for years of support.

The man came closer and closer. She vaguely noticed a blond mustache and long purposeful strides. She held her breath, bracing for an eminent collision.

He stopped short and whipped off his glasses.

A *tango* played in her head.

After the lecture from Karen, she bristled. "What are you doing here? Is Tony with you?" She tried to look past him but it was like trying to look around Whiteface.

He winced when she said Tony's name and stopped twirling his sunglasses. "He couldn't make it," he replied. "Something, er, came up. *You* never gave him your cell number." He paused and searched her face prompting her for an answer.

She swallowed her anger. After all, he was right. "I forgot, although a cell is useless in these mountains."

He nodded and then looked past her at an open table. "Let's have breakfast first."

"First? Evan, it was nice of you to come all this way to tell me Tony wasn't coming—"

"Don't you want to go canoeing? It's like gliding

on a mirror." As he spoke, he nudged her by the elbow toward a corner table where a hostess laid fresh silverware and gave him a knowing smile.

He pulled her seat out. No one had done that simple, polite gesture for her in years. Feeling awkward she sat.

"Foot okay this morning?" The corners of his mouth moved slightly upward.

Evan's smile. How she'd missed it. A small, but devastating smile, it drew the attention of several women eating at another table.

Her stomach clenched and her legs felt heavy. Good thing she was seated. "Ah, yeah... it feels fine." She removed the ring from the cloth napkin and spread the silky fabric in her lap, fussing with it to avoid looking at him until she regained her cool.

The waitress flipped some pages on her pad, and he ordered for the two of them.

Cassie held up her hand. "I want coffee, black, nothing more."

Evan and the waitress looked at her as if she'd sprouted wings and was about to fly away.

Evan's smile disappeared. "You'll need more than coffee for canoeing. Bring the lady strawberry crêpes for starts, then steak and eggs, and keep the toast coming," he said.

Any excitement she'd sensed at canoeing on the famous Mirror Lake disappeared like mountain fog on a blistering hot day. The way Evan took charge last night carrying her, wrapping her foot and then putting her to bed she'd accepted as part of his job. But assuming they'd go canoeing then ordering for her as if she were an incapable child?

She could make up her own mind.

She struggled to contain the fire in her gut. "Evan, I appreciate all you've done for me, but you can stop the TLC. I can order my own food."

He looked at her like he pondered a difficult

math problem and then nodded to the waitress who left to place the order.

Okay, subject dropped. No point arguing about food she didn't plan to eat.

Lounging like a king with his arms crossed in front of a pristine white Henley shirt, her surprise breakfast companion continued to study her. The smell of warm linen mixed with his cologne. He always smelled so good. And looked even better. Saying goodbye today would be tough, but necessary.

His intense scrutiny was too much. She spun in her chair to look at anything other than him. The tasteful country room, decorated in Adirondack-style, served as good distraction. Someday when she could afford it she wanted similar touches in her apartment. Maybe a whimsical little end table made of twigs or a lampshade covered in white and black-speckled birch bark. Since she was dreaming she'd like a grandfather clock made of split pine branches, twigs, and bark shavings like she'd passed in the vestibule. She'd add a nest on the top with a fake robin and her eggs to please Heather. The days of dreaming of Harden Cherry furniture, Waterford crystal and Wedgwood china were gone with her taste for the rich, powerful men who provided those things. Now, she dreamed of a comfortable modest home for Heather.

Her stomach cramped. All she cared about was getting Heather back, so they could be a family again. *Please, God, don't let me mess up again.* Through the picture window, the sun burst through the clouds. She held up her hand to shield her eyes from the brilliant shine reflecting off the lake. A kaleidoscope of autumn colors sparkled in the distance. The famous Mirror Lake rivaled anything else Mother Nature created on the planet. Its silvery surface beckoned to be touched. She longed to be outside climbing to the summit of another mountain, discovering another panoramic view. Heather must see this lake. Maybe they could camp at Heart Lake next summer.

Heart Lake. Her cheeks flushed. Why did she talk about it last night? Because Evan made her feel so safe she'd let down her guard and even mentioned the newly engaged couple. Because it was one of the most romantic things *she'd* ever seen why did she think *Evan* would care?

Thank heavens she'd fallen asleep before more foolish talk.

Hearing coffee mugs thud onto the table, she pirouetted in her chair. Evan still wore a puzzled expression. She shrugged. *Whatever.*

He answered by raising his elbows on the table and leaning closer. Another inspection? Did he notice anything different? Then again, her biggest changes weren't external.

Fidgeting with her silverware, she stole a peek under her eyelashes and snagged on those wide, muscular shoulders.

The less time she spent with Evan, the better.

****

Evan congratulated himself as he admired his breakfast companion. The morning sunshine bathed her hair into a golden halo and made her skin glow a pretty pale peach. He ached to touch its softness again. Her subtle, sexy fragrance wafted to his side of the table. His skin began to tingle. He tried to ignore it, like his conscious.

Getting Tony drunk last night was the right thing to do. A good co-worker and a top MRT officer, Tony had a "love 'em and leave 'em" attitude. At ZigZag's, Evan bought pitchers and did tequila shots with Tony until he passed out on the bar. This morning from the bathroom Tony asked him to apologize to Cassie for canceling. Evan had walked to his Jeep feeling a little guilty. Since seeing Cassie

47

at the bar in those flip-flops he was powerless to avoid her despite the attack of hives. Some kind of ancient, "caveman-gene," kicked in, leaving two choices: drag her by the hair to his cave or protect her. Not his customary approach to women. He never dragged anyone to his bed or had her fall asleep while pillow talking. Or make him break out in hives. Good thing he packed plenty of Benadryl, and patience. He longed to figure out why he felt like he tumbled in poison ivy every time they met.

He looked her over again. True, she was perfect—not only in body and face, but he always admired her spirit. Plus from watching her with her daughter, a generous heart.

Who wouldn't get nervous and itchy? If he found something wrong with her maybe the spell would be broken, the fantasies would end. He'd move on with his life.

A wiser man would retreat from a woman who looked as if she wanted to murder him half the time. But long ago she'd kissed him once the way he longed for her to kiss him, loved him like he never thought he'd needed, touched a place inside him no other woman had, and he suspected no other woman would.

The attraction he'd felt from the moment he'd met her years ago never faded. He'd wanted her from the first night he spied her at the hospital's New Year's Eve party. From across the crowded room. Only he hadn't noticed a man standing beside her. Probably because everyone in the room faded away when she smiled at him. But when he extended his hand to say hello and get her phone number, another man's hand appeared. The new doctor, Jake Hamilton, introduced his bride, Cassie.

His thoughts shifted to the present. What made her leave L.A.? With her starlet looks she'd be perfect out there. Did she miss home? Him?

Not likely by her scowl. He thought about calling her, but stopped himself several times. She didn't need someone who listened for the click of booby traps in grocery stores, woke up drenched in sweat, yelling for cover, or ripped apart pillow in his sleep.

And the worst, saw dead soldiers.

So why had he stopped at the boat rental before meeting her for breakfast, checking the availability of a canoe? Was his head still filled with powdered sand?

No. The opportunity to be with her this weekend dropped in his lap and he was going to ride this twist of fate for as long as it lasted.

Learn the hold she had on his senses.

See her naked. Once more.

She looked about the room, anywhere but at him giving him the chance to take a good look at her. Christ, in that sexy outfit last night she looked thin but in her clingy top today he could see some ribs. Before, her eyes sparkled like emeralds in sunlight. Last night, they resembled fading fall leaves, their radiance dimmed by some hidden pain.

His stomach clenched. He recognized the all-too-familiar signs of trauma.

The tingling sensation up his arms stopped. His fist fell on the table jarring the silverware. He wished he knew something about her stay in L.A. Anything. He'd avoided seeing Jake since his return from Iraq. They talked on the phone often enough either about Jake's practice or his new research. Jake mentioned Cassie was back in town but no other details.

When she swiveled forward again he tested her desire to be with him. "The lake's world famous. Tony said you like to canoe. I can take you."

One honey-colored eyebrow shot up, inferring she didn't believe he could stir coffee.

You're great for my ego, kid.
Too bad.

He looked forward to spending a few more hours with her. Negotiate the minefield. Win her over with his lack of charm. Her skin glowed when he ordered her strawberry crêpes. Now that he'd annoyed her she paled. She gnawed impatiently at her lower lip so long it swelled as if well-kissed.

His muscles tensed fighting the urge to squirm in his seat under her stare. Sweat on his chest began to prickle. This close to her without touching was killing him.

Minutes later the waitress reappeared and the table filled with plates of great-smelling food. She looked eager to dig in, not only eyeing her plate but his mound of food. Gratified he'd predicted her hunger he smiled to himself. Unresponsive to his canoeing offer though left him to wonder what her answer would be.

She inhaled deeply before her gorgeous mouth opened wide to receive a large slice of strawberry crêpes. Another fantasy flashed before his eyes. But after about two chews she choked and tried to hide it behind the veil of her napkin.

Shit. He knew the feeling.

His growing desire quelled as fast as his appetite. *She's hurting bad about something.* She'd been divorced from Jake for over four years so it could only be one thing: Some fucker in California put her through the ringer.

He stabbed at some pieces of steak and chewed harder. He'd stay clear of that subject. For now. "So, how's Heather?"

Clang. Her fork hit the china plate and bounced. Green eyes shimmered for a moment when they met his, then lost the fight and grew huge and vacant.

Way to go, ace.

She recovered her fork and bowed her head. He

noticed the puffiness under her eyes before her bangs hid them.

Should have eaten the food and kept my big mouth shut. Instead of rushing to her side to pull her into his arms or ask what was wrong he stiffened in his chair. He lowered his fork and wiped his mustache then tossed the napkin aside.

Eyes riddled with pain looked up. "Heather's living with Jake. She's adjusted well to her new school, made a good impression on her second grade teacher. She's been able to read and write since she was four. They're thinking of having her skip a grade."

She spoke with the dispassionate voice of someone reporting the evening news. Shaky fingers picked up her fork but she didn't try to eat only pushed the food around her plate.

How could he respond? Couldn't he get anything right with this woman who made his skin feel like it was going to molt any minute? Who was he kidding? He'd gladly molt to be with her.

Learn how to talk without offending her first, champ. "I figured Heather lived with you."

Bright red dots appeared on her cheeks and he realized he must have said something worse. He thought he saw her lips quiver but she pressed them together before she spoke. "Jake came to L.A. for a visit. I had some problems...adjusting. He took Heather away from me."

The last words were more to herself as she reached for her water goblet and took a small sip.

What the hell was wrong with Jake? How could he take Heather from Cassie? A smarter Evan would have known to change the subject to something neutral, like the weather, rather than take out his gun and aim at his foot. But this new Evan, the insane one, pulled the trigger.

"Sometimes things go wrong," he began. "You

have to regroup 'til you can make them right again."
Lord, did he wish he believed that. They were
canned words right from the New York State Police
procedure book.

Digging his grave he added, "It's good you left
L.A. At least you can see Heather."

She softly set down her water glass. "No. I've
lost all visitation rights. I've got to prove to the
courts I'm a good mother and can provide a safe
home for Heather before they'll let me have her
again. I'm only allowed supervised visitation."

Then she whispered something heart-wrenching
even to his seasoned ears. "I messed up bad in L.A.,
but I'm getting my life back on track. I want my
daughter back. I *will* get her back. I have to..."

Determination lit her eyes and dared him to
doubt her.

He managed a curt nod although his head
experienced negative g-forces.

It was worse than he'd thought.

"Thanks for the offer of canoeing," she said,
wiping imaginary food from her mouth with her
napkin, "but I think I'll pass. It's a long drive h-
home. I want to head back before the rush. Thanks
for breakfast."

She stood and turned to walk away then
stopped. A slender hand came toward him.

He grasped the smaller, tender hand in his
large, normally useful hand. It felt warm and
comforting. A place he never wanted to leave. Like
when he sat before a roaring fire in his living room
overlooking the water dreaming about what could
have been.

She pulled her hand free, making the decision
easy.

Best he left her alone.

Chapter Four

Setting out a sample plate of her homemade chocolate truffles, Cassie inhaled a deep sniff. The rich, velvety smell of her confections soothed her frayed nerves. The court date to regain joint custody of Heather was this week. With the success of her fledgling business, she'd regained Jake's trust since moving back. He'd agreed to weekend visitations with Heather. Cautiously optimistic, she'd counted the hours until her daughter's return.

From her stash of Hershey's kisses in the checkout counter drawer she unwrapped several kisses and popped them into her mouth. The chocolate liquefied and exploded, satisfying every taste bud. As she chewed she brushed away tiny pieces of tinfoil that littered the counter. Her counter. She'd made this business work on her own—no one else called the shots. All decisions, good or bad, were hers. Soon, Heather would be home. She'd be back to normal. No, better than normal. No ex-husband or ex-boyfriend. Dylan was a thousand miles away. No one could hurt her here.

When she'd first arrived from California, and with weeks before until her custody hearing, there was no time to establish herself as a realtor. Opening a chocolate shop was a childhood dream. The purchase of the two-family house in DeWitt, a busy suburb of Syracuse, was a great location for *Serendipity Sweets,* and according to Karl, a good investment. All the money she'd made selling real estate went for living expenses in L.A., the move back home and her lawyer, so the last of her savings from her divorce settlement had served as down payment.

Overwhelmed at first by her purchase, she conceded painting and major repairs were best left to experts. Still, some things she managed to do herself. Like the polished wood-pegged shelves she'd painstakingly refinished, hoping to hold lots of future inventory. And the white and brown dotted-Swiss curtains framing the display window. They reminded her of powdered sugar sprinkled over a chocolate ganache frosting. Dozen's of pleats took hours to sew but captured the perfect old-fashioned feel.

The wood trimmed display cases were a lucky find. Purchased at a restaurant sale, nicks and age spots looked like they'd been there decades. They only needed a good cleaning. Unlike the wide-planked hardwood floor she'd discovered after she'd pulled up layers of worn linoleum. Karl and Karen helped her sand and stain it a warm chestnut. Someday it would make a beautiful dance floor for Heather to practice ballet.

Her favorite part of the store was the kitchen. By the check-out area, it was big enough for a commercial refrigerator and boasted plenty of storage. The smell of her chocolate creations floated from the kitchen and infused the shop. Every morning when she walked from the upstairs apartment, the scent made her mouth water. Some people thought there was no better smell than coffee in the morning but if they walked into her shop they'd convert. She'd never tire of the aroma. Not only the smell of success, it would secure the return of her daughter.

She checked trays layered on pristine white doilies in the main display case. Her first experiment with her own recipe, the strawberry-banana cream filled chocolates were sold out. *Pretty good for someone who failed chemistry and didn't know a gram from a meter.* And thanks to Grandma's candy-forms, the heart shapes were perfect.

Not like that odd-shaped lake visible from Mount Jo.

After a tricky hike upward, the mountain trail narrowed between clusters of pine saplings and then broke open. For some reason a bubble of excitement rose in her throat. When she'd asked Karen, *are we here,* her tone sounded as excited as Heather's when they turned onto the L.A. freeway. Deep blue skies over a granite summit floor framed the breathtaking view she hadn't seen in years. She'd moved as close to the rocky edge as she dared to see the famous Heart Lake. From the distance, the puddle still looked more like a broken circle a child drew with a crayon. Hard as she tried, she never envisioned a heart.

She smiled remembering Evan couldn't either. What would have happened if she hadn't fallen asleep?

Nibbling a few more kisses, she noted how many truffles she needed to make for the week. "Evan is eye candy for any woman from thirteen to ninety," the little voice in her head volunteered.

Funny thing, in the past she compared Evan to a peanut cluster candy bar, all smooth and dark on the outside but hard and unyielding as rock on the inside. But after his gentleness this weekend he seemed more like a peanut butter cup. Probably why she'd spoken so pointedly at breakfast. Evan affected her senses like no man she'd ever met. Although their time together was short, Evan's rejection bothered her more than her husband's.

The front door of the shop opened with a pleasant jingle followed by a bang as it slapped against the wall. Karen entered a little breathless probably from running to keep up with her energetic sons. "You're open early this morning. Did you sleep well?"

"Yeah, no problems," she uttered.

Except the hourly review of Evan's questions and berating herself for discussing Heather. She could still see the awkward look on Evan's face.

Imagine, Mister, I-Can-Master-Any-Situation-Super-Officer, speechless. At least he'd gotten her mind off the court date.

Karen pulled one son away from a display of enormous pink papier-mâché petits fours. "I'm glad I started my Christmas shopping."

Cassie harrumphed. "You think you're Santa Claus."

Two tiny heads swiveled around, all ears.

"Aunt Cassie's joking, boys," said Karen. "She's friends with The Grinch."

Karen's sons took a step back from Cassie. She handed the boys two new coloring books, stashed under the checkout counter. Karen signaled the boys to go to the play area.

"So, tell the truth. How much did you think about that gorgeous mountainman?" Cassie rolled her eyes, causing Karen to laugh with delight at the direct hit. "That much? Great."

"We've been through this. Heroes make lousy husbands." *And it's clear he doesn't want me.*

Cassie's gaze drifted to her chocolate-smudged left hand. She rubbed the sticky stain with a dishtowel.

"There will be another ring on your finger, sweetie," said Karen.

She scrubbed harder. "The first one wasn't anything special. I came home from shopping and found a note on the counter with the small black box." She rinsed her hand and stared at the vacant spot. "We were married the day before with borrowed wedding bands."

Karen reached over and turned off the hot water faucet. "That's all in the past."

"I never realized how spoiled I was back then," Cassie whispered, still inspecting her finger.

"You were young and in love."

Karen's voice was full of understanding she didn't deserve.

"Youth is no excuse for what I did. I never should have lied about the pregnancy."

"But you were pregnant for a week," Karen insisted.

Cassie traded her barely soiled apron for a cleaner one. "One drug store test came back positive. I couldn't wait to tell Jake."

Karen tsked. "You were excited."

"I was on the pill, and Jake said I'd been careless. We'd planned to wait until after his residency. He was stressed about school and money. He was so angry he never even proposed. When I got my period I was so in love with the idea of being Dr. Jake Hamilton's wife I couldn't tell him the truth."

"Oh, sweetie. Don't be so hard on yourself." Karen's hand rested on Cassie's shoulder unintentionally making her eye level with Karen's platinum and diamond wedding set. The brilliant gems sparkled in the glow of the candlelight chandelier overhead.

Cassie pulled away. "Jake didn't love me, but I believed I could *make* him fall in love with me. When

Heather was four weeks late he knew I'd made up the pregnancy. *'To trap him into marriage he wasn't ready for,'* he said. Things were never the same between us."

Regrets stabbed her throat. She balled up the clean apron and threw it in the laundry basket.

A thump and crash sounded from the back of the shop, startling them both. She rushed to the sound followed by Karen. The boys were okay... but her special wedding display tumbled to the floor. Boxed chocolates she'd carefully stacked to resemble a three-tiered wedding cake scattered across the wide planked floor. None appeared damaged, but the porcelain cake toppers weren't so fortunate. She found the groom first. A little glue would reattach his head. Pieces of the bride were scattered everywhere.

Karen faced the boys. "I'm assuming this was an accident but I'm taking money out of this week's allowance to pay for the bride. Now go sit."

"It's okay," Cassie said, and retrieved the broom and shovel. "No harm done."

With slumped shoulders, the preschool boys lowered their tawny heads and walked away. Their sneakers scraped the hardwood floor as they dragged their feet to the Little Tikes picnic table and waited quietly. At four and five they were miniatures of their father.

Karen swept up the last shards of the bride from dips in the floor. "Let's get back to why you were thinking about Evan."

Cassie was careful not to throw the head of the groom out with the rest of the debris. She stared at the figurine's blond hair and dark eyes.

"Thinking about Evan?" Karen winked.

The playful taunt had the reverse effect. "He asked the most personal questions and didn't know when to stop."

Karen's face flushed. "That cretin. What did he ask you, honey?"

Cassie bit her lip and shrugged. "About L.A."

Karen paused to make sure the boys were engrossed in coloring then lowered her voice, "I thought he asked you something lewd, like do you want to do it outdoors tied to a tree?" Karen handed her sons some chocolate samples from the counter. She popped several in her own mouth then grinned like a monkey.

Cassie didn't rise to the silly bait. "I told him I lost custody of Heather, and I had supervised visitation."

Karen stopped chewing. "Oh, dear."

Her breakfast formed a sour lump in her stomach. "I told him I messed up."

Karen swallowed the large lump of chocolate in her mouth. "What did he say?"

"Nothing. I left."

She went to her drawer and grabbed some kisses then joined the boys at the Little Tikes picnic table to watch them color. Heather colored mostly outside the lines because she was so impatient to finish and show off her masterpiece.

"You have to stop beating yourself up. You've transformed this dreary, old thrift shop into a warm, inviting candy shop. Karl said if your revenues continue the way they did last month, you'd turn a nice profit this year. Do you know how hard it is to open a successful business in New York State? You, madam, have found yourself a nice little niche."

She tried to listen to Karen, but the image of Jake taking Heather's hand and walking out of her apartment played in her mind.

That day, part of her died.

"You are a good person who made some bad choices in the past. But that's the past. And you will get Heather back. Jake's willing to let you have visitation rights—he told Karl—but it's out of his hands. What day is the hearing?"

"Friday." Cassie opened the counter drawer and rearranged several bags of Hershey's kisses. Then she smoothed lotion on her hands.

"Good. In the meantime you need to stop pushing men away by telling them your darkest secrets."

At the time Cassie thought she was answering Evan's questions with perfect honesty. "I told you. I'm not ready for a relationship right now—"

Pounding footsteps interrupted. The boys raced to the counter wearing chocolate all over their adorable faces. "Boys. Don't run in the store," Karen warned.

Cassie went to the kitchen and returned with some wipes. Karen allowed her to perform the simple task. Did she know how much it meant to do little, normal things like this for the boys? That's why she designed the play area. To see the big-eyed, Christmas-morning faces on children when they walked into her store. Hear children's laughter as they played. On the longest wall, a local artist painted a secret forest mural, complete small forest creatures, wood nymphs and a fawn peeking shyly from behind the bushes. In the distance, a knight rode his steed to face a towering, flame-spewing dragon.

When the boys' faces sparkled with shine rather then chocolate, she stroked their beautiful little faces affectionately.

"I know you think you're not ready for a relationship now, honey, but if you wait too long you may miss out on something great." Karen's worried expression showed genuine concern.

Some people were so lucky to have a straight course in life instead of wandering one trail of broken dreams after another. She touched her chest to stop the pinch of pain her self-pity always elicited. Now wasn't the time to tell Karen about her night with Evan.

Karen checked her watch. "Look at the time. I stopped by to tell you I can get a sitter on Wednesday, to help make truffles." Karen finished her sentence with a huge sniff. "I don't know how you don't gain weight from the smell."

The heavenly look on Karen's face made Cassie grin for the first time since Saturday. These days it felt odd to form a smile. But she did remember grinning as she fell asleep the night in the motel room.

Something she said to Evan about sleeping positions...

"Cassie... did you hear me?"

"Oh. No. That won't be necessary. Alexi is coming every day after school this week. She'll mind the shop while I make them. I don't know what I would do without her."

At only twelve-years old, Karen's first born was a responsible young lady.

"Good. But if you need me, call, okay?"

That last remark had nothing to do with the shop and both knew it. She helped the boys put crayons away avoiding an answer.

Karen popped another piece of chocolate into her mouth and sighed. "You should bring samples of this stuff to court. The judge will hear and *taste* all you've done in such a short time and you'll have Heather back. Come on, boys."

The door closed behind Karen and the boys when the phone rang. Cassie wiped her hands on a clean towel before picking it up.

"Hi, angel face. Tell me you're ready to return to me and I'll have a ticket waiting for you at the airport. I'll take you to dinner at Spago's to celebrate."

Her breakfast threatened to come up. "Dylan, you're crazy. I told you we're through." She forced air from her lungs to answer. "Leave me alone."

"I miss you. You'll never get your kid back."

"Stop it." She touched the sudden stabbing pain in her forehead. Black spots appeared like jousting fireflies before her eyes.

"Come back to me, angel. You won't have to worry about a thing—"

"No!" she screeched then slammed the phone.

Dylan's calls were becoming more frequent. Why now? And what did he mean, she'd never get Heather back?

Did he know something?

He was beginning to scare her. She needed help. *Evan?* What could he do? They were only phone calls. No, she'd handle this herself. Dylan must want something from her, but what? He'd taken the only thing she ever valued.

She paced around the wedding display. He was insane if he thought she'd go to him that she still loved him. She hated talking to Dylan but the next time he called she'd have to play along and find out what he really wanted.

The front door jingled pleasantly again. She jumped at the sound, nearly giving herself a heart attack.

Yes, something needed to be done about Dylan, and soon.

Chapter Five

Evan stood before the large metal desk in his office sorting through six weeks of mail. A chair moved in the office next door and he heard the hushed voices of two people, one male, one female, through the pale blue concrete walls. The female's laugh sounded forced. Both were in the center of the room; he could envision where a body stood behind a wall by the smallest of sounds. Not a necessary skill back in the States, even for a police officer.

He forced himself to tune out the private conversation. Since his return, he rarely spoke to anyone. Without the few items and clutter on his desk his office resembled an abandoned Iraqi home. One wall supported a large calendar with work schedules. Another wall, flyers of wanted men and women, some missing children. A flag with the American flag still at half-mast, stood by the door. Three rows of file cabinets doubled as shelves on the opposite wall. Behind him, nothing. Not even personal. Framed awards were boxed in the corner. The one family picture that he displayed, Clay and Jenny in Lake Placid, stayed on his desk. Another picture remained in a locked drawer. He turned the key and removed the small frame. Cassie, Heather and Jake, snapped at a picnic during happier times. He touched Cassie's smile.

After a series of raps on the door, Tony entered and craned his neck at a box in the corner of the room. "Are you gonna start hanging those awards to make this look like a real office?" Tony's eyes were clear, unlike the red-rimmed eyes from yesterday.

Funny, Evan still felt no guilt.

"Maybe tomorrow." His standard reply.

"Yeah—makes no difference anymore. You'll be leaving us soon." Tony fished, looking for some information, inevitable with all the talk of Evan's bid for promotion.

"Don't go spreading any rumors." *Like telling a toddler not to cross the street.*

Tony's eyes lit with mischief. "No chance of that, although I started a pool." *What a surprise.* "Who's that a picture of, anyway?"

"Friends," Evan said, unable to let go of the picture.

"Hey, is that Cassie?" Tony gasped, then buttoned his lip.

Evan slid the photo into his top drawer. "Did you develop those pictures from Mount Jo?"

"Picked them up at noon. Any picture you want in particular?" Tony grinned like one of those deformed dogs on a birthday card.

Evan didn't take the bait.

"Got a great one of Cassie. I'm gonna post it on the bulletin board. The rest of the guys want copies. Bovard said she's the *Playboy* pinup of hikers."

Steam rose off the back of Evan's neck. "I'll take every copy, including negatives, rookie, unless you want duty at that middle school dance Saturday night."

"Ha! I'm kidding. Man, Ev, you've got it bad."

"Get going."

Evan ushered Tony out and slammed the door but Tony's laugh could have penetrate steel.

Sitting at his desk, Evan imagined what the photo of Cassie on Mount Jo would look like. Knowing Tony, he'd probably taken dozens from every angle. Evan opened his desk drawer and removed the photo again. His finger traced a lopsided circle on the glass. Cassie looked perfect with Jake and at the time he couldn't help a moment of envy. Someone's wife was off limits, invisible. But still, Evan couldn't deny the rush of longing that settled around his heart. He'd built a comfortable bachelor's life, let women know he wasn't the marrying kind and shared good times. He wanted nothing more. Until the night before he left for the war.

After one night with Cassie, suddenly he wanted it all.

Again he thought of this weekend, and slid open his cell. Maybe Jake would spill.

His finger paused over the keypad. He gazed at the picture again, snapped shut the cell phone. He gave the idea a minute's further thought before he turned to his computer. He squinting at the monitor's bright blue glow as it booted up.

Within seconds, he found what he needed.

****

Cassie cleaned the last of her spatulas of mocha chocolate cream. Her fingers ached. She left the frosting covered bowl to soak in the sink. Her cuckoo clock sounded five times. She'd greeted customers and made candies without a break. But no amount of activity made her forget Dylan's phone call.

His call made no sense. After what he'd done to her, how could he think she'd ever consider returning? More importantly, how did he know about the hearing? Did he have someone watching her? Could that be why she nursed the creeps all last week? She knocked some clean spatulas into the bowl of sudsy water. Her hands shook as she retrieved each one. Then from the checkout area Cassie heard Alexi's muted call for assistance. The pre-teen worked a couple hours each day before closing so Cassie could clean things up. Although shy, Alexi was polite to customers and good with numbers.

The kitchen door opened a crack from Cassie's light touch. Alexi, who rarely smiled beyond a grin beamed at someone on the other side of the counter and shuffled her feet. Alexi glanced at Cassie and rolled her eyes. She thought the girl mouthed, "holy-shit," but couldn't be sure.

Cassie feared the worst—robbery. Karl warned her if it ever happened to hand over the money. The place was insured. "Don't do anything to encourage him to be violent," Karl warned. With her knees knocking she reached for the telephone.

"Cas-sie! There's some-one here to seee-yoooou," cried Alexi.

No time to make that call. Her singsong voice meant *help!* Cassie reached for the nearest weapon. Her hands found and trembled on the broom handle. Splinters dug into her skin as she cursed herself for not calling the police at the first sign of trouble. The lightweight slatted door swung open with a hallow tap. She took a steadying breath and charged, broom handle leading the way.

"Go to the kitchen and wrap the petit-fours, Alexi. I'll see to the customer."

Her jaw dropped open when she saw the broom, and she took a step back.

Cassie tightened her grip on the broom handled and tried to sound natural as she rounded the counter to face the thief.

"Can I be of assistance, s-sir?"

Making eye-contact, her already weak knees

liquefied. Before she landed on the floor she managed to slide the register stool underneath her butt. Her heart thudded so hard her chest hurt.

"I thought you were a robber!" She looked up at the intruder, more terrifying than an actual thief.

Evan's cool smile disappeared. He came around the counter and crouched next to her. "Take a deep breath. If you thought I was a robber, why didn't you call the police?"

Why?

She looked at his gilded-blond hair that needed no sunshine to glow and chocolate-syrup eyes that she swore grew sweeter every time she gazed into them.

Why, he asked? Because ever since he'd carried her then put her to bed she'd been unable to think straight. She couldn't function properly in her own store. And it was all—his—fault.

"No time. I brought a broom." She raised it.

He frowned. One by one he removed each white-knuckled finger from the broom handle. Minus the broom she felt better and tried to stand.

"Easy. Don't stand yet. You're white as a sheet."

He pressed her hand into her lap. Then he disappeared through the swinging doors and returned with a tall glass of water. "Drink this first, then you can tell me about your security system."

She swallowed the water the wrong way and coughed.

He patted her gently on the back.

God, this is mortifying. He must think I'm totally incapable of running this shop. "I don't have any."

His eyebrows rose an inch, but he didn't comment.

"This is a pretty safe area." *Well, somewhat safe,* she thought. Dylan's phone call howled back into her memory.

His eyebrows lowered and she couldn't help but

think they were nicely shaped, not scraggly like some men's. They were smooth and thick, like the man before her. He scanned the room and then focused on her face.

"I've been here almost a year, and I've never come close to having a problem other than a broken lock," she added.

Now his eyes narrowed and those beautiful brows dove, accentuating his concern.

"I replaced it with a padlock." She couldn't tell if he was listening. He rose, put his hands on his hips and stared at her as if deep in thought. Feeling like a teenager who'd stayed out past curfew, she braced herself for a scolding.

But the lecture never came.

He glanced at the front door then back at her. "You need a panic button by the register. That will alert the police. Bolted locks, too. What security company set this place up, the Keystone Kops?" He strode across the room and checked the display window.

The cobwebs cleared from her head. "Wait. What are you doing here?" Her voice sounded shrill, but she didn't care. He scared two years off her life. And made fun of her store.

"There's a great deal of inventory here, more treasures than candy for a robber."

His gaze could ignite paper. Something inside her kindled, but she tapped it out. She didn't need anyone telling her how to run her store.

He walked behind the checkout area. "Where's your safe?"

"I keep a small strong box in my apartment, upstairs, and go to the bank twice a week." Her cheeks heated. "If you came for a gift, I can help you. But as you can see, we're quite busy, and—"

"How's your dad?" Evan said to Alexi, who'd emerged from the kitchen with a tray of broken chocolate.

The child took a big breath. "He's great. Mom said she saw you this weekend. Did you rescue any climbers?"

The warm smile he gave Alexi surprised Cassie. Maybe Evan frowned only when around her.

Alexi giggled.

Evan glanced back at Cassie then answered. "Not this weekend. For the past six weeks, I've been training recruits in mountain search and rescue."

Alexi nodded, doe-eyed, as if God spoke.

Oh, brother.

"Would you like some Belgian chocolate? Once you've tasted some, you won't be satisfied with any other." Alexi walked up to him and raised the tray like a Greek offering.

Again, he turned toward Cassie. "Is that true?" His face looked decadent.

Cassie's mouth went dry. She took another sip. The water trickled down her throat. Steam heated her cheeks.

Alexi didn't realize the double meaning of her remark and vanished back into the kitchen to find more samples. Evan waited for Cassie's answer, the corners of his mouth twitching like he was holding back a smile.

"Um...well, many people prefer it to, um, French chocolate, um, that has less sugar. Then there are those who prefer Italian chocolate, which seems to be the rage now. The Italians mix hazelnuts with their chocolate base."

She stammered like a nervous student presenting her first English report before the entire class. He'd leaned on the counter, inching closer as she spoke. Those rich fudge-colored whirlpools beckoned her into their swirling depths.

"*Why* are you here, Evan? After yesterday, I thought we'd never cross paths again."

He gave her more space, swept some tinfoil from the counter. "I wanted to make sure you were okay. You were pretty upset when you left. I didn't mean to say anything to hurt you."

"You came to apologize? First of all, it's not necessary. And second, you could have done that over the phone."

He shrugged and then walked over to a display adjacent to the counter. He checked the price tag on the largest basket, filled with imported chocolates.

"Is this the Italian chocolate you were talking about?"

"Yes. It's expensive, but well worth it." Out of habit, the line spilled out.

He smiled, showing straight white teeth. "Do you deliver?"

"Of course, I deliver." She set down the empty glass and moved behind the cash register, an automatic move she learned to close a sale.

He stared at her for a moment then said casually, "I'll take it." One-handed he set the large basket on the counter and the other presented a credit card.

Her heart contract briefly when their fingers brushed and an exquisite tension fill her body. Somehow she charged the order correctly, thinking he was watching her with his police instincts. Could he tell she'd lied? She hoped she wasn't that transparent.

"I came for one other thing."

He eyed the credit card receipt on the counter and walked to the kitchen door. "Alexi, I'd like to take Mrs. Hamilton to dinner." He leveled his gaze daring Cassie to object.

Alexi breezed through the doors. "No problem, *Evan.*"

Her traitorous assistant knew they were done for the day and preparing to leave. Cassie wanted to

70

tell him to go to hell, but his pen poised right above the slip of paper. He waited for her answer. He'd picked out the most expensive chocolate display basket in the store that wasn't in the cooler. Well, if he wanted to play games, she'd play along.

"Get your things. I'm going to dinner with Mr. Jorgenson." The counter drawer squeaked as she pulled it open. Kisses rolled around, but she found no scraps of paper. "Where did you say you wanted this delivered?"

Lines around his eyes softened. He signed the receipt, hastily scribbled an address on the back and then handed it back to her.

Her fingertips snatched the receipt like avoiding a bear trap. "Is this downtown?"

"The red brick office building with white pillars. You can't miss it." He hesitated until she looked up. "It's for a friend."

She shouldn't have felt one ounce of jealousy, but it was there. Since she'd be the one to deliver it, she'd see the lucky lady firsthand.

Something else to look forward to this week.

****

A manicured jasmine bush swayed in the ocean breeze outside Dylan Black's office window. His newly delivered black Porsche Carrara glistened like polished onyx in the early afternoon sun. If his business continued to grow he'd have a fleet of six-figured cars.

As long as he kept his new silent partners happy.

Right on schedule his cell rang. "Did you get inside?" he blurted. Even a thousand miles away, he needed to know her every move.

"Piece of cake," Stone said. "She's got no alarm system and the locks were from nineteen-ten."

Dylan held the phone away from his ear, wishing he could put Stone on speaker but someone

71

might overhear the booming voice. "What did you find?"

A siren whined, then Stone answered. "Nothing. No money in the till, and no safe in view or concealed."

"Are you sure—hang on, Stone. *Go away, I'm busy,*" Dylan bellowed. One of his assistant barged into the office. His Lycra-clad butt sashayed out the door. He had no patience for the moron today. Time was running out. He'd hoped for a better report from Stone. "You were saying?"

"I'm sure. That's what you're paying me for."

Stone had the audacity to laugh.

Dylan seethed and crushed his empty coffee cup in his hand. "She's either hiding it in her apartment or has it in a safety deposit box." The door opened again. His secretary tiptoed into his lair with some papers that needed his signature. He winked at her and she blushed. "I'm running out of time here. You'll have to approach her." He took the offered papers and signaled the girl to get him a pen. "But don't hurt her."

Dylan heard a gasp and looked up. With a shocked expression and pen poised like a dart, the new hire backed out of his office. He wondered how much longer she'd last. She gave great head.

"How much time do I have?" Stone asked.

"I need it yesterday." The idiot knew about the urgency.

"There's one other thing. She's got a boyfriend. He's like a bodyguard—showed up at the shop— checked her doors. He's on her like glue."

The papers he clasped flew across the room. "Who's the guy?" His heart skipped a beat at the thought of his Cassie with another man. She belonged to him and no one else.

"Name's Evan Jorgenson, a sergeant in the State Police."

Dylan kicked his desk chair. "Fuck. Look, I'm paying you top dollar to be quick about this. If you can't get the job done by the end of the week, you're fired."

"It would be easier if you'd let me rough her up a bit. Then, she'd talk—"

"No! I don't want her touched." *Overrated dickhead.* "Not one hair. Keep looking around and let me know where she goes. And fax me a full bio on Jorgenson. Today!"

Dylan cut the signal. Cassie should have been back with him by now. Why couldn't she forget what happened and come home? Without thinking, he slammed the cell phone onto the desk. Metallic pieces scattered about the room. He cursed as he pulled one chunk from his palm and wrapped a handkerchief around it to keep the blood off his silk jacket.

Christ. He hoped he didn't need stitches. He had to get control of the situation before everything he'd worked, sweat and stole for fell to pieces. And get Cassie back where she belonged, fast.

Chapter Six

Evan gripped the steering wheel of the Jeep as Cassie waved goodbye to Alexi. Any second now she'd give him hell. Since slamming the car door she'd ignored him and spoke only to Alexi about some big date this weekend. The way she sat with her arms crossed tightly across her chest spoke volumes to a man trained to judge the body language of suspects. When he made sure the doors were relocked, she stole a look his way and *tsked*.

Hell, her irritation only aroused him further.

"Do you like Thai?" he asked, reigning in his lust as he backed down the driveway and onto the street.

She uncrossed her arms and sat closer to her door. "What? ties? What kind of ties—"

"Thai food. It's like Japanese, but spicier."

No response. Probably thinking of a way to get out of dinner. He'd seen suspects lean against the car door just like she was in an attempt to jump out. The skin on his left forearm tingled.

At a stoplight he looked at her, prompting an answer.

Weariness entered her green eyes. "Why are you doing this, Evan? Do you think if you take me to dinner I'll sleep with you again?"

God, yes. "Or we can be friends again. I've been thinking about how much I missed our talks." The skin on his left arm burned to be scratched.

The traffic light turned green. Her throat worked like she wanted to say something but the driver behind them honked his horn, startling her. He drove for a few more minutes before she broke the silence.

"I can't eat anything spicy. I've been having stomach problems."

Relieved that she didn't ask him to take her home, his breath rushed out. "The Lemon Grass has non-spicy food, too." He felt like he was probing with a hammer on a crystal vase.

"I've been there before. Okay."

The rest of the ride passed quietly, partly because she gazed out the window. Preoccupied about her business? The shop seemed undisturbed when he'd entered. Maybe she'd added inventory today. There wasn't a speck of dust on any baskets. Earlier he gave the shop's address to one of his officers needing a special birthday present for his wife.

When they arrived at the restaurant Evan requested an secluded alcove lit by fat candles. He ordered an imported beer for himself and Cassie ordered a glass of white wine and then looked at her menu with what appeared to be eagerness. When the waiter returned she asked one question after another and settled on Tamarind duck, a house specialty.

"I'll have what the lady ordered."

Hell, if she ordered hay, he planned to order the same thing. He smiled at Cassie who looked suspicious but remained silent.

Like at Mirror Lake's restaurant, Cassie checked out the room, then gazed out the large expanse of windows. Outside the restaurant happy couples walked hand in hand to various destinations around Armory Square. She watched one couple until they disappeared around the corner, an unreadable look on her face.

He waited for her gaze to seek his. "So why open a candy store?"

"It's a chocolate shop."

He reclined back in his chair and focused on her lips. "There's a difference?"

"I don't sell bar candy or gummy stuff. My candy is homemade chocolate except the basket you purchased today." She folded her hands on the table and met his stare.

He nodded, noting the stiffness in her posture. "Quite a lot of chocolate in it." *Had she hurt her back stocking baskets on that shelf?*

"Actually that basket contained a variety of imported European chocolates," she said, barely breathing as she spoke.

Alexi wasn't much bigger than Cassie, so Cassie must do all the arranging on those high shelves. "You import all your chocolate?"

She barely moved her head when she nodded. "Some," she replied, rearranging her silverware. "My grandmother collected recipes and made candy all the time. My earliest memory is helping her stir chocolate over a double boiler. I think that's when I fell in love with the smell and taste of it."

In the soft candlelight the words, *fell in love,* hung in the air and stopped her rambling.

He drummed his fingers. *Keep her talking, Champ.* It helped him to ignore the stupid itch on his forearms. "I read somewhere it was first used for medicinal purposes."

She nodded. "In the 1700's it was sold in drug stores as a cure-all."

She licked her strawberry-red lips. Her shoulder

slumped, but the pulse at the delicate cleft of her neck still fluttered. His gaze slid across her collarbone to her cleavage. *Does it work on itches?* "I always wondered how they made chocolate-covered cherries. Do you know?"

"If people knew how they were made they probably wouldn't buy them unless they were homemade."

The lovely spark of distaste in her eyes made him laugh. "How so?" He rubbed the back of his neck where the itch began to set-up camp.

"They add a chemical to the cherries before dipping that makes them sweat out their juices. By the time the chocolate shell is hardened, the cherries have shrunk, and the clear liquid has oozed out and is trapped inside the chocolate."

Juices, hardened, trapped. Oh, yeah, he could relate.

"When they are bitten into, that juice is so laden with chemicals and the cherry so hard, well, I never cared for them."

He felt cross-eyed for a moment and she misinterpreted his discomfort. "Oh, excuse me, it never occurred to me that you might like those candies. I hope I haven't spoiled it for you."

Then, she snapped open her napkin, and for a moment, he thought he saw her grin.

****

Evan squirmed like a toddler in his seat. Smothering a giggle, Cassie watched him over the rim of her wineglass. When he stood up and excused himself, she wanted to pat herself on the back.

Served him right for forcing her to dinner. But the delicious smells made her anxious to try a few bites.

She pressed her hand over her tummy and silently coached her stomach to relax and enjoy the meal. As for her heart she begged it to stop hammering every time he looked at her lips. Evan was a great kisser and her lips hungered for one taste. Getting re-involved with Evan would be heaven but in the long run they had no future.

The waiter entered with two salad plates. Her stomach gurgled as she smelled the citrus vinaigrette dressing. Surprised that her appetite returned, she savored the micro-greens. As she stuffed another forkful in her mouth, Evan slid his chair from the table and re-sat. She thought she smelled a chemical odor but it wafted away under the tangy citrus fragrance as Evan dug in. He looked a little cross about something and stabbed at his micro-greens.

Jeez, they were only talking about candy. "Is everything okay?"

A flash of annoyance turned into a heated stare that made those dreamy brown eyes twice as luscious. "Tell me more about homemade candies. It sounds, er, fascinating."

"Well, let's see. Do you have a favorite?"

He put the salad fork down and thought for a moment. "I haven't had chocolate in a while but I remember getting boxes of the stuff when I was young."

The image of a blond hair little boy poking through a box of chocolates came to mind. "Oh, you probably got a Whitman's Sampler. They have the best variety of cream-filled chocolates. Do you like cream-filled chocolates?"

"Do you?" It sounded like he was choking on the words but he didn't have anything in his mouth.

She waved her hand. "Oh, I can spend the day with a box of cream-filled chocolates. It's always so much fun to see what's inside. Sometimes I can't wait and take a bite of each one. When I make my own for the shop I try to imagine my customer's surprise when they discover all the different varieties of creams and fillers I've hidden inside the chocolate. Sometimes I use liqueurs, too."

Evan tipped his head back and took a long swallow of beer. His Adam's apple bobbed on his throat. She leaned forward, remembering kissing that long column and the memory of his warm male scent filled her nose. No chocolate smelled as heavenly.

The waiter returned. Evan ordered another beer and did that squirmy thing in his chair again. She giggled into her napkin.

"Is that your only favorite?" His voice turned as creamy as cocoa butter, and his eyes re-focused on her lips.

The room grew warmer and she sipped more ice water before replying. "Well, I do have one all-time favorite but you're gonna laugh at me."

She kidded, but he didn't move a muscle.

Her turn to squirm. "I love kisses." His interest intensified. "*Hershey's* kisses."

Evan leaned forward on his elbows taking up all the space and air in the alcove. His irises glowed golden in the candlelight. "Why?"

Feeling breathless, she answered. "When I was little my father put kisses next to my cereal bowl. When he'd get home at night he'd say, '*Little girl, did you get my kisses this morning?*' and then give me a big kiss... he used to call me his Sweet Thing..." A smile tugged at her lips. Those were such happy times. "One day he lost his job. He couldn't find work and started hanging around Lou's Bar day and night. Money became tight, Mom said, and... well... I never stopped liking Hershey's kisses."

The night her father left her parents argued terribly. They thought she'd been sleeping but she'd crept onto the stairs. Mom was tired of working two jobs and he needed to find work. Dad yelled something back and then said that they didn't need him. The door slammed so hard the house shook and then her mother wept for hours. The last time she saw him was five years ago on Heather's second birthday. He'd left the area but sent postcards from places he'd been. Now and then he phoned. She hoped one day he'd return so Heather could get to know her grandfather.

The waiter cleared the salad plates. The entries appeared and both ate in silence. She glanced up at Evan but he seemed deep in thought. When the waiter cleared the plates again he presented Cassie with a dessert menu.

"Oh, I can't eat another bite, I'm stuffed." She'd cleaned her dinner plate without a twinge of stomach discomfort but didn't want to push it.

The waiter tucked the menu under his arm and started to walk away. "Let me see that menu." Evan's voice startled Cassie after such a long period of silence. He studied the menu while one hand absently scratched the back of his neck. Then he motioned the waiter closer.

"What did you order?" She imagined Evan served up as dessert. Her heart pinched and left her breathless again.

"It's a surprise." His sexy grin returned. "So, you like Hershey's chocolate. Ever hear of Hershey Park?"

"I've been to the park but never been to the spa. Someday I'll go there." Staring at the flickering candle, she wondered if that dream like so many others was destined to burn away.

"Spa? What kind of spa could be there?" He leaned forward on his elbows halving the comfortable space between them.

Between dry lips she swallowed more wine before answering. "Only the best spa in the world. They serve you chocolate samples from the moment you walk in the door."

"That's nothing special," he said, and then captured her hand as it fell from the wineglass.

Warmth stretched down her fingertips and across her wrist. Her traitorous fingers curled in his palm. "No, that's the beginning. They use chocolate products for all the spa treatments." His golden brows made a vee on his forehead, so she continued. "For a body scrub they use finely ground cocoa shells. Then, when they massage you, they use cocoa butter. And they have tubs of meltdown chocolate to bathe in."

His eyebrows rose. "Bathe in?"

"They bring you into this room and dip you into a tub of chocolate. Can you imagine the smell?" She took a deep breath. "You can wash yourself in chocolate syrup and bask in a bath for as long as you want."

She closed her eyes and rolled her head back at the thought of such decadence.

****

Evan watched Cassie close her eyes and imagine lying in a tub of chocolate.

Forget chocolate-covered cherries.

Give him chocolate-covered Cassie.

He'd picked the topic of her candy making thinking it was a safe subject. About as safe as watching porn on a first date. He'd already gone to the bathroom twice to pile on the hydrocortisone cream after her description of chocolate-covered cherries. Lord knew he'd never be able to buy a box of them again without getting turned-on, or itchy. If she knew all her talk of cream-filled candy made him ready to throw her on the table she'd probably leave the state again. Thank God she'd changed the subject and talked about her dad. He wanted to know everything about her, good or bad.

"Here's the dessert, sir."

The waiter set the plate down with two forks.

Hot fudge seeped out from under the cream. The decadent whipped cream-covered treat got Cassie's attention.

Point scored for her smile.

"I thought you might change your mind when you saw what I ordered," he chuckled, nudging the plate toward her.

Her eyes were glued to the dessert. "Maybe I'll take a little bite." She selected a small corner, swirled it around in the hot fudge syrup and opened that pink mouth. In went the fork then her lips closed on the tines. Her eyes fluttered shut as the tines slowly pulled out between her lips. "Mmmmm."

He bit the inside of his cheek envying the hunk of cake sitting on her plate. The tip of her tongue skimmed her lips searching for drops of syrup and he heard a *pop* in his head like a blasting cap exploding. "Have another bite," he coached, mesmerized by her lips. He cut off a large piece of brownie and held it up.

She hesitated a moment then opened her mouth. In went the forkful of cake generously soaked in topping. Some dripped on her chin. She laughed and went to wipe it off.

"Don't."

He raised his thumb and rubbed her chin then brought his thumb back to his mouth and sucked. Looking alarmed she stopped chewing and then swallowed hard.

He proceeded to cut a large piece and place it in his mouth. *Damn, that's good.* He never remembered a chocolate brownie tasting this good. He cut off another large piece and moved it into his mouth all the while watching her take smaller bites and thinking about how much he'd like to take his time exploring her mouth.

She looked up. Alarm left her eyes and he'd have sworn a newer emotion replaced it—maybe longing?

Did she still care? He had a gut feeling it wasn't the brownie she wanted and the thought alerted the interest in his pants.

She stared at the empty plate. Brilliant green eyes searched his. "Did you like it?"

"I've never had better."

****

Evan grew impatient as he watched Cassie fumble with the key in the old lock. He'd like to get his hands on the guy who remodeled the chocolate shop but ignored the door to her living quarters above the shop. One good kick would pop it open. A few more jiggles on the door handle and it creaked opened into a dim, cold hallway that he coaxed her inside.

She glanced up the stairwell and then faced him. "I want to thank you for a nice evening. And for the basket order of chocolates. I'll see it gets delivered tomorrow."

Then she stuck her hand out.

He almost laughed at the outstretched hand and tentative look on her face. Undaunted, he grabbed her wrist and pulled her into his arms. Her body tensed at first but as his lips neared, she softly sighed and relaxed.

A light burst behind his eyes as his lips touched hers. Not the blinding desert sun that baked a man's body and turned hope to ashes, rather the soothing yellow sunshine on a lazy summer day. Meeting with no resistance, he parted her lips and tasted the honey of her mouth. He kicked the door shut and moved her up against the wall, all the time tasting more of her sweetness.

Not even a mountain of chocolate could be sweeter.

Inflamed that she hadn't resisted, his control broke. Over and over he claimed her mouth, paying attention to caress every recess, invading her mouth the way his body desired to invade hers. The fiercer his kisses the more she wilted in his arms. She tasted like chocolate and the desire she was trying to deny herself. Need swept through every inch of him, begging to be satisfied, so he turned up the heat and added more pressure to the kiss. When she responded with a sweet moan, he pressed between her legs, consummating the kiss.

Somehow they'd moved to the stairs. She reclined on a step and he leaned over her. In the soft glow she reminded him of an angel sent to ease his torment. Only a few more steps and they'd be in her apartment. Once inside no way would he tuck her in bed again and leave.

He wished it were that simple.

Some sane part of him found restraint and he dragged his lips from hers. His blood accelerated through his veins, numbing the pain he lived with. *God, kissing her is more potent than morphine.* He looked into those eyes and couldn't remember why he'd stopped kissing her. Her hands cupped his face and the past fell away, back to the night in his apartment where he wished to God he'd confessed his true feeling. But too much had happened since then. Instead of kissing her again he rubbed his thumb over her swollen lip, marking the spot.

She pressed her fingers to her lips and stared at him, all soft and glowing and as amazed as he felt by the look on her face. His arms dropped by his sides and he backed through the doorway.

"I'll be seeing you."

Heading down the porch stairs, his lungs filled with the crisp, clear fall air. By the time he reached the Jeep he felt lightheaded. He paused besides the driver door to steady himself and looked back. A silhouette parted the upstairs curtains, waved and then lights out. His mind conjured up images of Cassie lying beneath him and he ached to go back inside and finish what they'd started. But what if he woke up screaming, feeling the searing heat of the explosion, and blinded by the white flash before the deafening thunder?

Inside the car he leaned over to key the ignition. The keys jingled as they landed somewhere on the floorboard. *Damnit.* His breaths came in white ragged puffs. The steering wheel suffered a punch that his useless fingers never felt.

Once again, he'd done the honorable thing, played the part of the hero.

Would there ever be more to his life?

Chapter Seven

Cassie closed the apartment door and fell back against it. *Oh, that kiss was divine.* It took her seconds to welcome Evan's kisses. Hot, intoxicating and focused directly at her, the power of his kiss pulsed clear to her toes. Like a rich chocolate desert she'd denied herself, his kiss poured through her system, filling the empty places and opening a door she'd nailed shut leaving her feeling exposed and vulnerable again.

Her fingers touched her lips still warm and throbbing. This kiss was so different from their goodbye kiss. She'd acted like a mother hen telling him to be careful, keep his head low, all kinds of stupid things to say to a man who'd been a police officer and a former soldier. On the verge of hysteria, they'd kissed like the world was ending that night.

This kiss left her wanting much more.

His mustache didn't tickle but felt soft against her mouth. His lips tasted like no chocolate she'd ever sampled, resembling a secret recipe that tasted rich and exotic and sexy. She'd never been absorbed in a kiss and so unconcerned for the consequences.

Superman nailed her with the kiss of the

decade, conquering and gentle at the same time, one that would linger on her lips for hours.

As she undressed, she wondered how that kiss affected him? Then a dubious thought occurred to her. Maybe he'd run off so fast because it didn't mean that much to him. He didn't even try to come in, or suggest they spend the night together. From the beginning of the date he'd made it clear he wanted to be friends. Maybe it was a reflex, a perfunctory end-of-date kiss?

If so, she'd be in big trouble when he gave her the real thing.

"When? No, there won't be a when," she shouted to her bedroom mirror, hoping her hormones heard it. Evan was off-limits.

He'd probably forgotten it by now. Twice, when the opportunity presented itself he hadn't tried to sleep with her. That bothered her more than she cared to admit.

As she changed into a tank top and flannel pajama bottoms, the memory of the kiss replayed in her mind like a radio tune that she couldn't get enough of. No, she decided. That was more than a goodnight kiss—a kiss that promised more to come, like an invitation to a good party. But was she ready for the man who came with it? As she slid between the sheets her muscles loosened. She snuggled under the cover and sighed.

When was the last time she felt this relaxed? All from one stupendous kiss after another. In the darkness of her bedroom she admitted the truth. If he hadn't stopped kissing her she'd have begged him to be in her bed right now. She'd gladly fall back into his arms if he wanted her, but then what?

Oh, thank God he stopped.

She rolled over on her back and threw the covers over her head. The court date was this week. One crazy man was calling. It took all her time and energy to run the shop and make candy.

She didn't need more complications.

Sleeping with Evan would complicate her life.

****

Evan heard the soft footsteps before the knock on his office door. He opened it.

He saw the top of her head first. A triangle of blue fabric held her hair away from her face, the rest fell over her shoulder in a long braid. She wore jeans and a gray sweatshirt and sneakers. A bland look on anyone else, but enchanting on Cassie. Her cheeks were flushed, maybe from the flight of stairs, or maybe, he hoped, she remembered their goodnight kiss. Never far from his thoughts, seeing Cassie's face made the memory of their kiss return in minute detail.

"Evan... you never wrote the name of the person getting this basket." The basket thumped on top of his desk. She wiped her hands on her jeans and snuck a quick look at him under her sooty eyelashes. A deeper pink glow flooded her cheeks as she waited for his reply.

Yeah, she's thinking about the kiss.

He suppressed the urge to lean over his desk and taste those parted lips but next time there would be no stopping.

"I'll take you there." He held the door open for her.

Hoisting the basket with two hands, some folders fell to the floor. "Oops." She knelt and began to pick them up which brought her eye level with the picture of Jenny and Clay. "Are these people family?"

"Sorta." When her brow crinkled with confusion, he clarified. "That's Clay and Jenny." He braced for questions. Surely, she'd heard the story of Jenny from Jake.

Instead of prying she carefully angled the

picture on the desk the way he had it.

He pointed to the door. "It's not far. You want me to carry that?"

"No. I have it." Two dainty hands re-grabbed the wicker handle and hefted it up. Pretty strong for a slip of a woman. "Lead the way," she ordered.

Five paces down a narrow hallway they ran into Dawn, who smiled when she saw him, but frowned at Cassie. The young temp threw her cleavage forward and opened her permanently pouting mouth. "I was on my way to see you, Ev—I mean, Sergeant Jorgenson. I have those reports typed that you needed right away. Do you want me to wait in your office?"

As Dawn spoke she assessed Cassie. Unconcerned with the conversation and teetering the basket on one knee, Cassie's expression remained unchanged.

"Leave them on my desk. If there's more changes I'll call you."

Anxious to get Cassie to the hub, he moved around the temp without waiting for her reply. Cassie struggled to hoist the basket. "That basket looks heavy," he said, reaching out a hand to take it.

She shook her head and adjusted the basket higher, resting it on her hip. "I'm fine. Lead on."

He continued down the hallway. The other secretaries better be on breaks.

After a few turns came the drones of a large office in full swing. Cassie winced at the noise and held her breath as he held the door open. Uniformed officers from several forces crammed the room, working hard on a breaking case.

Tony broke from the pack and ran up to her. "Cassie! How-ya-doin? Is Evan giving you the grand tour? What's with the basket?"

"Hi, Tony—"

"Let me help you with that," Tony said, giving

Evan a cross-look.

Cassie glimpsed around the room, probably trying to understand why about ten guys stopped working and stood at attention when Tony yelled her name.

Evan's hands beat Tony's to the basket. He lifted it from her shaking hands and set it on a desk. "After dinner last night I invited her for a tour. She's brought chocolates from her shop. Some are imported from Italy."

Cassie's head whipped around so fast that he thought it wasn't going to stop until it did one of those *Exorcist*-like spins. Her green eyes rifled his. "I thought it was for..." she halted when he leveled his gaze. He could swear smoke came out of her nostrils, too.

"*Serendipity Sweets*," she corrected, "that's the name of my chocolate shop." Her arms crossed beneath her chest and she tapped her sneaker but didn't add anything further.

She's magnificent when she's pissed. So he'd lied about the delivery and the tour. Why wasn't she grateful he'd drummed up a little business?

When he caved in to a chuckle her expression changed to delight. Either she'd realized his good intentions or she was plotting revenge. His gut told him the latter.

"Yes, Tony, these are for you and *your* men. Evan said he has some reports to go over. Maybe, if you aren't too busy, you could show me around and introduce me to your co-workers."

"Sure. Anything for you, sugar-cakes. I can't wait for the guys to meet you."

Only Tony's mother could have loved the devious sparkle in his eyes.

"And, Tony, you still owe me a meal," she added. That sexy smile made Evan want to handcuff her to his wrist and march her out of the station, straight to his apartment. Then she arched one perfect eyebrow as if to say, *What do you think of that?*

Tony grabbed the basket and Cassie's hand, and pulled her away before Evan could comment or give *her* an eyebrow.

Nothing could be heard over Tony's shouting, anyway. "Hey! Daemon... Bob... Palmer! This is the babe from Lake Placid I told you about!"

Palmer, an officer so large he barely fit behind his desk, rose with outstretched hand, ready for a shake. "Peaches?"

Tony waved his hands and shouted, "No, not the commando chick without her underwear."

At Cassie's quick intake of breath, Tony blushed. Retrieving the basket that Tony placed on a nearby desk, Cassie held it between her and Palmer.

"Chocolate body armor isn't going to help with this crew," Evan murmured.

Hanes hung up the phone and shouted from across the room. "The one *on* the mountain... the Supermodel?" He sounded like a kid asking Santa for a Christmas present.

Damn-it. Tony circulated those pictures.

Confused, Cassie looked at Tony and Tony looked back at Evan for help.

Evan could see Tony shrink under his glare. "Middle school duty next week, Officer Garibaldi."

Tony waved-off Evan's remark and took Cassie by the arm. He then ushered her from desk to desk. The biggest grumps in the office managed silly smiles when introduced to *his* girlfriend.

Well, she'd won this one. Let Tony take her to lunch. He'd probably take her to some Italian place in East Syracuse and not make another move on her. Or maybe Evan needed to remind Officer Garibaldi he could kill a man over a dozen different ways with his bare hands.

To make sure, he walked up behind Cassie and

placed both hands around her waist. She tensed a little as he pulled her back a step. "See ya later, sweetie." He eyed the room and made sure every guy watched as he kissed her on the cheek.

Shoulders slumped around the room. Cassie didn't reply but gave him a .38-caliber glare over her shoulder.

Inwardly he grinned. What he wouldn't give to turn that hot temper in another direction.

But first, they needed to talk.

****

With a name like Garibaldi, Cassie suspected Tony would take her to an Italian restaurant for lunch. What she didn't expect was a place so filled with, what was a polite word? Ambience?

Fifties-styled, but not mid-century chic, the place looked frozen in time. The chrome-legged tables were topped with bright red, pearly Formica surfaces. They were crowded back-to-back along white stucco walls with barely enough room for the pincushion-seated chrome chairs. She counted at least fifty seats in a room built for less than half of that. What did she expect? Linen tablecloths and soft candlelight? Once seated, and wedged between two tables, she took another long sniff. The place smelled like they'd perfected tomato sauce. Her mouth watered in anticipation.

Where was the waiter with a menu? Her stomach wasn't as jumpy as yesterday. Although she'd eaten about a quarter of her meal last night it settled nicely without the usual pain. No running to the bathroom in the middle of the night meant her first full night's sleep in a long time. But the sight of Evan in his uniform set her innards fluttering in a good way. She couldn't take her eyes off him. The dark gray uniform made his skin look more tan and his golden hair glistened. Although his move was sneaky, she'd grown weak in the knees when he pulled her back to his chest. By the look on Tony's face, she hadn't imagined the gentle brush of Evan's lips on her hot cheek.

Tony gestured to some men that called to him from across the room, yelled something she couldn't understand, and some swear words in Italian that she did. He appeared to forget she was seated there as he talked to a group at another table. She'd barely heard much of the police officer's conversation over the pounding in her ears. It started when she entered the building anticipating the reaction of the woman who'd receive a basket of chocolates from Evan. He knew she'd think the basket was for a girlfriend. Still, it was nice of him to try to give her the business.

But how dare he pretend they were intimate in front of Tony and his co-workers?

She remembered overhearing a conversation while he and Jake watched football one Sunday afternoon, and she repaired Heather's jeans. Jake tried to coax out information about Evan's "string of ponies," to no avail, and then teased Evan that he hadn't kept a girlfriend for more than a Saratoga racing season. And how many women did Jake estimate Evan dated at once? Two? Four? She'd chuckled to herself at the time, thinking about all those poor women.

Her thoughts jumped to the bonbon that stopped him in the office hallway. That come-to-my-bed smile was Ocsar-caliber. She wondered if they already dated. Come to think of it when she'd arrived at the new State Police Troop Headquarters, the young brunette at the front desk, Heidi, glowered before giving directions to Evan's office. Maybe they'd dated, too.

Forget tomato sauce. She'd better order soup.

The sound of scraping chairs interrupted her thoughts. Four athletic-looking, gray uniformed men seated themselves. The young men merged shoulder-to-shoulder around the tiny table, each more handsome than the last, and they were staring at her.

You'd think *she* was lunch.

"Cassie Hamilton, meet Mike, Chris, Daemon and Freddie. They work in Evan's troop, too. You don't mind if they join us for lunch?" Tony's smile seemed easy and comfortable and she didn't sense any problem.

The more the merrier, right? "No problem. Hi."

She smiled amicably but became more nervous when they continued to stare at her. Blue eyes, green eyes, gray eyes and electric-blue eyes watched her in expectation. She felt like a crime suspect they were aiming to break.

At that moment the waiter showed up with a fist full of utensils. Instead of setting the places he threw them across the table. They clattered like the firing of an automatic weapon. The men didn't seem bothered. Each grabbed a fork or knife and starting ordering drinks and bread with cheese and oil. Then all eyes turned to her.

"I'll have a glass of water, no lemon, and a menu."

"No menu, lady—it's on the wall." The man then ignored her and began to take orders from around the table. With his black hair slicked back using a wide-toothed comb, the rude waiter looked like he belonged on, *The Sopranos.* His stance reminded her of someone more comfortable holding a machine gun rather than a pad and pencil.

Tony ordered a meatball tunnel, *swimming*, and a litany of Italian food on the side. The waiter stared at her, making her self-conscious. "Do you want a meatball or sausage with your ziti, lady?"

Huh? When did she order ziti? She was still trying to find the *wall* menu.

"Bring her one of each, Leo," Tony shouted over the noise of hungry customers. It didn't bother her that Tony ordered for her especially when he gave her that adoring look. She found herself smiling in spite of her nervousness.

Tony gestured around the table with his fork. "So, Cassie, the guys want to know all about you."

She shifted her napkin in her lap. "Well, there's not much to tell. I own an old-fashioned chocolate shop called, *Serendipity Sweets.* I've always dreamed of having my own shop and I love chocolate so the decision was easy. I make everything except the baskets that contain imports." *That* sounded like an "F" book report in Mrs. Mulligan's English class.

No one moved. A few jaws twitched.

Again all eyes stared at her, leaving her wondering what more they wanted to hear. She looked to Tony for guidance but he spied the impolite waiter and motioned him over to the table. "The lady didn't get her water yet, Leo. And where's the parm and oil? We've got to get back to work in fifteen!"

Magically a tiny, smiling waitress appeared with hot bread, freshly shredded Parmesan cheese and a carafe of olive oil. The waitress passed Cassie a small glass of water. The men began grabbing chunks of bread and loading them with oil and cheese. *Where's the butter?* she wanted to ask but then a steaming plate of ziti appeared before her. It smelled so incredible that she grabbed a fork from the middle of the table, stabbed several ziti and prayed her tummy wouldn't reject the tomato sauce.

Hands and arms swung across the table, in front of her and behind her, as the men passed around plates of food. There was a brief moment of silence. They seemed to have forgotten she was there. Good. The rich flavor of the tomato sauce exploded in her mouth. The ziti was chewy but she decided she liked it that way. When had she ever tasted something this good? One by one the ziti disappeared from her plate. It tasted so good she wanted to kiss the chef.

Tony passed the cheese shaker and shook a blizzard of cheese onto the remaining ziti on her plate. "Ya know, Cassie, Evan's up for a promotion. A big one. All this terrorist stuff." He waved a forkful of spaghetti through the air and then deftly dropped the pasta into his mouth.

"Terrorists?"

Not again. She dropped a forkful of ziti onto her napkin.

"They want him in Albany to coordinate mobile response with neighboring states in the event they have to hunt terrorists. Evan's the best man for the job."

"He has to go to Albany to find terrorists?" The queasy feeling returned.

"No," replied Tony. "He'll be in charge of the teams that go in to catch the terrorists and assist the Canadian border patrol. There's a lot of rough terrain."

"He's got the job already," Freddie added and he stretched a fork across the table to steal some of Tony's green peppers. Tony didn't seem to mind. "Are you gonna eat your sausage, Cassie?" His fork hovered midair.

She motioned for him to grab it, having lost her appetite as soon as she heard the word, *Albany.*

Albany. How can he kiss me and act like he's dating me around his friends when he's moving to Albany?

That gigolo.

"Yeah, he's got that job all locked up," Chris said between swallows. "Hearts will be breaking all over Syracuse when he leaves."

His stone-colored eyes collided with hers for a second.

Tony grunted. "Hearts are already breaking

since Cassie walked in today." He used a slice of bread to wipe his plate clean and then added, "I've never seen a bunch of women scramble so fast to the ladies room. Heard crying when I walked past the door."

Mike smirked. "You mean *listened* by the door, Antonio Sleaze-bag."

"Ahhh—it'll be in the paper tonight." Daemon, the only quiet one up to this point, whispered, making the group bark with laughter. "So, are you moving to Albany with Evan?"

Count to five. She licked her lips to keep from spitting out her answer. "Evan and I are old friends that ran into each other this weekend. We aren't dating." *I'm the woman he makes love to before he leaves for war or a new job.*

All heads snapped up from their respective half-eaten plates.

She tried to look them all in the eyes, but faltered under their, that's-what-you-think, expressions.

She looked at Tony for help.

"You and Evan went out to dinner last night, right?" he said.

She nodded.

"And breakfast together at the Mirror Lake Inn, and before that, Evan *carried* you back to your motel room, and, well…"

"Well, what, Tony?"

The unmistakable voice pierced the clatter of forks on plates.

Four men rose in unison, downed their drinks or wiped their mouths, and disappeared so fast they made Chris Angel seem like an amateur.

"Hey, Ev—glad you're here. I forgot I have to be in court." Tony patted Cassie's shoulder gently. "Bye-bye, sweet-cakes. I'll be seeing you around."

Tony disappeared as Evan pulled up a chair

next to hers.

Being carried by Evan wasn't as uncomfortable as sitting at the table with him in the absurdly crowded, noisy room. Conversations from five tables could be heard but the silence at their table was deafening. How much had he heard of her conversation with the men?

Leo re-appeared holding another fistful of silverware and a slip of paper. "You want me to put it on your tab, Evan?" Leo snuck a glance at Cassie, and then smiled slyly.

Evan nodded and signed the paper. Without looking up as he wrote, he spoke low. "We need to talk. Let's get outta here."

Oh, yeah, they needed to talk.

"My shop's usually quiet this time of day." No way were they going to his office. This talk would be on *her* turf.

He followed her out the door. In the parking lot the smell of decaying leaves replaced the aroma of Italian cooking. Question after question popped into her head as she drove. She punched the radio panel but no station played tunes that could soothe her nerves.

He's leaving for Albany. How dare he do this to her again? By the time she parked her car and fumbled with two keys to unlock the shop door she was ready for battle. One key slid into the slot easier than usual. *That's odd.* She'd have to check the lock later, after they talked. Then she stepped on the *Open* sign that she was certain she'd hung on the door and turned to *Closed.* She picked it up and traced the large circle of dirt. A footprint?

"Something wrong?" he asked.

Searching the floor for the sign's missing nail, she answered, "I must have closed the door too hard when I left this morning."

The rich smell of chocolate permeated the air.

Taking several deep breaths she fortified herself as Evan crouched to inspect the nail hole with his finger. The door swung around and he peered at the keyholes.

Cassie marched into her shop, unconcerned with what he was doing. "Niagara Sparkling Water is the only beverage I carry. It's that or tea."

"Water's fine," he replied from the other side of the door, smoothing his thumb over the doorframe.

The front door slammed shut as she grabbed two bottles of Niagara water from the cooler and then waited on the bench of the Little Tikes picnic table. Evan took the wooden adult chair across from her. His long legs stretched out and rested next to hers.

She passed him a bottle. "Why does everyone in your office think we're dating?" Twisting the bottle cap off with too much force, she spilled some water in her lap.

He placed his unopened bottle on the floor. "We went to dinner last night and before that breakfast and before that—"

"I remember before that." She gulped her water.

His hands slid in his pants pockets. "Maybe because I've been with you more this week than any woman. The guys know that. They're being cops, drawing the obvious conclusion."

Evan dated so many women his dates were advertised. She couldn't afford to get caught up in his corral of "ponies." Besides, she needed to concentrate all her energy on her chocolate shop and didn't need any distraction or interference.

"We agreed to be friends," she began.

He stared at her lips.

"Kissing goodnight doesn't make a relationship," she added.

He leaned toward her but his eyes stayed focused on her lips. "Oh? And what makes a relationship? Does making love count?"

Her nipples tingled. She dug her fingernails into her palms. "That happened four years ago. *Things* change."

Something on the Little Tikes table drew his attention from her lips. "You're right, things do change. People change. But feelings if they're deep enough rarely change." His arms crossed over his chest and he leaned back in the chair like a king.

Evan wanted her to admit that night was important. Then what? Sleep together again, for old time's sake?

Barely keeping her voice down she began to shake from the strain of guilt and controlling her temper. "Feelings? What about fidelity, loyalty?"

"They're important. But when two people sleep together for the right reasons, that's special." His gaze never wavered.

He believed what he said. *So he's a romantic.* But if the night they made love was special to him, wouldn't he have found some way to contact her by now? Communicate how he felt?

She stared at the mural behind him. A little bunny waved from under a bush. Fishhooks of pain stabbed her throat. "What about Albany?"

He made her wait an uncomfortable amount of time before he replied. "There's a job opening there that I want."

"A dangerous job looking for terrorists."

"Not only terrorists, but yes, if anything happens I'd be asked to coordinate all agency responses."

"And you're moving there." He appeared so composed, she wanted to roar the words.

He stood up and righted his slacks. "I have an interview, that's all."

From the basket on the table he grabbed a Superman coloring book and flipped through the pages. Karen's boys scribbled red and blue on most of the pictures.

"That's not the impression I got from your men. They asked me if I was moving with you," she said, nervously twisting the bottle cap.

He cursed and threw Superman back in the basket. "I have no idea why they said that."

Unable to look at him, she looked at her lap. Evan was like every other man she'd met since her divorce. Perfect gentlemen, initially saying and doing the right thing so she'd sleep with them. The difference was he wanted to do it again, telling her up front this time that it would mean nothing. Well she'd had enough disappointments to last a lifetime.

She stood up and fisted her hands behind her back. "I have to get back to work. Thanks for the order...and the opportunity to meet your friends."

She started toward the front door. Instead of following her, he wandered through the store. In front of her wedding display he paused and peered at the figurine. The groom's head was tilted to one side due to a missing piece of porcelain. Evan tilted his head. "He looks like he's thinking about buying chocolate. Is this an advertisement for men?"

She reached up and swiped the figure off the cake, surprising them both with her adeptness. "He's the groom. The bride fell the other day, and was in so many pieces...I haven't the time to pick up a new one."

He turned over her hand and opened her fist. "Looks like you need a new groom, too."

No. Not again. The head re-broke in several pieces. Hot tears stung her eyes. Ridiculous. She felt like bawling over a ceramic groom.

Evan let go of her hand.

She closed her eyes and listened for the door to close. It shut so hard the chimes rang like hundreds of cymbals.

Only then did she allow her tears to fall.

Chapter Eight

On the drive to Karen's cabin, Cassie replayed what happened in court, or rather what she remembered.

Most of the proceedings were a blur. Another six months. She dabbed at the corners of her eyes. How would she manage another six months without seeing Heather wake up in the morning to "good morning, Sunshine," or tucking her in "snug-as-a-bug-in-a-rug" at bedtime? Fruit roll ups, cookie dough ice cream and vanilla wafers, all Heather's favorites, were purchased thinking she'd spend her first weekend. She'd fallen asleep on Heather's bed last night. Eleven months had passed since Heather slept there. All because she'd messed-up.

Tears plopped onto the steering wheel. She pulled another tissue from the box on the passenger seat. A horn blasted. She looked up and saw that she was headed straight for another car. She braked hard. Yanking the steering wheel to the right, her compact swerved in time to avoid the crash. The pings of gravel hitting the car lasted for several seconds until it lurched to a stop on the shoulder. She unbuckled her seatbelt and slumped onto the steering wheel, fighting for breath. That was too close a call. Automotive, or nervous breakdown, either way she'd never get Heather back.

She sat up and looked around to make sure she didn't cause the other vehicle to swerve off the road. It took a minute before she realized the other car never crashed and had moved on. After several gulps of Chai tea-to-go, and several deep cleansing breaths, she restarted the motor. Before pulling into highway traffic, she checked the map one more time.

Snow Lake was off Route 28. Karen printed the names of each road she'd pass before making the final turn down a long, winding, dirt road to Karen's cabin by the lake. She'd passed two roads, five more to go.

This was a good idea, she kept telling herself, driving further and further from civilization. Last weekend was loaded with exercise, but they never talked much. Karen promised this weekend would be different. They could play Scrabble and watch their favorite movies, *Someone Like You,* and *French Kiss.* Make S'mores by a roaring campfire. Lounge in the Jacuzzi while drinking wine and searching for falling stars. And talk. Karen made it sound so relaxing. It no longer mattered that she'd closed her business another weekend. Working hard wouldn't get Heather back any faster if the judge kept ignoring her financial report.

Cassie did feel guilty taking Karen away from Karl and the kids two weekends in a row, but Karen insisted that the overnight trip wouldn't be a problem. Karl was Cassie's friend too, and both agreed she needed this. It would be a good time to tell Karen about Dylan's last phone call, too. And maybe talk about Evan. As hard as she tried to forget, she thought about him often. By tonight, Karen would know everything about L.A., as well as the night she'd spent with Evan.

She slowed as a mother deer with her fawn waited by the roadside. As she turned down another road, that creepy feeling up her spine returned. She checked over her shoulder. Headlights flashed in her rearview mirror. For a moment she thought the beat-up car that followed her up Route 28 followed her off the exit, too, but after ten minutes of watching the rearview mirror, the car and headlights disappeared.

Her imagination working overtime again.

No worries. She'd be safe there.

****

Evan settled back in his recliner to read the sports section. The phone rang. He set the paper down and picked up the receiver.

"Hey, man, you're hard to find. What are you up to?"

"Clay. Where're you calling from?"

"Dublin. Still on location. Man, you should see it here. I never saw grass this color. It's like the Emerald City—fields of bright green everywhere, like dyed Easter eggs."

"Sounds beautiful. You wrapping up?" He folded the paper and slid it back into the newspaper rack. Clay's calls were infrequent, but long.

"I wish. Too many stars fighting over their lines. I should be back in the States by now. We're still on for the climb up Whiteface before the first snow, right?"

"Sure, if you get back in time. Too bad you aren't here now. The weather's been great in Lake Placid."

"Been there lately?" Clay's voice rose over sounds of people in the background.

"Yeah. Took another group of MRT trainees up there for a few weeks."

"So that's where you've been. Explains why you haven't returned my calls. I thought you found some new pony and rode off into the sunset with her."

A woman giggled in the background. Same old Clay. Evan never considered Cassie that way. She'd been all he thought about since Thursday afternoon. He'd seen a sparkle in her eye when he mentioned making love. After two sleepless nights he wanted to see her again. Less jumpy lately, he hadn't checked out every unfamiliar sound. Maybe he was getting better.

He decided not to tell Clay. Too many questions would follow. Questions he couldn't begin to answer.

"Naw. Slim pickings around here. We don't have starlets walking around the set like you. Who you with now?"

"No one in particular, although that's something I plan to change today."

Evan pictured the rakish look on Clay's face. Although his old friend wore a patch over his left eye from a childhood accident, women flocked to him. None stood a chance when he turned on the charm.

"Thought for a minute you got that Albany promo and left to apartment hunt," Clay added.

"Haven't even interviewed yet."

"Irrelevant. They created the job with you in mind. You know it. You're lucky I can't stay in one place for long or I'd be snatching that job from you."

The brag wasn't idle. Next to the Forty-Sixers, hikers who climbed the highest mountains in New York State, Clay was the best climber he'd ever known. High peaks were a challenge for most adults but for he and Clay altitudes over four thousand feet were plain fun. They'd toured the mountains in the three adjacent states as teenagers. Clay always led the way, with an instinct for climbing that couldn't be learned. You were born with a feel for a mountain, the smell of the wind guiding your path, a sense for reading stone formations, directing where to put a handhold or lodge a cam. Spiderman would be envious.

"Why don't you retire and come join us? We could use someone with your experience." Evan joked.

"No, thanks. That's your bag. I can't plan further ahead than two weeks without getting nervous." Clay added a shiver sound of dislike.

"No sign of that battery running down?"

Clay hooted. "Nope."

"Not even for leading tourists on the wildest whitewater rafting imaginable?"

It was a dream they shared for some time. When Clay came home for good they'd go into business together, open an Adirondack supply shop by Moose River. Evan stared at the framed photo of his camp on the wall, the place on Fourth Lake he considered his true home.

"Someday, but not today." Clay's voice trailed off the way it usually did when they talked about him settling in the mountains.

"Someday," Evan echoed. He worried about Clay, who lived his life in the most reckless ways he could find. Too many close calls, but Clay always laughed it off and lived each day like it was his last.

"Listen man, they're ready for my stunt. Must be they threw some of the windbag do-nothings off the set so we professionals could get some work done."

"Yeah. You're a pro." Evan chuckled and picked up the paper again.

"I wish you were here, man. Forget all that rescue stuff. Come join me. This stunt's so cool. I get to ride on the outside of a sea plane, and then hang upside-down from the rails until I get over a lake, then fall off."

"No can do. Better make sure that parachute has triple backup."

"What parachute?"

"Take care buddy."

Talking to Clay always charged him up. It was time to call Cassie. But a minute later, Evan answered his cell.

"Thank God, you're home!" Karen shouted.

"What's wrong? Kids okay?" Evan was already out of his recliner and walking to the counter to grab his car keys before he knew what was wrong.

"No, it's not the kids. It's Cassie. Oh, she'd kill me if she knew I told you—"

"Told me what?" Cassie didn't returned his call yesterday, or this morning. His skin itched, and it wasn't from seeing her. In a dream about her the night before, she was falling and he watched helplessly. "Is she okay?"

"Something happened Friday. I suggested that we go away to my cabin at Snow Lake where it's quiet, to cheer her up. But she's not there." Karen sounded like she was hyperventilating.

Friday she'd gone to court. A sinking feeling pulled at his stomach. "Did she get Heather back?" Cell in hand, he unhooked the jacket by the door and headed to the elevator.

"Everything went wrong. S-she took it bad, Evan. I talked her into going to the cabin to rest but she's not answering the phone or her cell. I'm so worried. She should have been there hours ago."

"Hold on. I'll lose you in the elevator."

The connection returned by the time he got into his car. He put the Jeep in gear before the key was turned completely in the ignition. With no idea where he was heading, at least he was moving.

"Evan? She may be okay, but—"

"Karen. Start with where I'm going."

Chapter Nine

Cassie lugged two bags of groceries into the camp. It smelled like the balsam needles Karen stuffed into little pillows scattered about the room. Whoever arrived first started dinner. Craving pasta again, she filled a pan with water to boil. Something screeched outside. Not an owl. It was too early. Ha. Karen's new car needed brakes. She'd be furious.

Humming to herself, she began to empty one bag of groceries. A funny tingle up her spine stopped her. Hearing heavy footsteps on the porch, she rushed to kick the unlatched door shut.

Too late. A man appeared. A beefy man who'd wedged himself between the doorframe and door. "Hello, little lady." His smile showed yellow teeth in his big round head.

"You have the wrong camp." She shoved at the door but it only opened further.

He shook his head. "Where's the money, lady?"

He didn't have a gun, but who needed one when you were built like a side-by-side freezer.

"Take my purse. It's all I have," she choked, but by the look in his eyes she didn't think he wanted her pocket change.

"You carry that much in your purse?"

His breathing increased and his focus jumped from her hobo purse on the counter to her chest. He kicked the door shut and bolted the chain.

She slowly backed up. "What are you doing?"

Goosebumps prickled her arms as she recognized the trouble she was in. *Remain calm.* No time to think. The man was so massive two steps closed the distance between the front door and where she'd backed up against the stone fireplace.

"Yeah, they all play dumb when it comes to money. Jesu, he left out that you're a pretty thief. Maybe we can get to know each other better." His gaze raked her up and down and settled on her breasts, which rose and fell uncontrollably fast. "And then you'll tell me where the money is." His smile never reached his lizard-like eyes.

She felt naked under his scrutiny. Air rushed from her lungs. *Here it comes,* she thought, the moment she trained for years ago, when she and Karen took a self-defense course to be near Karl.

If only she could remember those, *Steps-to-Protect. Nose, eyes, groin...*

His paws extended and swiped at her breasts. "Come on, lady. I don't want to hurt you. Play nice. Tell me where the money's hid or you'll regret it." He caught her shoulders and dug his fingers in. The pain shocked her. Gasping for air, her searching hand found the fire poker and lifted it. With one beefy paw, he swatted it away, and laughed. "Keep fighting me, beauty. I like a feisty lady. Be nice, and maybe I'll split the money with you." He gripped her arms until she thought they'd snap under the pressure, or she'd faint from the pain.

She'd go down fighting. "Who are you and what money are you talking about?" she hissed.

He relaxed the pressure on her arms. "Stop squirming or you'll hurt yourself."

"You're going to regret putting your filthy hands on me."

He cackled. "I don't think so. I think I'm gonna enjoy it. Let's have some fun before we hit the road, eh?"

Cassie tried to knee him in the groin but he pinned her against the wall. Twisting in his grip, her shirt buttons ripped apart. She'd tried to remain calm, but a bubble of fear forced out a bloodcurdling scream.

"Aw. Now I'll have to gag you."

Did she hear car brakes? "Stay outside, Karen," she yelled.

The front door slammed open by a high kicking foot. A body propelled inside the room. Through her tears she saw only colors, black and blue and red, moving toward her.

The intruder turned and a fist flew at his chin. *Smack.* He dropped backward like a freshly chopped pine. The cabin shook as he hit the floor. Legs that were supposed to protect her by either running or kicking gave out, and she crumpled to the floor. Then, everything went black.

Shaking her head, she tried to push herself off the floor. She must have gone down the same time as the big guy. As soon as she got on all fours, two hands grabbed her around the waist and elevated her in the air. Barely catching her next breath, she screamed. This time it was smothered against a warm, spicy scented shirt. A strong arm banded around her and a frantic hand threaded her hair off her face.

"Are you okay? Why didn't you bolt the door? Do you know what could have happened? God, say something, Cassie. Please say something, so I know you're okay."

Not Karl. Cocooned next to the body of the blur—or rather, the man who rescued her from certain rape, the voice registered. She opened her eyes and met a pair of hard, brown ones staring back at her.

She released a big sigh—followed by a bigger sigh—his.

"Thank God," she croaked. Every nerve ending applauded his timely appearance.

He lifted her chin with a fingertip. "You're okay, now." His smile faltered. She'd never seen that look on his face. Evan never got scared.

He walked her to the couch. She sunk into the over-stuffed pillows. A plaid blanket landed in her lap, then tucked around her. She snuggled further under the blanket, although she wanted to put her arms back around Evan, burrow into his solid chest and stay there.

"Karl must have some scotch in this place," he murmured. Cabinet doors creaked open and slammed closed. Heavy boots shuffled on the floor. Eventually a cool glass touched her lower lip. "Here—sip this." He said.

She parted her lips. Sweet liquid poured over her tongue and down her throat. She coughed. When it hit her stomach, it burned. Minutes later, a shock wave of heat penetrated her limbs. The tongue-and-groove knotty pine planks that were on the walls and ceiling came into focus. Along with burgundy and green plaid curtains, that matched her blanket. Karen's cabin looked unchanged. Where was Evan?

Crouched on the floor. Next to the unconscious intruder, checking the belt he'd secured around the man's paws. The man lying on his stomach had him by at least a foot, both ways.

Evan joined her on the couch. "Friend of yours?"

"He was looking for money and...oh God, Evan, if you hadn't come in when you did... I don't think I could have fought him off." She took a large swallow of scotch, blinking back tears.

Her watched her drink. "Got handcuffs in the car. Be right back." He stood and crossed the room in three steps.

"But...." *Don't leave me.*

He was gone. If her knees stopped knocking she'd have run after him but he returned seconds later carrying a red duffle bag. She took another sip, trying to look anywhere but the floor.

Cuffs slid from his back pocket and snapped on in two more seconds. Then Evan turned the beast onto his back. A massive red bag came toward her, held by a relieved looking Evan. He crouched in front of her then stroked her cheek gently with his fingertips until she looked up. His fingers were warm and rough. "The drink brought some color back in your cheeks." She leaned her face into his palm. He quickly withdrew it to remove the glass from her hands, and re-tucked the blanket under her chin.

Were his hands shaking? "What are you doing here? How did you know? Do you have some super-psychic ability?"

She almost said, "Super-man."

"Hmpf." For the second time in a week he touched her wrist with a thumb and middle finger. "You feel okay now?" He pushed her bangs from her face and smoothed his hands over her head. Then he patted her down from shoulders to hands. When finished he zippered his bag and sat next to her on the couch.

Blood rushed to her face. She wanted to fall into his arms but his fist rested on one leg and he looked a bit disgusted. How could she have left the door open? She turned away, unable to see the censure in his eyes.

"Karen gave me directions."

Her head swung around fast enough to make her dizzy. *Karen did what?* The intense scrutiny unnerved her but her back stiffened as her chin rose to meet his gaze.

"When I saw the second car I considered leaving." His gaze searched her face. "I thought he was your lover."

Her jaw dropped.

"Through the picture window I saw you backing into the room." His eyes narrowed. "I sensed he wasn't invited." A finger tapped her mouth closed and his gaze softened. "You're okay. A little scared, hmmm? You're heart's beating like a trip hammer." He pushed a strand of hair behind her ear. She thought she heard him utter something else about *being a tough lady*, but she was so beguiled by his smile and gentle touch she wasn't certain.

"Rest here for a bit. I've gotta make a call."

Then he leaned closer and his lips brushed hers, igniting a fire in her belly more potent than a bottle of Jamison's.

****

Cassie stared out the passenger window of Evan's Jeep. Most of what happened in the cabin was still a blur up to the point when Evan broke down the cabin door. What would she have done if he hadn't arrived when he did? She shuddered thinking about it. From the corner of her eye she saw Evan glance at her then turn a knob on the dash. The rush of warm air teased stray hairs about her face.

She didn't need heat.

She needed answers.

"Not that I'm not grateful, Evan, but I still don't understand what you were doing at Karen's cabin."

From the reflection in the window she saw him glance at her but not comment. He continued to drive a little further until the car began to slow and slow and slow.

"Shit, I don't believe this," he said.

"What?" She looked out the window, expecting a bear with her luck.

"We're outta gas."

Her head whirled around. "Out of gas? How could you be out of gas?"

The car rolled to a stop half on dried goldenrod and burdocks stalks as tall as her window.

He stared at the dash. "I left the house in a hurry... there was enough gas." He drilled her with molten-brown eyes that dared her to question his motives.

"Wait, let's back up. First, I didn't come up here alone. Karen was supposed to join me for a girls' night, like we used to... *Now* what's wrong?"

His mustached mouth frowned and he shook his head. "Karen phoned, worried you came up here *alone* and hadn't checked-in. She thought you were lost or broke down."

He flipped his cell phone open and punched several numbers then closed it. "We're outta cell range." He threw the cell onto the dash. Suspicious eyes looked her way. "She sounded freaked," he added.

She sat up in her seat and smoothed the bottom of the blouse. "Why would she be?" She'd die if Evan learned he was the number one topic of every conversation. She schooled her face and looked back at him.

"Yeah, why would she?" Evan's eyes narrowed.

She raised both hands. "I have no idea."

No answer.

"I went to court yesterday and she suggested we come up here—" Her lips slammed shut, unwilling to volunteer any more information.

"What happened in court?" His mustache lowered until his mouth nearly disappeared.

She entwined her hands in her lap to keep from shaking. "Jake had an emergency and couldn't make it. Court was postponed for s-si…"

As hard as she tried, she couldn't get the word *six* out. Instead she coughed on her own breath. Hot tears rained on her hands.

His seat belt unclasp, then hers released. Strong arms pulled her against his chest. The breath she held slowly found its way out but burned her throat. She inhaled another breath, then another and buried her head against his chest to hide a sob she couldn't hold back.

"I get it now," he said, his voice a soft rumble in his chest. "Karen thought you'd need a different kind of friend."

****

Cassie's head slowly lifted from Evan's chest. Although they were losing sun, Evan could see every fleck of color in her sad, green eyes.

"What do we do now?" she asked.

Evan wasn't sure which she referred to, her pain over losing Heather, or that they were out of gas on a backwoods road at dusk. A fine time to run out of gas.

Some help you are, Jorgenson. "The local police should be cruising by with the guy from the cabin. We can either wait for them and hitch a ride into town or walk back to the cabin."

She looked over his shoulder and then back to him.

The damn camping gear.

When her car wouldn't start he blamed a dead battery rather than disclose the engine had been tampered with. The trunk and doors locks were broken due to a prior electrical problem. She'd refused to leave her gear. Something about it costing more than her beat up Audi. Her backpack in his back seat was proof he'd lost the argument.

He'd arrived just in time. He pushed away an image of what he might have found if he'd arrived later.

"Your gear is safe inside my car. My doors lock," he joked.

She pulled out of his arms as if he'd struck her. "For your information, not everyone can afford a brand-new car. Some of us have to run a business, supplies to purchase, and take care of ch-children."

She breathed hard with fury. Good. If she needed to get her anger out, he could take it. What he couldn't take was the dawning horror on her face when she realized her reference to a daughter that no longer lived with her.

"Let's stay here and wait," he said gently.

She pushed back from his chest and swatted away the open arms he re-offered. "No. I don't want to stay here. I want to walk back." Her door opened and slammed shut before he could protest. The back door flung open.

To get the damn backpack.

He got out of the car. "Leave the backpack," he said sternly.

"I'm not leaving my gear. Anyone can come down this road and break into your car." She tugged the backpack halfway out.

That lit his temper. "No one is going to come down this road. It isn't even on the map. I don't know what possessed Karl to build a summer home in such a God-forsaken place."

Before he could rant further, mostly from embarrassment that he'd run out of gas, he heard the sound of breaking glass.

"Shots! Heads down."

Two more shots pinged the Jeep as he dove to her side of the car. He covered her with his body as three more shots fired. A ping breezed next to his ear.

He flattened her to the ground and jerked his gun from his ankle holster. "Stay low, as low as you can. I want you to run until I tell you to stop," he commanded, then he pointed her westward into the dense field of goldenrod. Wide-eyed she nodded then her sneakers kicked back sand.

He waited until she disappeared between the stalks to fire off a few shots, but stopped, thinking one might ricochet off a rock and hit Cassie. His hand stretched up to the open car door and in one motion, yanked the backpack though the door.

In a dead run, he took off after her.

****

Through a field of weeds that eventually led to the thick pine forest, Evan passed her and grabbed her hand making her run even faster to keep up. She didn't know how long they ran but was grateful when Evan said they could stop. Her heart thundered so hard her entire chest shook. Eager to collect her breath, she collapsed onto a log so decayed she sunk in and bit her lip.

Sand filled her mouth as she licked her wound. Her blouse stuck to her chest and she felt dizzy. Brown specks of dead thistle stalks dropped from her hair. A tissue from her pocket wiped sweat and tears from her face. The tissue smelled like lavender rather than the heady piney odor that saturated her nostrils while running. Burdocks snagged her hair and stuck to her clothing, but she didn't care. They were alive.

"I think Route 28 is west of this road," Evan said not even winded. Her breathing sounded like a fish gulping water. "I want to check the compass."

Compass? Where'd he get the compass?

He turned around and she saw it. Evan was wearing her backpack and holding the compass that she'd clipped to the outside of the bag.

She didn't know what made her happier, that he'd grabbed the backpack she spent a small fortune on and was using the water resistant, glow-in-the-dark compass, or that Evan was still there to protect her.

Okay, she was glad she was with Evan, who now turned in a circle trying to sense their direction. The setting sun caused his hair to glow like some super avenger. Something else was glowing. A dark streak on his jeans. This late in the fall, there were no berries on the bushes they passed. She walked up to him and checked the fresh reddish line on his jeans. She gestured frantically to his calf. "You're bleeding."

He continued to look around the forest, apparently unconcerned.

A small circle of denim was missing on his calf. Out of the black hole dripped dark cranberry liquid.

"You've been shot!" Her knees bent and she keeled to the ground. "Oh God, what's going on?"

Evan followed her down and caught her by the waist. He tilted her chin, and she opened her eyes. "I'm okay," he said harshly. "It's a graze. Can you walk a bit longer? We'll either find road or water if we go a little further."

He was bleeding, and he worried about her? She didn't want to disappoint him and nodded.

"You sure?" His large hands caressed the sides of her face. In the minimal light from the setting sun she could see his encouraging smile before warm lips lingered on hers.

Giving her the courage she needed to go on.

****

Surrounded by the dense pine trees, Evan had no idea where they were. If they kept walking North they may hit road or head into more rugged terrain. Cassie looked exhausted. The trickle of blood running down his calf itched. His sock felt soaked. To cover any trail, he'd kicked up leaves as they ran. He was pretty sure they'd lost the shooter.

Time to settle down for the night.

They'd stopped in a clearing where he could hear water moving not far off. Cassie gathered sticks and dry pinecones and pieces of bark for a fire while he set up the tent. Since the sky looked clear he rolled a small tarp on the ground to make a sitting area and then grabbed some stones to anchor the posts and ring a campfire.

Several sticks and pinecones fell onto the tarp. "Do you think we lost him?" Her voice was barely audible.

"Yep." He wanted to add, "you can relax," but he wasn't so sure himself. While running he looked over his shoulder every few yards seeing no movement or hearing footsteps the last hour or so.

Why would he become so desperate to shoot at them? Why go this far out of the way to get money from someone in the first place?

He glanced at Cassie's face, now illuminated pinkish in the setting sun. Two attempts on her life that he was aware of. There was something else going on here.

Nobody fired a gun unless they meant to kill.

Why would anyone want to kill Cassie?

"How could he escape from the handcuffs?" Her eyes rounded with worry.

"It's possible," he lied. The guy must be familiar with cuffs. Only one sheriff was available when he'd made the call. They should have stayed at the cabin until he arrived, but Cassie kept glancing at the broken door and unconscious man and he thought it best to get her home.

He anticipated her next question as they broke up the sticks into smaller pieces. "We're not too far in the woods that we can't find our way out. We'll camp here tonight, hike out the way we came in tomorrow." A butane lighter from her backpack brought the small pile of kindle alive. A search of her gear provided a great deal of supplies including a first-aid kit, bags of snacks, a flashlight which he'd placed inside the tent and a hunting knife which he hooked onto his belt buckle. He usually wore his ankle gun until he went to bed but he'd keep it nearer tonight. He shone the flashlight in the distance where he heard water and saw a reflection. "I'm going to get us some water."

She rushed to his side. "I'm coming with you." An owl cooed and some branches snapped. "Did you hear that sound?" Her hair swiped his face as she looked over her shoulder and then leaned against him.

His insides groaned. "Probably a deer, maybe a raccoon. We're close to a stream. Animals come out to eat and drink at night."

Using an expensive looking flashlight he carefully guided her through the fallen leaves that hid old roots, rocks and rotting logs. Something rustled in the darkness beyond the beam. She flinched and looked over her shoulder and then at him for more reassurance. "The fire will keep them away," he said. "Besides, we don't have any fresh food, only trail mix and Power bars."

The flashlight was low tech compared to his gear in the war, no lasers sites and infrared goggles for night maneuvers. Still the beam shone far and intense. He raised it to catch her expression. Yep, she was good and scared, more scared than someone should be of forest animals.

They reached running water and he handed her the flashlight. Once the canteen was full, he popped in a chlorine tablet and soaked his handkerchief in the icy water. The flashlight swung about in a large arc. Several pairs of eyes, low and high, reflected back. She gasped, and squeezed his fingers, tourniquet tight.

He pointed. "Beavers probably wondering why we're trespassing at their water hole." He couldn't hold back a chuckle. Light struck his eyes and he held up his hands. "Whoa. Don't go blinding me or you'll have to take care of the two of us."

The flashlight hit the ground and went out. Leaves crunched and he smelled fresh dirt as she scrounged with her feet to find it. He bent over the spot, flipped it over, then shone the light directly on the tent.

She *tsked*. "Obviously you're more experienced at this type of thing."

He stared at the tent. The image of them rolling around naked in the leaves, kissing her senseless, streaked through his mind. "I've been trained for this sort of thing." He bit back a grunt. If she only knew the other conversation going on in his head, she'd probably run and bunk with the beavers for the night.

Behind the small tent the last lines of violet and indigo of an October sunset reeled in the darkness. The night sky in Baghdad never had such colors. It turned from blood red to black in minutes. He focused on placing one foot before the other. A quick shake of his head cleared the thought.

Cassie sighed when they reached the tent. "What a beautiful sunset." She crossed her legs and sat on the tarp before the fire, then bounced back up. "Evan, there's blood on the tarp."

He looked down. Some drops of his blood glistened by the campfire.

"It's coming from your leg," she shrieked.

"That's not a graze!"

Chapter Ten

"You have to do something to stop the bleeding." Cassie dug into her pockets for a tissue and came up empty. Everywhere she looked she saw red.

Evan merely shrugged, unconcerned with all the blood on the tarp. Even in her alarm her heart did another spin, about the hundredth since he'd arrived at the cabin and led her to this spot in the woods.

Away from civilization.

Away from the shooter.

Alone with him.

He fit in so well with the ruggedness of the surrounding area that he took her breath away. So at ease, even with bloodstained jeans. Like some ancient Indian warrior, wounded but protecting his family.

Who was this man, that in the span of a week barged into her life and wedged himself deeper by the minute?

He didn't answer her, only dropped to his knees and poked his head into the tent, presenting her with a view of his taut behind.

Oh God, what was she thinking? She's losing it. Hiding in the woods from a killer, with a man who was dangerous in a whole different way. Her heart threatened to launch out of her mouth at every little noise and it hurt to breathe. But rather than be terrified she was cataloging the body parts of her sexy guardian.

Yep. Insane.

As if on cue he pulled his head out of the tent and looked up at her. The way the firelight danced off his face and hair he looked like an angel who wandered from heaven to save her.

His lips silently moved. She heard him the second time around.

"You're not squeamish, are you?" His brown eyes glistened in the firelight.

"Oh, noooo. Let me help you."

Her weak knees bent and gratefully landed away from the red puddle. She stifled a gag. The usual reaction to the littlest amount of blood, but she'd die before she'd let him see her fear.

He'd pulled off his boot and sock that was more red than white. That odor became stronger. Her body swayed slightly. *Toughen up.* He was bleeding because of her and now needed her help. After a calming breath she opened the kit, a real bargain thanks to hours surfing on the Internet, and gingerly grabbed one item.

"Wait—you don't need the scalpel, only antiseptic," he barked, kicking his boot and sock into the darkness.

Her hand turned the scalpel that she'd inadvertently picked up so it flashed in the firelight. Then she stared at him. The last time she'd held one she'd been forced to dissect an innocent dead baby pig.

Evan stopped the struggle of pulling up his pant leg and stared at her with a queer look.

Setting the scalpel aside, she found the scissors. "It will be easier to cut up your jeans. Unless you're attached to them." Her voice sounded eerily calm, even to her ears. He didn't move, so she expertly cut through the hem of his jeans. After all, in high school she'd shortened tons of her own jeans.

Cutting up the denim leg something warm wet her hand. It was sticky and smelled like dirty pennies. The scissors turned sideways in her hand.

Evan startled her when he swiped the scissors and reared back. "That's far enough."

He's behaving oddly.

He threw the scissors aside. One-handed, he started rummaging through the kit. The other held a rag over his leg. After a minute he dumped the entire contents of the kit onto the tarp.

"Hey." She'd spent hours neatly organizing it. "Now look what you did. Everything's dirty."

Evan ignored her and poked around until he found a small brown bottle. He tried to take off the cap but his hands were too wet with red stuff.

"I'll do that."

She could be bossy, too. The cap easily twisted off but left a smear of red on the inside of her thumb. Then she took the wet rag from his hand and gently stroked the back of his calf. The rag turned a dull shade of rust and she folded it over to a clean spot. He repositioned his leg toward the light. Red liquid trickled from the dark hole. Her eyes watered slightly from the pungent odor. The rag became warm and heavy with...

"There's the nick," he said, pointing to a small dark circle. "It's still trickling." He touched her hand. "Are you sure you're okay? It's only a graze, but it will heal better if it's closed. Pour some of the peroxide over it and then I'll have you suture it."

Tears burned down her throat thinking about how much it must hurt. He didn't complain when she spilled the entire contents of the bottle onto the wound. The spot around the hole bubbled, reminding her of the first time Heather fell off her two-wheeler and cried that it stung.

Heather. Would she ever see her daughter again?

The events of the day flashed like a heat lightning in her mind. She was hiding in the woods from a person she didn't know, who followed her to the cabin and tried to kill her and Evan.

Maybe she wasn't safe to be around Heather.

The empty brown bottle began to shake in her hand. Liquid fell on the red rag, turning it dark green. The smell made her stomach clench. She bent over and it stopped cramping.

"Wipe your hands with this and then you can suture the wound. It should only take two stitches. You can sew, right?" His voice floated to her from somewhere far, far away as he handed her a wet white square.

Of course she could sew. She'd made most of her toddler's clothes.

He handed a fishhook. Her slippery fingers nearly dropped it.

"If you can't do this, I can put on a regular bandage. I'll have to keep changing it, though, or I'll get blood on the tent floor," he calmly stated. "Pretend you're stitching a rag. Take the needle from one side to the other. Then pull, tight," the voice said.

She did as instructed, wincing while she stitched *the rag.*

"Atta girl, now the other side, and pull— t-tight."

Robotic fingers obeyed his command. She forced herself to concentrate on the voice even as all the red sticky liquid seeping on her fingers made it difficult to move them.

What if someone went after Heather?

"Great. You did great..."

Everything became quiet except for a ringing in her ears.

There must have been an earthquake because she was being violently shaken and didn't know what to do. She reached for a pillar. Was she standing in a doorway? Where was her baby? An animal howled in the distance, sounding like it was being tortured. Her throat pained, like she'd swallowed glass.

"Cassie… *Cassie!*"

Someone shouted her name. Her eyes popped open. Hot tears spilled into her open mouth.

Strong arms banded around her.

Warm, safe arms. Arms that would never let go.

The rocking slowly stopped.

And then, the screams.

****

"Cassie, honey, calm down. Everything's okay."

Evan tucked Cassie against him as she struggled. "We're safe," he repeated. He had to calm her down. Sound traveled far in these mountains. He gritted his teeth and willed her to stop shaking and screaming.

In a quieter voice, he repeated his words. "I'm fine, honey, but you need to calm down."

She felt like an ice cube so he removed his jacket and tried to wrap it around her.

"No!" She screamed and burrowed closer into his chest.

"I'm not leaving you."

Again he swung the thick leather jacket, this time resting it over her shuddering shoulders. Her teeth began to chatter and he feared there was nothing in the first-aid kit for shock. He was a fool for letting her tend to his leg. He should have let it bleed out.

"Cassie, please calm down. We're okay." His voice sounded thready, too.

Her sobs turned to whimpers, and he held her close until he felt her last shudder. Cold lips moved against his neck. "E-evan?"

He smoothed bangs from her eyes. "Yes, honey?"

"Are we g-going to be okay t-tonight?"

Eyes as innocent as a child's looked up at him. His heart lurched so hard it hurt. Nothing in his war training prepared him for this.

At her first scream, the chill down his spine froze his blood. He'd seen men torn apart, heard cries as they burned alive while he fought to get them out of the Humvee. He'd been moved to action, regardless of the searing heat; he hadn't frozen like some of the others. In the hospital, he'd talked to survivors, knowing what to say to ease their consciences. Clasped hands in prayer with some until they expired.

He knew how to rescue, how to kill.

He knew how to hide from the enemy until help arrived.

He knew how to motivate his soldiers, and train recruits.

But he didn't know how to ease Cassie's torment. He was as useless as an empty gun.

Mindful that her screams echoed in the woods, he kicked dirt on the fire. If the stranger followed them this far, he'd know their location. He listened for several minutes, but nothing heavy thudded through the woods.

"There's nothing to be afraid of. We've got food and a tent. We aren't as deep into the woods as you think."

She pulled away from his chest. "Do you think he'll find us?" Her hair flounced around her face as she searched the darkness.

Nice going, Ace. "No. He's probably on his way home to a warm bed," he tried to joke, but her eyes sparkled with unshed tears, so he added, "I won't let anyone hurt you anymore."

Her entire body shuddered in his arms.

Something terrible *had* happened to her in L.A.

And followed her home.

Again his trigger finger itched so badly that he rubbed it against his jeans until it numbed.

He'd deal later. Right now her eyes fluttered closed. Probably crashing from the adrenaline rush. He needed to keep her awake a little longer, hydrate and get some food into her and then they could bed down for the night. Not the way he'd imagined the evening would end when he drove away from the cabin but at least they were together. Until he found her stalker and learned why someone wanted her dead, they'd stay that way.

"Evan." He eased back her head in his hand, still cradling the back of her neck. "I'm so sorry I got you shot."

Tears cleaned lines down her pretty cheeks. He caught some with stiff fingers and rubbed them until they disappeared, wishing it were as easy to ease her pain.

"Does your leg hurt a lot?"

"Not a bit."

"I'm so sorry. I never wanted—" Her head fell back against his chest. She sobbed again, and the warm wet spot on his chest made him shiver.

"Shh-h-h. It's okay. I want you to forget about everything for a minute and have some of this protein shake you packed in this bottomless, Mary Poppins-like backpack."

She took a sip, and he got her to eat a bite of a power bar, and then drink more of the shake. While she drank he found a brush and pulled the burdocks from her hair. She even let him walk away for a moment to relieve himself, then held his breath the entire time she was gone. After cleaning the tarp, he activated some glow sticks he found in the backpack and placed several around the top of the tent.

The flashlight swayed back and forth. As she neared, he watched the barest hint of smile form, and then crumble off her lips. Crouching on the tarp, she hid her face in her hands.

"What's wrong?" He slid closer to her.

"It's the glow sticks. Heather picked them out. It was her contribution to, *something-special*, in our backpack." Her breathing hitched. "We'd planned to go hiking in the Sierras and did all kinds of Internet surfing to find the perfect supplies and latest gizmos. But she said we needed to have something for fun and since the backpack was already pretty full I told her it had to be functional."

She gathered the empty powerbar wrapper into a ball and placed it in the backpack.

"Sounds like a pretty terrific little girl."

"She is... I miss her so much sometimes... I can't... breathe."

He waited for her to add more, like what happened for her to lose Heather but she unwrapped her arms from her stomach and began to repacked the first aid kit.

In the neon lights from the glowsticks he watched her rub fresh tears from her cheeks.

He stifled a curse. "What was your contribution?"

"You're gonna laugh at me again."

"I promise I won't. What, silly-but-functional, thing did you pack?" He imagined some new high-tech gizmo.

She gnawed at her lower lip.

"Kisses. Hershey's chocolate kisses."

She waited for him to laugh.

How could he? That was the sweetest thing he'd ever heard, bringing kisses on a mother-daughter camping trip especially when the mother had a sweet tooth. "Like your dad gave you," he whispered, suddenly needing a bucket of water.

She nodded and stared at the dead fire.

He reached inside the backpack and pulled out a bag that he looked like balls of tin foil. He'd wondered what they were for. "How about we have some now." He grabbed a handful and made a small pile on the tarp. Then he picked one up, unraveled the foil and said, "Open up."

The tiny chocolate triangle disappeared in her pink mouth. He unwrapped another one to take its place. He fed her two more when she grabbed one for him. They repeated the ritual until the pile was gone.

He felt permitted into her world with the simple gesture.

They sat in silence a bit longer, until she rubbed her eyes and yawned.

"We're both tired. I think it's time we went to bed." He'd listen for trouble while she slept.

Her eyebrows rose. She glanced at the tent opening and back at him and then stood up. The boots he'd cleaned at the motel kicked off, followed by her jeans. Slender fingers began to unbutton her shirt.

Pow.

The force of a grenade kicked him in his gut. Air burned down his throat at his rapid intake. Fantasy came to life—the ink-black sky with its trillion stars silhouetting her body like an erotic painting. Her blouse parted, revealing skin he knew was as soft and creamy as the chocolate kiss he could still taste on his tongue. Moonlight reflected off long legs that he imagined dragging his lips up their length. Seated less than a foot away, he inhaled her musky, womanly scent. Rock-hard at once, he quickly flipped the top button on his jeans.

She concentrated on her fingers as she continued to carefully release button after button.

When she got to her navel, he groaned aloud. "Stop."

The sexiest eyes in the world looked down at him.

"It's warmer to sleep in your clothes," he bit out.

Frowning she sat down on the tarp and pulled on her jeans. One by one, shaky fingers buttoned her blouse and concealed what he'd waited a hundred years to see again. But, the last thing he wanted was for her to feel obligated to sleep with him.

Didn't she know him better by now?

Apparently not.

Apparently, she thought he'd take her in the helpless state she was in.

Only a monster would do that to a woman.

****

Evan held the flap of the tent open. She bent low and slipped inside. The sleeping bag lay half unzipped, the corner turned back, her jacket, pillowed and centered on the bag.

"Aren't you coming inside?" she asked.

He stared into the darkness. "I'm not very tired." His rolled-up pant leg fell down.

She didn't move. No way would she let Evan sleep outside. He was injured. What was he thinking?

He walked around the tent. By the time he got back, she'd returned to the tarp. She poked at the dead fire with a stick. "I'm staying up with you, then."

His hands rested on his hips and he searched the night sky. Maybe he knew where they were by the stars. He watched as she finger-combed her hair. "You need rest. I can stay awake for days."

"Did you have to when you served in Iraq?"

He hesitated. "Yes."

She found a few orange embers in the campfire ashes and pushed them around. "What did you think about all that time?"

He didn't answer but the way he looked at her made it feel like she sat before a blazing inferno. *Making love to me?* she wanted to ask, but if he said yes, then what would she do?

Tired to the bone, she *tsk*ed, and tried another approach. Dignity be damned. She needed his arms around her.

"I don't think I can sleep alone tonight."

The muscle in his jaw ticked but he made no reply. Instead, he looked away and seemed mesmerized by something in the distance.

She held a breath.

Please don't make me beg you, Evan.

He scratched the back of his neck, and looked at the tent's entrance. His face turned to stone, and so she braced herself for rejection.

"Go inside," he said softly.

She hooded her gaze before he saw her hurt then shuffled inside. After zipping the tent closed, she crawled on top of the sleeping bag and congratulated herself for not being a bigger fool by asking if he'd recalled making love to her during those lonely nights in Iraq.

He'd fought for his life. Knowing Evan, the lives of others, too.

A few minutes later she heard a low hiss. The tent flap flew open. The flashlight beam found her curled up form as she huddled to one side of the sleeping bag.

She heard crickets in the distance, an occasional frog croak and the pulse of her heart speeding up.

It took a minute before he spoke. "Do you want me to leave the flashlight on?"

Did he think she was afraid of the dark? Or maybe he thought she feared him. Well, neither was the case. "I like it dark."

The flashlight dimmed, then went out. She

shuddered.

His large body slid into the sleeping bag next to hers. She held her breath until he settled on his back and his arms crossed behind his head. A minute later, he chuckled.

So now he thought this was funny? She tumbled over and nearly crashed into his face. "What's so funny?" she bit out, trying to mask her hurt feelings.

He pointed to the ceiling. Irregular circles of yellow, pink and green light filtered through the tent. "Looks like a disco in here."

She smiled despite her nervousness and drew crooked circles in the silky slice of fabric between them with her fingertip. They lay facing each other searching each other's face for the moment in the faint, mismatched light. She wondered what he was thinking as his eyes roamed her body, then stopped and focused on her lips.

Dark, depthless eyes collided with hers. "You're so beautiful," he said, and he reached for her, pulling her closer.

She trembled from the sudden contact and the evidence of his desire pressed against her belly. Evan wanted her.

He ran a hand through her hair, and then tilted her head back to look up at him. "You have the prettiest eyes I've ever seen." With the back of his hand, he stroked her cheeks and underneath her chin. "And the softest skin."

Evan hesitated like he wanted to add more. Then he muttered, "Oh, hell" and pressed his lips into hers. He kissed her lazily, brushing his firm, full lips back and forth over hers, as if they had all the time in the world.

A fist of lust drove her forward, and she flattened against him, wanting to feel every ridge and valley of his chest. Desire rushed across her skin and spread down her back, and then squeezed between her legs where liquid pooled. He pulled her into a firestorm of pleasure that she couldn't break free, even if she wanted to.

And she did not want to.

Then those warm lips pressed harder on hers, not for a moment tentative, for they were past that little ruse. His tongue probed the seam of her lips and she opened for him, tasting the chocolate kisses on his tongue, and his desire. He did things to her mouth that were a foreshadowing of making love with him. He set her wits spinning, her defenses crumbling and any moment she expected him to pull her clothes off.

He pulled away.

His forehead rested on hers, and between pants he spoke. "We'd better get some rest." Turning her to face the tent wall, he then bundled the sleeping bag around her. She immediately felt chilled. Unshed tears ached her eyes, and some trailed down her cheeks anyway.

Evan's rejection hurt. To make matters worse, he stroked her arm and kissed her hair affectionately like he wanted her. She'd mistaken concern for a deeper emotion, again.

He uttered something, then he tucked her back against his chest. "You're going to be okay, I promise," he whispered.

She nodded, but she knew the truth.

She'd never be okay.

Chapter Eleven

The next morning Cassie woke to the smell of dead campfire and the sound of deep breathing. She released the shirtfront that she clutched like a security blanket, and lifted her head. Evan slept on his back, legs bent, barely fitting in the tent made for two, a bicep as her pillow. The events of the prior day came rolling back. She should be dead. How could she ever thank him enough?

She doubted a basket of chocolates would be suitable repayment but making him coffee would be a good start. She began to rise but a heavy hand clamped on her shoulder, holding her down as he slept. She'd freaked on him, and he'd been nothing but understanding. Odd for a guy so big and at times, ferocious looking. She sighed. It felt nice to be held so tenderly all night.

He stirred slightly, working his shirttail out of his jeans. His exposed abdomen was well sculpted. A light brown swirl of hair down his midline extended into his pants. She noticed the bulge in his jeans. Gnawing at her lower lip she averted her gaze upward. Three little buttons of his pullover were open, exposing more skin. Little tuffs of golden hair escaped but instead of tanned like his face the skin was unnaturally red.

Sun burnt from the campfire? They didn't sit by it that long. And his face wasn't burnt. She gingerly lifted the collar of shirt.

"Sleep well?" he said.

Her fingers paralyzed. How long had he been awake? The large hand that held her down squeezed her shoulder and tucked her closer. A renewed thrill of apprehension washed over her body. "Ah—yes. You?"

"I slept okay." He glanced down at his pants, closed his eyes, and added, "a little uncomfortable but it was worth it."

She opened her mouth to reply but his fingers had pulled back the collar of her shirt and began kneading, uncoiling muscles she didn't realize were tense. Heat poured over her skin. She rolled her neck, marveling at how all the kinks disappeared. Who wouldn't be tense after spending the night with this golden giant?

Daylight dappled through the tent zipper, illuminating his reclining form. The last time they spent the night together they got little sleep. In the morning he woke her to make love one last time before he departed. Amazingly, she'd survived a night with Evan without falling into his arms and begging him to make love to her.

Evan stretched for a sec, and then held her so tight the buttons on her blouse probably left dents on his skin. Heat rolled off him. Beads of sweat rolled between her breasts. This close to his face, she could see his beard grew in swirls. She followed one swirl under his chin and down his neck, and gasped. "You're loaded with mosquito bites."

He raised his head to look at the little "V" of skin. "I'm used to it by now." He dropped his head back, closed his eyes, as if ready to fall back into a deep slumber.

She wiggled out of his tight hold. "Haven't you heard of all the diseases mosquitoes carry? I packed my lotion. The stuff is great. It sooths and prevents bites."

She stopped babbling and unzipped the tent flap. He uttered something as she crawled out of the tent to dig through her backpack. Mister macho-nature boy didn't probably believe in mosquito repellent.

Unscrewing the tube of lotion she re-entered the tent. Resting on his elbows and looking like every woman's dream lover, her feeble attempt at seduction last night came back. Long ago she'd felt so cherished but clearly he wanted to be friends. Even though he'd kissed her goodnight, a steamy, heart-melting, never-want-to-leave-you-again kiss, she was another search and rescue mission for him.

You made the rules, fool, and with good reason. She'd lost her heart once to her rescuer. It took her years to get over him.

The tent flap gaped open, spotlighting the morning light on his neck. She sat back on her heels, squirted a large amount of lotion in her hand, and braced herself. "Take off your shirt."

For a moment he didn't move, only looked from her hands to her face. Neck muscles corded and his jaw ticked, twice.

Well? she thought, raising an eyebrow like she did when Heather played dumb.

He rose slightly. One hefty arm pulled out, and then the whole shirt went up like a curtain over his head, exposing one gorgeous chest, covered with ugly red blotches and huge welts.

With both hands she lunged at him, attempting to treat all the welts at once. "Why didn't you say something last night? I could've put lotion on you then."

"Didn't bother me last night."

Reclined on his elbows he watched her hands as she worked the soft-as-silk lotion over his chest, shoulders and biceps. She went back twice for more lotion, moving from his chest to tummy. There was so much skin to cover. Warm, golden, irresistibly touchable skin. Skin she touched a thousand nights in her dreams. Skin she remember leisurely exploring with more than her hands.

Her hands yanked back. "Turn over and let me see your back," she ordered. "Oh, Evan. How can you stand this? You slept in a nest of mosquitoes."

She attacked his back, wildly wiggling her fingers from shoulder to shoulder, then from his neck to the dip of his back, skimming the waistband of his jeans. Squirting another handful of lotion she wondered if she'd run out of it before she ran out of skin. When she turned with another handful, he'd sat up. His handsome face inches from her nose.

A chainsaw-like buzzing went off in her head as his lips moved. "Maybe I did. Maybe we both did. Do you feel itchy?"

Like anticipating a bite of expensive chocolate, her mouth watered. "A little."

"Then I'd better check your back." He took both of her hands and rubbed them until all of the fragrant lotion transferred to his palms. "Turn around."

She turned and lifted her blouse.

"Yeah, you've got bites. One here and one here, and one here." He touched one shoulder blade then the other and then the nape of her neck. Each touch intensified the tension in her belly. Warm lips nipped her earlobe and brushed the dip of her shoulder. "Do you think you have any more bites for me to take care of? I still have plenty of lotion."

She nodded and faced him.

His hands dipped under her blouse, walked up

her spine and released the clasp of her bra. A stare capable of fusing her blouse buttons fastened on her breasts as his knuckles skimmed the top of her bra and removed her blouse. "Got one there," he said, touching the cleavage between her breasts. "Think you got bitten anywhere else?" With a flick of his fingers her bra tumble off.

Goosebumps rose on her arms with his sexy intake of air. Her nipples contracted even before he touched them. Opened-palm he massaged lotion on one breast, paying particular attention to one erect nipple, then the other.

His breaths were short but not labored. He sat back on his knees, soldier-still.

"Lie down."

The tent grew brighter. Chirping, birds were celebrating the dawn of another day. She was heady with the knowledge that Evan desired her, again.

He pulled her jeans off in one tug.

Cool air teased her legs and bottom. She was completely exposed to him, thrilled at the way he took his time looking at her. Then he grabbed more lotion and lingered on her thighs. The slight friction from his calluses emptied a bellyful of heat low into her abdomen. By the time he massaged all the way down to her toes, she wanted to throw her legs apart.

He kissed behind her knees. A ripple of pleasure raced up the back of her legs to the juncture where her body was overly ready.

"No bites here, but I wouldn't want to take any chances."

His mustache tickled as he nipped up her thighs adding pressure to a system on the verge of climax. His gaze stayed with his hands as they moved higher until a finger slipped inside her, coaxing the ache that throbbed for release. He played with her and she lost all sense of time and place. She opened her mouth, exhaling a moan as his thumb moved faster, then came apart.

When she opened her eyes he was crouched on his knees between her legs gazing at her with that intensity that made her want to pounce on him, but she was too sated to move. His hand fisted and closed, fumbling with his half-open zipper.

"Let me."

She brushed his fingers aside then lingered her fingers over the soft, happy line of hair that disappeared into his pants. The muscle in his jaw twitched frantically. He hissed when her fingernail skimmed one side of his erection. "I think I see more bites," she whispered. She turned to get the lotion, but he reached the bottle first and threw it aside.

"Next round," he said through clenched teeth, and showed her where he wanted both hands.

Warm, musky male scent filled her nostrils. She squeezed and stroked, loving the soft feel of his skin. As her rhythm increased, he bent over and latched onto a nipple, biting at first carefully, then harder. The tent walls changed from beige to honey. The feel of his wet tongue clamping around her nipple while she touched him was one of the most erotic things she'd ever felt.

"Damn," he said between puffs, "gotta slow down."

She dropped her hands by her sides. While she writhed on the cool sleeping bag he opened his wallet. After the condom was in place, he took her waist in one calloused hand, tilting her hips until her legs slid up his thighs.

His mouth sought hers and his tongue pushed inside, piercing her over and over in time with the slow strokes of his hand. She moved further and further into the center of pleasure that only Evan could create. Logic, reason, location, vanished from her mind. Evan's smell, the feel of his warm skin, and the thought of how good he made love to her were the sum total of her universe. He plundered and promised and purloined with his lips and hand, until she cried out for him.

He pulled back, searching her eyes. "You're ready for me."

She didn't know if it was a question or a statement, but she knew the answer.

Her body had been ready for him since he picked her up and carried her home. It had taken her brain a little longer to realize the inevitable.

Would her heart be next?

"Come here."

They switched positions. He easily handled her, reminding her how powerful he was, making her hotter and wetter. Her breasts landed on his chest, something that pleased him immensely as her legs spread-eagled over him. He lifted her by the waist, lifted right off her knees, and positioned her hips.

"I've waited so long, it feels like a dream," he murmured, and then lowered her. Her legs quivered, and she sunk around his fullness until she could no longer move. Gasping for breath, suspended about him, she gloried in the feel, the strength, the length of Evan.

"So beautiful." Spoken low and gravelly, the words hinted at something more. Something dangerous that sent skitters of excitement down her spine. He lifted his hips making her legs stretch further apart to take all, down to that sweet, intoxicating spot. She reached for his shoulders and dug fingertips into muscles, fighting to gain air, needing him more.

It was everything she'd remembered. Pure and powerful and breathtaking. "Not a dream."

She could come in one thrust, but that night together he'd taught her to be patient, to wait. He rose up on his elbows and she tucked her hips forward and rocked. A toe curling ache began, and she inhaled a ragged breath before he pulled her face down for a powerful kiss, one that went on and on until he broke off and commanded, "Ride me, Cassie."

His gaze held as she hesitate. Sensing her timidity, his hands rapped around her hips, guiding and driving her upward. Her body came alive. Perfume mingled with his scent, and the earth and forest that divided them from the world. His breathing set the rhythm, tight with need. Needing her.

Moisture collected like sparkles on the walls of the tent, and the air grew warm and hazy. Gazing into the softest pair of eyes in the world, her body responded. She moved faster. Past memories braided with the present, pushing her to let go. The Evan she'd remembered. The one she'd dreamt about and prayed for, waited for, wished for, kissed her. That end-of the-world-kiss, the one that pushed her until she though she'd die in his arms. Then he stiffened and gripped her body tight against his, and she did.

They lay cocooned in silence, arms and limbs and souls entwined. The nylon tent had collapse around them, and smelled of wildflowers, spice, and passion. The warmth of their bodies slowly seeped away.

He lifted her hair, knotted and stuck to her back, and traced a hand down to the base of her spine before anchoring her closer, prolonging the tiny tremors that still fluttered in her body. Her hands explored his arms, his shoulders, any skin within reach, noting a loss of tension and wishing she could explore the planes and valleys of his body at her leisure. She remained slack but sated, unprepared to let go.

Just a few more minutes.

Cassie could count the number of men she had

slept with on one hand. Although this lovemaking was not as hurried and frenzied, but still incredible, as soon as the afterglow cleared and her breathing became normal, doubts resurfaced.

She'd made a big mistake.

Had a moment of weakness. Who could blame her with someone as desirable as Evan.

But he was moving to Albany. Going after terrorists. Leaving her again. And how could she forget Heather? She needed to focus all her energy on her business to get her baby home.

Nothing had changed, and her heart wouldn't survive another breakup.

This could never happen again.

She tried to rolled away, but a heavy arm across her back barred her from rising. Evan lifted his golden head, mussed from her fingers, making him look more desirable. His eyes narrowed. "Where're you going?"

"To get dressed."

Knuckles traveled lazily up her backbone, leaving desire in their wake. He searched her eyes. "Why?"

She closed her eyes to tap down the tremor that his touch created. "The sun's up, and I want to get out of here. I visit Heather on Sundays."

In Wrestlemania-styled fashion he reversed their positions, trapping her beneath him, their faces so close lips nearly touched. His expression didn't change, but uncertainty passed through his eyes, so she said what she thought he wanted to hear. "You were good."

Short of crushing her, he pressed her into the sleeping bag. His gaze intensified, so she looked away. His breath pet her cheek, and she wanted to take the words back, wanted to empty her heart to him, stay under him until they were old and gray. Instead, her rational mind rallied.

"We both knew this would eventually happen," she said facing those dark, wary eyes. "Now it's over."

Not so gently, she pushed at his chest. He shifted slightly and she wiggled her way out from under him, grabbed her clothes and started to dress. By the dead fire she waited for him to come out, bracing for an argument. Men like Evan rarely took no for an answer. He'd have more question, ones she never would answer.

A few minutes later he came out of the tent, fully clothed and towered above her. "What's wrong?"

"Nothing's wrong. We had sex. Now, I want to leave and forget this happened." The last words she said low, unable to put the firmness behind them that she needed to sound convincing. She concentrated on tying perfect bows in her sneakers, hoping he'd let it be.

He crouched eye level, a fierce scowl on his face. "Why?"

"You know why."

She forced herself to look him in the eye. *Like you forgot about me the last time*, she'd wanted to say. She pursed her lips instead.

He stiffened. "No, I don't, but I'll take you to see Heather. Later, we'll talk."

She nodded, all the while thinking, *No way*.

****

Cassie didn't look at him once the entire time he repacked the gear and took down the tent. She seemed to have withdrawn into a golden cocoon. Gone was the beautiful open woman he'd made love to.

And he had no clue why.

He should have been happy. He'd gotten what he'd wanted. Making love to her again was more than any fantasy he'd ever created. The years apart from her seemed to fade away. He'd nearly died in her arms. So what went wrong?

Maybe she'd felt the change in him. The tent spikes in his hand slipped from is fingers. They formed two X's on the ground.

She was right. They should forget it happened. Forget how much he wanted to get her to the cabin, where he could light the fire and make love to her on the bearskin rug, and ...

None of that was going happen. His fantasy woman looked at him like she wished him dead.

They hiked in silence and emerged into a clearing when he first heard the helicopter. He looked up and waved. MRT. Probably found the car. The image of a Tomahawk dropping a gurney to take his sergeant away flicked across his vision. The whip of the blades came closer and closer. Then the forest burst into flames.

Where was Cassie? Lost in the flames?

Pain sluiced from his hands to his head.

Agonizing pain.

In a minute he'd black out. Instead of darkness, there was light. He spied Cassie. She walked toward him, looking relieved that their ordeal was over. Sweat dripping from his brow stung his eyes. He wiped it away with a shaky hand. Nothing compared to the way his insides shook.

A few minutes later, they met a small group of men, led by Tony. "Scared us, man. We found your bullet-riddled car. You two okay?" Tony relaxed his rifle by his side as he spoke.

Evan clenched his fists to control the trembling. "Cassie's fine. Did you get the guy in the cabin?"

"Bad news, the local sheriff's assistant lost him. We found the guy unconscious in the cabin. But we got a good description of him and the car. He won't get far. They're cleaning for DNA now. Found footprints all over the place, including the woods.

And gun shells."

"Ohh," moaned Cassie.

He should have yanked Tony aside before they started to talk. "Keep it down, Tony. She nearly shocked once. The guy scared her good."

They watched another officer walk Cassie to the helicopter.

"I've more bad news, Ev. We have a Complaint in the office. It's against Cassie. An arrest warrant on a felony charge from Orange County, Los Angeles."

"What? What for?"

"Embezzlement," Tony replied.

"There's no way Cassie stole money, you know that. It must be a mistake." Evan swatted the air and started toward the helicopter.

Tony followed. "Listen, how much do you know about her? You haven't seen her in years. Do you know she's lost custody of her daughter?"

Evan stopped and faced Tony. "That's not relevant."

"Ev, she's beautiful and nice to talk to, but are you going to throw away your career for her? Word's around the office that promo's yours. Getting mixed-up with this lady could get your name pulled."

Too late, Tony, I'm past the point of mixed-up. "I'm taking her to see her daughter. I don't know anything about a warrant. But make sure it's left on my desk to serve. Are we clear?"

Tony looked like he wanted to say something else, but Evan climbed into the helicopter, to leave with Cassie.

Nothing Tony had to say could convince him to leave Cassie.

Chapter Twelve

Heather smelled like strawberries and sunshine. Cassie looked down at the long blonde hair, so like her own, and wished she could stay on the swing with her daughter forever.

"Mommy, you promised this time you'd take me home with you," Heather said as she pet her little kitten.

"I know we planned to be together this weekend, sweetie. Something came up." She combed her fingers though a knot in Heather's hair, but the child didn't protest.

Heather's chin raised and her nose crinkled up the way it had since she was a baby. "You smell different." She pistol-pointed a tiny index finger. "You weren't making chocolate." Her expression changed to concern. "You went camping. I smell the mosquito lotion." Large blue eyes narrowed and her bottom lip quivered. "You were supposed to wait for me."

"Oh, sweetie. It couldn't be helped."

She couldn't tell her daughter the entire truth, but she couldn't lie, either. "We'll go camping some other time. Besides, it's getting too cold outside."

The glider swayed back and forth as Cassie waited for Heather's reply. The kitten fell asleep. With Heather tucked by her side and the familiar creak of the swing, she felt better, almost like home. She closed her eyes and soaked up the moment. They needed a glider. Garage sales weren't over yet. She'd check the paper tomorrow.

"Did you use the tent?" Heather asked.

"What—er—Yes."

Heather settled closer, although her little arms couldn't have been wrapped tighter around Cassie. "Weren't you cold?"

"No, Mommy was warm."

"Did you use the glow sticks?"

Cassie nodded. "They were a big help." She knew that would yield that "proud of herself," arrogant smile for that comment. It was so like hers.

"Were you alone?"

"No..."

"That man?" Heather pointed to Evan, waiting by the garage doors. She studied him for a moment, her cherubic face so serious that Cassie expected her to say something negative. "Evan rhymes with heaven, Mommy."

Sigh.

The kitten awoke, and both watched as he scampered away. "Daddy says Evan's a good man. He saves people. Did he save you, Mommy?"

So Jake *had* talked to Evan. How much did he tell Evan?

Cassie pushed harder with her feet. The glider soared back and forth through the air. Heather laughed that child-like giggle that was music to her ears. They sailed higher and higher, "to touch the sky," she told Heather.

She didn't want to talk about Evan, but Heather wasn't detoured. "Did Evan like the glow sticks?"

"He said they made the tent look like a disco."

Heather's head popped up. "He did?" Her eyes shone. She looked in his direction again. "What else did he say?"

He said he wouldn't let anyone hurt me again. "He thought you were very smart for thinking of them."

That got a bigger smile. She loved how Heather's smile went from one side of her little face to the other. Such a beautiful child, and she would have done anything for her.

"Did he like *your* something-special?" Heather asked.

Her face warmed with memory of how Evan fed her kisses. "Yes."

"He has a sweet-tooth like us." Heather frowned and added, "Grandma Hamilton says all my pretty teeth are going to fall out if I don't stop eating kisses. Is that true, Mommy?"

Curse Jake's mother for trying to take candy from a baby. "Brush your teeth, and they'll stay pretty. Hershey's kisses never ruined my teeth." And to do something silly, Cassie opened her mouth wide and acted like she was going to swallow Heather up. Once she had Heather laughing, she began to tickle her, and that signaled it was time for a tickle match.

Satisfied Heather was distracted, Cassie changed the subject. "You haven't mentioned school, honey. You usually talk about that first."

"I don't like school anymore." Heather crossed her arms and pouted.

"Why?" Cassie restarted the swing.

Heather's little mouth hardly opened as she answered. "Jeffrey Braningham. He said I talked funny, and Billy Gaines stuck up for me, and they got in a fight. Billy punched Jeffrey *right* in the nose, and it didn't bleed much, but he cried anyway." Her little fist flew through the air, reminding her of the way Evan's fist collided with the stranger's in the cabin.

"That wasn't nice of Jeffrey, or Billy." *Yes, Billy!* "What did Mrs. Patterson do?"

"She made them shake hands and 'pologize to each other. Then she made Jeffrey 'pologize to me. Hmfp." She turned her nose up in the air, exactly the way Cassie perfected at the same age. "I told him, a fool's born every minute. That's what Grandpa says."

"Grandpa? Grandpa Joe was here?" Cassie's toe caught the ground and the swing slowed.

"Yep, he came by with a be-belated birthday present for me. A fairytale book, and a bag of kisses in Easter colors. The ones you like, he said. Said he saved them special."

"How long ago was this, honey?"

"Last week. I talked to him a little, but Daddy talked to him a long time."

Cassie's stomach sank to her knees. Her father was back in town and he'd contacted Jake first. That meant one thing.

"Billy Gaines got suspended from school for two days," Heather continued. "Before he left, he told Clare he liked me." Her smile of pure female satisfaction made Cassie's heart swell.

The boys aren't going to stand a chance with this one. She'd make sure her daughter wouldn't make the same mistakes she'd made. "Listen, sweetie. Forget those boys and concentrate on your schoolwork. You still want to be a doctor like Daddy someday, don't you?"

Heather thought about it for a long moment. "I don't think I want to bandage people up anymore. I don't like the sight of blood." Her nose scrunched up and they both laughed.

She hugged Heather closer. "That's okay. You have plenty of time to decide what you want to do."

Heather smiled impishly. "But I do know. I want

to be a chalk-la-tear like you, Mommy. Then I'll eat chocolates and smell like chocolate all the time, too."

"Oh sweetie..." She looked from her daughter to the man walking out of the house. Jake followed. As her heartbeat picked up, she told herself to calm down. Jake wouldn't tell Evan what happened in L.A., she was certain.

It was up to her to explain, and the sooner the better.

****

Through the deck's sliding glass doors, Evan watched mother and daughter head to the swing set. The last time Evan was here, they'd celebrated Heather's third birthday. He'd been to more birthday parties and christenings then he could count. One after another he'd watched his high school buddies wed. He had a couple of godchildren, who he'd spoiled on birthdays and holidays, and that he'd treasured like his own. After all, they would be as close as he'd come to having kids.

Jake handed him a beer. Sipping the beers, they watched Cassie play with Heather. "Has Cassie told you about L.A.?"

Evan stared Jake in the eyes. "I can't believe you took Heather from her."

Jake looked weary. "Did Cassie say that?"

"No. We haven't talked about it yet." He felt exceptionally tired, too.

"Good. It's important you hear her side first."

Evan stomach clenched. "She'll tell me when she's ready."

He followed Jake onto the deck. A chill wind blew, scattering a pile of raked leaves. Winter was coming. It would only get colder.

"I'm glad Cassie has you to help her," Jake finally said. "She's had it rough since the divorce. I blame myself. She needs someone she can trust."

Evan nodded. Jake's face was lined with worry.

A good man. Something terrible must have caused him to take Heather.

Bullets of fear slammed into his spine. He had to get her to talk about L.A.

His gaze captured Cassie, now looking with Heather at a birdhouse posted by the garden. Cassie picked Heather up for a peek inside, followed by a stream of giggles.

His heart did a weird double-time step. Her relationship with her daughter was one of the things he'd always admired. If she wasn't talking about Heather, or playing with her, she was making something for her. He'd never seen a more devoted mother. A mother who deserved to have more children. He could picture her with a little boy. Cassie wouldn't raise a Momma's boy. Her son would be rough and tumble, more like a bull in a china closet. The way his grandparent's described him. He must have broken every vase and picture frame in their house that first year, not to mention the living room window due to a baseball tossed too close to the porch. Boy, did he get punished for that. But they doled out a lot of love for an unruly, lonely orphan.

"Have you heard about the Albany job?" Jake asked.

He spun the empty beer bottle on the picnic table. "The job covers a large portion of New York State. There are a lot of qualified people." He tried to sound like it wasn't a big deal.

Jake watched the bottle spin, too. "When will you hear if you received the appointment?"

Heather squealed and pointed to a large pumpkin in the garden. Cassie wrapped her arms around her from behind. They swayed together as they watched a butterfly dance from one pumpkin to the next. He felt the tug in his chest tighten. He stopped trying to rub it away. "I have an interview in Albany in a couple of weeks. After the governor's last commission report, they're looking to start something up right away."

"Would you start immediately?" Jake said.

"There's that possibility." He watched Cassie twirl Heather around in a circle and then both tumbled to the ground. They got up and did it again, this time Cassie feigning she couldn't get back up. Heather landed on her stomach. The sound of their laughter filled the air.

He could watch them play all day.

Jake sighed and pointed. "They're like this every visit."

Evan clenched his jaw. All smiles for her daughter today, there were no signs of the last night's torment.

She continued to amaze him. How many women after losing a child would have the guts to start a business? Most would probably bemoan their situation, expecting others to solve their problems.

Cassie looked in his direction, and waved. A satisfied smile shone on her face.

He'd make a terrible father.

He worked long days and was on call for emergencies; unable to attend T-ball or soccer games like his parents. The new job would require more traveling, less communicating if he was chasing down terrorist's cells. He'd be cut off from the outside world, like in Iraq.

Family life would become impossible.

"I haven't decided if I'm going to leave," he said. His gaze never left mother and child. The dream job would carry him though the next ten years. Then he could retire from police duty. He'd still be young enough to start up a small business, maybe hiking excursions in the Adirondacks. Unlike Clay, he had no desire to explore other mountain ranges. His heart rested in those mountains.

Cassie walked closer, carrying Heather. He

could hear the song they were singing. *I love you I walked with you Once Upon a Dream...*

The smile on Cassie's face was bright enough to light Times Square. He thought she was beautiful when he made love to her, but this was a different Cassie, a playful, vibrant woman. No fear or hesitation marred her face. She was the Cassie he remembered before she went to L.A.

He wanted her back.

The warrant, his mind warned, but he batted the thought aside.

He knew his next move.

****

After a dozen hugs goodbye, Cassie got in the unmarked police car and the tears started. Evan reached in his pocket for a clean handkerchief, and she took it. She faced the passenger window but he could see her tearstained reflection, hear soft sobs.

Acid scorched his gut. He slammed his hand on the steering wheel causing her to jump in her seat. "Sorry. A bee," he said.

"Did it sting you? Let me see." She reached for his hand.

Both hands gripped the steering wheel. "No."

Great, now she looks like I hit her. "I'm okay. My apartment's not much farther."

One dark-blonde eyebrow rose slightly. "Why are we going there?"

Her cheeks turned that pretty shade of pink while he took his time answering. "I need my other gun."

Her eyes opened so wide, her eyelashes touched her brows. "Do you think—"

"I think we lost him in the woods. I wouldn't have taken you to see Heather if I thought otherwise. But, there's a chance he'll try your home."

She shuddered and then lifted her chin. "I'm not leaving my home. Monday's the day I order supplies

154

and receive shipments. Nervous brides seem to call first thing."

"I figured. That's why you're getting around-the-clock protection."

"Police protection?"

"The best."

He expected a protest, or at least more questions. Her hands folded and unfolded his handkerchief. Silently they drove the rest of the way to his east-side apartment. He garaged the car, punched a security code to open the complex door and led her up two flights of stairs. Still no questions about the twenty-four hour surveillance. The pink color had drained and she clutched a photo on her key chain.

He unlocked the apartment door and waited for her to enter. That scared-kitten look still marred her face as he turned on the lights. Inside she looked chagrined as he slid three bolts in place. Footsteps tapped behind him as he reached the end of the hallway. "The living room is off to the left. Be back in a sec."

She nodded but stayed in the hallway. He turned to the right.

In his bedroom he strapped on his shoulder harness and grabbed more bullets. He kept the ankle harness on but replaced the clip. A change of clothes, shaving kit and more bullets dropped into his gym bag, enough for a couple of days. Out of habit, the latest Michael Crichton novel dropped into his bag then he dug for it and tossed it back on his nightstand. He needed to focus on Cassie tonight. Ready to leave, he found her in the living room, studying something in his trophy case, the only piece in the room that didn't resemble motel furniture. The piece had been passed down from one generation of Jorgenson's to another.

"This is where I crash during the week," he

explained as she pressed the cabinet light switch.

From the inside the case, the fluorescent light spotlighted her face as she surveyed his awards. "Do you still have the place up north?"

"Yep. Get there some weekends and vacations." He placed the gym bag by his desk.

She pointed to something in the case. "I've never seen a trophy for rappelling. What's that?"

"Going down a mountain with a rope." His speed came in handy rappelling down one three-story building in Iraq to avoid capture.

"Oh. I remember now. I tried it once. You have to have strong arms and a lot of guts to jump off a cliff." She bit the tip of her thumbnail while she continued her perusal.

He didn't know why he'd kept those trophies. Should have chucked them a long time ago, but he carried them from one apartment to another.

She pointed to the lowest shelf, and laughed. "This one's cute—Best T-ball player. It looks like someone used clay to make it." Her finger touched the glass and then she pointed to the case's door handle.

He nodded, allowing her to open the door and remove the trophy. "It's modeling clay."

The ugly brown hunk rotated in her hands like she held a child. "Let me guess. You lost MVP, and you made your own trophy."

He shook his head, feeling his cheeks heat.

Her lips pursed, ready to laugh at it.

Shit. Why did she have to see that hunk of stone? Expecting an answer, he gave in. "Every player and parent knew I had that trophy locked up. The catch was you had to be at the last game to get a trophy." He paused, remembering that day. "I missed the game because of my parents' funeral."

He expected a look of pity. Instead, she traced her finger over the lettering and smiled sadly. Then she carefully placed it on a higher shelf, in front of the shiny brass, "rappelling" trophy. "I think a trophy like that deserves to be in a special place." She checked the other trophies but her eyes strayed back to the clay one.

Before they left, he checked his messages. The answering machine light blinked three. He clicked the first message. "Where ya been? You should've seen me today. The stunt was outrageous. Call me."

Evan lowered the volume after Clay's booming voice. Next message. "Hey. I'm having a small get-together tonight. You can bring the whipped cream." No mistaking Dawn's syrupy whine.

Cassie's focus remained on the trophy case. Part of him wished she'd reacted to the message.

The last was from Tony. "Got the digs on the warrant—"

Evan cut the message.

Dammit, Tony, don't give me any more info about the warrant. Cassie should be getting booked right now.

Another good reason why he should stay with her.

He could add a dozen other reasons to the list but it boiled down to one thing. Now that he'd slept with her again, he didn't want to leave her side for a second. She'd confused him when she backed off right after they made love. Anger indicated deeper emotion.

Maybe she was scared? Not of him. He'd cut off his shooting arm before he'd hurt her.

"Was that Tony?"

"Yes... probably wants the day off. I'm ready. Let's go."

She stood and aimed for the door. He was a step behind her when she stopped and turned. "Why do you have the gym bag? Are you going somewhere?"

"I'm staying with you." She was in real danger.

157

Would she continue to push him away?

Her eyes widened and her lips parted. Probably thinking of ways to object. He braced her reply. "If you think there's going to be a repeat of what happened in the tent, you're wrong." Her chest heaved up and down.

He gazed at her lips, held her with his eyes. Her breath caught in her throat, exciting him further. *No, you're wrong, Cassie.* "I can send a car by to watch your house but without an alarm system it's possible he'd sneak in your house without you knowing."

He paused, wishing he didn't have to convince her of anything.

She hooded her eyes. "Okay. But only until I can get a security system installed."

"Deal."

Then he pulled her into his arms and kissed her hard. He'd been waiting to kiss her again for hours. When she leaned into him, he deepened the kiss. He loved how she kissed with her entire body, stretching every inch to make contact with his. She tasted so good it overloaded his senses.

God, he couldn't kiss her even a little without wanting her naked beneath him. She filled his senses with her smell, her taste and feel. Would it always feel like this, or was it just the threat of danger heightening his senses?

Reluctantly, he broke off the kiss. They need to slow down, or they'd be spending the night in his apartment. "Only for a couple of days?" he hushed.

Her arms were thrown around his neck and her body pressed against his, silently requesting a repeat of this morning. He wanted to set her straight and carry her to his bed and take them both into orbit.

She caught her breath and then pulled back. Lips that moments before pressed against his, formed a hard line. "Yes, but... please don't kiss me again." Cool eyes raked his face with icicles before she added, "I mean it," and gave him frostbite.

Damn. She was right. What was he thinking?

His job was to protect her from a killer. Put a lid on his lust, not torch it. He stepped back and opened the door. "Only if you ask. Let's get to your place before dark."

In the car, he watched the road with one eye, and the rear view mirror with the other.

Cassie glanced over her shoulder. "Are we being followed?"

"Not that I can tell but I'll feel better when we're there."

Minutes later he pulled the car to the curb across from the sweet shop. No traffic. By morning, the street would be swollen with rush hour traffic. It was a great location for a business, and someone would have to be very careful to break in unnoticed. That thought relieved him somewhat. But at this hour, the street appeared desolate.

She hurried ahead of him. When the shop door swung open before she'd placed the key in it, his worst fear was confirmed.

"I'm sure I locked the door."

Confused she looked at him.

He pulled her behind him, removed his shoulder gun and crouched low to the floor. No time to put her back in the car, besides he didn't want her out of his sight. There could be more than one perpetrator.

He signaled her to stay low, behind the candy counter, and then checked the kitchen area. The cash register was locked. The shelves stacked with chocolates. The aisle clean and clear. Nothing looked disturbed. No intruder in the shop.

"Stay down here," he whispered.

He crept up the back stairs to her apartment, with Cassie close behind him.

Chapter Thirteen

The back door to her apartment seemed secured and untouched but Evan entered cautiously. Gun in hand and listening for any sound, he managed to check the rooms in the dark. No shadows moved. The only sound was the wind beating on the windows. He breathed a sigh of relief and holstered the gun before turning on lights. Then, he went back for Cassie. "You can come in now."

Her face paled. "Are you sure? Did you check the closet?" Her eyes scanned the apartment faster than any radar device.

"I checked everywhere. You can relax."

Holding her icy hand in his calloused, scarred one, he led her through the kitchen into the small living room. Relief swept through him when her shoulders lifted and she pushed her bangs from her eyes.

In front of a narrow white door, she took off her jacket and reached a hand out for his.

"I'm going back to the car for your backpack and my bag," he said. *And to look around the perimeter to make sure there were no open windows or doors to encourage a second attempt.* "I have to make a call.

I'll be back in a few minutes."

As he stepped onto the back stairs landing, he heard the phone ring. Karl and Karen were notified when MRT found them in the woods, but Karen would want to hear Cassie's version of what happened. Good. He liked knowing someone cared for her. He bounded downstairs to the back yard.

Outside, he checked the first floor windows. Besides the picture window in the front of the store, the kitchen window's locked was painted shut. Another downstairs window, in the bathroom, was more for ventilation than light. The perp would have to be an elf to get through it. That left only two ways into her upstairs living area, break through the front door, not an easy task during the day on such a well-traveled street, or break the bolted steel back door, impossible without tools and a lot of noise.

That front door was history tomorrow, no matter what she said. He knew a hardware store that specialized in beautiful imitation wood doors that were actually solid steel. He'd install a four-inch bolt, remote controlled lock. And wire it.

Evan wiped sweat from his brow and released a breath he unknowingly held. He never enjoyed this part of police work. Mountain rescues were more his style. But after Iraq, searching was ingrained. He looked up at the roof. Luckily, there were no attached porches, front or back, to make the climb easy. The perp would need a rope or a double-hung ladder for the upstairs windows. No sign of a ladder in or behind her garage. The rosebushes that ran along the perimeter of the home all looked undisturbed. Not a handful of dirt looked kicked out of place.

Something snapped behind him. He raised his gun and dropped to his belly. A large German Shepherd loped from the neighbor's yard through a broken fence, stopped next to him, poked a nose into his face, sniffed, and then rambled down Cassie's driveway.

Evan smirked. Even the animals looked out for Cassie.

There was still the third way in: through the front door, *during* business hours. The thought made his stomach ache. In this crowded small business district someone would have to be desperate to attempt that. Desperate men had nothing to lose. With winter months on their way, the sun set before six. Soon it would be dark by five o'clock. She'd still be working. *Add a panic trigger button for underneath the front counter.*

Satisfied with his house inspection, he noted the number and make of the neighbors' parked cars. He texted the numbers to the police computer. He'd have a report by morning. Then he grabbed the bags from the car and re-entered through the back door.

Still on the phone, Cassie glanced up when he walked into the kitchen. That concerned look returned in her eyes.

He nodded his reassurance.

Her features relaxed.

At last, some sign of trust. Enough to talk about L.A.?

All day he'd fought not to guess what could have happened. Being a police officer had its disadvantages. The things people were capable of doing, especially to former loved ones, amazed him. The thought of someone hurting her made him want to punch something.

Clenched fists pounded together as he surveyed the tidy room. The kitchen was freshly painted a beige color. White metal cabinets hung above a small counter space along one wall. A stainless-steel percolator with an old cloth-covered cord sat on the counter. No microwave, toaster, blender, or food processor. No wonder she was thin.

Against the longest wall was a drop leaf table with one chair pulled away from the table and one tucked in. On top of the table, one vinyl placemat and a small wooden bowl filled with apples were set. An outdated, mismatched refrigerator and stove stood on opposite sides of the room. A shiny copper teapot waited on a burner. The refrigerator door displayed an abundance of crayoned artwork and photos of Heather.

Cassie's gaze followed him as he exited the kitchen. He carried the bags into the living room and set them by the couch. The front window curtains drifted apart. He didn't recall that window being open.

Worried, he checked the street again. Headlights on a Taurus turned on and then the car sped away. *Shit.* That car wasn't there earlier. Too dark to get any plate numbers or a true color. He'd have to call for a cruiser, now. While he made the call, he checked the apartment's layout.

Off the living room were three doors. The bathroom boasted a decorative circular window, but a toilet and sink. Looked like a recent remodel, with fresh sheetrock on one wall. The second door led to another bedroom that appeared like she'd used it for storage. The third door was closed.

He text-messaged the address for the cruiser, then put his cell phone on vibrate for the night. Resting his hands on his hips, he looked around the living room. On the floor in the corner sat a small, unplugged T.V. No plugs nearby. The stereo next to it wasn't hooked up, either, and wires wrapped around the bases of two speakers. Some CD's sluiced out from an opened cardboard shoebox, as if a search had been interrupted. Two black plastic cubes, tipped on their sides, doubled as a coffee table. Both were filled to the top with magazines and paperbacks.

At last, he examined the narrow, tan sofa. He gauged its length to be about five feet. *Now, this is going to be an even longer night.* The other option was a ladder-back rocking chair. Sofa... chair... floor? He looked at the bare floor. *Been there before, won't kill me.* He glanced at the archway to the hallway a few feet away leading to Cassie's room.

Maybe he should sleep in the car.

"You don't have to stay. I'll be okay."

How did he miss her pad barefoot into the room? He forgot about his error when he turned and noticed her eyes glistened. She'd been crying. He went to raise his arms toward her, waiting to kiss the tears away. Slay any monster that came within a thousand miles of her. Instead, he ran his palm over the fabric of the couch. "I checked outside. The apartment is secure, except the store's front door. You may like its old-fashioned appeal, but it's too small for the frame. Makes it easier to kick in."

She flinched.

He squeezed the arm of the sofa, leaving deep impressions of four fingers. "I'd feel better with a new door," he added... "And remote locks, fully wired to an alarm system."

She shrugged, causing her sunny blonde hair to drift over her shoulder. "You're right. But you still don't need to stay."

He didn't answer. He looked at the sofa. The word, *need,* echoed in the room.

Her shoulders slumped, probably too worn out to argue. Then she looked kindly at the ugly piece of furniture. "It's not as bad as it looks. When I sleep on it, I love the feel of sinking into the cushions. It feels like a warm hug." She stroked the worn sofa as she spoke. "And the fabric's as soft as velvet."

He'd bet not as soft as her skin. The skin on the back of his hands tingled. *Damn.* He'd thought that reaction was history after this morning. He looked up at her, and thought of this morning. It must have teleported to her brain. Her hand jerked off the sofa, and she nervously backed away. He looked at the sofa, then the floor. "I'll manage."

She sighed, the same low sounding tone when she came in his arms. "I'll get you a pillow and blanket."

The sway of her hips as she disappeared into the bedroom intensified the itching. He thanked his lucky stars that he threw some Benadryl capsules in his jacket pocket. He dug for one. She returned and placed his bedding on the sofa.

She pointed to the small bathroom, said something else, maybe about something cold in the fridge. Then she walked through an archway. Her bedroom door snapped shut, clicked and a bolt slid into place.

Nice try, sweetheart. Locks and bolts won't keep out a man trained to disarm IED's.

Now wasn't the time to imagine holding her again, but he did. He thought making some coffee would distract him, and help him through the long night ahead. He knocked on her bedroom door to ask how to use the percolator and heard the gurgle of running water. His forehead fell on the door. Playboy-like images of Cassie soaping up in the shower popped into his head, followed by the fantasy of him washing her off. He pictured her long hair hanging like wet ropes that he could wrap around his fists to hold her in place as he kissed her breasts. Then he'd pull her down onto his lap and make love to her until she screamed.

Cassie in his arms again, screaming his name was the sweetest sound in the universe.

He stroked the slick white enamel paint. The skin on his arms crawled with an itch. He hoped the Benadryl kicked in soon. With heroic effort, he reined in his fantasy before he broke down the door.

He'd figure how to use the damn coffee thing or eat grounds. But, first he wanted to take a better look behind the other closed door.

Door number one opened. Light spilled from the ceiling lamp, a crystal globe that resembled a pumpkin-shaped carriage. A large sleigh bed angled across the narrow room, its wooden headboard stenciled with pink roses and green ribbons. The shinny bedspread was pale green, trimmed with pink bows. On the nightstand sat a ceramic lamp painted with a princess trying on a glass slipper held by a prince. Little mice tumbled around the lamp. Hair ribbons overflowed from a large glass slipper.

In the corner, a massive wooden wardrobe with curvy scrollwork matching the headboard took up the entire wall. On the top of a smaller dresser sat a crystal-framed photo of Cassie and Heather with a big theme-park cartoon dog, a memento of happier times. The walls were papered, and the hardwood floor partially covered with a shaggy, white oval rug. A rocking chair was stationed in the corner. Its white paint chipped, but it looked sturdy, like it ushered many generations gently to sleep, and now guarded the room. A pink, stuffed bunny and a patched teddy bear occupied the seat. The entire bedroom ensemble looked big bucks.

A room fit for a princess, all right.

"Here you are."

The voice from a distance startled his thoughts but he didn't move. Her scent teased his nostrils. It reminded him of a drink he'd ordered while vacationing with Clay in Cancun. Some kind of fruity drink that went down smooth, but packed a helluva punch. He imagined her walking on the white sandy beach, her long hair floating in the breeze. She'd look amazing in a thong bikini. All that beautiful skin. On second thought, Cancun was too crowded. He'd take her to some secluded tropical island. Somewhere they could make love in the sand, uninterrupted.

He could hear her breathing. She was directly behind him now. He pictured her in a towel. "I'm making some tea. Would you like some?" When she moved next to him, virtually lost inside a terrycloth robe, a fire ignited inside his belly. She wrapped her arms around her shoulders as if the air in the room had chilled.

"I'd rather have coffee. Nice room." He pointed to the bed and dresser.

She nodded and crossed to the bed. There, she fussed with one of the pillows and smoothed the bedspread of non-existent wrinkles. Her gaze found the photo. She touched her hand along the glass frame, and massaged it as she spoke. "Heather hasn't seen this room. She's a bit of a tomboy. I put her in dance classes in L.A., but she hated being indoors. She plays tennis, softball, soccer... and climbs every tree she sees." He expected Cassie to smile a proud-mother smile, but the corners of her mouth dropped lower. She continued to polish her fingers over the frame.

He stepped closer. "She must like fairytales."

In the light from the chandelier her eyes glistened like emeralds. He pictured a cluster of emeralds around her neck, or maybe an ankle bracelet. It would be a fun party putting either on m' lady.

"Both, to be honest." She shivered, looked around the room, then gazed up at the brilliant light. "I guess I went a little overboard."

"Not a bit."

She stared at him for a long moment.

Do I measure up, sweetheart? Can you trust me enough to tell me your secret? "I think Heather will love this room."

She picked up the picture with both hands and

then sat on the edge of the bed. Toes curled under the robe, and the collar folded up and caressed her face. She continued to caress and gaze at the picture, lost in some memory.

His gut pained like he'd eaten glass. Heather should be here, now. If he ever had a child he'd go crazy if they were separated. How did she stand it? He wanted so badly to wrap her in his arms and hold her, to let her know that everything would be okay.

He took a step toward her. The floor creaked but she didn't notice. It was on the tip of his tongue to tell her how much he'd missed her in Iraq. Dreamed of her day and night.

Feeling like an intruder, he left.

In the living room the stack of blankets and pillows on the sofa had toppled over.

Why he was doing this? She was safe for tonight. If the stranger from the cabin were in that Taurus, he probably wouldn't be back.

He could keep watch from the car.

Again, he smelled Cassie, this time headed for the kitchen. The back of his neck itched. He followed at a safe distance. The fluorescent kitchen lights were brighter than the light in Heather's bedroom. They shone on her simple robe, some shade of gold that covered her from head to bare toes. He pictured her dressed in a ball gown with her hair done up. When she bent to check the gas burner, curves and valley accentuated, and the imaginary gown disappeared. He kicked out a chair at the table and sat, leaning forward. The Benadryl must have kicked in, or he'd have been scratching his skin off.

"The percolator will take a few minutes. I left towels for you in my bathroom if you want to clean up." She turned on the faucet and started filling the metal coffee pot.

When the coffee was set to go, he gestured to the opposite seat in the table. "We need to talk."

She didn't hesitate to sit but took her time adjusting her robe over her legs before looking up at him.

He got up and began to pace in the small area. He returned and leaned over the table. "Who would want to kill you?"

Her eyes popped open.

Shit, tone it down. She wasn't a prisoner. "Look. I'm not buying that guy followed you because he knew you owned a store. He could have robbed you here, or another store. He wanted you alone for a reason. Then he escapes and tries to silence us both. Why? Why kill someone over an attempted robbery charge? Or is there some other reason."

"I honestly don't know." She rose from the chair and removed a teacup from a narrow cabinet. "I've never seen him around my store. Although—" Her knuckles turned so white on the cup handle, he waited for it to snap.

"Go on."

"I've had this strange feeling, ever since the hike in Lake Placid, that I'm being watched." She set the teacup down hard on the counter. "At the time, I thought it was you. But the feeling continued when I walked into my store." Crinkled lines formed around her eyes. The tip of her nose turned red and she rubbed it.

"Usually when people get a feeling like that, it's because they're worried about some trouble they're in," he prompted.

She looked down at her feet.

"Are you in trouble?"

Her back straightened, and her chin tilted up. "I haven't done anything."

"Good. Then we'll assume the guy's a stalker. They're usually more predictable. More reason for you to not be alone. If you think of anything that can help…"

Her breathing increased. She pursed her lips. *Damn-it.* Those perfectly bow-shaped lips weren't divulging any information tonight.

He picked up the sugar bowl. "I checked the neighborhood's police reports. Very little happens here. This neighborhood was a good choice."

"I've liked it since high school. Karl said it was a safe area." She set the cream pot on the edge of the table.

"Still, you can't be too careful. All it takes is one wrong customer, maybe even someone you think you know, to mess things up."

Her eyebrows moved slightly. "I know that."

The whistle on the teakettle hissed. She went over to the counter and he watched her fix a cup of tea. With her back to him she took several sips.

"I'm trying to help."

No response. A minute later her shoulders slumped and the teacup found the counter.

"I'd like to shower and call it a day," he said at last.

No voice called to him as he walked away, but he heard a cabinet door bang shut.

In the doorway to her bedroom he halted. Her scent drifted to him as he crossed the room. The business in his pants ached. A breeze from the open window offered some relief. He opened the blind then window and stuck his head out. Breathing quickly through his nose made him dizzy at first. After several inhalations of the crisp night air his head cleared. A cold shower would help his lower half.

Her bedroom overlooked the unlit driveway.

Install floodlights around the periphery, too, he noted. Lucky she didn't have trouble sooner. A beautiful woman, alone, anyone could... He should have called her as soon as he got back from Iraq. How could he leave her alone this long? He took a large swallow of air and held it until it hurt.

When he pulled his head back inside his shoulder bumped a shelf full objects. Wizards holding crystal balls, and dragons of all shapes and sizes. The largest dragon stood on a large crystal ball, its wings spread ready for a fight, mouth open in a silent growl. It's huge glass eyes glared at him. Not one princess or knight in the bunch, only an odd collection of lizards. Maybe she was into *Dungeons and Dragons?* Or were they talismans meant to protect her?

He righted a small dragon that had wiggled close to the edge, wishing he knew more about her. He wished he could talk more freely about Iraq. Wished he could be a different man. Maybe the reason she didn't open up to him was that he'd never opened up to her.

Feeling vulnerable, he faced the room. Moonbeams filtered through mini-blinds and stretched bars across her bed. After Heather's room, he'd expected a room befitting a queen, maybe a fur bedspread and satin sheets, a crystal chandelier, and dozens of scented candles.

Not this.

A full-size mattress set on a headboard-less frame, covered with a milky white comforter. A slender nightstand, big enough only for a square clock radio and an office-style black lamp, crammed together on top. A sole dresser, half the size of Heather's, angled in the corner, stripped of most of its green paint, and listing to the right. It looked like something someone threw away.

Photos of Heather at various ages covered one gray, cracked wall. He paused before the largest one which faced the bed. Turquoise-colored water and sunshine behind her, Heather knelt on a pristine white beach and proudly presented a conch shell to the photographer. His stomach soured thinking of the injustice of keeping those two apart.

A floorboard creaked behind him. "Evan? You forgot your bag."

She walked into the moonlight, her robe glittering like fairy dust. The bag landed at his feet. Red-rimmed eyes looked up at him.

The urge to hold her in his arms and kiss those tears away was so strong that he swayed forward. It tore at his gut to see her in pain.

Please make this easy on both of us, sweetheart, and ask me to sleep with you.

She went to the nightstand and began twisting the knobs on the back of the alarm clock. "I have to set this thing or I'll never wake up. What time would you like to get up?" When he didn't answer, she hesitated, and nearly dropped the clock. A tinge of pink painted her cheeks.

Any other time, he'd have cut the crap and laid her on that bed. But her trust was way too important. She needed to make the first move. He reached into his bag, taking his time to gather his shower stuff, all the while aware that she watched him.

He walked into the bathroom and set each item down, further delaying his response. When he finished, he leaned against the sink, crossed his arms over his chest, and waited.

He watched her chest rise and fall faster and faster.

He moved to the doorway, stared her down. *Invite me into your bed.* When she didn't speak, he said, "I don't need a clock."

She set the clock on the nightstand so hard it nearly bounced off. Clutching the lapels of her robe together, she looked at him warily. If only she could see what he saw. She needed to be in his arms, like last night, even more so tonight. *Screw this and come take a shower with me,* he wanted to say. "I'm leaving early. First thing in the morning, BL Security will be here. You'll get locks and wires up here, too."

The lapels on her robe twisted under her fingers. "Good. Thank you again for... everything. I feel safer with you here. Someday, I'll be able to repay you."

His fingers twitched from wanting to touch her. "Friends help friends." Like the night she came to him, only what he'd felt that night wasn't gratitude.

Her eyes widened and she took a step into the doorway. "Still, I want you to know I'll never forget your help, even when..." Her breath hitched. "W-When this is all over."

The bedroom door slammed shut before he could respond. The mirror on the back of the door rattled. His image shimmered for half a minute, and then cleared.

There was no doubt why she ran. It was written all over his face.

****

Cassie's strength at times amazed her. If she'd stayed in her bedroom one more second with Evan looking at her that way she'd have been undressing him and begging him to make love to her the way he did this morning. He was too gorgeous to be real. Every time their eyes met, she remembered the tender way he made love to her. His last look was so intense it stole her breath.

Weakening, she looked at the closed door.

No. I can't.

As much as she wanted to feel his arms holding her again and taste his kisses, she had to resist. Making love again would only make it more painful when he left her this time. Like with her favorite sweets, one little bite was all she could control. Too much, and she'd gorge.

Before she could surrender, she went to the living room, grabbed the latest issue of *Chocolate*

Desserts, and found sanctuary in the kitchen.

The ad on the back cover, of a beautiful woman tempting her lover with a box of chocolates, made her stomach cramp. Evan deserved better. She'd rather cherish the memory of his passionate stare than face loathing, or worse, hatred.

The smell of coffee perking filled the air as she flipped through the magazine pages. So much had happened since she'd bought her favorite magazine on Wednesday. One corner of a page was turned down, the recipe for the chocolate truffle cake she'd planned to make with Heather. Gulping down her lukewarm tea did nothing to quell the burn in her stomach, or ease her mind. Not only didn't she have custody of Heather, but she didn't know if it was safe to have her daughter.

Unsafe to have her baby in her home? What was happening?

Who wanted her dead?

Away from Evan, she finally processed just how much trouble she was in. A burst of fear flamed through her. Her hands shook uncontrollably. The picture of the chocolate truffle cake, blurred. One fat teardrop fell on the page. She found a tissue in her pocket and wiped her cheeks.

Evan didn't need to see any more tears.

Sipping the last of the lavender-tea, she envisioned the incidents up north. It made no sense. She didn't have any enemies—had broken no laws since coming home. Dylan was the only truly dangerous man she knew. Sick bastard that he'd become, his phone calls indicated he still worshipped her like in L.A. But why now after all these months?

Evan was right. She'd given little thought to a security system. In California, she'd seen lavish systems on multi-million dollar properties. Had her lackadaisical attitude put her in danger again?

Thumps came from the bedroom. It sounded like

shoes being thrown on the floor.

What if she heard a frightening sound during the night and she needed Evan? He'd come running. The warmth she felt all over had nothing to do with the fresh cup of steaming tea. Now that it was ready, she transferred the perked coffee into a carafe to keep warm for Evan. What was she thinking, telling him to leave? Evan was there to protect her. So far, he'd done a great job. She'd faked anger at Karen's interference on the phone earlier. She'd be in a hospital, or dead if Karen omitted that call. Or in jail. If she had gotten a better hold of that fireplace poker, she'd have killed the man. Killing even if it was self-defense, would be too much to bear. Judge Hinckley would've use that against her, making it impossible to get Heather back. Her knees felt weak, so she grabbed the counter until the feeling passed.

Thank God Evan arrived in time.

And she *had* planned to replace that old door, as soon as she earned a little more money. Why hadn't she told him? Why was she fighting Evan's help? What was wrong with her?

The telephone rang as she rinsed her teacup. She hesitated, but picked up the receiver.

"Hey, don't mean to interrupt, but I forgot to ask if you still need me at the shop tomorrow."

Karen's voice relaxed her more than any herbal tea. "No, but I may need you later in the week. I ran an ad in the papers. I'm hoping to catch a few winter wedding orders."

Holiday weddings used to be her favorite.

"Love those winter weddings. A bride in a white velvet gown has to be the ultimate to behold."

Carrying American Beauty red roses.

Wearing a lace-edged veil that drifted to the floor as she moved, and a snowy fur stole with matching gloves to keep her warm, until she reached her groom. And when his hand touches hers, its warmth would keep the cold away, forever.

"Yes."

"Oops, I forgot to tell you, Karl went to the cabin to check on things. He said they were towing the Audi. The police said something about checking the engine for tampering. You'll get it back in a few days."

"Good thing I don't have far to walk to work." The news frightened her, and she fought to hide it from her voice.

"The offer still stands to stay with us. I can come and get you now," Karen said cautiously.

"Not necessary. I have a bodyguard."

Karen's squeal was so loud that Cassie pulled the phone from her ear. "Oh, sorry, I didn't mean to wake you, honey," Karen whispered to Karl. Then in an excited voice she added, "It worked. I knew if you two were alone long enough, you'd spontaneously combust. One little detail, please, and I'll never mention it again, unless of course, you want to tell me all the little details."

"Karen."

"Is he as good as he looks?"

She shook her head. "I'm not going to discuss any of this."

"Is he next to you now?"

Karen, responsible mother of three, sounded like a thirteen-year old.

"No. He's in my bedroom—"

"Waiting for you. Oh, honey, I'm sorry I called—" Karen's voice sounded elated.

"No, Karen, it's not like that... I'm in the living room... he used the shower—"

"Did you take one with him?"

"No! He's here in case the stalker comes back." Cassie's cheeks burned, imagining soaping Evan's naked body.

"They can send a car to watch your house," she

gleefully added. "He's there because he's smitten. Oh, this is so great. And *you* didn't want to talk to him in Lake Placid." The gloating adult returned.

"He's not—"

"Don't be in denial, kiddo. Besides, wouldn't you rather have a warm body next to you? What Karl... oh, Karl wants me off the phone so he can sleep. Yeah, right, Karl." Cassie heard Karen's giggle, and then a long pause. "Okay, I gotta go. Karl wants me to put my big mouth to better use. Sweet dreams, sweetie."

Cassie hung up and walked over to the white door. Counting to ten didn't help. Dragons had lit a bonfire in her stomach, but now the feeling drifted lower. Damn Karen for putting thoughts in her head again. What happened in the tent was a fluke. Something they both needed to get out of their systems. She recalled his fingers moving up her spine. Her face burned. She wanted *more*. But more wasn't possible.

In the living room, she waited in her rocking chair.

I wish he'd leave. I wish he'd leave. I wish he'd leave.

The bedroom door slammed opened. Evan walked into the living room wearing black jeans and T-shirt, and a zipped up black nylon jacket. His eyes were polished black stones, impossible to read. His gym bag was in one hand, car keys in the other.

Her heartbeat tripled. She stood up. "Are you leaving?"

No mistaking the sound of disappointment in her voice. *Be careful what you wish for*, her mother used to say.

Would he really leave her?

He paused, and looked her up and down. If he held binoculars, he couldn't have been more thorough. "I want to cruise the neighborhood one last time."

Relief flooded her veins. "Will you be long?"

"A while. I've got your keys. Don't wait up." His hair was slicked back and little drops of water dripped and stained his collar. His black eyes glowed fever-bright. She wanted to tell him he could use her blow dryer, but the door shut before she could reply. No man had a right to look so handsome, and so dangerous. She wanted to kiss that scowl off his face and pull him into her bedroom if given ten more seconds. Good thing he decided to leave.

She laughed. Saved again, this time from herself.

Back in her bedroom, there was no sign of Evan. Nothing was moved, but it didn't feel the same. The air seemed electrically charged, like the atmosphere after a sudden thunderstorm. She smelled something—Evan's scent. In the bathroom she spied the birth control pills she'd forgotten to pack. She swallowed two, just to make sure. Good thing she'd stayed on them to keep her periods regular. The last thing she needed was to get pregnant and have another guy marry her out of misplaced honor.

But a baby with Evan... Her arms rose, cradled her elbows and swayed. She couldn't explain the current of excitement. She'd always wanted to hold another baby in her arms, maybe a boy. Evan's son would be a handful but a beautiful baby. And smart.

She dropped the unused towels she'd gathered in her arms, and collapsed onto the commode. It was wrong to think she'd ever have another baby when she didn't have Heather with her.

After another good cry, she turned off the bathroom light and walked into her bedroom. At the foot of her bed she opened her backpack, and retrieved Heather's Kitty. It no longer wore the bright red satin finish of a new stuffed toy. The red faded to a fragile rose-color. Whiskers were missing on one side of its enormous face. Its neck had been stretched and the head flopped about, but he still wore that grin.

Kitty smelled vaguely of strawberries.

Holding Kitty tightly to her chest, she turned off the light and slid between the sheets, painfully aware, of being alone.

Chapter Fourteen

Cassie tossed and turned under the covers. Only when Evan returned about an hour later did she relax and fall asleep. She woke up, feeling refreshed, and hurried to the living room. Blankets and pillows were stacked neatly on the sofa. Evan was gone.

In the small half-bathroom off the living room, the snowy white towel she'd left for him was untouched. The only sign that Evan used the bathroom was a tube of toothpaste tossed in the garbage pail. Even the gym bag was gone.

She pushed away the tinge of disappointment as she pulled open drawers and tossed some work clothes on her bed. As she dressed, she recalled how large he looked in her bedroom. *Everything about him is too big,* a small voice warned. He didn't fit in her home, and he didn't fit in her life. If it weren't for Karen's meddling or the shots by the stalker, he'd probably be pursuing another woman by now, someone who could move to Albany and didn't worry about dangerous missions or terrorists.

Someone who hadn't messed up her life in the worst way possible.

Fear crept into her belly. She hated that

emotion. With Evan nearby, she'd been safe, even when hiding in the woods. Safe enough to last a lifetime?

Funny, her heart should have been in too many pieces to consider a future with anyone, but somehow it glued back together without her noticing. Her chest no longer hurt every morning, and food stayed down. As she sipped her morning tea, she wandered into the living room. One indented pillow smelled like Evan. She'd never forget his smell. Too bad they hadn't met under different circumstances. Karen was wrong. She wasn't in denial. He was helping her because he felt sorry for her, otherwise, he would have stayed last night. After his shower, he acted like they were strangers. In L.A. she'd prayed he would write and tell her he was okay, maybe slip her a note and say he loved her. She'd bargained with God to keep him safe. Prayed she'd see him one last time. For three years, she'd waited. Then she met Dylan.

The hand that raised the teacup to her lips shook uncontrollably. The teacup fell to the floor and broke in half.

She had to keep Evan from discovering what happened to her in L.A.

Once the security system was installed today, there would be no reason for him to stay, she thought, as she mopped up the tea and picked up the china pieces. Besides, the police would find the stalker. A man that large was easy to spot, even in a crowd. She and Evan gave the police a good description. It would be over soon. Then she could concentrate on her business, and prepare for Heather's return.

And mourn the loss of Evan all over again.

As she sprayed on her perfume, the phone rang. She ran to answer it before the machine picked up. Thinking it was Evan she couldn't hold back an excited, *Hello.*

"Hi, Angel. Sleep well?" a deep, scratchy voice shouted. She hated that nickname.

"I told you not to call me anymore," she replied, and lowered herself onto the arm of the couch.

"Can't do that. Can't stop thinking of you, either. You're on my mind even when I sleep. Forget that candy store. I need you, Angel. You can be on the afternoon flight, and we'll be together tonight."

His voice hissed. How she'd ever found it exciting, she'd never know. It wasn't creamy or comforting like Evan's. "You're crazy. There's no way I'm taking a plane or getting within a thousand miles of you. You're the reason Heather isn't waking up in her room this morning." Her forehead began to throb and she ran her fingers over the ache.

"How many times do I have to tell you I'm sorry for what happened? Things didn't go well in court Thursday? Too bad, Angel—"

Her hand dropped. "How do you know about my court date? Are you spying on me? If you had anything to do with the man who attacked me this weekend—"

"Whoa. You were attacked?" The alarm in his voice sounded real.

"A man followed me away to a secluded cabin in the woods and wanted money. Then he fired a gun at me and nearly killed my friend—"

"Wait. Are you hurt?" He actually sounded concerned.

"I'm scared! And your phone call is making me feel worse. For the last time, leave me alone." Her footsteps echoed in the room as she paced.

"Wait, Sugar. There's something you should know—"

She hung up the phone as hard as possible, feeling some satisfaction at the loud noise it made.

What would it take to be free of Dylan?

****

When Evan walked into the shop a few hours later, Cassie's heart fluttered. Always the first part of her body to react to his presence, she no longer fought the feeling but relished it. He stopped to speak with John from B.L. Security, who'd supervised the lock change and alarm installation. The electronic system didn't make her feel better about the stalker, or any future intruders. Seeing Evan in her shop did.

The kitchen timer buzzed for the second time. She hurried into her kitchen, needing to stay on task. To take her mind off Dylan's call, she'd made a huge pot of chocolate base for her cream filled samplers, enough for a week's worth of candy making. One look at Evan in a dove-gray tailored suit, looking like he'd stepped out of a GQ ad for Armani, made her forget what she'd set the timer for and what planet she was on. Knowing a gorgeous body hid under that suit made her breathing difficult. Chewing a piece of chocolate helped a little.

The door swung open. "Smells great. Neighbors must love it. I can see why you love making chocolate." The smile on Evan's face could have meltdown chocolate without a double boiler. Judging by the amount of heat pouring through her belly her insides were melting, too.

She nodded.

"Smells like something other than chocolate. I can't place it." His brows crinkled, making him look like a thoughtful Robert Redford.

"Lavender. My grandmother added a touch to her base. It gives the chocolate a special taste and smell," she said, feeling her cheeks grow warm.

He paused, his stare X-raying her so sharply that she felt her bones weaken. "I'd say it's very special."

To avoid that unwavering gaze, she pretended to

have lost something on the counter. Her act backfired when her clumsy hands knocked over the crock filled with wooden utensils. He didn't comment as she took several minutes to replace them the way she liked, fanned out by size for easy access. She patted the package of bamboo skewers, which stayed put.

The corners of his mouth twitched, before he spoke. "What are you making?"

"Hmmm? Oh... bonbons." She'd been staring at his lips.

"Like the ones we talked about at dinner?" A bamboo stick twirled between his fingers.

Those fingers were so skillful.

She nodded.

"Let's see."

Damp fingers accepted his skewer. "Oh, okay."

She poked a small square of homemade strawberry nougat, dipped it carefully, three times, into the base and then placed it on a stainless steel drying rack. She felt his eyes on her and was certain she dipped the next one too many times.

"Looks like fun. Need some help?"

His smile looked younger. *He must have been such a handsome teenager. I wonder how many disappointed tears were shed by girlish crushes. As many as she shed over four years?*

"Aren't you working today?" She stammered. All the air seemed to have sucked out of the room. That happened a lot when he was around.

He looked away. "Done for the day."

Unlike last night, he appeared unusually happy. *Maybe he has some good news. About Albany?*

When he blasted her with that dazzling-white smile, she caved. "Well... I did make an extra-big batch of dip."

Another sexy smile.

Her heart fluttered til it hurt. A million nerves

184

fired under her skin. She was certain she blushed red all over.

Evan removed his jacket, washed his hands and allowed her to tie on an apron, but it fell loose since the ties were too short for his brawny frame. Then he put on a pair of latex gloves that barely fit, and a Yankees baseball cap for his hair.

Jeez. Even this getup looked sexy on him.

"What do you want me to do?"

Pose for the next issue of, Chocolate Desserts. Women would stampede to the grocery store. Bookstores would have to hire security. Demand from women all over the world would force a re-issue. The editors could retire and live the good life in Tahiti.

She cleared her throat. "Let's see. I have more batches of nougat to flavor. You can do the dipping." A raised skewer issued the challenge.

His eyes twinkled. "Okay. Show me again."

"Simple. Dip, drip, dry." She demonstrated once more. Once the skewer passed hands, she left him to the task. A grin stayed pasted on his face. She was dying to know what put him in such a good mood, but afraid to ask him if he'd heard about the Albany job.

He caught on quickly with little mess, and soon made a full tray ready for the drying rack. Her mouth watered as those strong arms flex as he dipped, swirled chocolate on the morsel and waited for the dripping to stop. Her gaze flew to his mouth. His lips were compressed in concentration and she imagined running her tongue along the line to coax his mouth open for her eager tongue. He'd suck it inside and taste the heat of her desire for him and have them upstairs in her bedroom before she could whisper a protest. There, he'd take her clothes off and allow her to do the same and before long they'd be making love.

She shook herself back to the present. After the third tray he not only spread chocolate base all over his gloves, but some splattered on those strong arms exposed below cuffed-up sleeves. A touch of base smudged one cheek.

Lick it off his cheek, a devilish little voice dared. Instead, she wet a towel and approached him. "I can't imagine what Tony and your men would say if they saw you."

That erased the grin. A stony scowl formed.

What'd she say?

She showed him the wet towel and focused on his cheek. "You've got some chocolate on your face. It always happens to me." She touched the towel to his cheek, but before she could pull her hand away, he trapped it with his larger one.

He moved her fingertips to his mouth and kissed each one. "They'd be jealous."

Breathe.

Powerless to pull her hand away, she watched as he lightly kissed the inside of her wrist, too, reminding her of those lips on her breasts. She wondered how they'd feel someplace else.

"Let me take you somewhere for dinner," he said.

Her large intake of breath was embarrassing. "Okay, but my treat, since you made so much candy."

He held her wrist firmly and shook his tawny head. "No way."

"I insist." She stared into those divine chocolate eyes. He let go of her wrist and it flopped boneless by her side.

"Okay, but make it a burger joint, " he said, flipping off the apron and hat.

She quit the kitchen, locked the front door and turned the sign to, *Closed* "Nonsense. I know a little place that has great spaghetti."

Evan reached for the door handle. "I'll get the car."

The corners of her mouth rose. "That won't be necessary. It's not far."

****

Cassie couldn't remember when she'd enjoyed cooking a meal more. Evan acted like the simple dinner of spaghetti, meatballs, and Caesar salad were the best meal he'd ever eaten. "If you ever get tired of candy making, you can open a restaurant. This homemade sauce is terrific. Where did you learn how to cook?"

"I took lessons when I got married," she replied.

Evan lowered his fork and wiped his mustache. There was so much he didn't know about her; he stared like a man with a thousand questions.

She explained as she cleared plates. "I could've burned water. Jake's mother sent me to cooking classes. I learned the basics then bought a few cookbooks and tried different recipes. Jake joked that he never knew what he ate from day to day but he had the best leftovers of all the interns."

Hot steam bathed her face as she added dish detergent to the water. Funny, she'd forgotten those happy times.

"I think that great dinner deserves a great dessert."

Her pulse pounded in her ears. She turned around. He'd leaned back in his chair. Dressed in a black pullover and black jeans with black boots, he resembled an outlaw. His skin was more golden against the black, and his dark eyes pierced the shell she'd tried to erect around her heart. She'd missed his touch, and yearned to feel her hands all over him. And his smile was so sexy she wanted to scream for him to stop.

Her hands dove into the steaming dishwater. "What did you have in mind?"

Evan didn't answer. A chair scrapped. Footsteps thudded behind her in time to her pulse. The large ceramic spaghetti bowl appeared on the counter next to the dishdrain. It needed saran wrap. She wiped moisture from her forehead with the back of her hand. After several failed attempts at opening the kitchen drawer, he put a hand over hers and tugged it open. Aware he watched her hands, she briefly struggled with the plastic before she smoothed it neatly over the bowl. He grabbed a dishtowel from the drawer before closing it. The drawer slammed shut like it was made out of cardboard rather than solid maple.

A waterfall of lust pounded through her.

She knew what she wanted for dessert.

In silence, Evan dried while she washed. She tried to ignore how sexy he looked holding the pink and brown polka-dotted dishtowel. Maybe she was ovulating. She always got overly aroused in the middle of her cycle.

"Do you still like chocolate ice—"

She startled when he loomed over her.

He deftly caught the falling wet dish. "I noticed the Ice Cream Shop around the corner." In a blink he'd dried the platter and put it away with the others. He closed the overhead cabinet and stepped closer, until his mouth was inches from hers.

All she had to do was lean forward and the gates of heaven would open.

"I like everything chocolate," *especially your big, brown, bedroom eyes.*

Her hormones were becoming an embarrassment, she thought, and dried her hands on a SpongeBob kitchen towel.

"I have to make a call and then we can walk over."

"I'll get my coat."

Wishing there were a suit of armor inside, she

opened her closet door.

****

Rehashing his terrible day, Evan waited impatiently for Cassie to get her coat. Maybe he got a half hour's sleep last night, tops.

Ordinarily, sleeping in a sedan wasn't a problem, a luxury after months of bedding on rocks. But a series of images: Cassie in the shower, Cassie lying naked on her warm, white bed, Cassie bending over him, kept his mind active. The same way in Iraq his mind worked overtime thinking about her, except he didn't need his old fantasies. The satiny soft, gorgeous woman was twenty-four stairs, fifteen paces, and three doors away from his car. He'd wanted to creep inside her bedroom, pull down the sheets, and slowly reveal her beautiful body.

Settle on top of her and make love until they knocked each other out.

Despite the overnight near-freezing drop in temperature his driver's side window remained open, needing the crisp pre-winter air to soothe all his aches. The moon had a hazy blue band around it, typical for this time of year. As a child, he'd been fascinated by the moon, and at one time dreamed of to becoming an astronaut, the first to investigate the dark side of the moon or maybe blast off to Mars. As a soldier, he'd seen the dark side of the earth, the darkest side of humanity.

Thoughts of Cassie had kept him from slipping into the darkness.

In two weeks Cassie soothed his guilty soul more than a dozen army shrinks. Brutal images, nightmares that replayed even during daylight, visited less and less. He doubted the nightmares would ever completely disappear but she was a balm to his tired soul.

He wondered what would it take for her to trust him.

There was never a falling star when he'd needed one. He'd remained alert until the first tendrils of a red dawn appeared on the horizon and the sunlight paled the darkness. A golden sunrise followed, ushering in another rare Indian summer day in Central New York.

And there was no place in the universe he'd rather be.

Inside Cassie's kitchen his neck muscles coiled, feeling like a boulder rested on his back. He sat down at the kitchen table and ran his hands over his face to keep awake. Although his body was weary he knew that between eating her homey dinner, coupled with being that close to her untouchable curves, it would take a powerful sleeping pill to knock him out tonight. And tonight he knew the one thought in particular that would haunt him: What if he could spend every day this way?

His cell sounded. The call from Tony he'd been waiting for.

"Got an address on that car you saw," Tony said. "With your description and the plate numbers, we got lucky. The guy's named Stone... a solo operator new to the area. Idiot used his own car. Must be he thought it was going to be a cake job. We've got a search warrant for his place, and an APB out for the car. Oh, and the prints they found in Cassie's car are a match, too."

The perp tampered with Cassie's car. His blood iced. "Great, see what else you can dig up."

Tony paused. "You better shop for a new Jeep, too."

Evan righted the chair he'd been sitting in. "Bullet holes can be fixed." The Jeep may have a lot of miles but even more history.

Tony hesitated. "They found a nick in your gas line."

Evan cursed. "That explains a lot."

"Want me to see if anyone you canned got out of prison?"

That bastard spied him around Cassie's shop. That meant he'd been stalking Cassie over a week. It was easy to get at his Jeep in the parking garage. On the chance that this could be about him, Evan agreed. "Good idea. Have them check surveillance camera's in my parking garage."

"Done." Tony hesitated. "Listen, Evan... about the arrest warrant on your desk... You should bring—"

"Wait."

Evan checked to make sure Cassie's bedroom door was still closed, before he answered Tony. "I'm on vacation, Tony," he stressed. "And don't let anyone else into my office." The cell phone creaked in his hand.

"You can't clear her when the arrest warrant is from another state. Only the guys from L.A. can do that. I can call and feel them out... see when they are planning to pick her up—"

"It could take months before they hop a flight," he answered harshly. Depending upon how much heat they get from their D.A.'s office.

"Theft of money, even a large amount, has to be bottom of the list these days." Tony added. "I'd hate to see Cassie sit in jail, too, but she may have no choice."

Evan stormed over to the living room window and parted the curtains to check the street.

"She's not going to sit around in jail for something she didn't do!" His frustration grew by the minute. "Run those warrant numbers. Get me information on the person filing the original complaint."

While pacing the room the toes of his boot knocked over a pile of CD's. His head ached so badly it sounded like a round of bullets firing.

He shook off the pain and refocused on what Tony was saying, rather than the shuffling of papers. "Thought you'd want it. I traced the complaint back to a guy named Dylan Black, some L.A. independent movie producer. He had a foreign film up for an award a couple years ago."

Dylan Black...what was his connection to Cassie.

I messed up real bad in L.A

"See if he's got a rap sheet, check for any alias. Where he went to high school. Find out everything about him, okay?"

The shuffling stopped. "Are you sure about this, Ev? Maybe you should bring her in and let the D.A. handle the rest—"

Cassie entered the kitchen wearing a thick tan sweater so big it swallowed her slender frame. She pulled it around her shoulders and looked at him with expectant eyes.

"I've never been more certain of anything in my life. Call me when you have something."

Evan snapped the cell shut, although he wanted to crush it between his hands. He was running out of time. Having Tony talk to the D.A. was a last resort. When the D.A. learned about Evan's delay in serving the warrant, he'd have some explaining to do to a lot of people. Earlier, he'd called the best criminal lawyer in Syracuse and filled him in on Cassie's situation. After he'd explained about what happened this weekend, Porcelli agreed to help Cassie. The earliest the attorney could schedule a meeting with Cassie was Thursday.

Three more days to keep Cassie safe from the stalker and away from that warrant issue.

Cassie snuggled deeper into the sweater and tracked his hand as he pocketed the cell. "Did they find him?"

He wanted to ask her about Dylan but then he'd have to explain about the warrant. "No, but it won't be much longer until we bring him in." He walked toward the front door, expecting her to follow.

Her feet shuffled toward the front door, then stopped "Are you staying again, tonight?"

Why did she sound tense and look more scared than last night? They'd set the new security system and had good news about the assailant. Lines formed around her eyes and mouth that weren't there this morning.

"One more night, two at the most," he replied, gauging her reaction.

She swallowed and nodded.

"Can you stand me that long?" He tried to sound casual as he held the apartment door open for her, even forced a smile for her. The look on her face didn't change. Terrified.

Didn't she realize she was safe as long as he was around? Unless the stalker wasn't the only problem. Could there be more going on here? Enough. Tonight he'd get her to talk about what she was hiding. Then, he'd explain the warrant when she no longer had to worry about it.

He followed her down the stairs and watched her set the alarm and key the locks. They walked in comfortable silence down the sidewalk to the ice cream shop. He wondered if she remembered their walk in Lake Placid. He'd loved the excuse to hold her in his arms again and wished for another reason to carry her. Dry leaves scraped along the road. Her heels snapped against concrete sidewalks and her breathing slowed as they walked. His breathing slowed, too, and his tense shoulders dropped. An older couple walked past them, arm and arm. He started to pull his hands out of his pockets but then shoved them back.

At the right moment he'd bring up L.A. Not much farther to the ice cream shop.

Arms tucked in her sweater, she looked pensive,

frowned. She looked so different when she smiled, especially after they'd made love. The feel of every feminine curve and sexy little sound echoing off the tent canvas were embedded in his mind. In all his fantasies he'd never imagined the first time they'd made love again to be in a tent.

The way she'd kept him at arms length seemed like she'd completely forgotten the experience.

Inside the parlor she chatted with the young ice cream attendant like an old friend. The guy had a silly grin plastered on his face. She ordered a small chocolate cone with chocolate sprinkles. He preferred hot fudge sundaes and gave her the cherry. Her lips formed an "O", and her eyelashes fluttered on her cheeks as she inserted the cherry in her luscious mouth. Watching her conjured erotic thoughts. Hell, watching her eat spaghetti turned him on. He imagined feeding her chocolate covered strawberries and drinking champagne while in bed after they made love in a hundred different ways.

Their shoulders bumped as she moved around other customers to find an open table. Any slight contact was like flint on metal. He was like dry kindle ready to burst into flames at any moment. Her expression was cool enough to flash-freeze ice cream.

A table opened up and she motioned for him to sit down on a dainty wrought-iron stool. He passed and leaned against the wall next to her and enabled him a full view of the room and exits. She eyed him as her tongue lapped the chocolate dome, carefully catching the drips and keeping a peak. His gaze darted from the door to her mouth. *Great idea to go for ice cream, champ.* At least the Benadryl he'd popped earlier still worked. There was only one cure for the interest in his pants. She thought she hid a giggle behind her cone.

She'll pay for his torture.

To take his mind off her, he surveyed the room, noticing the sherbet-colored walls and floor and brightly painted posters of kids enjoying mountains of ice cream. The room overflowed mostly with young families and tons of kids. For once, he didn't image something jumping out of the corner, unless it was a three year old. The place was too crowded for a serious conversation.

His gaze worked back to Cassie. Her cone tipped sideways for more efficient licks. "What else do you want to do tonight," she asked. "I mean it's kinda early to go to bed—" She stopped licking her cone. Her upper lip was smeared with chocolate and her tongue darted out of her mouth until the ice cream disappeared.

His jaw locked until he thought it would shatter. He was dying. One kiss. That's all he wanted. Pretty soon he'd have to do something about her reluctance or they'd be picking out his gravestone.

He forced his jaw to unhinge. "I'll leave that up to you."

Chapter Fifteen

Cassie enjoyed nightly walks around her neighborhood and tonight was no different. Unless you considered walking with a bodyguard that commanded the attention of every female over ten. The ice cream shop stares were harmless. Mothers with children looked her way and smiled pleasantly. But as she entered the corner drugstore, the looks from some young girls waiting in line were reminiscent of his office, lovingly at Evan, evil at her. Thank goodness she didn't have to worry about being with him often. She might grow warts.

She shivered and pulled the collar of her sweater up to her cheeks.

Some kids ran past them, and Evan's shoulder bumped hers again. Although she'd worn layers of clothing even with the slightest brush felt skin to skin. Details floated forward, like how hot and satiny slick his skin became after he'd found his release, and it's salty taste that lingered on her lips.

"Are you looking for anything in particular?" he asked, moving in front of her to lead the way through the store. He did that five second scan of the room again, like in the ice cream shop. When his hand bumped against hers, and her fingers curled around it.

"There's some magazines I need," she answered, relieved he didn't look over his shoulder at her, but instead searched the aisle signs. His hand squeezed hers and her heart constricted. Then he let go.

He waited as she flipped through magazines. He purchased, *Motorcross World,* 'to read later,' he said. The way he said *later* sent a tremor through her body, followed by the image of them rolling on her bed the way they had in the tent. Grateful for the darkness, she led the way out of the store, certain she was redder than Superman's cape.

Earlier her mind began bargaining for his kisses when they stepped into the ice cream shop. 'One won't hurt,' and, 'What's the worst that can happen?' or 'You can always say, 'no.' And now, 'Just-do-it.' The internal dialogue made her crazy. She'd trashed a half-eaten cone. Now she'd lost her appetite for the bag of Hershey's caramel kisses she'd bought.

Walking down the sidewalk slightly ahead of him she reminded herself she had to endure one more night of his masculinity—his sexy scent, dreamy body, and that reassuring smile. Ignore her hormones and fantasies and listen to her better judgment. This was the new Cassie, the successful businesswoman who made decisions with her head. What came over her at the ice cream shop to tease him that way? At the worst times she suffered a bout of amnesia and forgot about getting Heather back, or the fact that he was a player. And that he was moving to Albany.

She glanced over her shoulder. *Darn it.* Every time they locked eyes, she wanted to place her head on his shoulder and feel his arms around her. Part of her longed to confide what happened in L.A. As a police officer, Evan would understand her side, wouldn't he?

Silently they window-shopped around the rest of the block, but not even the cool night air reduced the heat that flared in her stomach. They strolled past a new art shop that displayed local talent, and a gun shop with bars on the windows. Evan paused in front of that window. With his hands resting low on his hips, he looked like a gunslinger, waiting for a bad guy to make the first move. She wished it were that easy to shoot the bad guy in her life. Then her and Evan could ride off into the sunset.

He turned to her and smiled, the one that made her knees weak.

"Isn't it time we headed back to the apartment?"

She practically ran ahead.

****

In the sanctuary of her kitchen, Cassie made some tea while Evan went to get his bag from the car. When he didn't return right away, she peeked out the front window and spied him talking to someone in a State Police car parked in front of her house.

Now the neighbors would be curious. The older couple next door always worried about her, so they'd be happy. So did the woman across the street, unaware that her husband looked for any excuse to approach her when his wife left on errands with the kids. Maybe he'd stop bothering her now.

Evan entered the apartment with the same gym bag, a little fuller this time. He unrolled the magazine he'd purchased and settled into the rocking chair where the light was best. The lines on his face softened. Did he feel relaxed with her? The night they made love before he shipped out, she was certain the tension left him. That's why she'd been so crushed when he never wrote her. Not even once. Never one to believe in love at first sight, Cupid's arrow struck her heart that night, but not his. She was ready to go to the ends of the earth for him, if only he'd asked.

The magazine she'd bought sat unopened on the kitchen table. She listened to the coffee perk as she sipped her tea. Tea usually calmed her stomach at the end of a long day. *Goodness.* The cramping was oddly missing this past week, actually, for a little over a week. That's how long she'd been with Evan. Funny, it felt like she'd known him her entire life. She'd read somewhere that meant something. After drinking her tea, she washed the cup, nibbled a few kisses.

Evan's head popped up when she yawned and entered the living room. "Bedtime?" His smile bordered carnal.

She bumped into the sofa. "I'm going to change for b—sleeping."

Lord, when did the living room get so small? Had he moved the furniture around? The hallway wasn't moved, so she aimed for it. "Goodnight," she said over her shoulder.

When he answered, "sweet dreams," his sinfully gorgeous eyes matched his smile.

Rather than dawdle another second, she rushed down the hallway. A cool breeze slammed shut the bedroom door. She reached for the bolt then stopped. Chilly air soothed her overheated skin, and the cold floor beneath her bare feet felt refreshing as she crossed her room to close the windows. The moon was still low, a huge white snowball above the horizon. Small crystals formed in the corners on the glass. Indian summer-like weather was over. She hated turning up the thermostat so soon. She decided to change into her hoodie and sweats for bed. She wondered if Evan wore sweats to bed, or slept naked—finishing that thought sent a lick of anticipation to her core.

No. He'd never take his clothes off. What if he had to run outside? Or into her bedroom if she needed him? She wouldn't need her hoodie or sweats to stay warm. His skin was always so comfortably warm. Who needed blankets?

Jeez. She sat on the edge of her bed, willing her contracting muscles to relax. Moisture welled between her legs. *Stop thinking about him naked!* It was all Karen's fault for planting ideas in her head. Think of monsters. Dracula, Frankenstein, the Mummy, the Wolfman, not the Hugh Jackman-kind, sigh, but Lon Chaney, black and white version, the one with scary voice and face. Her breathing slowed to normal, until she heard a noise.

Opening her bedroom door she peered out and spied him rising from the chair and stretching. His shirt lifted, and a band of his abs winked. She crept down the hallway, quiet as a church mouse. That gorgeous body moved to the front windows. He checked behind the blinds. She checked his behind. Extreme thirst struck her. She needed water, or preferably, a gallon of tea, but retreated to her bedroom.

Back in her bathroom she noted her flushed skin. After shaky hands removed what little make-up she'd worn and moisturized half of the bathroom floor, she put on an ugly gray robe. Dylan never liked her in it because it zipped up the front. He preferred sashes. Once he'd tied her hands to the bedpost and it felt awful, like she was a sex toy. Afterward she'd blasted him, saying if he ever did that again she'd have him arrested.

The thought of Dylan being raped in jail pleased her.

She caught her gray reflection in the bathroom mirror. She wished the robe was a suit of armor, and that she owned the courage of a knight. After all, as a cheerleader for the White Knights of Williams High School, they never lost a game. The memory used to make her smile. Seated on her bed, she brushed the wetness from her cheek. The smell of strawberries made her pull Kitty out from under her. Reminded of Heather's smiling face, she hugged Kitty once, and then tucked Kitty between her pillows in a more dignified pose. Her bedside clock read eight-thirty pm. She'd never fallen asleep this early. There must be something to do. Work might keep her mind from thoughts of her bodyguard.

Without alerting Evan engrossed in his magazine, she padded into the kitchen and refilled the kettle with water. Sitting at the kitchen table she went through her grandmother's recipe box looking for the divinity recipe. Grandma Macey always made it for the holidays. Her recipes often left out the exact quantities of certain ingredients, calling for handfuls or pinches instead of measurements. So she practiced all grandma's recipes in small batches.

As she sipped her brew, her finger slid down the list of ingredients on paper as thin as an onionskin. The recipe seemed simple. The clock read nine pm. Not the latest she'd ever started to cook, so she opened the cabinets and gathered the ingredients— sugar, vanilla. Where was her vanilla? Did the eggs need to warm to room temperature? Was Evan still reading?

Holding her herbal tea, she moved to the archway to sneak a peek at Evan.

He still sat in her rocking chair, engrossed in whatever he was reading. The high-wattage bulb from the stand highlighted his hair like polished brass. She remembered how soft it felt when she slipped her fingertips through it the last time they'd kissed in his apartment. It still amazed her how the warmth of his lips could linger on hers, warmer than hot tea. Maybe he'd kiss her goodnight tonight. No. He'd adhered to her hands-off decree. But—if he knew her thoughts, what would he do?

A sip of tea went down the wrong way. His head rose, and he smiled. She covered her cough but the lack of oxygen inspired her. The recipe box returned to its place in the cupboard along with the ingredients. She removed a cellophane bag from the kitchen table's drawer and turned off the kitchen light.

"Would you like to play a game?" she asked as she entered the living room.

The rocking chair jerked upright as he stood. His magazine landed under a rocker runner. "What did you have in mind?"

Sergeant Jorgenson stood at attention as if he'd never been absorbed in the article to begin with.

A quiver of desire circuited her belly as she inverted the top of the makeshift coffee table, revealing a battered black and red checkerboard pattern. Mr. Poker Face wasn't surprised. Her bag of Hershey's kisses from the kitchen landed on the checkerboard.

Sitting cross-legged on the floor, she signaled for him to sit across from her. "Heather and I like to play checkers this way. She thought of it." Silver triangles tumbled onto the smooth surface from the cellophane bag.

"Smart kid." He reached for the silver foils and made quick work of putting them on the board while she undid the wrappers for her unwrapped set. "You must have played this a lot. I've never seen kisses unwrapped that fast," he added.

Out of habit, she popped one piece in her mouth. The chocolate flavor exploded on her tongue. There was only one thing better than a Hershey's chocolate kiss.

Evan waited for her to finish another kiss before he continued. "My friend loved checkers, too. We played until she won."

Cassie stopped unwrapping her kisses.

He hooded his gaze and quickly unwrapped the rest for her, sampled one himself, and then said smugly, "Of course, I rarely lost, so we played for hours."

His cocky gaze found hers.

The bag of kisses emptied onto her lap. He gathered up the kisses in her lap with one scoop, twisted the top of the bag, and readied the board. "Your move."

"Huh? Oh." She fumbled with a few kisses before selecting her first move. Some of the chocolate melted on her fingers and she absently licked it off.

He didn't take any time deciding his first move. His tan fingers were on his kisses as soon as she moved hers. He seemed to move without thought, recklessly. Sometimes their fingers would bump.

She could play that thoughtless, too. The first game went by fast. To her delight, she won the first, and second game. "Some player. You're a pushover," she snarked.

He didn't reply, but watched her with an unreadable stare. He'd angled his body closer, moving his left arm and fingers to move his silvered pieces. His quiet stare began to unnerve her.

"Are you letting me win?" she asked, and jumped a piece he placed right in her path.

"No chance of that. You're a great player." He triple-jumped her pieces and popped all three kisses in his mouth.

She harrumphed, and then moved another piece that he promptly double jumped. Four unwrapped kisses remained. She sat up on her knees and confronted him. "Where'd my other pieces go? You're cheating."

"You're not paying attention. Bet I know what you're thinking. You're wondering if the friend I referred to was Jenny."

She sat on her heels. The cellophane bag slid off

her lap and kisses tumbled onto the bare floor. "Oops. How clumsy of me," she said, and corralled kisses with fingers as flexible as wooden spatulas.

He reached over the checkerboard, and grabbed her hand. "Ask me whatever you want to know about her."

She tried to pull her hand away. "It's none of my business—"

"It is... now that we're friends. Aren't you the least bit curious?" He opened her palm and placed several kisses in her hand.

She closed her fingers around the kisses. "Was she the girl you dated in college?"

"Yes."

"And you were in love..."

He stared, then nodded.

"The forever kind?"

His gaze went from her lips to her fist. She opened her hand. The kisses were crushed together.

She wanted to punch him with the fist full of pancake-kisses but she was bursting with questions. The next question caught in her throat. "How did she die?"

Evan got off the floor and moved to the couch. Outside, the wind moaned, and a band of dry leaves jammed against the living room windows. The air in the room grew cold. The first snowfall of the season was coming. She'd have to turn the heat on tonight.

"Come here."

She tossed the mutilated kisses on the checkerboard and then joined him on the couch.

His face tensed, and then he began to speak. "For years Jenny had been Clay's bratty little sister, following us everywhere. One day she came to visit Clay at college. I couldn't stop staring at her. She'd turned into the most beautiful girl I'd ever seen."

He paused and looked at her in the way that made her uneasy.

"We dated about a year when the accident happened. Our senior year, the weekend before graduation. It was Clay's idea to hike the Cascades at Lake Placid, celebrate our success by smoking some pot at sunrise. May was still too early in the season for climbing, but it sounded too cool to resist."

He bowed his blond head, lost in some thought.

She moved closer, until her knee rested against his thigh. "A lot of kids smoked pot."

He blew out a sigh and continued. "Clay's parents spoiled him after his eye accident, and Jenny, well, no one could say no to her. The prior summer we'd gone hiking every weekends and thought we knew everything about hiking mountains." He shook his head. His tanned face lost color.

Small shivers made her curl her toes under the robe and slip her icy hands inside the sleeves.

Evan's expression grew grave. "But this time was different. We wanted it to be us guys, so I broke the news to Jenny. She threatened to follow. Clay teased her and said we were going to climb to the top of Algonquin and she'd never find us."

She rubbed her arms. "But, isn't Algonquin quite a hike, second to Mount Marcy as the tallest mountain in the state?"

He nodded. "Yeah, but its trailhead is three miles shorter, so it starts off easier."

She thought about it for a minute. "I remember seeing it from the summit of Mount Jo."

Evan nodded. "It's a strenuous hike, about a three-thousand-foot elevation gain in less than four miles. The first three aren't bad, but the last mile is all rock over some major ledges. You have to be in good physical shape and mentally strong because some ledges make you feel like you could fall off the world."

His exhale hissed through his teeth. The room

had grown so cold she needed a blanket, but didn't want to interrupt. Evan put his arm around her. She snuggled closer.

"We woke up that morning on the summit of the Cascades and saw the most beautiful sunrise we'd ever seen, then got high. We stayed up there for hours and talked about everything. Clay and I had been friends since kindergarten, but we knew after that morning that we'd be friends for life, no matter what."

"He sounds like a good friend." Cassie thought of Karen.

"When the first sirens sounded, we were so stoned we thought they were the cops coming for us. We ran down the Cascades from the High Peak Trailhead. The descent is like running down a ramp for about two thousand feet. We made it in less than a half hour. When we ended up at the base, which is at Heart Lake, we laughed at our stupidity. That's when we heard some climbers talking about a rescue."

Although Evan spoke clearly, she could hear the underlying effort it took him to speak.

"'Some amateur had been climbing Algonquin alone and fell,' they said. Clay and I looked at each other, thinking the same thing. He nearly killed us driving the short distance, passing all the emergency vehicles."

"Oh, Evan."

"Clay's mom's car was there. Some troopers stood by it. Clay ran up to them, asked something and then took off up the mountain. I ran after him. Clay was always the better climber, always led the way."

Eyes that knew terrible loss looked at her. She didn't know what to say.

"Because it's a protected alpine zone, they don't allow a helicopter's, so they couldn't drop someone in and belay her up. They didn't know how far she'd fallen... maybe above Wright Peak Trail. 'Morning dew conditions probably made the sheer rocks that straddle the face, slippery, possibly iced,' they'd said. I followed Clay down the chasm. There were rocks and holes and downed trees everywhere. Later we learned that the EMT's and firemen followed us. It took over an hour to get to her."

Cassie squeezed his frozen hand.

"Clay went up to her and said, 'Fun's over Jenny, you can get up now.' He kept saying it, and then shouting it. I ran to her. She'd worn all her gear—helmet, daypack, crampons, heavy-duty hiking boots. She looked perfect, like she was sleeping, except her neck was cocked at a funny angle. They say it took three guys to pull me off her."

The knuckles of his fist turned white. His hand was like holding a snowball.

With her other robe sleeve, she wiped away hot tears streaming down her face.

He looked at her, his eyes devoid of emotion. "We didn't mean for it to happen. We wanted to go away, make a memory. We killed her."

"No, no, no. Jenny wouldn't want either of you to think that. I'm certain." She caressed his cheek. "She'd tell you it was an accident. It wasn't your fault."

"But it was."

Evan's other fist opened and closed, his only movement throughout the entire story. His face, sharp planes. Expressionless.

"You didn't know she was going to follow—"

His head swung around. "I never should have left her behind."

"You shouldn't feel guilty. It was an accident." Exasperation choked her voice.

He looked at her with eyes she didn't recognize. "She was so brave. She tried to climb Algonquin by herself. I wanted to tell her...I was so proud of her."

He got off the couch and paced the room.

She didn't know what to do or say to help him. The entire story was so tragic she wanted to run to her room and cry into her pillow.

He grabbed his magazine from the under the rocking chair. After he slapped it on his leg, he threw it. It landed on the checkerboard and scattered kisses. Then he leaned toward the door, listening for some inaudible sound. He did that a lot. Checked behind the curtains, too. He came out of his trance, remembered she was there and returned to the couch. Somehow, his face softened and he even wore a timid smile. "So, now you know about Jenny."

"Thank you for telling me. I always—" She didn't want to admit the last part, a morbid curiosity at the time.

"Wondered? What else did you wonder?" His eyes turned a silky black.

She held a shaky breath. He'd been so honest with her. "I wondered if she was the reason why you never married."

The smile vanished. He pushed off the couch and gave her his back so she couldn't see his face. When he turned, she'd never seen such a raw look of need. "No."

He grabbed his jacket off the coat rack and then stopped by the open front door. In a few steps he re-crossed the room and lifted her off the couch. Dark crescents appeared under his eyes. "I've got to check outside. Lock the door. Don't wait up for me." Then his thumb traced her lower lip, reminding her of their last kiss. Bruised eyes searched her face. She wanted to kiss that look off his face, but he released her.

She locked the door behind him and then staggered over to the couch before she put her face in her hands, and wept.

****

Cassie didn't recall putting on her cream-colored blouse and beige slacks, her low-heeled suede shoes, or even walking downstairs and entering the shop's kitchen. Still in a dream state, she gathered supplies. The banging on her front door awakened her from a trance. She'd placed some utensils on the counter. The clock read 9:32 AM. The street door should have been opened at nine. She ran to unlock the door.

"Hey." Karen breezed through the door. "You sleep in late today? I'm here to help you make bonbons, but if you want to spill your guts about what happened last night, I'm all ears."

Cassie hooded her eyes. "Nothing happened. Evan feels it's his duty to protect me. It must be out of loyalty to Jake."

Karen snorted. Her short hair swung around her face. "Jake has nothing to do with Evan's actions and you know it. The guy's crazy for you. Why can't you admit it? What are you so afraid of?"

She walked away from Karen without replying.

Karen followed. "Okay, that was out of line. I know how skittish you are about men, especially after Dylan—"

"I can't talk about Dylan, especially now that, well, never mind." On tiptoes, she removed ingredients from the top of the storage cabinet.

"Okay, okay. But what did you do last night if you didn't mess around?" Karen sat on the counter stool and opened the lid of her take-out coffee.

Cassie quickly recapped the dinner, dessert, and walk, but left out the game of checkers and Evan's story. She didn't want to share that moment with anyone. All the ingredients to make the bonbons were lined up on the counter by the time she finished explaining.

Karen put on an apron and turned around for

Cassie to ties the strings. "Sounds like quite the homey little evening. I knew you two would get along. Is he staying tonight?"

She paused and then tightened the ties on her own apron. "No."

"Why not? Has that crazy guy that tried to kill you been caught? You're not staying here alone. Pack a bag and come home with me."

She stopped and took a deep breath before she insulted the best friend a girl could ever have. "I won't invade your *home* with my problems."

Karen pushed up her sleeves and soaped her hands. "Good. Then Evan gets to spend another night, 'cause I'm sure he'll look for any excuse to keep an eye on you for one more night." She winked and added, "Now, don't waste another night eating ice cream or taking long walks. Greet him at the door wearing that sensational red teddy—"

"I can't do that." She'd bought it on sale after Valentine's day, thinking she'd surprise Evan when he had his first leave from Iraq. She tried to measure out a cup of liqueur, but shook so badly half the bottle of Amaretto spilled on the counter. "Oh. Look what you made me do."

"*I* didn't do that, sweetie. It was the thought of what Evan would do to you if he caught you in the red teddy that caused you to shake like an eight-point-oh earthquake."

Karen sponged up the liqueur with a dishtowel, smiling like it was the most enjoyable task in the world.

Cassie collected herself long enough to measure the proper amount of liqueur into the creamy concoction, and transfer it to the bowl. Sweat rolled down her back as if she'd measured nitroglycerin. Resting on her stool, she wiped her forehead with the edge of her apron. "I don't think I can be around him another night. He smells too good. My whole apartment smells like him."

Karen sniffed. "Before I leave today, I'm going up there."

Cassie ignored her and continued. "He barely fits on my couch and I swear the apartment's gotten smaller. I can't concentrate on the simplest task. It's like someone's offering me an endless supply of chocolate truffles and all I have to do is agree to taste one. I keep waiting for the catch." She capped the bottle of Amaretto. "He left early for work this morning before I woke up and I was so disappointed I forgot to open up."

"Wait a minute."

Karen left the room and returned with two bottles of Niagara water and a small dish of dark-chocolate coconut clusters, her favorite, from the display case. "Okay, keep talking about Evan." She swallowed a large gulp of water and popped two candies in her mouth.

Cassie took a long drink, and then continued. "I keep thinking about him, even though I know it's wrong. He's the kind of guy that's impossible to forget, know what I mean? If he finds out about L.A., I'll die of humiliation."

Cassie absently measured other ingredients, and added them to the mixing bowl.

"You can tell him. He'll understand," said Karen softly.

Cassie shook her head. "I have to concentrate more than ever on making this place so successful that no judge would ever deny me custody. And Heather needs my full attention. There was some trouble in school the other day."

Karen chewed another candy. "Heather will be fine." She waved her hand. "Back to Evan. Do you want to sleep with him again?" Two more candies shoveled into Karen's mouth.

"I'd be lying if I said I didn't. Even though we

were in the tent, it was amazing. I wondered what he'd be like in a bed, ya know, not rushed."

Cassie stopped mixing ingredients and imagined Evan's tanned body on top of her comforter, stretched out, waiting for her.

Karen held her hand up. "Okay, stop there. I'm outta candy and from the look of sheer ecstasy on your face I'd love to hear more but I'd have to have Karl close by."

"You ate about two-thousand calories of chocolate, not to mention the sugar high you'll get in about thirty minutes."

"Yeah, but it was worth it. Listen to me. Do yourself a favor. Don't think. Don't worry. Tonight, if Evan says he's spending the night, agree. If he doesn't make a move on you, which he won't because he's in his super-cop-mode, then you make a move. You need this, sweetie. Let him love you."

"I can't do that—"

"Yes, you can. Call me tomorrow."

Karen hugged her tighter and longer than usual. "Do it!"

Chapter Sixteen

Whack.

Thud, whack.

Thud, thud, thud... Whack.

"Hey, keep that up and they'll have to order a new kick bag. Who is she?"

Evan squinted as sweat drained into his eyes. Despite the sting, he kept on pounding. He didn't need to see to know who'd spoken to him.

He stepped away from the bag, did a spin-kick, and unleashed his energy. The center of the bag popped and caved in, then it swayed and moaned. He bent low to catch his breath before replying to Clay. "What wind blew you in? I thought you'd burn a few more weeks before you wrapped up the movie." He tapped both mitts against Clay's held-up fists.

"My stunts were perfect from the first take, as usual. They always plan more time than I need."

Clay grabbed the swinging bag and held it steady for Evan.

Evan's arms screamed for a rest but he resumed punching. He didn't stop until they felt like he'd been holding hundred-pound bazookas. Exhausted, he used his teeth to pull the knots from the boxing mitts. Then Clay pulled the gloves off.

Evan's fingers flared apart and his arms dropped by his sides. "Thanks, Hanson."

Clay promptly put the gloves on and began a series of short hard jabs. Evan watched the play of Clay's muscles. Still on the lean side, Clay delivered a stinging punch, known to knock out the best fighters in gyms and the occasional bar fight. His reach was long and his strikes always fluid and efficient. The low thuds of a well-abused bag echoed in the gym.

When Clay took a time-out, Evan threw a few more kicks at the bag, bounced on his toes and then uncoiled and released more pent-up energy. Satisfied the bag looked like it needed replacing, he turned to Clay. "How'd you find me?"

"When you didn't answer your phone or cell, I figured you stayed with someone, or came here. You forget. I know your habits."

One wing-like eyebrow rose up and down like *The Rock*. Clay continued, "since you're here, could it be you got turned down... wait, no one ever refuses you when you turn on the charm, even my sister caught Evantitus."

Evan grabbed his water bottle and took a long drink, then poured some on his head. They hadn't talked about Jenny in years.

King-Kong-like, Clay banged his chest with the red mitts. "Natch, in time you were putty in Jenny's hands. I've yet to see anyone fall as hard and fast as you."

Evan wiped sweat off his face with his arm and then walked over to the bench press. He loaded up the bar with several hundred pounds of weights. His chest tightened, compressed by the sudden flood of memories.

"What aren't you telling me, bro?"

The weight Evan lifted off the floor stopped

midair. "Your sister was special."

The words came out less forceful than usual, less effort to say.

"I know you'll always love Jenny," he said softly. Then Clay bent and picked up another weight and secured it on the bar. "Sit down."

Evan lay back on the bench, checked his grip on the bar, and squeezed. Clay spotted while Evan straight-armed the weight. "Got it."

Clay released his hold on the bar and stepped back. "People fall in love, again. Happens all the time."

The heavy bar rose and fell rhythmically over Evan's chest without pause. He kept up the grueling pace until his muscles started to burn. Sweat poured from his body and his shoulders slid slightly on the vinyl bench. Pushing himself harder than he'd ever done he continued to lift and drop the bar but couldn't purge any of his frustration. Being so near but unable to touch Cassie was hell. Christ, he hoped by now the smell of her perfume would be replaced by the stench of the gym. It hadn't. Breathing got harder and harder. He saw a red haze but somehow he kept raising and lowering the bar.

"Jenny would want you to be married and have a family."

Clay acted like he was going to reach for the bar and so after one more rep Evan held it above his chest. His elbows locked, and his breaths came in short bursts between clenched teeth but Clay continued to preach rather than grab the bar. "I mean it, Ev. Don't blow it. I know you like this lady or you wouldn't be trying to kill your body."

"Grab the bar," Evan hissed. His gut shook worse than his arms.

"Okay. But promise me you'll think about what I said."

Clay's fingers touched the bar.

Evan's vision dimmed from the strain but Clay's stare was clear. He wasn't kidding around.

"Take-the-bar, Clay."

Evan's hands hit the floor a second after Clay took the bar and set it to rest. Huge draughts of air rushed into his lungs. Too dizzy and spent to sit up, he told himself it was from pushing too hard.

It had nothing to do with how badly he wanted to believe he could someday be normal and have a family.

After a three mandatory months in a psych ward he convinced everyone he was well enough to head back to the states. He'd been sleeping in a bed, ate lunch at the table with other patients and focused long enough on the living to win a hand or two playing poker with his doctors. He'd successfully buried the events of the war in the farthest corner of his mind and won his ticket home.

But on the long plane ride his newly molded reality somehow slipped away. In the airport he walked up and held out his hand to say hello to a fallen soldier, happy to see he'd made it, too. The guy was there one minute, dressed in uniform and smiling broadly then the next instant, disappeared.

He went in the men's room and puked. After that he kept his appointments with the psych docs at the V.A. hospital in Syracuse. The docs were great, doing their best to teach him coping mechanisms when he slipped back into combat-mode. By sheer force of will he passed the psych evaluation to earn his place back on the force.

Lately he thought he had a better handle on his emotions. The visions during the day were non-existent since he started to protect Cassie. But Cassie shifted his paradigm like the bomb-ravaged terrain he'd patrolled in Quatar. She responded with such understanding about Jenny, he didn't know how to deal.

Maybe she had heart enough for both of them. Still, he couldn't take any chances that he'd wake up with his hands coiled around her throat. He'd rather spend ten years in Iraqi prison then hurt her. Course, he left the apartment like a bad wind.

If he'd stayed last night maybe she'd have talked. Stupid move. But like a tripped landmine, he had to blow her apartment. The room shrunk to the size of a hiding hovel. Ghost crowded the shrinking room. Jenny, his parents, the men he lost in Iraq, so many people in pieces on the streets. Once outside the apartment he scouted around the block for hours, investigating every sound and scanning for snipers. Only the sign, *Serendipity Sweets*, brought him back to reality.

In another life, he'd planned to take care of a wife and kids and become a hiking guide. That guy could have handled kids. Not a soldier who fought wars and crime and sometimes didn't know the good guys from the bad. Cassie deserved a man that could hold her at night without screaming for a medic. A man who could give her a slew of kids.

No one so fucked up should have kids.

Feeling lightheaded he sat on the end of the bench and crouched forward. Too embarrassed to put his head between his legs he closed his eyes to recover. Imagines of children with green eyes and golden hair made his heart beat faster than the discharge of a hundred rounds of ammo. He heard children's laughter. His men were handing out candy to some kids. Then everything went white. He shook his head, forcing the blood to flow to his head and opened his eyes.

"You okay?" Clay threw a clean towel at him.

"What do you care?" He slapped the towel against his palm wishing he felt something.

Clay's cocky grin dissolved. He opened his mouth and then closed it.

"Shit. Sorry, man," Evan said, wiping gallons of sweat from his chest. "This case has me stumped."

Clay had no idea how bad this last tour messed him up. Trouble was, he didn't have it buried away. Like a cracked raw egg, he held it at arm's length, waiting for it to break completely open from the pressure and let the insides ooze out. Sometimes he wanted to throw it against a wall and be over with it but the thought of doing that made a scream rise up in his throat.

Clay sat next to Evan on the bench. "Anything you want to talk about? Juice bar in the lobby should be open by now. Got no plans for today, so I'm all yours, sweetheart."

Evan wiped more sweat from his eyes but more rolled in. His muscles still trembled or he'd have been up and walking. Sweat turned to steam. Jeez. He'd pushed himself too far. "Yeah, sounds good." Tony wouldn't check in for a couple more of hours. "Give me another minute."

"Sure, old man." Clay's cocky smile was back. He never could stay serious for long.

The juice bar was quiet this early. Once he'd downed a couple of juices he felt better. He told Clay about the cabin, the shots fired, playing bodyguard, and the warrant, deciding to save the war talk for some other time.

Clay whistled low. "Sounds like your lady brought big baggage from L.A. Who's the ex?"

"I think he's Dylan Black."

"Think? Hasn't she told you? Hey, that name sounds familiar."

"Part of the problem. She won't talk about L.A. I need fingerprints to see if he has a record."

A check of her closets might turn up a gifts. It was a stretch but they could still have prints. And prints could last a year. He hated to snoop, yet he couldn't ask her without revealing the reason. Back to square one. Gain her trust.

Clay whistled through his teeth. "If she won't talk to the army's best interrogator, she's good. Have you tried torture?"

Evan grunted.

"Maybe you shouldn't get involved with her if she's gonna be trouble. You don't want to jeopardize that job in Albany."

He looked at Clay but didn't take the bait. His gaze must be black for Clay to shut up.

Evan rubbed his hand over his day-old stubble. The Albany job. The last time he thought about it was days ago. It was all he thought about for weeks prior to meeting Cassie. He wanted the job bad, bad enough to relocate, moving him further from his Adirondack home and closing the final chapter on his old life.

"Albany's the last—"

"Hey. Look who's here," a nasally voice interrupted. "Evan and Clay-ton. You guys up for a game? Scheduled partners are a no show. Or, are you getting too old?"

Evan turned around slowly.

The two members swinging rackets and talking trash looked at Clay's eye-patch with victory on their artificially tanned faces. He didn't need to look at Clay's face. Clay never shirked a challenge. So he answered for them. "You're on, Sampson. Care to make a little side wager, ole man?"

Clay stood up and pulled out a wad of fifties. "I'm in."

Blood roared in Evan's ears. He needed someone to beat on.

The two Syracuse attorneys were meat.

****

That evening Evan treated her to dinner at a new steak house with a Manhattan ambience. The floors were bleached hardwood, but the furniture was lacquered either black or white. Anything white glowed purple under the blacklights hidden behind plastic ceiling panels. The faint smell of charred steaks mingled with the fragrance of jasmine from bushes that flanked the entrance.

She wore a simple black and white striped dress and twisted her hair off her neck. He wore a white tuxedo shirt, black pants and boots, and a black leather jacket, drawing stares from every woman there. Proud to be his date, but nervous, she kept sneaking peeks from under her lashes. Every time she glanced up, he was staring at her, too. Her body hummed with desire amplified by her conversation with Karen.

During the meal, the conversation flowed easily from sports to politics. Evan was so relaxed that laugh lines were the only lines on his handsome face. He didn't do that scan thing or look sharply at everyone who arrived. Only her. It was the best opportunity to confide about Dylan but the night had been so perfect, she didn't want to ruin it. Besides, as soon as they found the stalker, he'd have no reason to stay. She'd deal with Dylan. At least she'd have this beautiful memory.

Back at her apartment, the awkwardness missing the entire evening surfaced. Her answering machine blinked three messages. While he checked the rooms she checked the caller ID memory. Dylan phoned twice. Her stomach instantly hurt and her head began to pound like she had some instant-flu as she erased the calls. What if he called back when Evan was there? She put the ringer on mute and before Evan removed his jacket, she decided to confront him.

She moved her bangs off her forehead. "You don't have to stay tonight. The security system's installed and certified."

His gaze never left hers as he walked forward

until he trapped her in front of the refrigerator. His hands rose and cupped her face. A sunflower magnet bounced off her shoe. The postcard of the Golden Gate Bridge surfed the air until it landed, one of the places she'd like to visit. "No system is one-hundred percent. Besides, it may take a while for a police car to get here. A lot can happen by then."

The backs of his fingers traced her jaw line from ear to ear. The hairs on her arms stood at attention. She wanted so badly to lean into him. He waited for her reply, his eyes giving none of his feelings away. She ordered her body to stay equally calm, although her stomach did a double-flip when he tugged her twisted hair and tilted her head at the perfect angle to be kissed. Mesmerized by the intensity of his gaze, she splayed her hands against the refrigerator door.

"Do you want to take that chance?" he added softly.

Her heart kicked. A thousand thoughts ran through her mind. If she said *yes*, would he leave her? Would she be safe without him? Ever see him again? Last night she'd learned the soft center beneath the tough shell Evan showed to the world. Could a man who loved so deeply once, ever love again?

She looked at he kitchen floor, this time spying an Empire State Building postcard from her friend in Manhattan. She'd planned to take Heather to New York City before Christmas. "No."

"Good." He'd leaned forward so that his chest molded to hers. His lips neared and she closed her eyes and braced for his kiss. Instead, a cool breeze teased her lips. She opened her eyes. His fingers combed through the ends of her hair as he backed away. Then he left her in the kitchen with the hard steel of the refrigerator door for support.

She counted to ten before she straightened then pulled the clip from her mussed hair. Her fingers thread through her hair until it felt smooth and carefree.

So she had to survive another night with Evan. No doubt he'd keep to the bargain, but why was she the only one who wanted to renegotiate?

Over the pounding of her heart she heard furniture shuffled around in the living room. She removed her heels and padded into the living room. Evan had removed his jacket and rolled up his sleeves. "It's still early. Do you mind if I hook this up?"

She let out a pent up breath. "I've been meaning to get an extension cord for it..."

Evan picked up the TV like it was hollow chocolate and placed it on one of the magazine cubes near an outlet. A nervous laugh bubbled up her throat. In the tuxedo shirt he looked like a Chippendale television repairman. "Er... thanks."

"No problem. Want to join me?" He held up the remote and adjusted the picture. She pictured him throwing the remote and stripping for her.

As if he read her mind those bedroom eyes zoomed in on her. Her pulse knocked under her hot skin. Backing out of the room, she felt for the furniture, unable to stop staring at Evan. "Maybe later."

Without waiting for his reply, she headed to her bedroom and breathed a sigh of relief when she heard a game show blasting.

After a long soak in the tub, she dried her hair and then combed it with a boar's-hair brush until it rippled like silk. Deciding she needed a cup of chamomile tea, she put on a pretty blue bathrobe and crept down the hallway to the kitchen. Maybe after hot tea and a good book, she'd be tired and get some rest.

Fat chance. Even with the long soak her body hummed from Evan's touch. This was the last night she'd have to survive this attack of her senses by one hundred percent all-American hero.

On the way to the kitchen she spied Evan sitting cross-legged on the floor looking through her CD's. He looked up and pointed. "I hooked up the CD player." He pushed a button and the GooGoo Dolls filled the room.

Her music.

She wandered slightly dazed into the living room. There was a time when she couldn't drive in a car, or clean house, or rock Heather to sleep without listening to her tunes. She bathed to music. Slept to music. Made love to... "I've been meaning to do that...Thanks."

On bended knee, Evan looked up. "Interesting collection. Everything from rock, to the Bach, to musicals." He turned over a CD. "Then there's my favorite, Beauty and the Beast—" He fumble with the CD case.

Heather's favorite. She waved her hands to stop him. "No. Not that one."

Evan's finger hovered over the play button. Confused, and looking way too gorgeous, he sat down on her floor surrounded by her old CD's. She needed that tea, but her feet didn't move. He pointed to another neatly stacked pile of boxes that weren't there an hour ago. She'd accidentally knocked them over after court and didn't have the strength to pick them up.

"Quite a collection of games." His grin disappeared when she moaned.

She fled from the living room before he saw the tears in her eyes. She didn't want his pity. His footsteps sounded behind her.

As she ignited the burner under the kettle, she decided to explain. "Heather and I played games before bedtime. Her favorite was Yahtzee."

Her voice sounded abnormally cheery as she

stared at the blue flames the way people sound when someone close dies.

"Mine, too. I never lose," he bragged.

She pivoted and faced him. "I never lose, either."

He crossed his arms. "Sounds like we'd better play a game."

The game was set up on the checkerboard when she returned carrying a tray with tea for her, coffee for him.

He had no idea what he was in for.

****

Evan suggested hooking up her TV as an excuse to get her out of the kitchen. When the music didn't work he found himself scrambling. Good thing he'd noticed the games.

As Cassie shook the dice in the cup, Evan admired the view. The slight arm gesture caused her breasts to sway under that sensational fabric of her robe. The cloth played catch and release with her nipples. He'd have to take ten Benedryl to sleep tonight. Last night he was delighted to discover this competitive side of Cassie. He never would have guessed she'd take playing games so seriously.

"That's four sixes! I'm going to bonus on top. You're never gonna beat me now." Her green eyes sparkled like Fourth-of-July fireworks.

"The game's far from over. How would you like to make a wager on the outcome?"

His tone made her sit up on her heels. A silky mass of yellow hair fell forward to cover her breasts. He hoped it was only a matter of time before he'd be seeing all of her again.

"What do you mean?"

He didn't answer and rolled all five dice.

"Oh, you have two threes. If you get two more threes, and then four twos on another turn, *you* can bonus on the top, too."

He admired her mathematical skills.

Three dice fell into the cup and he slowly swirled them around. He didn't throw them down until she stopped checking the math on her score sheet.

"No help there." She smiled. His chest hurt from longing to see more of those smiles.

"What do you want to bet I throw at least one three on my third toss?" he said, loving the anticipation in her eyes.

She licked her lips, something he discovered she did when she was nervous. "What's the bet?"

"If I get one three, or more, you have to take something off. If I don't, I take off something."

She studied him. "That's not fair. I'm wearing less than you."

"True. But you've been on a lucky streak. Think it will continue?"

He swirled the cup. The *click, click, click* of the dice filled the silence. He watched every play of emotion on her face as she considered his proposition. He figured she was game when her lids half-covered her eyes like they did before he kissed her.

"Okay. Roll."

He belabored the shake a little longer until she *tsked*. He didn't need to look at the roll only her satisfied grin.

"You lose," she said.

He rose up from the floor, and in one quick motion pulled his shirt over his head. The sharp intake of her breath fueled his already heated blood. He'd been teasing her all game by deliberately touching her fingers every time they passed the cup. He'd watched her flinch or her eyes as they narrowed. This time when their fingers brushed, she stole a look at his chest. He'd abused his body today at the gym because of her and was glad his muscles were primed.

"Your turn."

She threw twice. Before she rolled again, he stopped her. "Call what you want. You still need a full house."

"I thought it was only on your turn. At this rate, we'll run out of clothes before we finish the game—" A little squeak came out.

He swallowed a laugh. "That's possible. What are you worried about? You said you always win."

Her chin lifted and she looked down her nose at him.

Poor kid. Her pink blush betrayed her. She rattled the dice. "I'll go for the full house."

He tried to look upset when he whipped off his belt. He'd removed his boots before he got the idea for strip Yahtzee.

On his turn he lost. This time he removed his ankle gun. As she shook the dice she glanced at the gun.

"What's wrong?"

Her face pinked, and she shrugged. "Nothing. I've never seen a loaded gun up close."

"Don't worry. Safety's on."

It killed him not to take her in his arms and kiss that worried look of her face. Thoughts of rolling on the floor sent such a shock wave of heat that his back slicked.

She pointed at the gun. "It doesn't count as an article of clothing."

"Fine by me." He moved the gun to the top of his pile of clothes, away from her, but near enough to reach. He pulled a sock off.

She looked sheepish all of a sudden.

Oh sweetheart, why are you fighting this? I know you want me as much as I want you.

"Tell me more about L.A.," he said.

She threw the dice in the cup and vigorously shook them and averted her gaze. "There's not much to tell."

Tortured by the way both nipples pebbled against the fabric as she shook the cup, he almost forgot he needed information. "Did you enjoy selling real estate?"

"It was okay."

A large straight rolled out on the first try.

He took off another sock. "Meet a lot of interesting people?"

"Some. Your turn."

He waited for her to finish scribbling on her score sheet. "I think I'll try for those twos again."

He rolled four of them.

She untied and removed her belt. Her deep cleavage and the swell of both breasts flashed before she managed to snag the robe closed. He adjusted his position on the floor.

Now, what were they talking about?

Thankfully he lost another turn and took his pants off, carefully replacing his gun on top. He knew she'd spied his erection through his boxers when he heard her quick inhale. She all but threw the cup at him.

He put the cup aside and slowly rolled the dice in his fingers. "How about upping the stakes?"

"What more do you want?"

He grimaced. "All or nothing. First one to lose a roll has to take everything off."

"And what if the game's not over?"

"Oh, it will be over by then."

He let her think about his words while he openly stared at her red thong exposed by the poorly closed robe. "What's wrong? Don't you still feel lucky? Or do you want to give up now?"

The pulse at the base of her throat fluttered. "I never quit. Do *you* want to concede?"

"Not a chance."

For the next two turns, both rolled what they

wanted.

He studied his score sheet. "Yahtzee left. Whoever rolls it, wins. Your turn."

This time when he handed her the dice his fingers circled her delicate wrist. She didn't pull away as he placed the dice in the palm of her hand, one at a time. Cool fingers skimmed his before they circled the dice. She cupped them and rolled.

"You're off to a great start," he said.

Her chest rose and fell so fast, he thought she'd hyperventilate any minute. Instead of keeping three sixes, she kept two fives. He opened his mouth to say something but she'd already tossed the dice again.

Her robe descended off one shoulder, half exposing one breast. "Five's always been my lucky number in Yahtzee. Wanna bet I can't throw three fives?"

"Throw the dice."

She did. Up in the air. They bounced off the walls and skidded on the hardwood floor. "There are three fives on the floor. I win." Her breathing hitched.

He studied her a minute. "Come here."

She moved off the couch and stood above him.

"Down here," he commanded.

Kneeling before him, her robe flared out. He felt his cock lengthen when she met his gaze.

No rushing tonight. He wanted to love her the way he'd imagined in a thousand desert dreams. "I think you should get on the floor with me and look for those fives." As he spoke, he leaned toward her.

Her eyes darted from the floor back to him. "And what if I don't?"

"Then I guess I win."

He removed her fingers from the robe. She watched his hands as he pushed the robe down her arms.

He'd only seen parts of her in the tent, so he

took his time looking at her now. Her skin was smooth, a beautiful peachy color, her breasts, round and high. The nipples were small, and puckered under his stare.

He leaned closer. "Ask me to kiss you."

She swayed toward him. "Kiss me."

He barely brushed his lips over hers. His tongue licked the seam between her lips and when they parted, he delved into her mouth. He licked every surface, wanting to linger there, marking his domain.

He pulled back. "Ask me to make love to you."

She hesitated, searched his eyes. His breath caught in his throat. If she refused now, he'd go insane.

"Make love to me, Evan."

His skin prickled with the relief that flooded his system. "Anything you ask."

He trailed kisses from her neck, across her collarbone to her breasts. Lifting one breast to his mouth, the other hand arched her backward so he could feast. Her eyes fluttered closed and her gasp made his lips move faster, tasting every surface. She tasted like honey and smelled like an exotic spice. Her hands anchored in his hair. He lapped and sucked until she whimpered, then repeated the action on the other one. Her hands skimmed down his back and around his sides and worked his boxers off. Before her first caress down his length, he was rock hard. Her circling fingers explored then squeezed and his breathing stopped.

Two can play that game. He sucked hard on one nipple then blew on the moisture until it hardened to a peak that he took between his teeth. Her arms limped by her sides. He laid her gently down. Hooded lids fluttered open as she watched him roll the condom.

"Now, let's see those positions."

Carefully, he turned her over onto her hands and knees. He pulled down her thong and brushed his hand between her lower lips, feeling warmth and wetness. She moved her knees farther apart and arched her back. He held her hips still as the head of his cock buried into her. Her breaths hitched as he gave her another inch. Teasing the opening, he pulled out. He circled her waist and stroked deeper. Her head reared back and rested on his shoulder.

"You okay?" He said, as his lips wandered the curve of her neck to her shoulder while he held still inside her.

"Ummm."

"You sure?"

He pulled out, and tried again. He moved his hands, gently kneaded her weighty breasts, and then pushed in halfway. "Don't want to hurt you."

She leaned back onto his lap, taking more of him. He withdrew and pressed slowly into her, then withdrew again. He repeated the motion, feeling about to explode from both the snug sensation and realization she was in his arms again.

"Oh, Evan," she cried when he surged deeper.

He held her in place, fighting the need to piston into her. "You feel as good as I remember," he whispered in her ear. He smeared kisses over her blushing cheek while his hands never stopped roaming her breasts, tummy, thighs, attempting touch her everywhere at once.

She ground her hips, tensed.

"Tell me how to make it better."

"Better?" she half-laughed.

He tilted her hips upward, changing the angle of penetration, then began short, hard strokes.

She gasped. "That feels s-oo good."

He pinched her nipples while keeping up the rhythm, moving a fraction further. "Still good?"

"Don't stop."

She wilted against his chest. He smiled and wanted to roar. He wished he could stay inside her forever, it felt so incredible. He wanted to kiss every part of her, and to take her in every way imaginable, but that would take a lifetime.

At least they had tonight.

****

Cassie melted like well-tempered chocolate.

At first, when Evan's lips touched the curve of her neck, a current of heat shot to her core and flamed. Anticipating his next move, she remained still. Then he pushed into her, stretching her until she thought she'd break, but instead a glorious pulse began. As he pressed deeper, his thickness raked every sensitive nerve and sent tendrils of pleasure up her spine. It seemed like he pushed into her forever, until he bottomed and then held himself there.

"You coming?" He whispered against her neck, sending chills along the sensitive skin behind her ear.

"Cl-ose."

Seconds away from a sweet, powerful orgasm, she held still, feeling him pulse deep inside her, seeing how long she could prolong her release. When he reached a finger between her legs and rubbed her, she bit back a groan and bucked against his lap.

"Come for me," he said, and then pumped, sliding further. She walked her hands forward on the floor, then lowered her head and raised her hips. In the gray-green reflection of the television screen she watched Evan rise up on one knee and move over her. She couldn't take her eyes off the screen as he moved back and forth, focused on his task, making her delirious.

Moans slipped between her pursed lips, until she cried out, some from shock, more from pleasure. "Evan! Oh, God, Evan." Locked in Evan's embrace, she joined his rhythm. The top of his head, hair mussed by her fingers, was all she could see now in the reflection, besides the occasional arch of his back as he drove higher up into her. How was it possible to feel so many lingering sensations at once? His lips never left her neck except to nibble her earlobe. She liked the feel of the weight of his chest as it slid over her back and the brush of his abdomen slapping her bottom. And those hands. His hands were magical, knowing exactly where to touch her and whether a graze or heavy stroke would set her aching further. His tempo didn't stop. Deeper inside her, every push or pull raked her with so much blinding pleasure, pulling her higher to the summit until his fingers parted her lips and pushed hard on her nub.

"Ohhh... Evan." She bucked back as he kept the pressure there, part torture, part thrill. *Evan was inside her, loving her.* Seconds later her release triggered a cascade of ripples, each exceeding the other. Her shoulders shuddered with the force of her orgasm and her mind exploded with the heady knowledge that it was Evan that brought her to this point.

Her Evan.

She never thought they'd share a moment like this again. It exceeded every erotic dream she'd made up. She squeezed her eyes shut, but several tears escaped and ran down her face before she could stop them.

Pressing back against his strength she rode the wave of pleasure, holding on to the memory of him inside her.

Enough to last a lifetime.

****

Evan couldn't believe he held back his release so long without dying. He'd intended to keep her hanging near an orgasm for a while determined to give her the most mind-blowing climax possible. Call it male ego but he wanted to erase from her mind any memory of another man's touch. But once she breathlessly groaned out his name, nature took over and he pumped faster. He thought he'd die when she ground his lap, causing his cock to push against her barrier. It sent a rocket of pleasure to his brain and back. He stroked, near collapse, fighting back his own orgasm several times, feeling it pull at the base of his spine, his balls aching for his release, but he held back.

The sound of his name on her lips when she came over and over was worth waiting for.

Through a thousand lonely nights he'd yearned to hear her say it exactly that way. Breathless, desperate, shouting his name loudly, the second time she screamed his control snapped and he surged a final time, taking a deep breath, straightening his spine and focusing all his energy on the explosion that was seconds away. He came so hard his muscles locked. He surged forward twice, savoring his release, until his muscles gave out. When he came to, he was lying on his side, his cock still pulsing inside her. His arms and legs trembled. His body slicked with their sweat. He swallowed huge gulps of air until his vision cleared. He was so exhausted he couldn't pull out of her even if he wanted to.

He never came so hard that his body collapsed, or he lost all thought.

He couldn't wait to take her again.

His mind worked on how he could make it even better, last longer. Part of his mind screamed this wasn't great sex but he was too stunned to understand. The last time he felt this bouyant was paratrooping school. The first step Airborne was a doosy, his stomach dropped to his feet and his head ballooned, but the euphoria from the ride was so worth it.

"You okay?" She was equally still.

He skimmed her back with his knuckles. He'd planned to go slow, kiss every inch of her from the tip of her toes to her fingers but that much restraint wasn't in the cards, er, rather dice tonight.

"Mmmm. I'm great. Why do you keep doing that?"

"What, kissing you?" He rubbed the back of his hand between her shoulder blades, and followed the trail with kisses.

"No, touching me with the backs of your hands." She flipped over and grabbed his hand before he could pull back. She checked one hand. Sat up and grabbed the other.

The haze of good sex left her eyes as they widened. "What happen to your palms?"

He pulled them away, bracing for a lecture, or worse, hysteria. She sat up on her knees, and looked down at him. "Something happened to you in Iraq, didn't it? Those are burn marks on your hands. How did it happen?"

He rolled away from her. "That's classified information." Seeing her so upset hurt more than the burns.

"Then I'll guess." She hesitated, and then gasped. "You pulled someone out of a vehicle on fire?"

"No." He rolled back to face her and grabbed both of her wrists. "Let it go."

She'd paled. By the stubborn tilt of her chin, he knew she'd keep guessing. The information wasn't classified.

He released her hands, but his mouth remained clamped shut. She ran a finger over his abs, and then dipped it in his navel. "Please, tell me." Shimmering eyes stared at him. She bit her lower lip, causing a little dot of blood to spill.

"They're powder burns from a flash bomb. I was lucky. My burns were minor, but my men...." Searing

234

pain flared in his mind. He closed his eyes and silently counted to ten until the worse of it passed.

Her fingers yanked off his chest and froze in midair. He braced for the tirade. By now he knew her temper and waited for the fire in her eyes to ignite.

Cool green eyes like a new blade of grass searched his face. She picked up his hands and kissed each ugly palm. "I never told you how proud I am of you for serving your country. You're the bravest man I know."

Then she took both of his palms and placed them on her breast. "Can you feel this?" He watched her move them over her nipples and listened to the IED explosions go off in his head, then fade away until all he heard was her sultry voice. "I can, and I don't want you to feel like you can't touch me like this." To prove it, she held his palms against her breast and her body swayed as she spoke. "Touch me, Evan. I want to feel your scars and take away the pain."

His hands obeyed. They roamed all over, from her breasts to her shoulders, neck to tummy. Like the night before his deployment, when he'd measured and memorized her body, thinking he might never see her again.

Her eyes closed but from her expression he knew she wasn't repulsed. He imagined the softness of her skin and every dip and curve. Then he saw the scars against her beautiful skin, and stopped.

Through hooded eyes, she looked down at him. "Don't stop touching me. I missed you so much."

This was not fever-induced dream. Cassie clung to his arms, flesh and blood woman, wanting him as fervently as he wanted her. The look of longing on her face ricocheted through his chest, until it melted the metal bars he'd kept around his heart, unlocked desires he'd buried deep inside him, made him break free of his self-induced prison. Filled all the hallowed-out places forged in battle, making him feel alive again.

He thought the war had taken everything, emptied his soul, left a shell of flesh that posed as a man. But here was his Cassie, with a heart as big as the mountains he loved, thinking she could take away his pain.

And she thought he was a hero.

He needed her again, needed to show her how much she meant to him, to make up for all the time they'd lost. She yelped as he lifted her off the floor, high in the air, threw her over his shoulder, and headed for the bedroom. She pounded on his back, a token protest.

It would be a late night.

Chapter Seventeen

Before Evan went to work the next morning, he had made love to her once more. Cassie basked in the memory of how sweetly he took her in the light of dawn, with plenty of kisses, making love while lying face to face. His favorite position, he said. He loved her so thoroughly, she'd never felt so sated or at peace.

In no hurry to get up and lose that feeling, she rolled onto her side and imagined him still sleeping. His mussed-up hair, the absence of worry lines on an even more handsome face, the feel of his skin as she roamed the pads of her fingers over his chest. She wished he were with her right now.

She rolled over on her stomach and curled her pillow up under her head. Her bed still smelled like the man. Spicy. Sexy. Dangerous. Tender. Unselfish. She considered staying there until he returned, but the note he left on his side of the bed said he'd be back later this morning.

The dent where he'd slept warmed her palms. As she smoothed her hand over the sheet she thought about his burns. At first she froze with terror. But then he allowed her to examine his palms and she felt relief and pride. They looked calloused, and there was a big pucker of flesh in the center of his left palm. Evan was right-handed and the skin on those fingers was thicker, explaining the lack of sensation.

Knowing Evan, if he could have traded places with his men he would have done so. Certain there was so much more to the story, at that moment all she wanted was to take away his pain the way he'd taken away some of hers with his presence. If only she weren't so sure that he'd be repulsed by her secret she could have imagine a future with Evan.

Images of her dream home filled her mind—a large house in the country, not too far from the city, with a big backyard and certainly enough room for a playroom and nursery. Wanting four children, two boys and two girls, so they'd each have a brother and sister, she pictured a big, salt-box style house. With plenty of bedrooms and two fireplaces, one in the family room and one in the master bedroom. With those big muscles, Evan would have no trouble keeping the woodpile stocked.

That yarn made her bolt upright.

She was doing it again, spinning fantasies about a man she had no future with—only plenty of hot sex. She bent her knees and laid her head on crossed arms. She needed to regroup but disappointment burned her throat. Sleeping with Evan was a nice reprieve from her life. She'd be lying if she said she regretted it but there was too much at stake.

Besides, he wasn't the kind of man she wanted to marry. She'd be worried sick about him all the time. Didn't she want someone to be there for her and the kids rather than serving the needs of others?

She should be in her shop preparing for customers rather than lounging in bed. Didn't she want to concentrate on her business and make it such a hit that she could one day move Heather to a real home? Someday, when Dylan no longer bothered her or someone stalked her.

Reality bites.

The shower was cold and brief. With so little time to do her hair, she pulled the damp curls back into a ponytail and twisted it. With her hair slicked back and pinned up, she looked like one of those successful shop owners in her dessert magazine. Only those elegant women didn't have a baby to get back or a stalker.

Or a sexy bodyguard.

Something was wrong with her reflection in the mirror. She set down her hairbrush and leaned on the bathroom counter. At first, she thought it was the steam from the shower that altered her appearance. After several swipes over the mirror with a hand towel, the vision hadn't changed.

She looked different.

Her skin glowed like polished with rose petals, dewy and healthy, not the pale pallor she'd worn since leaving California. She'd lost some wrinkles around the eyes. Her cheeks were less angular and bore a natural blush. But the eyes that looked back at her were the most changed. Dazzling, as if lit from behind, like green beacons. A more vibrant, excited, definitely confident person looked back.

Evan put that look there.

The realization of what it meant made her gasp. Evan was going to complicate her life.

Breathing deeply she towel dried some drips from her hair. As she flung open drawers in her bedroom her chest felt like a dragon sat on it. Several pieces of underwear fell to the floor. A thong and bra that she threw on the bed tumbled into the dent from Evan's body. The crevice ran from top to bottom of the mattress. He slept on top of the covers without even a throw. Something about being too warm. No matter. She liked looking at his naked body and touching it while he slept. She collected her underwear and put it on then grabbed her camisole from another drawer.

He'd looked so large next to Heather when they said goodbye Sunday. Everything about him was too big. He didn't fit in her bed, her home and logically thought that he didn't fit into her life. She wished they'd met under other circumstances. Considering all her problems, she was lucky to have shared last night with him.

Maybe she should tell him about Dylan.

But then she'd have to tell him the rest of the story. Her stomach cramped. No man would understand what she went though and then want her. She sat on the bed, picked up the dented blue pillow and hugged her cheek to it. The cramping eased.

She pulled a rose-colored camisole over her bra then layered on a lacy, low-cut blouse. The sleeves were sheer, but could be pushed up to her elbows. A pair of camel slacks and low-heeled mules completed the ensemble. In the bottom bureau drawer, she found her jewelry box and selected some pieces. With her hair up, exposing the long column of her neck, she appeared more feminine, daintier, and lovelier than she'd felt in years.

As she posted her earrings, the phone rang. She ran, but the machine tripped on.

"Cassie, this is Dylan. Look, we need to talk. It's important. Call me on my cell as soon as you get this message."

The slippers skidded to a halt. The telephone cord coiled like a viper, inches from her extended hand. *Yeah, right. I'm gonna call you to hear more crazy talk.* She backed away from the machine. What was Dylan up to? Imagine Dylan's expression if Evan called him back. Her smile evaporated. No, she didn't want Evan to know that part of her life. No one else believed her side of the story, so why would he be different?

Because of the tender way he made love to me?

The phone rang again. This time, she checked the caller ID before she answered.

"Hello, Cassie," her lawyer said. "Karl asked me to call. I hear you had a setback in court."

In the past, his upbeat British accent had been comforting. Now, his voice sounded hallowed, like he spoke from the end of a long tunnel.

"Hello, Mr. King." She rubbed the sudden pain in her stomach before it radiated, making speaking difficult. "The judge wouldn't read a thing without Jake present. The proceeding was supposed to be simple—"

Mr. King interrupted, "I'll try to move up your court date. Trouble is, one of our judges retired, and the other is having chemo treatments. The judge you saw was on loan from Rochester."

"That explains a lot," she said trying to hold back her bitterness.

"They hope to have more judges in a couple of months. I'll phone the clerk to get you in then."

"Do you think you can get a court date before Christmas?" Cassie looked at the calendar on her kitchen wall. Her fingers walked off the days to Christmas Eve.

He paused long enough for her stomach to pitch. Her custody lawyer was always completely honest with her. She wished she could have afforded to have him in court with her the other day. This phone call alone would cost her over a hundred dollars. "I'd planned to have Heather spend Christmas Eve with me." She added. "It's okay with Jake."

He cleared his throat. "I'll do my best, but under the circumstances... keep up the good work with your shop. By the way, my wife was wondering—" his voice faded.

There was a chance she could get back into court and Heather would be home for Christmas.

Her spirits soared as she walked into Heather's room. Another morning ritual. A breeze stirred the hair around her face. The window was open a crack. *Maybe Evan opened it last night*, she thought as she dropped the sash and turned the window lock.

Were those footsteps? The hairs on her arms stood up. She looked around the room, even opened Heather's armoire. Nothing seemed out of place. The only sound was her hammering heart. She lingered before closing Heather's bedroom door.

Walking across the living room to check the locks on those windows she noticed a pillow on the couch and a rolled up quilt. Carrying them back to her bedroom, she made her bed and folded the quilt on the footboard, where it had been the night before. The footsteps were probably squirrels on her roof. In the backyard she'd left bits of nuts for them. They like to run in her gutters, although that sound was more scratchy, not thumpy like footsteps.

Now she was being silly.

Dylan's call rattled her. The windows were two stories up and locked. Her business was wired with a security alarm system and she had a personal bodyguard.

How much safer could a girl be?

****

A bad day to make Divinity, she thought as she counted the number of choco-nut Pina Colada clusters in the display case. Normally, Wednesday was a slow day, the perfect day to replenish inventory. Even with only four ingredients mixing Divinity was time consuming. All the activity helped to keep Dylan's phone call off her mind. The door chimes and the small timer clipped to her blouse went off simultaneously. She ran to shut off the mixer and returned to the counter in time to greet two women.

"Are you the owner of this charming shop?" The taller of two nicely dressed women asked while the other walked up to the wedding cake display.

"Yes. Can I help you?" Cassie tugged at the strings of her apron, and threw it on a shelf under the counter.

"I'm looking for Italian chocolate. My husband sampled some at work the other day and raved about it so much that Sarah and I want to try it." The woman carefully searched each shelf of the display case.

"I think you're looking for these little nuggets of bittersweet chocolate with roasted hazelnuts on the inside. The Italians called them, *Bacio di Dama.*"

Cassie removed a tray with the pieces. "Actually, they are very simple to make but I import the real thing because they contain Piedmontese hazelnuts grown only in Italy." Cassie walked over to a display of baskets while they chewed. "These baskets contain bags of *Bacio di Dama*, along with other Italian chocolate."

Both woman sighed and licked their fingers. Cassie handed them scented wipes. The taller woman, wearing at least three inches of gold bracelets, studied some of the larger baskets. "My Italian's rough. *Dama* is *lady*... but I can't remember *bacio.*"

"It means, 'kiss of a woman.' It's the Italian version of chocolate kisses."

She enjoyed the look of delight on their faces, similar to her first taste.

"Oh, Sarah, look at how pretty these baskets are."

"They're gorgeous, Paulette."

Hours surfing on the Internet eventually yielded the right style and color of basket in her price range. She couldn't suppress a proud smile. Counting

Evan's, it was only the fourth basket of Italian chocolates she'd sold.

"Is your husband with the New York State Police?" she asked.

The woman beamed. "Jerry Palmer. Do you know him?"

"I'm not sure, I met so many of Ev—Sergeant Jorgenson's colleagues when I delivered a basket."

Cassie wondered if Officer Palmer was one of the men she'd lunched with.

"My husband's a fireman. His unit's got a sweet tooth," said Paulette.

"Our club meets once a week for girls' poker night. Don't tell our husbands," explained Sarah. "They think we make scrapbooks. Your chocolates sounded perfect for dessert."

"And there's no calories," Cassie joked. She liked these women. There'd been no time to make friends in her neighborhood.

Both women laughed. Each grabbed a large basket and set it on the checkout counter. Sarah pointed to the display case. "Paulette... look at the fudge. Lynda, loves fudge. Who makes it?"

Cassie removed a sample plate. "I do. Does your sister prefer any particular flavor?"

"I think she likes anything with nuts," said Sarah.

"Here's one with hazelnuts, macadamia, and one with pistachios." Cassie pointed to tiny triangular pieces of each.

Paulette tasted the samples, and passed some to Sarah. "You try a piece. I can't decide what I like better."

"Take a pound of each. One for your sister, and two for you and me to split later," Paulette replied. "I'll take that basket of Italian chocolates on the counter, too. Oh, and a pound of the chocolate amaretto truffles. My mother-in-law loves those.

Can you deliver them today?"

"No problem." Cassie drew dollar signs on a scrap piece of paper. If this continued, she'd have to hire a delivery boy. She'd phoned Franco, owner of the pizza parlor down the street, to borrow Jessie to deliver a phone order placed earlier. She wanted to shout a cheer for her success. "Will there be anything else?"

Sarah thought, and then answered, "I did have a question about freezing chocolate. I get so much as Holiday gifts. How long can I freeze it?" Sarah moved over to the sample tray, and popped a divinity morsel in her mouth. Her eyes rolled back as she savored the morsel.

Cassie stopped tallying the order to explain. "If it's milk chocolate, it can last for a year, frozen. But be careful to warm it slowly to room temperature. Wipe off any condensation, or it will make the chocolate watery."

"Oh—that's fabulous. What's this fluffy stuff?" Sarah asked.

"It's called divinity. Freshly made."

The woman winked to her friend. "Mmmm. I'll take a pound of it."

After Cassie rang them up, she barely had time to add Irish Crème liquor to the latest batch of divinity candy and drop them on the cookie sheet to dry for three hours. The recipe took very little time to make but the temperature of the mixture had to be perfect, then beaten continuously for ten minutes in her largest copper bowl. Grandma's recipe suggested candied cherries, yuk, or coarsely ground walnuts in the mix. Cassie needed time to experiment with more contemporary flavors, like key-lime, or pomegranate martini.

Sampling the newest batch of Irish Crème divinity, the chimes sounded, again.

Yet another customer? She clapped her hands

and whispered a Williams White Knight victory cheer, and nearly back-flipped to the counter.

****

At the police impound lot, Evan checked the trunk of the abandoned car registered to Hugh Stone.

Clean.

Like Stone knew a forensic team would eventually scrub it for prints.

Something yellow glowed under the jack. A can of Fix-a-Flat. He removed it with his pen and called for a bag.

"Have the prints run today." Evan placed the can in a plastic bag Tony held open. "Did you run that address?"

"Yeah," Tony replied. "It's a phony. Used to be a drug house, but it burned down a year ago."

Evan winced. *Don't make this be about drugs.* If Cassie were involved with drug dealers, he'd be powerless to help her.

"Tires are bald. The guy did a lot of traveling," Tony added.

"Yeah, I bet. Maybe to Lake Placid," Evan replied while prying open the glove compartment.

"You think he followed Cassie there?" Tony removed his latex gloves and threw them in the back seat.

"It wasn't a random attempted theft. Someone tampered with my fuel line. Cassie's shop door looked tampered with, too. This guy was hired to find something. Question is, what?"

"Could be the money. It's a coincidence that she's got a warrant on her head for embezzling a hundred grand."

Evan frowned. "Why would you send a thug when you have a warrant? It makes no sense." The glove compartment slammed shut with the force of a nail gun.

Tony tore off his latex gloves. "Unless this Dylan wanted to shake her up a bit first and use the warrant as a last resort."

Evan punched his fists together. At least one of them thought clearly. A chill ran down Evan's spine. How far would this guy, Stone, go? They had to find him fast. "Check the other homes surrounding the burned drug house. Maybe someone wants to trade a night in a jail cell for information about a former neighbor. And get Cassie's car delivered. Techs are done with it."

Tony stepped back then turned. "Cassie might be safer in a jail cell."

Evan bit his tongue. He didn't know how much longer Tony would follow his orders, a blatant disregard for police procedure. He straightened and simply shook his head.

"Okay, okay. I warned you." Tony threw his arms up in the air. "It's not going to look good for you, Ev," he said as he stalked back to his car and it skidded away.

Evan hated fighting with Tony. He was right, of course. Cassie might be in serious trouble. Porcelli was due back in two days. He had to get her to talk about Dylan before then.

After spending the afternoon in the forensics unit he couldn't wait to see Cassie. A patrol car watched the shop all day, and he checked with the officer by cell phone every hour to make sure she was okay. After one call he found himself on the wrong highway, halfway to Oswego before his thoughts cleared. But racing back to Syracuse his thoughts drifted back to Cassie.

Another night like last night and they'd need a stretcher for him. The last thing he'd wanted to do was sleep. He couldn't get enough of her. When she kissed his scars, something snapped in his head. He wanted to lose himself inside her and never pull out.

Two more nights of trying to keep her safe from both the stalker and the warrant, he thought, rubbing his aching forehead. He had no idea how many hours she'd spend in jail after the warrant was served, so tonight had to be special. The corners of his mouth turned up as he recalled her competitive side.

Her love of playing games gave him an idea.

Porcelli said he'd get her out in an hour. If only Evan was so certain. His fists tightened around his steering wheel, whiting his knuckles. Before Iraq it had been so easy to avoid the enemy. Keep low, listen to every sound and never stop scanning the horizon. Ironically, the enemy was now his profession.

How far would he go to keep Cassie safe?

****

Dylan stormed around his studio looking for something or someone to hit. "What the fuck are you doing, Stone? How'd the cops find you?"

"I-I had to ditch my car. That c-cop boyfriend of hers musta remembered my plate and found my former address." Stone stuttered the reply, badly gulping air. "He spooked the old neighborhood so bad that one jerk called me for money to keep his mouth shut."

"Shit. Okay, you're outta this. I'll take care of everything from now on."

Stone dragged loudly on a cigarette. "What about my fee?"

With two pillows propped behind his head, he watched a starlet enter the sound stage.

"It's in the mail. Don't put me down for a reference." He snapped the cell shut, and then threw a prop that resembled a ceramic stallion against the wall. It made a satisfying boom as plaster spattered on the satin bedspread. He slicked his hair back from his eyes and righted his Prada leather jacket

248

before reclining again.

The girl didn't seem afraid of his wild behavior, instead appeared intrigued.

"Get me a drink," he winked and spoke in his charming Texan drawl.

The first time he laid eyes on Cassie, she'd reminded him of Princess Grace Kelly, polished, aloof, almost untouchable. The perfect woman to legitimize him, neutralize his bad-boy image, his ticket into more sophisticated circles in the old Hollywood crowd that still ran things.

The only down side was the kid.

The night he'd discovered the box filled with returned letters to some guy in the service at first he'd panicked. Later that night he'd concocted the plan to make her forget the boyfriend. A bonus was he got rid of the kid, too. So now he needed to think of a way to get her back plus get his silent partners off his back permanently.

Think, Dylan, think. Seven nights in a row he'd phoned without her answering or a returned call. Only one option left. He called his assistant. "Book me a flight on the red-eye to Hancock International, one way. If Fields comes looking for me, tell him I went to the East Coast for a few days. Yeah, I know he's going to be pissed. Too bad. He's waited this long. Do what I said."

Ending that call he phoned Stone back. "I've got one more job for you."

"Okay," replied Stone.

"Find me wheels and pick me up at Hancock." He shook out two pills from a prescription bottle.

Stone paused. "Is the check still in the mail?"

Dylan put his hand over the cell, and mouthed, *Fucking loser.* "I'll have cash with me."

"What time?" Stone sounded bored. What else did that thug have to do?

"Get to the airport and wait. I'm catching the

red-eye."

He ended the call and slipped the cell into a hidden pocket. He should have handled this himself a long time ago. It felt like years since he'd touched Cassie.

The girl returned with two glasses of *Jack*. He knocked the first one back washing the pills down and feeling an instant buzz. He took his time on the second while she slipped off her robe and removed the costume she'd worn for the scene. Then she crept onto the bed. The hiss of his zipper let out a smidge of the anger he'd brewed all day. He adjusted the pillows behind his head again. The girl bent over him as she parted the fly on his leather slacks. Her large breasts hovered over his mouth as she removed his flaccid cock and began to stroke him. He pinched her nipple and pushed her head toward his cock. "No time for fun, angel. Do me quick. I have a flight to catch."

He closed his eyes and thought of Cassie.

****

Cassie lost count how many times she'd run from her kitchen and back to the checkout counter that afternoon. The last batch of divinity over beat, and had to be thrown away. After ringing up another customer she generously poured lotion on her extremely dried out hands, a hazards of pulling gloves on and off all day. The plunger clogged, so she'd left the cap off spilling some on the counter. She inhaled the odor as she pulled the counter drawer open to nibble a few more Hershey's kisses before resuming kitchen duty. Every time she'd rung up a customer she'd smell the lotion and remember that day in the tent.

While the morning had been busy the afternoon was plain crazy. She'd managed to make a couple batches of divinity while ringing up sales until a young woman entered in tears. Cassie grabbed the box of tissues from under the counter and handed her several. The distraught woman explained that the pastry chef for her wedding this Saturday ran off with his lover and she no longer had a wedding cake.

"I can't find anyone to make one with three days' notice who doesn't want a fortune. My aunt told me about this place. She was here earlier in the day and saw a cake made of boxes of chocolate."

Cassie gazed at the display with the new bride and groom on top. "I'm afraid it's very expensive."

"Ohhh. I don't know what I'm going to do. Isn't it bad luck to not have a wedding cake? Maybe I should call off the wedding." She blotted the tears that rolled down her blanched face.

Cassie came around the counter. "No. Don't do that. We can think of something."

"Can you?" The tears slowed and her pretty gray eyes sparkled.

"Have you ever heard of petit-fours?"

"The tiny French cakes?"

"Yep. How many guests are you expecting?"

The bride frowned. "One hundred and sixteen have RSVP-ed. The cake served two-hundred."

Cassie pushed the bags of Hershey's kisses aside as she located the calculator from the drawer. "Let's see. Then you'd need about twenty-dozens. How much did you budget?"

The cake made of petite-fours fit right in the bride's budget. She'd drop off her grandmother's antique silver platter to display the cakes. Before leaving the blushing bride paid in full.

Cassie dreamed of days like this when she first envisioned owning a candy shop. Could things get any better?

Who needed a horseshoe nailed over the front door when she had Evan?

****

When Evan arrived at five o'clock, he found

Cassie with her head on the counter. His heart slammed to his feet. She'd found out about the warrant. "Are you okay?"

As he stepped around the counter she picked up her head. "Hi." A euphoric smile greeted him.

He rubbed his moustache to conceal his relief. "Hi, back."

"How was your day?" she purred as she spread lotion on her hands.

He wanted to take her upstairs, then and there, and make her purr some more. "Mine was okay, but yours was—"

"Great. Thanks to you."

The sultry voice rippled through his nervous system like a storm surge.

"Me?" He stepped closer, opened his arms to receive her.

Pressed against him her arms coiled around his neck. He kept his lips loose in order to fully absorb the sweet pressure of hers. Air, heavy with chocolate, mingled with the soft scent of her lotion. He'd never be able to eat chocolate again without thinking of her kisses. Adrenaline rifled through his system, making every muscle prepare for her touch. He raised her off her toes, taking over the kiss. Bruising, even to his own lips, his kiss met with no resistance, only more softness, and a heat that rolled over his skin and nestled in his belly. What would it feel like to be greeted every day like this? To begin the day making love and then knowing this ecstasy waited for him?

Bells sounded, followed by the slam of the door. A throat cleared, and cleared again.

He should have locked the damn front door.

He eased away from her lips then slowly lowered her reluctant to lose the connection with her body. The instant he lost contact, he felt icy.

The throat cleared again. A kid stood in the

doorway, pulling at the collar of his hoodie. Cassie's eyes opened but she still hadn't noticed her guest. Her sparkling green eyes were focused on his lips reliving the kiss. Wide-eyed, she looked as awed as he felt.

"There's someone here, sweetheart." He grazed the side of her cheek with the pad of his thumb until her head turned.

"Oh, may I help you—Jessie!" Cassie smoothed back a few stray hairs from her face and tucked one behind her ear.

The lanky kid shuffled from leg to leg. His Adam's apple moved up and down, but no sound came out. He probably had a crush on Cassie and got an eyeful.

"You're here for the deliveries," she said, still breathless from kissing.

Jessie nodded. His head disappeared inside his hoodie. A well-worn sneaker toed the floor. "Yes," he squeaked, and burrowed deeper into the hoodie.

"I have three, but they're all nearby. If you can't handle them all, it's okay." Cassie spoke over her shoulder as she walked.

The kid remained rooted.

"I think Jessie can handle all the orders, right?" Evan offered.

Jessie's hood bobbed.

Evan remembered those days, when his arms and legs grew faster than the rest of his body. His grandparents never complained about his need to eat every two hours. In fact they found it amusing. He signaled for Jessie to walk into the store.

Cassie disappeared behind the checkout counter and reappeared hefting three large boxes. She added chocolate colored ribbons to the white boxes, carefully snipping the tips. "I appreciate the last minute help, Jessie." She handed him the addresses and some money. Cassie gave him a huge, grateful smile.

Snatching the slips, the kid's fingers grazed Cassie's. His eyes darted Evan's way, and he squeaked before replying. "Anytime, Mrs. Hamilton. See ya," said a deeper voice. Long arms easily wrapped around all the boxes and after one last peek at Cassie, Jessie left the shop.

Cassie locked the door behind him. A different smile appeared as she strolled toward the counter that Evan leaned against. He removed his hands from his pockets.

"Delivery boy?"

She quirked her head sideways and that unruly piece of hair fell over her cheek. "The pizza delivery boy from Franco's next door. I borrowed him." She re-tucked the piece of hair behind her ear and then grabbed his hand and pulled him through the kitchen doors. "I want you to try something."

Visions of sex on that stainless-steel counter bounced through his head. "Okay." The swinging doors slapped his back. Utensils and pans littered the small counter. Definitely no room for an on-the-counter quickie.

She turned and raised a platter of white shiny balls level with her chin. "I made these today. This is one of the few batches that I didn't ruin. Ya know why?"

"I have no idea."

"Because more customers walked in here today than all month." Carefully, she removed one of the white spheres off the plate.

"Is that so?" He stepped closer.

"Uh-huh. And they all knew a certain sergeant with the New York State Police." She raised one and stared at his mouth.

He opened and bit. "Hmm. Heavenly."

"Close. Divinity. It's my grandma's recipe, some sugar and egg whites and flavor. These are flavored with Bailey's Irish Crème."

First it liquefied on his tongue, then the mint flavor burst. His mouth watered and he found himself wanting more. "Any other flavors?"

"Black cherry and chocolate caramel, today." She held up another darker piece.

"Of course."

He swallowed it whole. "Mmmm. I think we need to celebrate your success."

He wanted to push everything off the worktable and sate his need, but settled for a kiss as a chocolate-flavored bomb went off in his head. He kissed her with all the emotion he felt tumbling forward. He devoured her mouth, every taste sweeter than the last. His crotch pushed against her belly to show her how crazy in lust she made him, how she intoxicated him better than any confection she could conjure up.

Something clattered to the floor, sending him out of his lusty haze. Her eyes twinkled like a kid on Christmas morning as she struggled for breath. "What did you have in mind?"

Give me a minute to choose, he thought. In three minutes he could have her up those stairs undressed and in bed. Her hand slid down his chest and the backs of her fingers grazed his erection. *Make that two minutes.*

Then he remembered the warrant. "Ever been to Turning Stone?"

"The casino in Verona? No, but I've always wanted to go there."

"Then get ready and I'll pick you up in an hour." He kissed her goodbye. The taste of sweetness lingered on his lips, with the promise of heaven to come.

****

Evan hadn't been gone five minutes when she heard a knock on the front door. Walking down the aisle, she noted all the gaps on the shelves. What a day. She needed to restock before she opened tomorrow. There were so many things she needed to buy for the store but her first purchase with today's profits must be a Christmas outfit for Heather. No longer afraid of Santa's lap, she pictured the smile on her daughter's face wearing a green velvet and lace dress. *If she could talk Heather into wearing a dress one more year.* Maybe if she added boots she'd agree. She had to keep planning that they'd be together soon, or she'd go crazy.

A shadow darkened the frosted glass window. Thinking Evan forgot something and returned, she punched in the code and flung open the door.

"Did you forget—"

A man entered as the chimes merrily sounded. "Hello, Sweet Thing."

"Daddy!"

Chapter Eighteen

Chad Martin plodded through the store behind her until she approached the checkout counter. He backtracked and looked around, surveying the area as if contemplating a purchase. Cassie found her stool and sat down. She needed a moment to recover from the shock of seeing him after six years with no phone calls in between, not even when she got divorced. He'd been at Heather's first birthday party. The years went by so fast.

His perusal also gave her a chance to study him. He wore a mismatched suit that had seen better days. The pants were too short. The jacket pulled at the seams. In one spot the thread didn't match. A tall, bulky man, her father was leaner than she remembered. He checked the price of one of her imported baskets as he stroked a short beard, then turned and winked.

The years faded away.

"Sure have a lot of fancy chocolate in here. What made you decide to open a candy store?" He strolled down to the end of the aisle toward the front door.

She raised her voice to answer not trusting her legs to walk yet. "I found Grandma's recipes one day.

I thought it would be a fun business... fill a niche... something this area didn't have and might be receptive to." Part of her wanted to run, hug him. Part of her held up a tinfoil shield.

"Good idea. Rich folks like spending money these days, showing off to their friends. Keep your prices high, they'll buy more." He stopped at a small basket of samplers, squinting a bit.

Probably still hasn't bought reading glasses. He needed those ten years ago. Stubborn man.

"You make all this stuff?"

She walked around the counter, finding her legs quite strong. "Yes. Those samplers are my own recipes. I fiddled with Grandma's to make unusual flavors like cappuccino and boysenberry crème." She hungered to hear his praise.

His smile didn't reach his eyes. "You were always a smart one. Too bad you were too crazy about Jake to use your brain."

She reared back and gasped. Tears stung her eyes.

He'd started to walk away, but stopped. "Excuse me, Sweet Thing. That was out of line. I know how much you loved that boy. Enough to follow him off to college with no job or money."

"Daddy—" Her hands wrung her apron until she heard a tear. The comment burst the small bubble of joy that had formed around her heart.

"Do you still love him? Is that why he's got Heather? Having money doesn't take the place of a good mom."

Relieved Jake hadn't told him about L.A., she hedged, "It's a long story—"

"Yeah. I figured. And you probably don't have the time to tell your dad about it because there's nothing I can do to help you, is there?"

She rearranged some baskets to make the empty spaces less obvious as she answered, "Daddy, it's—"

"No. No need to explain. I haven't been there for you in a long time. I messed up bad, didn't I, Sweet Thing? Is it too late for an apology?"

Mirror images of her own, his eyes met hers as he came closer. He put a hand in his pocket. For some bizarre reason she held her breath and flinched.

His shoulders slumped as he pulled a wrinkled brown paper bag from his pocket. "I brought these for you. It's kinda silly since you own a chocolate shop. You've probably outgrown them."

The bag tipped. Out tumbled a bag of Hershey's kisses, heavy in her hand. She blinked back tears. "I still eat them every day."

"That's my girl." His smile changed his face, reminding her again of the hero of her youth, her dad.

Her heart threatened to come up her throat. "Would you like to go upstairs and have a cup of coffee? Or, maybe you can stay for dinner?"

He looked around the room again, up at the ceiling and down to the floor. "No. Can't stay. I'm leaving town tonight. I'm starting a new job, selling insurance."

"Oh. That explains the suit."

His cheeks darkened. "Trouble is they're sending me to Cleveland for training. I told them it was no problem that I have the cash to get there but I'm a little short. I've gotta catch a bus."

Fifteen minutes later Cassie still sat in front of the open drawer of the cash register. Deep black grooves stared back. The three hundred dollar sale from the bride was gone, along with all the sales of the day and anything else she could spare.

She closed the drawer of the replica antique cash register. The *click* broke the silence. She glanced at her watch. Evan would be there any minute. She grabbed the bag of Hershey's kisses her father left on the counter and tossed them from hand to hand. Funny, no matter how hard she tried to keep the men she loved in her life, they always walked away. Another reason not to tell Evan about L.A. One more day of happiness, was that too much to ask? Then she'd force Evan to leave. Make up some story. *I'm planning to repaint my apartment... Oh, don't worry, I'm staying with Karen for a few days.* Not actually a fib. She'd grown sick of those ugly gray walls in her bedroom. Maybe lavender walls? And chocolate-painted walls in the kitchen would look lovely. After a year, the place began to feel like home.

Feeling better, she opened the counter drawer and placed her father's bag inside with her other bags of kisses. From the staircase she looked at her store one last time before shutting the lights.

The butterflies in her stomach felt at home, too.

****

A light rain fell in Syracuse, but the temperature remained well above freezing so the highways weren't icy. Evan drove with one eye on the highway and one admiring Cassie. Gone were the pale shades of vanilla and pink she favored for workclothes. Dressed in a red clingy top and black slacks, she looked sexy as hell. He'd meant to introduce the subject of her ex-boyfriend and broach the topic of her warrant before they arrived, but his brain cells were scrambled. Hell, after last night and that amazing kiss that left him lingering in a cold shower he had to remind himself what planet he lived on.

The Turning Stone visit seemed like a good idea this morning. He needed to stall the warrant discharge another two days until Porcelli returned to represent her, rather than have her take a chance with a court-appointed attorney. Although Turning Stone Resort and Casino was in the heart of New

York State the land was owned by the Oneida Indian Nation, with a separate legal system. When visitors arrived on the Nation's property they were in another country, and U.S. warrants were served only in extreme criminal cases.

So far no one from the courts tracked down the missing warrant. If his captain unlocked his office to retrieve the warrant he would be powerless to interfere with the servitude. Still, if Cassie didn't want to go to the casino, he'd find another way to keep her safe.

He glanced at his passenger. She'd been unusually quiet. He expected her to be in a good mood from this afternoon but instead found her waiting by the door in a big hurry to leave. Her lips didn't move when he kissed her hello. Rattled by her appearance he didn't register that something must have happened until he got on the Thruway.

"If you changed your mind about going to the casino say the word and I'll take you home," he said, noting her small frown.

She smoothed her pants and placed her purse on the floor. Then she released her seat belt and slid up next to him. A soft breast pressed against his arm as she kissed his earlobe. "I don't want to go home."

"Hey, put that back on. I can't drive with you unbuckled."

Much as he liked the feel of her tucked next to him, he nudged her back to her side. A healthy color appeared in her cheeks. Damn, he loved it when she blushed. His grip relaxed on the steering wheel. "When we get to the casino, you can get as close to me as you want." He slid another quick look at her and readjusted his seatbelt.

Sitting sideways in her seat but fully belted, she reached across the gearshift to stroke his arm. He liked the contact and the sexy look in her eyes and the fact that she couldn't keep her hands off him.

Concentrate for ten more miles, or they'd be pulling off into a parking area, or better yet, the blind from a radar trap for a quickie. Christ, then he'd really be acting like a lovesick teenager.

The next time they made love would not be in a tent or on the floor or in a car.

He sat up straighter. "Did something happen when I left? Did you get another big sale?"

Her jaw dropped open then slammed shut again. She hooded her eyes and his heart sunk fearing the worst: Stone contacted her.

****

"I was thinking of all the inventory I went through today," Cassie answered and leaned her head back against the headrest. Closing her eyes a distant memory came forward. The first time she found kisses by her cereal bowl and the bear hug and laughter when dad came home. For years after he'd abandoned them she fought her anger by eating kisses, a silent offering for his return.

Evan's fingers touched for hers. Like a compass needle finding the magnetic pole she laid hers inside his needing his strength. His thumb tapped hers in a secret code as he sped down the road.

"Any visitors?" Perceptive eyes darted to her face.

"Umm, a window shopper, that's all." The tapping slowed but his expression remained thoughtful.

Without her profit she'd been tempted to cancel. Her street was busy and she'd toyed with extending the shop's hours to see if she'd pick up some evening traffic. But when he'd pulled up to the curb and she spied him through the front window the first tingle of sexual desire beat a path to her core.

Now his rhythmic thumb taps amplified the sensation to her marrow. There was no turning back.

Tonight he wore black trousers, a charcoal gray

leather jacket, and a sexy smile. Funny, when she was married she'd thought he was another good-looking guy, and now, well, she couldn't think of one woman in the world she'd trade places with. The night of his deployment he'd been her warrior going off to battle. They were frenzied knowing little about each other except the need to comfort. Now she knew the man, knew his tender touch and his amazing power to make her soar in his arms.

And his endearing desire to protect her.

After last night she was certain they were beyond the friendship stage. As hard as she tried to fight it, he'd weakened her resolve. Maybe he'd be fair and not judge her based upon what happened in L.A. A kernel of hope had taken root inside her when he held her last night and whispered the many different ways he would pleasure her. He didn't allow her to sleep until he made good on all his promises.

To make love so thoroughly must mean something.

He glanced at her again. She'd learned by now how insightful those dark eyes were. His gaze penetrated and probed but didn't threaten. Knowing he was there and cared for her welfare made her feel so safe. She wanted to curl up in a ball next to him and listen to his breathing.

Those alert eyes narrowed. He sensed something. Should she tell him about her father? Would he understand?

He'd probably think she was foolish to give away all her money but she'd do anything for someone she loved. It was her money and for once no one told her how to save or spend it. At first, the responsibility of handling money on a daily basis frightened her, more so than when she sold multi-million dollar mansions and handled large escrow checks. The checks were her responsibility until deposited in the business account. Cashing out her shop's sales drawer everyday was very different. Finding she was good at handling cash and credit receipts had been a relief to a math-phobic. One day the heady realization came that she was dependant on no one. And the best part, she was on her way to getting her daughter back.

He glanced at her again, this time his eyes hooded but one corner of his mouth lifted. Maybe he sensed her arousal. Evan's instincts bordered on animalistic. His ability to hear or see things before she did surprised her. Or maybe he'd found out her secret. Her fear of discovery loomed larger every day. Maybe he'd checked her incoming calls and he noticed the calls came from L.A.

No, if he knew the truth he wouldn't be so relaxed. Her secret was still safe but her hands still grew damp.

How long could she keep it from him?

"You okay?"

She adjusted the seatbelt over her shoulder and pulled her jacket collar around her face. "I'm a little tired. I'll be okay."

His gaze left the straight road and assessed her again, twin brown pools that left her soft like meltdown chocolate. Her smile trembled, overwhelmed with longing.

"Turning Stone's up ahead."

In the distance, she saw a hotel tower silhouetted against the velvety black sky. He pulled into the long drive, past fountains. A huge boulder turned on its axis.

"Doesn't that monument have a special meaning to the Oneida's?" She stared at the oval bohemic as Evan drove around it.

"It's a symbol for the Oneidas. This venture represented a turning point for The Nation, in their cultural rebirth and economic independence."

Evan stopped the car by the hotel entrance. The valet opened the door for her. Curious to see the stone up close, she crossed the road to the small park. She heard Evan's boots and then felt his arms smooth over hers before wrapping around her waist.

"So much has changed lately," she whispered, half to herself. She listened to the spraying water and leaned back against Evan's chest. After a few minutes he turned her in his arms and placed a soft kiss on her lips. She gloried in the feeling of safety and offered a silent prayer as they kissed again.

"Ready to go inside?"

"I'm ready," she replied. The rebirth of strength and confidence hammered through her veins.

Inside the hotel, she pointed to a tall rock waterfall with real palm trees. "That wall is so cool!"

Evan touched her elbow and led her toward it. "There's lots more to see. Did you stay away because you don't gamble?"

"No. I like to gamble. Before I moved to L.A., I planned to come here with Karen but Heather had the flu. I wouldn't leave her with a sitter."

In a little while she'd call Heather and wish her, *sweet dreams*. Evan held her elbow tighter as they walked with the crowd, all headed in one direction. Toward the casino. She heard people talking, bells ringing in the distance. It took her a moment to notice they'd stopped before a fountain.

He pointed to the center. "Make a wish."

"I love wishing wells." She dug a fist into her small purse, fishing for change.

When she came up empty handed, Evan handed her several pennies from his jacket pocket. "This is a special fountain. Any wish is destined to come true."

She accepted the pennies. "Then I'll have to be very careful what I wish for." She threw three pennies into the fountain. He tossed in one. Their pennies joined the layer of pennies on the bottom.

"Do you want to try the slot machines first?" he asked. They'd walked into the first room, filled wall-to wall with flashing machines, bells and alarms, and people, young and old.

Excitement bubbled up her throat. "I want to watch blackjack and roulette."

"Why watch when you can play? You had a great day today." He looked at the purse she held close to her side.

Cassie felt her face heat. "I planned to pay some bills with that money. You go ahead. I'll watch."

Evan wore his cop expression.

Here comes the interrogation. Please don't ask me about the money.

Relief flooded her when he looked away and walked up to a blackjack table. Then he surprised her when he handed her a hundred-dollar bill.

He gestured to a vacant seat between an older man and middle-aged woman. "Play."

"Thanks, but I can't take your money," she said, stepping back.

He gave her a cool x-ray gaze, and smiled. "Lead the way then."

****

They wandered across the crowded, smoky, gaming floor. Evan's splayed hand touched the bare skin where Cassie's sexy, red top dipped in intersecting vees down her back. The front of the silky blouse fell in folds of fabric low enough to expose the tops of her breasts and a generous amount of cleavage. Fitted black pants skimmed long legs to her dainty ankles. Three-inch heels were in for most women, but Cassie wore black-and-white low-heeled sandals exposing her beautiful feet.

He half expected flip-flops.

He loved how her hair smelled like some exotic fragrance. She'd pulled the glistening blonde mane back in a tight ponytail tonight. The long length swished back and forth as she walked or rested between them when they stopped. It fell like a third hand over his heart.

Her earrings were gold ribbons that dropped from her lobes the length of her neck to tap her collarbone. He knew the taste of that spot. He couldn't wait to place kisses there again.

All eyes were on her wherever they walked. He smiled at the women who noticed. Never a possessive boyfriend, he found himself smothering several growls. "She's mine," he wanted to shout to one guy who gawked then followed her to the ladies room. The young stud made skid marks on the floor, reversing directions, when Evan walked up behind Cassie ending the attempted pickup. Delighted in his juvenile display of jealousy, her feathery kisses unclenched his jaw.

A couple of times they ran into other officers with dates. The first time, he tested her by introducing her as a friend. Her temptress eyes sparkled, but not in anger. One satiny eyebrow raised. "Friend? And here I thought we were on a date."

"Would you prefer I introduce you as my girlfriend?" he teased, and followed it with a kiss. To voice aloud that she was his warmed his insides.

Her smile made blood rush to all parts. He'd never wanted to please a woman the way he wanted with her. In return, she drove him wild with her little moans of pleasure and constant touches. All day he'd replayed the sounds in his ears, enough to make him forget about Stone and the warrant for awhile. He scanned the room without her noticing. Not easy when she glanced at him like he was her hero. His mind wandered into orbit.

"The poker room's not much further. Are you sure you don't want to play?"

She glanced sideways at him. Her face was way

to easy to read. "Oh, look! There's that game with the dice that they play in the pits." Her hand hooked his arm and pulled. "Let's go watch."

"Craps."

She looked at him with her mouth slightly open.

"It's called craps. We'll watch a bit, then you can try."

Her eyes didn't leave the table once. They darted back and forth from the boss to the dealers to the players placing bets. After about ten minutes of observation, she turned around. "It's a lot like Yahtzee," she said, her back to the table. Every guy playing, including the pit crew, tried to check out her ass. He placed his hands low around her waist.

He grunted and then whispered in her ear. "We have to keep our clothes on here."

An elderly woman walking by overheard his remark, gasped and rushed away. His face heated. Cassie burst into giggles.

****

Cassie tried to listen as Evan explained the crap game, but it took a Herculean effort while every brain cell clamored that he'd called her his girlfriend. Whether she was ready for this next step or not, it was happening.

"The game's basically simple," he said. Then he went on to say more.

"Okay, that's easy." He looked so great in that leather jacket.

"See that black disc?"

"The hockey puck?" she pointed and again every guy looked at her. Her cheeks warmed.

He smiled that sexy bedroom smile. "It has two sides, the black side says *Off* and the white side says *On*."

"Like a light switch."

Evan nodded and went on explaining the game. There were a lot of rules and her brain cells switched to gossiping about his sexy mustached lips when he spoke.

"You got that?" he asked. Another new expression, quizzical, but extremely sexy made her want to kiss him long and hard in front of everyone. *Nod your head to whatever he says,* floated up from some functioning corner of her brain. He smelled so good that she sniffed.

One brow quirked. "No questions?"

"Is there more?" Why did she have so much trouble hearing?

"Mostly the different ways to bet but you've got the basics to start playing. Here, take these chips and go up to the bar and place a chip on *Come.*"

Come? Her brain cells uncorked like a magnum of champagne. "What for?"

"'Cause the point has been established." He chuckled. "You'll get your own point."

Whatever. Cassie leaned over and tossed a chip on *Come.* "Why is that one man in the middle staring at me?" she said to Evan.

Evan whispered in her ear. "He's the boxman. He sees everything."

She liked the delicious tingle of his breath on the shell of her ear. She whispered in his ear hoping it would have the same effect. "He's no longer looking at me."

"Yes, he is. Every guy in the place is looking at you."

She looked at every guy. They were focused on the game. Evan acted paranoid a lot.

"Eight-the-hard-way," said the man wearing a tuxedo shirt and holding a bamboo stick. He openly stared at her.

"What's he do?" She pointed, and the man grinned.

"The stickman controls the dice. He's waiting to see if you're joining the game," Evan said and trailed his fingers down her back. A tingle traveled to her toes. Then he handed her some chips and pointed to a spot on the table. "Now, lets hope the shooter rolls anything but a seven. You win on a roll of eight."

"Seven, all bets off. New shooter," the stickman said and looked expectantly at her. Then he turned over a glass dish with five red dice and pushed them to her.

All eyes focused at her.

"What do I do with those?"

Were they a gift for playing?

Evan leaned up against her and murmured. "Pick out two. You're the new shooter."

Feeling everyone watching she selected two die and then rolled them between her hands.

"No!" Everyone shouted. Fumbling fingers nearly dropped them on the floor. Her face warmed and her mouth felt hot. Her ponytail slapped Evan's chest as she turned on her heel. *The nerve of him to grin while heat poured off her face.*

"Use your fingertips. Throw them against the cushion."

She picked them up, intending to throw them hard, hating that she'd looked stupid but everyone seemed to have friendly smiles, so she relaxed and lofted them.

"Seven. Win-ner!" the stickman shouted.

Several people cheered. Evan squeezed her shoulder.

She turned around. "I won?"

"Yep. Doubled your money." He pecked her on the lips and spun her around. The stickman pushed the dice back to her and nodded.

Like a dirty diaper she picked up the die. "Again?"

Evan's muscular arm snake forward and put some chips on the table. "Keep rolling."

"But don't they have to take the chips off the

table?"

His eyes narrowed. "Didn't you listen when I told you the rules?"

She was so embarrassed her arms blushed but then strong fingers massaged her neck until she looked up. "You're doing great," he said. "I'll tell you when to throw the dice until you get the hang of it, okay?"

The dice sailed and bounced off the curve. She braced for more stares but no one minded.

"Six," said the stickman.

"Is that good?" she asked, feeling the excitement of the crowd.

Evan picked up some chips and put more down on other numbers. "Yep. I'll tell you when to stop."

The stickman shouted one number after another, sometimes with words like *hard* or *yo*. Evan looked so sexy leaning over the table. His dark eyes sparkled like black diamonds whenever he looked at her. The pit was shoulder-to-shoulder with people placing bets, but all eyes followed her hands as she tossed again and again. It became eerily quiet. She lost track of time.

"Am I doing okay? I haven't thrown a *sex*, I mean, *six."* Several chuckles and grunts, made her cheeks broil. *I'm probably redder than these dice.*

"You're doing great." Cool lips skimmed her hot cheek. "No seven," he whispered.

She promptly threw a four and a three. Seven.

"Ohhhhhhh," could be heard around the table.

"SEVEN. You lose. New shooter," the stickman shouted.

She put her hands on her hips.

He had the nerve to wink. "What's wrong?" His grin was twice as large as when she'd started.

"What's wrong? I lost 'cause you whispered in my ear, 'Don't get a seven.'"

He pointed to the bar. "It's okay. I bet it."

She looked down at the chip bar and saw a long, long line of striped chips. "You won all those?"

"*We* won," he corrected and showed her a pocketful of chips.

Her arms flung around his neck and she laid a big kiss on those *sexy* lips. She didn't release him until she heard a low whistle. It came from the pit boss. "Had a nice run there, miss." He nodded and then turned his attention back to the game.

Evan lifted her throwing hand and kissed every knuckle. "Come on. Let's go to the Diamond Shop and buy you something nice."

She hesitated. "Do you think I could have the half the money instead?"

His expression darkened. *Here comes the interrogation.*

He lowered her hand and took a deep breath. "Let's go to the lounge. There's something I need to tell you."

"Tell me what?" she began, and stole a look over his slumped shoulder. No, it can't be! All her breath stole from her mouth as she screamed.

"It's him! Over there! The man from the cabin."

Chapter Nineteen

Evan looked in the direction Cassie pointed. The back of the man's head was visible.

"Stay here. I'll be right back."

He took off in a dead run. The large, boxy man wore a dark plaid jacket, easy to track as he maneuvered around startled patrons. At the cabin Stone wore a baseball cap. This guy had thinning hair and a bald spot. For a wanted man his quarry moved slowly. Evan tried to recall more details about Stone. He didn't remember a limp either. Maybe one of his shots in the woods connected.

Closing in, Evan shouted, "Stone!"

A crush of people turned around and stared at him. He thought about drawing his gun but some event let out from the showroom. Too many innocent bystanders. The massive man moved toward a back exit to the parking lots. Evan raced toward the figure at full speed. Less than ten feet ahead, the man slipped something small and black from his jacket pocket, turned and aimed.

****

Stopping once to fling off her shoes, Cassie kept Evan's tawny hair in sight. The fleeing man leveled something at Evan.

"No!" she yelled, stumbling to a halt. Holding her hands over her heart, she braced for the bang.

Evan jumped the man who had the same refrigerator build. But his face didn't look the way she remembered. No gunshots fired, but she thought she saw blood. "Evan!"

Evan released the struggling man. "I didn't take anything. You can check. This is mine," twanged the man. Not the evil voice that would live in Cassie's memory.

Evan head twisted over his shoulder. Barefooted, she skidded into his back. Her knees buckled and she reached for one leather-clad shoulder before she fell to the marble lobby floor.

He caught her around the waist. She moved her hands over Evan's chest looking for a hole in his shirt, or a trail of blood.

"Are you hurt?" She patted down his chest, growing hysterical.

"I thought I told you to stay behind."

Lines formed around his mouth and eyes.

"I couldn't," she cried.

"I'm fine," he replied, and turned the black object over in the big man's paw.

The big man fanned the black square in her face. "Hey, lady. This is *my* Diamond Card. Here comes my wife. She'll tell you. We're celebrating our thirtieth wedding anniversary. We don't want no trouble."

He handed the card to Evan, who'd showed his badge. He checked the card and looked sideways at her. The lines on his face deepened. He shook his head. To Cassie, he said, "You okay?"

"What's going on, Alfred?"

A short, stout woman in knee-high Uggs and a two-piece red suit bounded up to the big guy, followed by two security guards. "I can't leave you for five minutes. What did you do now?" The top of the woman's teased up ruby hair reached her husband's shoulder.

The man stooped over and held open his paws. "Nothing, Reba." He turned to Evan, silently imploring him for help.

Reba huffed when Evan showed his badge. "Look, I'm sorry to have bothered you. We—I—thought you were someone else. Have a nice anniversary." He hauled a handful of chips from his pocket and handed them to Reba.

Flashing her Chiclets-sized front teeth, the little woman accepted the chips. Satisfied, she hooked her husband's arm and entered an open elevator.

Evan eached for her and she rushed between his arms. "I saw you fall and I—I thought you were dead!" she said, burying her head in his shoulder.

When another set of elevator doors opened, he pulled her inside and up against the wall. Green buttons flashed and the elevator moved. Her stomach tumbled as his mouth covered hers in a bruising kiss. She opened her mouth and his tongue pushed inside, searching for its mate.

The elevator doors reopened and he grabbed her hand to lead her around an ornate table with a large purple and orange centerpiece into a long corridor.

"Where are we going?" she said breathlessly. Her pounding heart felt ready to burst from her chest. Dozens of hotel doors whizzed by. Her excitement peaked.

Evan stopped and checked up and down the hall, then leaned her up against the wall opposite a painting of a mother and child and deluged her mouth with kisses. His thickness pressed into her belly making the throbbing between her legs increase until a pinging sound rang in her ears.

"This way." He grabbed her by the wrist and turned a corner, then they were running again.

As she ran double time to keep up with his strides, shoes flapping by her side, she stumbled around a forgotten dinner tray. He took a breath then picked her up and continued even faster. At the end of the hallway he halted, shoved a black card into a door slot, kicked it open and carried her inside.

Deep-piled carpet tickled her bare toes. His jacket came off before the door snapped shut plunging the room into darkness. Casino chips clicked like a round of applause, spilling from his pockets.

She strained to see but it was too dark. A distant door slammed shut and a shower ran in the room next door. The smell of Evan's cologne grew stronger. Fingers touched her neck as he unbuttoned the back of her blouse. Cool air touched her freed breasts but his warm lips on her nipples caused her to shudder with anticipation. She was moving again. This time he guided her deeper into the darkened room, only stopping to open the zipper on the side of her pants. They slipped down her bare legs.

All that remained was a dewy, black thong.

She peered into the darkness trying to make out his shape, eager for her turn. Twin table lights flicked on, momentarily blinding her. When her vision adjusted she faced a king-sized bed. She turned and found him standing behind her.

Large and handsome and all hers.

He'd removed his shirt, exposing rows of muscles and tanned skin. He tossed his wallet onto the bed while desire guided her hands to undo his belt and zipper. When the fly to his pants parted she freed him. His hiss of pleasure sent forth an unexpected sense of tenderness. "Cassie, what you do to me," he said, leaning into her hands. His voice was so strained that it shattered the last threads of resistance in her heart. She teased, touched and explored the thickness, loving the velvet feel of his warm skin, wanting to make him equally crazy with need.

He kicked off his pants and wildly resumed his kissing, trapping her hands between their bodies and crushing her breasts against the wall of his steel chest. She took short breaths as his arms banded around her. He broke her hair tie, freeing her ponytail. With hands fisted in her hair he maneuvered her backward against something cold. She gasped. Her body had caught fire against his, but her back became so chilled goose bumps rose on her arms.

"I've been waiting for this all night," he rasped. "You nearly made me crazy down there." His open mouth came down on hers for a heady kiss, that left her lightheaded. His tongue darted in and out of her mouth, pausing only to add more praises: *God damn sexy... Made for loving... All mine tonight...* Then his hand pushed aside her thong and his fingers probed. She bit his lower lip lightly as he fanned his fingers, bringing her close to orgasm but she fought it, wanting him deep inside her when she came apart in his arms.

A new desperation enveloped her. Desperate to feel his body above hers. Desperate to release her from every fear and heartache. Desperate to make them one.

She brushed his fingers away and positioned him at her opening. "Now, Evan."

"Not yet," he said.

He stopped kissing her and laid her on the bed. Then he found and opened his wallet. Her chance to look at what was so cold against her back. The cold wall was actually a enormous framed mirror. Feeling like a goddess on the golden duvet she stretched seductively.

Watching her in the mirror, his eyes burned like

black coals.

Foil ripped and her pulse kicked. He handed her the condom and knelt before her. She licked the tip of the condom and then slowly rolled the thin material down, teasing his straining flesh with her fingers. One hard squeeze of her shoulder was his only indication of the torment she inflicted. Heady with the knowledge of the power she wielded over this warrior, she wondered how mindless she could drive him. But as soon as she removed her hands he hauled her off the bed and back against the mirror. Urgent kisses stole her breath. She fought to match his. Never had she wanted more to be possessed. A moan of surrender ripped from her throat as he lifted her legs around his waist and positioned himself. So ready for him he easily drove into her. She took his entire length to his base. Slick coldness from the mirror cooled her back as he steadily pumped into her, massaging her inner walls, turning her insides molten.

"Christ, I want you so much," he breathed between kisses. He alternated kisses with strokes keeping her off balance with sensations. Ripples of pleasure built as he raked all of her tightness until finding the spot that drove her wild. Whimpers replaced her moans. Bit by bit she was falling to pieces.

He changed the angle and drove upward, pumped faster. Absorbed in the sensation, she didn't open her eyes until the first pulse started. Words weren't necessary. He knew. In his eyes she saw fierceness coupled with a conquering smile that she'd never seen before.

She liked this Evan.

"Damn," he whispered on her lips. "You okay?"

Nod.

She gripped his shoulders to keep from falling although it was unnecessary. His look softened, hinted at a smile. Her heart tumbled over.

Each raking thrust sent her to the edge of sanity. Without mercy he continued. Her legs tightened around his waist, until they turned to rubber.

"You ready to come, babe?" he whispered.

"Oh, yes."

He sent her spiraling upward, and when she thought she'd never reach the crest, she went over. A liquid heat pulsed over and over as she hung on to his arms, unsure where she'd end up. By the sound of his curses, he'd followed her. Weakened, but thrilled, she was barely aware of where he set her until she saw the golden covers. While basking in the afterglow, in an amazing feat of stamina, he moved his hips in time with her breathing. In the mirror's reflection, she admired his naked back and taut behind. What a sight. Tight muscles rippled with power. Power he carefully controlled, despite the desperation she glimpsed in his eyes. To see better, she moved her head over to the side so she could watch. She was spread naked on the bed. Her lover above her. She hung off the edge of the bed supported by his hands around her hips to keep her from falling.

Her body blushed pink.

Evan looked over his shoulder. "Want a better view?"

He pulled out of her, his erection proudly jutting forward. Then he set her on her feet, facing the wall-size mirror. He stood behind her.

"Watch."

His one word thrilled her close to another orgasm. His thick arms snaked around her waist, one hand headed for a breast, the other between her legs. In unison, they played with her body. He looked over her shoulder, concentrating on the task, pausing to nibble on her collarbone when she lolled her head to one side. Already master of her body, fingers of one hand plucked at her nipple and the other fingers moved rhythmically in and out. She couldn't take her eyes off the mirror, loving how he touched her like she was a precious object.

"This is making me crazy," he grated. "Lean forward. I need to be in you."

A warmth of emotions spread through her from her tummy to her fingers and to her toes. As he assisted her movement, he tenderly touched her skin like she would shatter, a type of reverence reserved for the mind of poets and artists. When he feathered a kiss up her neck, she felt more cherished than Francesca in Rodin's *The Kiss*, eager for surrender.

And she'd gladly surrender not only her body, but her heart.

If he'd have it.

****

Evan dozed and woke up feeling fantastic. Cassie cuddled next to him, sound asleep, and looked so beautiful lying on her stomach. *We really knocked each other out*, he thought, gliding his knuckles down her spine and moving behind her. He leaned over her and kissed her from shoulder to shoulder. He kneaded her bottom until she stirred, then parted her cleft and positioned himself against her slick core, needing to be inside her like he needed oxygen. He surged forward and thought he'd die from the sensation. He'd never felt such an insatiable urge to be with someone. Entering her slowly he memorized every gasp and sigh. He stayed fully inside her, rocking against her cervix until they both climaxed. Fighting for air, he spied his own smug smile in the mirror. "Got any more positions?"

Cassie rolled out of bed and faced the large mirror. She stretched her arms over her head and swayed to imaginary music. He leaned back against the headboard, crossed his hands behind his head to enjoy both views of her naked body in the reflection. She raised her hair off her neck and slowly gyrated her hips, watching her movements in the mirror. He could look at her for hours and never be bored. *Years.*

Her forehead wrinkled as she tapped the mirror. "When did you get a room?"

"Earlier."

An eyebrow lifted. "That sure of yourself?" She started moving her hands over her breasts, caressing and squeezing and kneading them.

His tongue settled like a lead sinker in his mouth. Every muscle, including those in his throat, locked like invisible hands strangling him. Gale force heat poured off his body. She snuck a look at him and then raised her breasts to the mirror like an offering. Nothing but a hot breeze escaped his throat.

"This mirror is unusual. Are they in every room?"

Her body resumed the gyration. Afraid to break the spell with words, he forced air through his teeth. "Most." She tossed her hair over her shoulder and he sat up, eager to see what she'd do next.

She turned her head this way and that, an inscrutable look on her face. "It makes the room look twice its size." Delicate fingers trailed down her ribs, dipped into her navel and continued downward. The fingers disappeared between her thighs and her eyes closed as she touched herself.

In a blink his blood quit his head and rushed to his cock. "I don't think that's what they had in mind," he said robotically. He moved to the edge of the bed, encircled her waist, and planted a kiss between her shoulder blades.

Her eyes turned a glassy green color as he kissed lower. "Grab another condom," her thready voice whispered.

She knelt between his legs, and reached for his face. Her kisses circled his mouth, careful not to touch his lips. Her scent filled his head as she trailed her tongue down his neck and veered down the side of one collarbone. She circled a nipple with her teeth, bit gently, and air whooshed from his lungs. Anxious for her lips to move lower, to where his body throbbed for her attention, he struggled for patience.

This was her show.

A lock of her long yellow hair rested on his knee. He relished watching her spend time kissing every rib, and when she put her tongue in his navel, he fell back on his elbows and sucked in his breath. She kissed every abdominal muscle he'd spent a lifetime abusing. Once again, he thought of how his whole life changed direction in a week.

More blood rushed to his cock as her breasts settled on it.

When her licking brought her above his cock, she sat back on her heels and looked up at him. He brushed his hand over her cheek and touched his thumb to her mouth. She opened her mouth and sucked his thumb. Using both hands to pull at his cock, she treated his thumb to the same rhythm. His breath hissed between his teeth. Then, she released his thumb. He held the next breath as she cradled him and took him in her mouth.

"Slow down," he grated with the next exhale ripping apart one cell at a time.

Her hands joined her mouth in torturing him.

"I mean it."

He squeezed his eyes shut, fighting the urge to spill himself.

She stopped and looked up at him. "Can't take it?"

Oh, he could take it. He might die, but he could take anything she imagined. At least he thought so until she took him deep in her mouth, and then he did die. When he opened his eyes and could breathe again, he pulled her away.

"That's enough." He lifted her onto the bed and plunged into her so hard she slid up to the pillows.

"Ohhh, Evan. That's so good I can hardly stand it."

With the last of his strength, he threw his body into a few more deep strokes, every muscle straining until they gave out.

The feeling was so amazing. He never wanted to make love to anyone else.

Oh, God. He'd forgotten the condom.

Panicked, he rubbed his hands over his face. He tried to sit up, but she sighed and wrapped her arms around his neck. Velvety, vanilla-scented skin snuggled closer. Her heat seeped to his marrow. He never bought into the whole romance thing, and as a true skeptic, never believed passion could soothe his battle scars. But the ghosts that shadowed his every waking moment were vanquished when he was with Cassie.

He stroked her back, let out a pent up breath, and closed his eyes. No images of war. Only new fantasies of Cassie, like making love to her in a warm, Caribbean-blue sea. Walking along some isolated sandy shore hand-in-hand as they watched the sunset, or maybe one of the volcanic black, sandy beaches of Hawaii. He'd gone there once, alone, after Iraq, had a shitty time, even contemplated throwing himself in a lava flows to feel warmth again.

Still shaken, but needing more contact, he rolled her until she draped her over him. He opened his mouth to tell about the condom, but a tremor racked her body.

Warm tears fell on his chest. "When I was in L.A., I met the wrong man," she whispered. He forced his hand to keep moving down her back, silently encouraging her to continue.

"He was the kind of guy that had it all—looks, money, connections. I was fascinated. He talked constantly about anything from sports to politics to art, even religion. He always seemed to have an audience whenever I'd see him at parties."

"One day we were introduced. The first time I met him, he said he was going to make me a star." She lifted her head and looked into his eyes. "But those schoolgirl dreams were gone. I had Heather to think about. Mac, my stepfather, said I took to real estate 'like I was born to sell,' and I was on my way to a successful career. Heather and I were so happy."

Evan met her wet gaze. "What happened?" His fingers curled loosely around her arm, but inside his guts coiled.

"I refused to see him. But, that only made him more determined. He called a lot, sent me flowers, tickets to movie premieres, or Lakers games. I returned the jewelry. After he threatened to ask me out on a theater marquee, I gave in."

One flash of those green eyes and any man would be haunted. Obsessed. As she spoke, a sharp pain began to form in Evan's chest. Now it felt like an axe wedged there. It hurt to breathe.

She watched a finger as it circled his nipple. "He treated me the way I always dreamed of being treated. Spoiled me with gifts, and attention. He phoned constantly and was kind and understanding. I could talk to him about anything..." The saddest green eyes glanced at him before she averted her gaze and cuddled next to him.

She'd never mentioned *loving* the man. He filed away that information with more relief than he thought he required.

She sat up, put some space between them. The sheets twisted beneath her fists. She sniffed and wiped her eyes. "One day, well, it ended badly. I didn't handle it well and I lost Heather in the process." Her shoulders slumped, and her green eyes held that faraway, bruised look.

He pushed her hair away from her face until she looked at him. "Would he try to kill you?"

She buried her face in his chest. "No! I—I can't believe he would—"

"Shhh. It's okay. Tell me his name so I can check him out."

Wetness spread over his chest. Her teary eyes implored him to understand. "Dylan. Dylan Black."

He caressed her face and used his thumbs to wipe her tears. "Do you have anything of his? Maybe a gift he gave you?"

All the color left her face, even her lips. She swallowed and then said, "I threw out everything he gave me."

The axe pulled free of his chest. He banded his arms around her waist, happy she'd trusted him with her secret.

"That's okay. I'm glad you told me about him." He gave her a soft kiss. Then another. His kisses turned urgent. He sensed there was more to the story but was confident she'd tell all soon. He flipped her on her back, and dried the last of her tears with his kisses.

Her trust was everything to him.

He couldn't tell her so he decided to show her.

Chapter Twenty

The next morning, Evan woke up to someone tracing his abs with something sharp. It didn't feel like torture; he could move his hands and feet. Was this some new trick to get him to break? His first instinct was to put the person in a headlock and escape, but he hesitated. A yellow-haired angel looked down at him, and her nails circled his navel. "You're back. Took you long enough to wake up," the angel said.

Thank God he'd held back.

He'd intended to sleep in the chair.

He tried to get up and walk off the adrenaline pouring through his system, but she began to kiss his face. The kisses were so light, so opposite of torture that he wanted to cry with relief. Instead, he wrapped his arms around her waist and deposited her on his chest. "I thought I told you to stay there."

His voice came out sore-throat hoarse. She looked puzzled, so he ran his knuckles down her spine and lifted her bottom over his erection. Easing him inside her, she sighed. "Good morning," she said, between long, wet kisses. She rose and stretched.

His hands trailed up her stomach until he cupped under her breasts and his thumbs parted her cleavage. "That's more like it," he said, and rolled his hips beneath her, not in any particular hurry to do anything but watch her eyes shining with passion.

"Need a backrub?" He massaged her breasts until the nipples pebbled.

"Are you offering?"

"Unless you want to try out the Skana Spa. They have a couples' massage room with a shower."

She brightened. He'd love to photograph that smile and look at it all day. 'Course, she'd have to be wearing clothes. He reached for his cell to use the camera function. Maybe one picture. "It's not Hershey's syrup, but we can go there next." It came out like a joke, but he realized he was dead serious. One more Cassie fantasy he was determined to fulfill.

Last night, he'd clicked off about a dozen from his list. She welcomed his every touch and suggestion, and he accommodated a few of hers, like sitting up with his arms spread wide clutching the headboard while she rode him.

He took the picture and showed her.

"What are you gonna do with that?" Even the tone of her voice changed since he'd found her in Lake Placid. No longer hollow or stilted but more playful, the way she used to sound, only better. "Let me see that." She took the cell from his hand and then aimed at his face. Her hand drifted lower, down his chest to his—

The cell phone rang and Cassie flinched in surprise.

Should have left it on vibrate.

One slender blonde eyebrow rose as she read the caller identification. "Dawn?"

Christ.

Cassie flipped open the phone. "Evan's phone,"

she said cheerfully.

He needed a great excuse as to why Dawn would call this early, but he blanked.

Cassie smirked. "Yeah, it's me, Tony."

Heat rolled off Evan's face, and he tickled her side until she yelped. She'd pay for that little gag. His sex-fogged brain cleared, followed by a chill that started at the base of his spine. A 7:00 A.M. call from Tony meant big trouble. Or, maybe good news, like they'd caught Stone. He let her keep talking while he unlocked his jaw.

She grinned at him. "He's right here." She kept listening to the phone and nodding. "Yeah, things are going well. Stop by the store sometime. I'll give you a sample of the Italian kisses— *bouche*, as they say in Tuscany."

Evan motioned for the cell phone. She said bye to *Romeo,* and sat on the side of the bed, facing the mirror. Between her naked image in the mirror and her teasing kisses down his back, he was so distracted he nearly missed Tony's remark.

"Time's up," Tony bellowed, "Captain's pissed. He gave me the warrant. You still at Turning Stone?"

Evan shut the cell phone with a loud snap. He watched her thread fingers through her hair. As much as he hated to admit it, after last night's mix-up, maybe Cassie was safer in jail until they found Stone. He faced her. "We have to leave."

She didn't ask why. Instead, she grabbed her clothes and exited the bathroom about ten minutes later, face scrubbed and her hair pulled back. So beautiful. And innocent. He had no idea what to say when they got in the car.

After a few minutes on the road, he stopped at a drive-thru coffee shop in Vernon, picked up a quick breakfast, and then headed down Route Five. A longer drive back to Syracuse, but at least he'd avoid

Tony or anyone else on the Thruway.

"Did you find the stalker?" They'd been driving about ten minutes. An untouched chocolate chip muffin sat on her lap. Her coffee cup was drained.

He should have figured that she'd draw that conclusion. As hard as he tried to school his face he probably looked concerned. His stomach couldn't handle even a sip of coffee. "No new leads. We have a different problem."

"What?"

They were at a stop light. He looked at her. "You."

Her brows lifted and she switched her ponytail over the other shoulder. "What about me?"

Christ, he hated to dump this on her after what they shared last night but there was no other way out. He signaled and pulled the car into a strip mall. He parked and unbuckled his seat belt. "There's no easy way to tell you this." He paused. He hated that look of uncertainty on her face. "Tony has an arrest warrant from Orange County with your name on it. The warrant is for the embezzlement of a hundred-thousand dollars."

Hundreds of prisoner interrogations had taught him to fasten his gaze to her face for the telling initial reaction. Loss of eye contact, eye twitches, blinking. Her jaw dropped, then her eyes widened. "What? What are you talking about. I never stole any money from anyone in my life!" In her anger she'd slid halfway across the front seat.

He studied her. She stared boldly. Either she was telling the truth, or she was a good liar, an actress.

"I need you to think hard. Who would make up such a tale? Out-of-state arrest warrants are hard to fake. Someone must have proof of missing money."

As soon as the words left his mouth, he knew he sounded accusatory.

Blank, lifeless eyes stared at him.

"I'm not accusing you of anything, but this is serious."

One eyebrow lifted, the corner of her mouth trembled. "How long have you known about the warrant?"

"That's irrelevant."

Delicate white fingertips that he'd so recently kissed gripped the dashboard. "When were you planning on telling me? After we made love again?" Her voice shook.

Shit. He didn't want to brush her off, but they didn't have much time. "I didn't plan on telling you until I found out more details, so you wouldn't be frightened. Did you ever deal with large sums of money?"

Her arms retracted and crossed over her chest. A large family hurried past, walking to their parked car. For a long minute she stared at the windshield, watching the father load the baby in a car seat, kids in the back seat and checking the van door was safely shut.

Evan feared he'd lost her trust, until her arms uncrossed. "I sold real estate with my stepfather. I dealt with large sums of money all the time. People gave us retainers, and we'd put the checks in a special escrow account until closing. My stepfather would never do anything illegal or fabricate my stealing money."

His sigh of relief nearly rattled the car windows. "How long have you known him?"

"Mom's been married six years, but she's known him all her life. They were neighbors growing up." A sheen of moisture formed in her eyes and she chewed her lower lip.

"Okay. Did you meet anyone else with that kind of money?"

He watched her eyes as she hesitated. They said

yes. "Our clients had money but no one I would consider a friend."

She became breathless. Fear did that to suspects. She'd fail a dozen polygraphs with that tone.

But she didn't fidget with her hands, or squirm in her seat, only looked thoughtful. Unable to meet her gaze while she lied to him, he listened intently. "I knew a lot of people, business associates. My mother took me to the yacht club and introduced me to doctors, lawyers, actors."

She'd stammered on the word, *actors.* Her lips formed a straight line, as if zippering her mouth shut.

He pushed aside his need to comfort her and narrowed the distance between them. "Actors, movie people, they can be deceitful. Selfish, manipulative people who don't hesitate to hurt others to get ahead," he offered slowly.

Her face pinked. He was getting close. Her lower lip began to quiver and her eyes closed.

"Was your boyfriend an actor?" His voice became guttural, void of inflection.

Her head bobbed. "A movie producer. Dylan owns *Midnight Movies.*"

He noted her breathing, gauged her pulse-rate and waited for pupil dilation when she opened her eyes again.

"Sometimes a casual friend can get you in big trouble, trouble you had no part in but trouble that follows you wherever you run." He stopped speaking abruptly, waiting for her to confess.

"Did you borrow money from him?" He'd grown so still he stopped breathing.

"No. Can you do anything about the warrant?"

Bongo drums banged a solo performance in his head. She still didn't trust him. "You have a lawyer. The best."

Her breath swooshed out. She leaned against the door. For a moment, he thought she was about to jump out, but instead, she pushed down the lock and closed her eyes, shutting him out.

He passed a mileage sign for Canastota. From there, it was three hours to the Canadian border.

Insanity nearly took over.

Instead, he threw his jacket over her shoulders and sped the last ten miles to Syracuse.

****

"Tony will be here shortly," Evan informed Cassie while she rinsed and re-rinsed her teacup in her kitchen sink. "You'll have to ride in with him. He has to handcuff you."

Her towel drying paused. She'd taken a shower and packed up some things like he'd told her. Although they didn't let you bring anything to jail, he'd wanted her to have a fresh change of clothes ready for court. She hadn't said a word since the stop in Oneida. He needed to hold her, to kiss that scared look off her face, so he grabbed her as she brushed by him.

"No," she said and pushed his arms away.

He engulfed her in his arms.

"Yes," he said. In a heartbeat, he'd have traded places with her. She struggled, her head buried so deep in his chest he thought she touched his heart.

Wetness seeped through his shirt. "I didn't do anything."

Evan stroked her hair, desperate to comfort her. "I believe you."

Her head came up and twin green mirrors reflected the pain he shared. "Then why do I have to go to jail?"

He swallowed the lump in his throat. "The warrant has to be served. You have to wait in jail until your bail hearing. It should be all over in about an hour."

"Are you sure?"

He hesitated, wanting to spare her feelings but she needed the truth. "No."

"Is that why I packed a bag?" She looked down at the small suitcase.

He drew her head back up. "Anything is possible. I don't know how much evidence they have in L.A. The judge may want to talk to the D.A. first. If he thinks you're a flight risk, he'll deny bail."

She stiffened in his arms. "What does that mean?"

"Don't worry about it. The best criminal lawyer in the area will be right next to you."

She pulled away from him and picked up the phone and gasped. "I need to talk to Heather but this early she's in school. We talk at least once a day. If she doesn't hear from me, she'll be confused."

"You can call her later," he said. "As often as you want. I'll see to it."

She dialed a number and talked rapidly. After a few minutes, she hung up. "Karen'll be here in about an hour. She's able to run the shop. There's a wedding order for Saturday." Her voice sounded eerily calm, but she wrung her hands until they reddened.

Thursday morning. Worst-case scenario, she'd still be in jail Saturday. He told her so. Her expression hardened. She looked like a beautiful porcelain doll, one that would break with the slightest touch. But his Cassie was made of sterner stuff.

"You're not going through this alone. I'll be with you."

Her chin rose and distant eyes gazed at him. She didn't believe him.

And he knew the worst was yet to come.

****

Evan watched Cassie's slender stiff back as she

walked down the center of the hallway, led by Tony. The jail was crowded with police officers and arrested individuals waiting their turn at lockup.

Don't look back. Show them what you're made of. I'm here, sweetheart. Keep walking.

If only his thoughts could transfer directly to her mind. She looked so out of place next to the scum sitting in chairs or smoking by phones. The handcuffs looked enormous on her tiny wrists. He knew that helpless feeling that swamped a person in cuffs. He prayed she'd forget the feeling quicker than he had. At least there'd be no scars as reminders.

Upon arrival, twice the normal paperwork. The time wasted ate away at his patience. In the field, there wasn't time for paperwork with a machine gun in your hand, only common sense and trust in fellow soldiers. She didn't say a word while being fingerprinted or searched. A female officer did that. Fists by his side tightened until his wrists cramped. He'd attack anyone else who touched her. Anger blurred his vision, anger directed at the situation, at the system, at himself. As soon as Tony served the arrest warrant, Cassie had stopped looking at him.

He'd let her down.

The lockup area at the holding facility loomed ahead, guarded by a large, gray steel door. The door creaked open, his signal to say goodbye. He stayed by her side as much as procedure allowed, but kept his eyes on the guard leading her. If Cassie looked at him sooner, she'd have seen the anguish that he couldn't mask.

"Goodbye," she said, in voice stronger than he felt. The pulse beating rapidly at her throat betrayed her anxiety.

His jaw unlocked, and he said loud enough for all to hear, "I'll be back soon."

She didn't answer and wore a lost, glassy-eyed expression.

The look would haunt him.

Desperate to hold her and kiss that wounded-puppy look off her face, Evan settled for squeezing her hand. It felt like holding a snowball.

"Don't worry," he mouthed. *If I could, I'd trade places.* Hell, he'd attempt murder to be locked up in there with her.

Her eyes shimmered but she didn't cry.

Then, the attendant pulled her away.

He wanted to roar at the injustice of Cassie behind bars. Sometimes this system sucked. He calmed himself and reserved his energy for plotting his next moves. First, he'd get her out of jail, get the charges dropped, and then he'd go after that bastard. Black would pay for all the pain he'd caused her. He didn't care if he had to go all the way to L.A. to dole it out. But where the hell would he begin?

Her eyes held his for endless seconds, glowing like emeralds on fire.

She turned away and the world went gray.

****

Evan paced in the parking lot. Tony watched for a moment, probably gauging when it was safe enough to speak. "She'll be okay, Evan. You got a lawyer for her?"

Tony's voice sounded as hollow as Evan's chest.

"Porcelli."

"He's the best. He'll get her out on bail." Tony didn't sound enthusiastic.

"He'd better. She's not going to stay here one more minute than she has to. I don't care how many favors I have to call in or judges I have to beg."

Evan began walking toward his rental car.

Tony frowned, looking like he wanted to add something, but put a hand on Evan's shoulder instead.

Evan's cell rang and he checked the number. Clay. He'd call back later. He pocketed the cell and growled. "Someone's setting her up."

"Or she's protecting someone." Tony's frown deepened. "Who would she go to jail for?" He took off his hat and scratched his head.

Evan rubbed both hands over his face and then answered. "Only one person. Her daughter."

"That reminds me, I got more details on the warrant," Tony began half-heartedly. He walked over to his cruiser, away from a group exiting the building.

Evan followed. "Go ahead, tell me." He squeezed his eyes shut tight to try to stop the sound of automatic weapons firing in his head.

"Says in the warrant her boyfriend has been calling her and trying to get her to give it back, claiming she took the money to buy a home and open a store. I've got the phone log of all his calls she received from L.A. According to the avadavit he filed, he had no choice but to go to the police."

Car bombs went off in his head. He rubbed his scarred palm across the back of his neck. "I don't buy it."

"Costs a lot of money to start a business," Tony warned and then added, "There's more."

"Go on," Evan said, turning away from Tony's cruiser.

"I did some checking. Cassie doesn't have a mortgage or business loans." Tony paused until Evan stopped and turned around. "She paid for the place with cash."

"She sold real estate in Laguna Beach. Commissions are large there." Evan shook his head again to try to clear the nightmarish blur of images—smoke-filled streets littered with bodies, children crying, soldiers wandering around in shock.

Tony's face paled. "You look wrecked, Ev. Go home and get some sleep. She'll be okay tonight. Nickelson's the guard on duty. He's got a daughter her age."

"She's not staying the night," Evan hissed.

Tony's eyebrows lifted. "Whew. How'd you arrange that? There's no court today."

It was like the full force of the IUD explosion hit him squarely in the chest. This time he didn't fly backward or wake up eating ashes. His mind whirled with images of Cassie.

He shook off the pain in his head and hurried to his car, shouting instructions to Tony. "Get a message to Cassie. Tell her I'll be back as soon as I can."

I've got to find a judge.

****

The smell inside the county jail, a mixture of stale smoke, raw gasoline and body waste, burnt Cassie's nostrils. The gasoline came from all the Meth lab arrests, quite the daily routine according to the guard. She tried to breathe through her mouth but she could never do that, even when changing Heather's dirty diapers. She took a full hit of the acrid stench, and gagged.

Further down the hallway, past occupied cells, the odor got worse. Banging sounds and curses filtered through the stench. Shadowed faces looked at her from behind bars. She couldn't make out any eyes, but could feel them watching. The hair on her arms stood and that creepy feeling galloped up and down her spine.

She walked faster in front of one dark, eerie cell, but lost her footing on the slick floor. An arm snaked between the bars. "Hey doll-face, let me help you." The face on the other side of the bars was unclear, but his breath reeked of smoke and alcohol. "Put the h-hooker in my cell, pig," he slurred to the guard.

Rising without any assistance she continued down the hallway where the lights were brighter. The cells she walked past now were empty. The attendant said she'd be alone, unless they arrested a lot of prostitutes tonight.

Arrested.

The first time she'd heard the word she thought Tony was telling someone else. She even looked around the shop to see if someone had walked in right after Tony, but it was too early for customers. Her mind instinctively blocked what Evan told her in the car until that moment. In a surreal blur, she'd ignored him and checked her daily planner to see what to make today.

The cell door clanged as the guard locked her inside. It was so tiny she began to struggle for air. It smelled worse inside her cell, like raw sewage. The floor was sticky and slippery in parts, so she carefully selected her steps to safely cross the room to the cot. Finding one reasonably clean spot, she sat on the edge of the cot. The mattress was as thin as a pancake and cold as marble. Feeble light came from the one ceiling light.

There were dark corners everywhere.

Dank chilly air stole Evan's lingering warmth from her skin. She wrapped her arms around her shoulders and wished she'd worn her long sweater. No, she wished for Evan.

He said she'd be there for about an hour. She hoped Evan phoned Karen, who'd be worried to death by now. Without her watch, she had no idea what time it was.

Dylan had gone too far this time, making up false charges about her stealing money to get her back to L.A. The man was certifiably insane, but obviously more powerful than she'd figured. He probably paid off some dirty judge to sign the warrant. It didn't take her any time to realize where he came up with a figure of one-hundred-thousand-dollars. The down payment on the mansion in Laguna Beach. Dylan wrote a check for that amount to her stepfather's real estate business. She put it in escrow but he probably neglected to tell the judge the deal fell through and he got the money back.

A master at manipulating people, he'd once bragged.

After last night she desperately wanted to unburden herself and decided to confess everything about Dylan to Evan. But this morning when he'd admitted he knew about the warrant and didn't tell her, she'd felt betrayed.

Was he doing his duty? First to protect her, then to find out information about the warrant because it was his job?

Her heart revolted at her mind's logic.

Not Evan. He cares about me. Trust him.

But her head had listened too many times to her heart and now she'd paid the ultimate price.

This trumped-up charge would be impossible to explain to any judge without proof. She'd returned the escrow check. Accountants would have to audit her stepfather's books to clear her, which would take time. She'd concentrated all her energy on Heather's return or she would have gone after Dylan sooner for his role in losing Heather.

She was breathing too fast. If it didn't slow she'd hyperventilate. She cupped her hands over her mouth. Something tickled her arm. Something large and brown and long legged. She knocked the roach off and shuddered as it scampered around her feet. It ran under her cot before she could stomp it.

Anger rippled down to her toes.

She was going to spend every second waiting for release figuring out a way to get back at Dylan.

Someone in L.A. must want to bring him down.

If the Orange County police wouldn't help her, then she'd sell her shop and hire a private investigator to find his enemies.

She wouldn't rest until Dylan paid for all he'd

done to wreck her life.

Tears stung her eyes. Hot air pushed up her throat. The more she tried to stop, the harder she gagged. With her sleeve she wiped her futile tears. No one would listen to her before when she tried to explain she wouldn't have allowed Dylan to baby-sit Heather. He'd lied to her mother and taken Heather before Cassie knew what happened. She didn't want to think of her baby while in this awful place.

How could she convince anyone of her innocence?

"You okay in there?" a voice whispered. Someone tapped the bars until she raised her head.

Fisting her hand over her mouth to hold back a scream, she murmured, "Yes."

The concerned look on the bulky guard's round face sent a frisson of warmth through her numb body. Handfuls of tissues extended through the bars. "You don't worry yourself. Evan will have you out of here in no time. This is a formality to make those idiots in Los Angeles happy."

Tilted sideways, the entire box of tissues came through the bars. She took the tissues and wiped her eyes. "Thank you."

The guard smiled. For a moment, something in his expression reminded her of her father. She blinked away a fresh drip of tears.

"I'll be here all night," he said. "If there's anything you need, yell for Nick. Anything. Even if you want to talk."

She sniffed and nodded.

"Lunch is coming in about a half hour. Evan's picking up food. You're a lucky lady to have him for a friend." His entire face smiled.

No way could she eat in this place. The burning pain in her throat prevented a reply.

"He's a good man. If he says you're innocent, then you are. Sometimes good people get mixed up in

things that aren't their fault. Judge will figure that
out."

"I hope you're right." She hiccupped rather than
sobbed.

"I've known Evan since he came to the force.
Young gun. Wanted to save the world, and he's still
trying. Gotta admire that. Some join the force and
get disgusted with the system. Too many criminals
walk these days."

She warmed at the thought of Evan's heroism.
"He's a good friend." Her hiccups prevented more
words but at least the tears slowed. A tremor racked
her body, but somehow she'd calmed down.

Evan believed her.

Muffled voices down the hallway distracted the
officer. He left without a goodbye. She appreciated
the company and the kind words. She forgave Evan
for not telling her about the warrant yesterday.

He didn't deserve her wrath.

Dylan did.

****

"What do you mean she can't see Novak today?
She's already sat in that stinking hole for three
hours." Evan slammed his desk drawer shut. The
desk shuddered along with everything on it.

Tony reluctantly poked his head further into the
office. "Sorry, Ev. Seems Judge Novak can't make it
back for one case. Besides, the warrant was for last
Monday between twelve-to-five. You can't ask for
any favors. He doesn't care you missed the date for a
family emergency. Judge Meyer's got a full load
tomorrow, but he'll squeeze her arraignment in first
thing."

Tony ducked out and shut the door.

Evan stared at the paneled door. He hated to go
back to Cassie with bad news. No way was she going
to stay in that jail cell all night alone.

He phoned Porcelli.

"Yeah. I got the news," Porcelli said. "Sorry, Evan. No time to look for another judge. If it was a murder charge or rape, we could get somebody. We're lucky to get her on the docket tomorrow. In these situations some people wait days for a bail hearing. And some stay months, waiting for the serving state's pickup."

Evan rubbed his neck. Like hell would he allow Cassie to wait that long. "All right. See you in court tomorrow."

"Stay cool. I'll get her out on bail. Course, if she's guilty—"

"She's not."

"Of course not."

The line was silent for a moment.

Evan held his breath.

"You might want to retain a criminal lawyer for her in Orange County," Porcelli said.

Evan's guts sank. He'd never be able to go with her to L.A., but he'd help her as much as he was able. "I want the best. Do you know of anyone?"

"I'll check on it. May take a few days. Let's see what happens in court."

The tightness in Evan's chest grew volcanic. He struggled for the next breath and the one after that. Pain radiated in hot spikes from the center of his chest to his arms. He sat in his chair and tried to meditate, find that kernel of peace inside him. The exercise helped him so many times in the past during battles and imprisonment but this time it denied him.

His cell rang. Mechanically, he answered.

"Hey. What's happening, amigo? How are you making out with the lady?" The humor in Clay's voice was loaded with subtext.

Evan cleared his throat. "I'm kinda busy now."

"Okay. I'll be quick. I remembered where I heard that name, Dylan Black."

"Go on." On his computer, Evan pulled up the file on Midnight Movies.

"He's bad news, man. Hasn't made any money producing movies in years but still has tons. Gossip around town says he's in with a drug cartel," Clay said.

"Fuck."

"Sorry, man," Clay replied.

"Thanks for the info. Gotta go." Evan squeezed the cell so hard, it cracked in his hand. Little fragments that he didn't feel stuck out of his palm. He closed his fist.

Porcelli better work a miracle. If the DEA stepped in, she'd either be part of the problem, or they'd want her as a witness to put Black away. Either way, Cassie stood to lose everything and he might have to stand by and watch.

He felt something warm on his hand.

Blood oozed from his palm.

For the first time since Iraq, he felt nauseous.

****

Hancock International Airport was no LAX, but Dylan wasted time searching for Stone. *If that weasel tries to fuck me again...*

"Hey. Black. Over here," a voice called from behind him.

"'Bout time. Where the hell have you been?" Dylan stifled the urge to smack the guy.

Stone took off his baseball cap. "Traffic's bad this time of day."

"Midnight?" Dylan snorted. "Forget it. Where's my room?"

"Downtown, like you asked. Ya need me for anything else? Otherwise, pay up."

Stone had more balls than brains. "Give me the keys." Dylan pushed past the bear of a man. "You'll get your money."

"You look beat. I'll get your bags," Stone offered

and then grabbed both bags.

Asshole. "If you'd taken care of things, this trip wouldn't be necessary." Dylan walked through the automatic doors. The damn car was double-parked. A yellow ticket waved in the breeze, but no cops in sight.

"As long as I get my money," Stone mumbled, throwing Dylan's luggage in the trunk of the beat-up Civic. Stone spent more time than necessary and Dylan suspected he was looking for money in his luggage.

Stupid idiot.

Dylan reached into the pocket of his jacket and handed Stone an envelope. "Here's half of what I owe you. When you bring me back to the airport in a few days, you'll get the other half."

Stone's mouth twisted but the jerk was smart enough to keep it shut.

Dylan looked sideways at the hulk of a man as he drove away from the terminal. Last time he'd use someone he didn't know for a job. Stone must have scared Cassie to pieces. Why didn't he kill that cop when he'd had the chance? The element of surprise was lost, or he'd have ordered Stone to try again.

His thoughts turned to Cassie.

Hopefully he could produce enough charm to get her to cooperate without having to resort to other means. One way or another, he wasn't leaving without her and what she'd stolen.

Chapter Twenty-One

Hearing heavy footsteps, Cassie jumped up and rubbed her eyes. It took a minute to recognize where she'd spent the night. Behind bars in a dank, fetid cell. How had her life come to this?

Evan showed up at the jail last night a little past six. He'd brought a game of checkers with Hershey's kisses but she didn't feel like playing. She even refused to eat any. Seeing the bag of kisses in his hands brought tears to her eyes but brushed them away before Evan noticed. He'd looked so worn out. She had to remain strong for his sake.

He moved two folding chairs together, and wrapped a new wool blanket around her so she'd be warm. She put her head on his shoulder and listened to his heartbeat, so strong and true. She dozed and when she woke up during the night, smelled him first and expected to be in the hotel room. Not expecting the interior of a prison cell, she panicked and jumped.

"Easy, easy. Come here." Evan pulled her onto his lap and held her tight until her shaking stopped. He whispered in her ear, words she couldn't make out but the cadence of his voice relaxed her.

Cocooned in his warm embrace, she wished he could hold her all night. Officer Nickelson had already said he was breaking procedure, allowing Evan in the cell. Evan said he'd take full responsibility. Officer Nickelson whispered something to Evan, locked him in with her, and then never came back.

After a long hug, Evan informed her the bail hearing wasn't until ten tomorrow. She wanted to protest but one look at the anguish in his eyes made her stop. He appeared as exhausted as she felt. So many new lines etched his face, lines that she'd put there.

How had she ever thought that face was made of stone?

****

Cassie looked better than Evan expected.

Tough lady.

"When I get out on bail, what's gonna happen to me?" she asked.

He bowed his head, fatigued to his marrow. Rubbing his eyes, he tried to brush the cobwebs from his mind.

Could she take more bad news?

Before he could get the words out, she read his thoughts. "They're going to take my business, aren't they? They think I used stolen money to buy the house and open the shop."

His eyes popped open and he stared into alert green ones. "The D.A. will put a lien on your checking account and notify the bank of a possible seizure of the property until this is settled."

She shook her head. "If I don't have money to buy supplies, I'll go out of business. I'll never get Heather back."

Her eyes were still red rimmed and he wondered how long she'd cried before he'd gotten back to the jail. "How could they do this? Don't I have any rights?"

Evan's head dropped. "You have the right to an attorney and you've got the best." Then, he looked her straight in the eyes. "Mr. Porcelli will want to know where you got the money to buy a house and start a business."

She got up and paced the room. "From the divorce. Jake was a resident and didn't have much money. His mom wrote me a check and told me to get far away from her son."

"Okay. We'll get a copy of the canceled check. That's a start. How much was the check for?"

"Seventy-five thousand dollars. I cashed it and kept the money in a safe deposit box here in Syracuse, in case I needed it quickly. The money I made selling real estate went for rent and living expenses in L.A. When I came home, I used most of it to buy the house and set up the shop. I swear I never stole anyone's money."

At last, some answers. Now he could help her out of this jam. "I know. I'll call Porcelli's office first thing and let him know. They can subpoena records of the canceled check from the bank."

She raked her hair away from her face and sat back down.

"Cassie. Think hard. Why would Dylan accuse you of stealing money?"

"Honestly? I think it's his twisted way of controlling me. He's been trying to get me to return to L.A. since my first week back."

"When was the last time you talked to him?"

She hesitated and then said, "Yesterday."

He heard the sharp intake of his own breath. "What did he say?"

"What he always says. 'Come home... I love you. Forget about Heather.' He knew I didn't get custody. It scared me. I'm sorry I didn't tell you."

All the ways he'd learned to kill a man with his bare hands went through his mind. "Is that all? This

307

is a lot of trouble to go through to get someone back."

Her lips trembled as she spoke. "I can't think of anything else."

His heart sank, followed by an icy numbness. He averted his gaze and pretended to look up a number on his cell phone. "If you think of anything, let me know."

She nodded *yes,* but her hollow eyes said *no.*

****

The courtroom smelled like fresh paint and lemon-scented cleaning products. The United States flag and New York State flag added strokes of color to the stark white walls. The low-nap carpet dampened the sound of footsteps of her lawyer and Evan as they found their places. Having heard a case prior to their entrance in the courtroom, the Judge was seated, looking grim and unfriendly.

But he wasn't looking at her.

"Before I begin, I'd like to address Sergeant Jorgenson," he said.

Evan left his seat and stepped up to the bench to face the judge.

"Sergeant Jorgenson, this court would like to remind you that only the most severe extenuating circumstances are accepted for a tardy arrest warrant discharge."

"Yes, Your Honor."

The judge turned to a laptop. Light flashed off his glasses as the pages scrolled down. Evan continued to look straight ahead. "Says here the warrant was to be served at nine o'clock Monday morning, October 12th. Is that correct?"

"I never read the warrant, Your Honor."

"Did you leave anyone in charge of the discharge of warrants in your absence?"

"No."

The Judge looked up from the screen. His face grew severe. "That's highly irregular and against procedure, isn't it?"

"Yes, Your Honor."

She looked around the empty court room, heaving a sigh of relief that Tony or Evan's men weren't in court to see the reprimand.

"Am I to understand you had an emergency that kept you away from all contact with your office?"

"Yes. A family emergency, Your Honor."

The judge frowned. "The next time, you will be held in contempt."

"Yes, Your Honor."

He'd known about the warrant for three days. She was the family emergency, and now he was in trouble. The thought of Evan losing his job because of her made her stomach cramp harder.

Evan didn't stay with her to get information. He'd been on her side. A rush of emotions made her lightheaded.

"I'm sure your supervisor will have more to say."

"Yes, Your Honor." Evan didn't glance her way.

Dismissed from the judge, Evan faced her with a grin that made the knot uncoil. He looked like a boy that had told the teacher the dog ate his homework and gotten away with it. She licked her lips, wishing she could run up and give the big hero a kiss. She envied his ability to deal with this situation. His dark, heated gaze riveted her until he took the seat behind her. It brought lightness to her heart, a strength and hope she never thought she'd feel again.

And something else she never felt before but was afraid to name.

Judge Meyers motioned her lawyer to the bench. They talked for some time. Someone read the complaint aloud. She picked out a few words. *Embezzlement...fraud...immediate return.*

Horrified, she concentrated on standing with her legs locked so she wouldn't collapse.

With the exception of her divorce and custody hearing she'd been in a courtroom only one other time, when called to jury duty. The room was so overcrowded with potential jurors then that she'd felt claustrophobic, and couldn't wait to be excused. This small courtroom was empty but the feeling of walls closing in crushed her chest.

"Your Honor, my client is not a flight risk and we request the minimum bail be set."

"Bail is granted until the marshal arrives for transport to Orange County for the trial."

The last words sounded in Cassie's head like a death sentence. Would she have to spend time in a jail cell again? Evan was the only reason she hadn't lost her mind last night. There was no way he could come to L.A. He'd arranged for her to phone Heather twice last night. No one in L.A. would do that for her. Where would she find the strength to fight this charge when everyone she loved was so far away? Her knees began to buckle. She leaned on the table to keep from falling.

Bang, bang, bang. The judge wielded his gavel, bringing her out of her miserable thoughts. Judge Meyer's voice rose above his hammering. "No one is allowed in this court. Bailiff, get him out of here."

"I have information about this warrant that will help the defendant, from the Orange County District Attorney," said a familiar voice.

Cassie began to shiver.

"Let's see it. And you are?"

"Black. Dylan Black, Your Honor."

****

Evan watched Cassie crumble into her seat. A dawning horror crossed her face when the judge mentioned she'd have to go to L.A. for trial. He saw the moment when the full extent of the trouble she was in hit her. He started to leave his seat to go to her.

310

Then, *he* walked in.

Dylan Black.

The bastard strolled down the aisle like he'd done so a million times. An actor playing a role.

Evan gripped the handrail of the bench until his knuckles turned white. *Creak.* The wood gave beneath his fingers. He couldn't wait to get his hands on the asshole. The guy played it cool, knew what to say aloud then lowered his voice and said something inaudible to the judge. He must have friends in high places if he knew where this bail hearing was being held. The notice only hit the dockets yesterday.

What's he up to?

Evan glanced at Cassie. Her shoulders slumped and she was deathly pale.

"If you look at page three, Your Honor, you'll see this was all a terrible mistake. An accounting error on the part of one of my associates." Black passed a packet of papers to the judge.

At the word *mistake*, Cassie's open mouth snapped shut. She shot to her feet.

Porcelli motioned for Cassie to sit down, then he approached the bench. "Your Honor, what's going on? Am I to understand my client has spent the night in jail for an accounting error? I request immediate dismissal of all charges."

Black smiled and adjusted his tie.

Judge Meyers returned to his computer and typed something. He looked down at Black's document and typed some more. It seemed hours until he turned to face the courtroom.

"Mrs. Hamilton."

Cassie stood. Color returned to her face and she gaped at the judge.

"The court owes you an apology. On behalf of the state of New York and the state of California, this case is dismissed. Bailiff, call in the next case."

It was over.

Evan let out his breath and reached over to hold her. Black cut in, his hand extended.

She swatted it away and grabbed Evan's hand.

His heart exploded with emotion. He wanted to pulverize Black's face as much as he wanted to cover hers with kisses. Instead, he shoved his hair back from his face and buttoned his jacket.

"I'd like a word with you, Mr. Black, outside the courtroom."

Black acted like he noticed him for the first time, shrugged, and turned back to Cassie. "There's something I need to tell you, sweetheart."

She ignored Black and rushed into Evan's arms. "Let's leave."

Black tried to pull her from Evan's arms. "Honey, wait. I came all this way."

Evan shot Black a lethal stare, one a SWAT sharp-shooter would be proud of, and held her tighter.

The sick bastard had the nerve to laugh.

Gathering Cassie by his side, Evan led her out of the courtroom.

Tony waited in the hallway, his forehead lined. "Captain wants to see you. Now. I've got a court appearance, but I'll find somebody to take Cassie home."

He'd gotten off easy in court. Not with Captain Young. He let go of Cassie's hand. Her look of jubilation faltered.

After a soft kiss on her cheek, he whispered, "I'll see you soon," then to Tony, "Don't leave her alone. And call Palmer to follow Black."

The courtroom doors slammed open and Black emerged. "Cassie, don't go anywhere until we talk."

Her mouth twisted. "You want to talk? Okay. I'll give you two minutes, then if you ever call again, I'll file harassment charges."

"Can I talk to you alone?" Black had the gall to act contrite.

The evil glare she gave him could have made a man drop to his knees and start praying for redemption.

Black began to babble. "Listen, honey. I'm sorry about what happened. I haven't been in the office much lately, and my new accountant found the discrepancy. He thought it was his job to report the missing money to the police without asking me. I tried to tell you on the phone, but you kept hanging up. I flew all this way to help you the only way I knew how. Come back to L.A. with me. I love you and I miss you, sweetheart. I can't stand being away from you any longer. Please come home."

Evan squeezed Cassie's hand, but pictured his fist rearranging Black's face. All he needed was five minutes in a dark alley, like the one behind the courthouse.

****

Cassie wanted to throw herself at Dylan's face, claws first. "You are out of your mind. For the last time, I don't love you, and I never want to see you again."

One corner of Dylan's mouth quirked into a smile that didn't reach his eyes. "I know differently, Angel. I know how much you love me. Maybe you need a little reminder. Maybe your boyfriend here would like to see how much you love me."

Dylan's enunciation of every word sent a chill down her spine. Memories of their last meeting in L.A. hurtled through her mind. Retaliation was his specialty.

He reached in his pocket and held up a black box. No—a tape. He scanned the room.

She started to sweat and felt faint. She raised a hand in protest. A cry of rage stuck in her throat.

Dylan gave Evan and Tony a chilling smile.

"Want to see my newest porn star?"

Movement in the hallway stopped. Uniformed people that had been passing by stopped to stare. The tape shook like a tambourine as Dylan turned around in a circle, a barker with his wares. All eyes focused on his raised hand. Then his wicked gaze returned to her.

In seconds a cold sweat soaked her blouse.

Evan released her hand.

Shooting pains seared her stomach as she watched Evan's reaction. First he stared at the tape, eyes narrowed. Then his gaze dropped to Dylan's face for long seconds, hardening like hot glass on a cold surface. Those same eyes found hers. The loathing in them made her step back. It didn't seem possible, but he no longer looked like the man who had held her in his arms in a jail cell all night promising he'd take care of everything. Harder than granite, his eyes condemned her with each breath that burned through her lungs. Her heart beat slowed and slowed and slowed. How could he hate her after all they'd shared?

"I take it you didn't tell your friend what you were *really* doing in L.A.," Dylan said. "Come on, let's go." Dylan's arrogant voice sliced up her heart as he stretched out his hand.

Several other uniformed men shook their heads, looked at Evan, and then hurried away.

Evan remained eerily silent, his face twisted in a mask of hurt and pain as he looked back at the tape then at Dylan. Tony looked horrified and began to pull Evan away by the shoulder.

Evan turned away.

He can't even look at me.

Brokenhearted and not wanting to cause Evan any further embarrassment, Cassie lifted her hand to Dylan's outstretched palm. He smiled savagely, grabbed her hand and yanked her down the hallway.

The opposite direction from Evan. Numbness tingled over her limbs but somehow her feet still touched the floor and moved her forward. Through a sheen of tears she glimpsed back once more to see Evan gesturing to Tony and shaking his golden head. Silently she implored Evan to look her way one final time.

What does he think of me now? Does he think I'm dirty?

Her face blazed with shame. Such a decent man, Evan wouldn't want her now, even if she told him the entire truth. Laboring for air she grasped her constricting throat with her free hand. She felt the loss of Evan with every cell in her body.

Evan, the man she'd come to love more than she'd ever imagined possible, hated her. She'd fallen hopelessly in love with him. Her heart knew she loved him from first time he touched her. And now she'd never see him again, never feel his strong arms around her, never hear another comforting word.

Never have a chance to say, *I love you with all my heart.*

It was a mistake to keep Dylan's treachery from Evan. Her mistake cost her the man she wanted to spend the rest of her life with, to have babies with.

Revenge was all she had left.

She'd go back to L.A. with Dylan, find his enemies and do whatever it took to bring him down. She didn't care how far.

Hopefully to hell.

Maybe the same district attorney who filed charges against her would listen to her story. She enjoyed a new respect for the police after meeting Evan. But she'd never find another person so devoted to helping her. A large gasp of air burned down her throat as acid rose to meet it. No time for tears. She needed a plan.

If she ever wanted to see Heather again, Dylan

had to be destroyed.

It might take years. Years apart from her baby? She choked on a sob. *Oh, why didn't she fight harder for someone to listen to her in L.A.?* Someone to watch the tape. At the time, all she could think of was running after her baby.

The courthouse doors opened and the bright sunshine blinded her. She tried to put her hand up to shield her eyes but Dylan grabbed them both with one large paw. Ironic that the sun shone brightly overhead while her world disintegrated.

"Finally, some sunshine. This place is too dark and gloomy. You belong in L.A., where the sun gives you color. You've gotten thin and pale. Good thing I came back for you."

While he rambled, Dylan opened a car door and pushed her inside, as if she were a suitcase.

"I've got two seats booked on a flight that leaves in a few hours. It's gonna be good to have you home." He reached for her and tried to kiss her. She slapped him away with all her might and bloodied his lip.

He swiped a handkerchief against his mouth and smirked. "I thought you'd be happy I saved you from jail. Once you're home, you'll come around. Who was that guy—your boyfriend? He didn't put up much of a fight for you." He sniffed and added, "cops on the East Coast are pussies."

She refused to be baited. He wanted information and she knew he'd only use it to hurt Evan.

Minutes later the car pulled into her driveway. Dylan knew her address, which didn't surprised her. He walked up the left landing toward her upstairs apartment. The wind kicked up, a shocking, frigid breeze. Indian summer was over. Soon, there'd be snow in New York. In her sweat-soaked clothes, she shivered as she keyed the front door. Inside the hallway she took her time climbing the flight of stairs and digested all that Dylan disclosed.

Someone here fed him information, maybe a private investigator. The guy who wanted the money?

The keys to her apartment shook in her hand and the entire set fell to the floor. Crouching to her knees, she knocked them away, stalling for time to think.

"Give me the keys. You'll never get the door open that way."

He selected the right one, turned the key hard and pushed the door open. She tumbled forward into her living room. He didn't help her up.

Moving past her carrying two pieces of luggage and her purse, Dylan disappeared into her bedroom. In the darkness of her apartment, her mind illuminated one piece of the puzzle. *Dylan hired the man who stalked her and then tried to kill her and Evan.* He wasn't taking her to L.A. He wanted her dead.

So why was she still alive?

With her cell phone out of reach in her purse running for help was her only chance. But if she took off down either flight of stairs, he'd catch her. She needed to immobilize him long enough to get out of her apartment to run for help. She scanned her barren living room for a weapon to use against him. No fireplace poker, nothing heavy enough that she could lift. She'd have better luck in the kitchen.

The percolator.

One knee buckled as she entered the kitchen. At the kitchen table, she sat for minute to gather her nerve. Evan's coffee mug was still there from the other morning. A small dark circle lined the bottom of the cup. She held it to her chest and crossed to the sink. Boot heels clicked against the living room floor and muted when she turned on the hot water faucet. Filling the old percolator, she formulated a plan.

"When we get to L.A., what then?" she shouted. The water shook inside the percolator as it filled.

"You want to talk about L.A.?" Dylan's skeptical voice boomed from the living room.

"Yeah," she yelled back, turning the faucet off.

Using both hands, she gauged the weight of the filled pot. With an electric base and filled with hot water, the stainless steel pot might be heavy enough and knock him out. She'd have to hit him good and hard on the head.

The pot slipped from her hands as she set it down. Hot water spilled over her fingers. She toweled the water from her fingers and the counter and cleared her voice before speaking. "Aren't there a lot of fires lately? So many mansions are burning up. I don't think it's a good time to sell real estate."

She snapped on the lid, faced the doorway, and waited.

"Where's the damn tape, Cassie?" Dylan bellowed from the living room.

She frowned and didn't move. "What do you want a tape for?"

Wood scrapped wood, like a drawer skimming the wooden floor. *Thud.*

Glass shattered. Her T.V.?

She set the pot on the counter and entered the room. The rocker was inverted. Contents of one plastic cube of her makeshift coffee table were spilled on the floor. Magazines and paperbacks swamped his feet. Heather's games were opened and scattered about the room. Tiny houses and dice, tokens and cards were strewn everywhere. A card with a smiling gingerbread man peeked out from under her toe. Her television laid on its side, a large hole in the picture tube like it had been kicked. Her speakers were lying sideways, slashed to shreds.

"What the hell are you doing?" she screeched.

He flung the empty cube. It hit the wall and splattered white plaster through the air, sprinkling the floor with what looked like ashes. His shoulders heaved. "What does it look like I'm doing?"

With one kick of his snakeskin boot, the mound of magazines parted. He went to her couch and picked up the cushions. Something shiny switched between his hands, then she heard fabric ripping. Yellow foam vomited from each cushion onto the layer of magazines.

"Stop that!" she yelled but took a step back. The long, thin object was a jackknife.

He ignored her and stomped on the foam. Muttering to himself, his eyes bulged from their sockets and flicked everywhere at once. He waved the knife around.

Deciding what to slash open next? Her hand covered her throat, and she fought to exhale.

He'd gone insane. And he had a knife.

She gauged the distance to the front door. She'd never make it around him. Her feet shuffled as she backed to the archway.

In the kitchen she tugged the handle of the utensil drawer where she stored a set of butcher knives. The drawer stuck but after the second, hard tug, the drawer and contents crashed onto the floor. A knife nicked her knuckles as it fell. She ignored the sting and the blood as she searched through the silverware for the cleaver.

The kitchen floor trembled as Dylan stomped in. He stopped in front of her knees. "Where is it?" His voice went terse with anger.

Empty pillow covers landed next to the pile of utensils. "What are you talking about?" she said calmly.

He pulled her to her toes and pinned her against the counter, hurting her back. The whites of his eyes were red and his nostrils flared. "What are *you* doing?" he said, and kicked the knives under the breakfast table.

Will he use them on her?

What will become of Heather?

She'd made a deadly mistake. Rather than look for a knife, she should have run down the back stairs but her first instinct was to fight back.

Fight the man who drugged her and then videotaped her rape.

Fight the man who caused the loss of her daughter.

Fight the man that she hated and now wanted dead.

His hand flew back and she braced for the blow that would seal her fate. Instead, he slapped her. She twisted and caught the edge of the counter. Then he stormed around the kitchen, pulling out the rest of the drawers until they, too, fell to the floor.

Her lower lip burned and she tasted coppery blood. She huddled next to the counter. Maybe if she didn't speak or move, she'd be invisible. She held her breath.

"Did you hide it in here?" he demanded, kicking potholders and dishtowels with his toe.

Something solid and warm poked her back. *The percolator spout.*

Without taking her eyes off Dylan, her fingers felt for the handle.

Dylan still muttered to himself and inched closer, emptying lower cabinets. Her fingers were slick with sweat and she fumbled for a good grip. With the other hand she held the counter to steady her legs. She glanced at the kitchen door that led to the shop. It was bolted. She'd have to run across the apartment to the unlocked door, down the front stairs, and onto the street.

Only one more step and he'd be within striking range. He ducked into the largest cabinet, right in front of her. When his head came out, she took a big breath, then swung with all her might, flinging the pot at his head.

He dodged an instant before it connected. "Hey!"

The pot grazed his raised shoulder and crashed to the floor, spilling hot water over her feet. Stepping away, she slipped, falling hard on her knees but scrambled toward the archway.

He hefted her off the floor by the neck of her jacket. "Are you crazy?"

"Yes!" She screeched and got a couple lucky punches in his face and kicked something soft as he carried her out of the kitchen. He dropped her on the couch, closer to the front door.

She pointed to the mess in the living room and screamed again. He hated screams. "Look what you've done to my house!"

When his head turned, she bolted for the door. Bloody fingers grazed the glass doorknob but it turned. Arms snaked around her waist and heaved her away as the door swung open.

He spun her around, shouting hot breath into her face. "You're not going anywhere. Did you think you were going to blackmail me with that tape someday?" He snarled and shook her by the shoulder.

Her head throbbed. "You've got the tape. You had it in the courtroom." She could barely breathe in his crushing grip. Would he hurt her? Dylan loved her, in his twisted way. He had a knife and didn't threatened her with it. *Yet.*

"It's a blank!" he yelled. "Every time I phoned, I kept waiting for you to name your price. My partners know it's missing and they want it back. I'm not leaving without the tape you stole from my office. Now, where's it hidden?"

She couldn't answer. It made no sense that he would come all this way for the tape she stole. How could she blackmail him? What partners?

He shook her again. "God damn it! You have no idea how much trouble you've caused me since you took that fucking tape. My partners wanted to come here and get it but I knew they'd kill you first. I don't want to hurt you, Cassie, but I'm not gonna die for you. Where is it?"

Tears blurred her vision as he shook her harder. Her head pounded. She let out a moan and his grip loosened, buying her precious seconds to figure out an escape. She had no intention of telling him where she'd hidden it; its location kept her alive this far. She needed to get him out the apartment. Maybe inside his car she could jump free. "It's not here."

"Where is it then? Back at that damn cabin?"

The shaking resumed until her head began to flop around. Pain sliced from the back of her head to her forehead. She tried to nod, *yes,* but the shaking didn't stop. Dylan's crazed eyes loomed closer.

Her last thought before surrendering to darkness was that Evan had arrived to save her.

Either she was dreaming, or dying.

Chapter Twenty-Two

Evan cursed the late-day traffic on Route 690. Adrenaline still poured through his system, making him wish he could knock the cars off the road the way he'd thrown the chairs around in his office. Tony informed him that a bad car accident in the city detained all available vehicles.

It tore up his gut seeing her leave with that monster, but he'd had no choice. He'd be kicked off the force if he disobeyed a direct command to see Captain. If he lost his badge he'd be unable to help her. It took every ounce of restraint to keep him from flattening the puke-bag in the court room.

Even more to let her go.

The last image of Cassie flared before his eyes, so scared and alone.

The siren blasted and cars moved out of his way. Precious time wasted away listening to Captain's punishment. He'd been forced to take an unpaid leave of absence. No problem. The governor waived the formal interview and ordered he leave for Albany right away.

He'd renegotiate that part later.

Captain wanted him out of Syracuse, away from

the lady causing all the trouble. Evan wanted to explain what happened in court but to get out of the office faster he'd agreed to everything, signed his resignation papers, accepted the Albany job, and then hit the road.

What was going through Cassie's mind now? He hoped to God she'd kept her cool and knew he'd eventually come for her. If Black hurt her in any way—

Her apartment line was still busy. No answer on her cell, either.

While driving like a fugitive through downtown Syracuse he checked the flights leaving for L.A. There were several departures, one leaving in a few hours. Dispatch would check the passenger manifest and warn the flight marshals not to let Black or Cassie on board.

Cassie, in porn? That was rich. Evan believed it for all of two nanoseconds. He knew a con-man when he saw one. The shocked look on Cassie's face confirmed her innocence.

No way my Cassie did porn.

She was a good mother with a great job and Black fucked it all up. There had to be more to the story. Cassie doing porn unwillingly crossed his mind.

He buried the gas pedal to the floor.

Christ. She was too embarrassed to tell him what happened. Black probably shot some video when they were having sex and then threatened her with its exposure. The bastard had something else on her or she wouldn't have left without a fight. There could only be one reason why she went with him so easily.

Revenge.

Don't do anything stupid, honey.

He reached for the car radio and called for emergency backup. Braking the car in front of the apartment, he saw the second story curtains swaying. Two silhouettes wrestled in the window. He jumped from his cruiser. As he took the apartment stairs two at a time, he heard sirens approaching. No time to wait for the backup units. With his blood roaring through his veins he rammed the apartment door until it broke off the hinges, tossing him into the room. Through a red haze he found bodies struggling on the floor.

"Get off her, you asshole," he hollered, and knocked Black into the wall. Cassie lay with closed eyes and a face whiter than fresh snow, except for the red swell on her forehead. Evan kept his eyes on Black as he shouted, "Cassie. Cassie, answer me!"

No response.

Acid boiled the back of his throat.

Black charged and threw a fist at Evan's gut. Evan pitched sideways and slammed several hard blows to Black's midsection. When Black doubled over from the pain, Evan spun around and kicked him in the face. Blood trickled from Black's nose. Most men would have been out cold but Black shook his head and dove at Evan, head first. The two fell backward through the open doorway and tumbled down the stairs.

On the landing, fists flew again. Evan took a dizzying blow to the face but he barely stopped to acknowledge it. He charged Black squarely in the gut. They sailed through the air.

When they hit the sidewalk, several hands pulled Evan off Black. "I've got him cuffed, let him go." He heard Palmer's voice and punched Black's bloody face twice more before he stood up. Evan's knuckles bled. His mouth tasted sour but Black's jaw twisted sideways, hopefully broken.

"Take him to the station. Charge him with assault." Without wasting another breath, Evan took to the stairs.

To his immense relief Cassie was sitting up and rubbing her forehead. "Evan, is that you?" She tried to get up but slipped on the magazines underneath her. Sunbeams through the front windows cast a spotlight on her face. She squinted. "Are you really here?"

His knees hit the floor and her arms circled around him. A million thoughts had exploded through his mind on the ride over, all ending with her death. Now that she rested safely in his arms, he didn't think he could let her go.

With shaking hands, he raised her face. Besides the red bump, blood covered her hand and lip. "I'd better get you to the hospital."

Her hands tightened on his shoulders. "No hospital. Can you hold me a little longer before I stand?"

He smoothed her hair from her eyes. They were glassy but not dilated. "He won't hurt you anymore."

Hot tears wetted his neck. "I thought he was going to kill me."

"He's gone." He looked around at the mess in the living room. "Was he still looking for money?"

Cassie lifted her head from his chest. "There was never any money." Her eyes begged him to trust her. "He went crazy." She shook her head and began to cry harder.

"Okay. Let's go get you checked out."

"I don't want to go to the hospital. I'm f-fine," she argued.

"Then I'm taking you home."

****

For most of the ride Cassie tried to doze, but Evan changed the cold pack on her forehead every time her eyes closed. He held a small ice pack against his lip, too. He kept her awake to make sure she didn't have a concussion, even turned on the radio and sang along to oldies. She never knew he could sing so well. There were still so many things she didn't know about him, maybe now that Dylan was taken care of, they'd have time. Maybe he wouldn't get the Albany job and they could have a fresh start.

Soon her forehead no longer ached. Checking in the rearview mirror, a small pink dot remained where she'd banged her head and thin red line by the corner of her lip. Thankfully Evan had arrived when he did.

Evan came back for her!

The thought sent giddy shivers up her spine. He didn't question Dylan's accusation, simply said he was taking her home. And now he kept smiling at her. She'd never seen him smile so long. Maybe he wasn't the same as all the other men she'd met. No. He definitely wasn't the same.

Her heart no longer ached with pain but joy.

She loved him.

A call came through on the speaker. "Is Cassie okay?"

"Yeah, she'll be fine," Evan answered Tony, his relief clear by his tone.

"I thought you'd like to know we think we have a lead on Stone. He was seen at Hancock earlier."

"Go on," Evan said, switching to headset. He scribbled some numbers on a note pad.

Evan had everything under control, and she relaxed. The scenery looked familiar, a mix of tall evergreens and pines and some maple trees still hanging on to their harvest-colored leaves. Perfect as a postcard picture.

Before long they turned down the road to Evan's camp on Fourth Lake in the Adirondacks. From a distance, dark green mountains fenced the lake, protecting all inside. The air was crisp and smelled stronger than pine incense. Winter arrived here earlier than Syracuse. Soon, all the leaves would shed, the lake would freeze over and everything would be covered with a downy white blanket.

God's country, she'd heard Evan explain more than once.

He held the car door open for her and waited patiently while she absorbed the surroundings. He placed his jacket over her shoulders and tucked her beside him then led her down the gravel walkway to his home. The warmth from his jacket penetrated to her bones. She pulled the corduroy collar up, smelled Evan's cologne and snuggled deeper inside. "It's so peaceful and beautiful." A few yards from the two-story structure, she halted and surveyed his home nestled between dense pine trees. "You've done a lot to it."

Evan nodded. "Six years ago I added the garage and the bay windows in the front for a better view of the lake. Otherwise, it's pretty much the same." He pointed a remote control and the garage door swung open. The space was neatly filled to the rafters with sports equipment.

"Looks like you need to build a new one," she said, suddenly shy to be alone with him. She'd expected *home* to be his apartment.

"It looks that way."

He led her around a small car covered in a tarp to a set of stairs. While he fumbled with a fistful of keys, she marveled at all the sports equipment. Jet skis, mountain bikes, four-wheelers and kayaks crowded the floor. Skis, snowshoes and snowboards were stored along shelf units or hooks, along with fishing and camping gear along the walls. A large wooden canoe hung from the rafters. She noticed two motorcycles in different colors, and two sets of golf clubs. "You seem to have two of everything—" Her lips slammed together. Maybe he brought girlfriends here. She didn't want to think of other women with him.

"Clay stores his stuff here. 'Course, this is the only place he'd use half of it." He keyed the door.

"Why doesn't he leave them at his home?"

That remark got an endearing, boyish grin. "He doesn't have a home."

"No home? Where does he live?"

The door to his cabin swung open. "In a trailer, roaming the country—" He paused mid-sentence and gazed at her. The light from the garage illuminated his face. When he looked at her that way, she felt the heat of his kisses all over again. His eyes softened like smoke. "I can't wait for you to meet him. He's gonna love you."

Like you love me?

The lights flicked on and she sucked in her breath. The living room was large and earthy. She and Jake dropped by once after a day with Heather at the water park in Old Forge, but hadn't gone inside. Evan wanted to give them the grand tour but as usual, Jake had early rounds the next morning. As Jake drove away she remembered hiding her disappointment from Heather. Dropped in the middle of a forest, far from civilization, she envied Evan this little hideaway.

Inside, her shoes sank into a brown carpet. Evan turned on more lights. Knotty pine slats covered walls and ceiling in a V-shaped pattern aged to deep amber. She struggled to look at everything at once, dark maroon leather sofas and chairs, Adirondack end tables with bark trim, a large chandelier made of deer antlers. An enormous fireplace.

Flat rocks stacked from floor to ceiling took up the entire wall around a cavernous hearth. Evan bragged once that he and his grandfather spent an entire summer building the fireplace. Added he'd never sell the place. The mountains would always be his home.

He leaned over the hearth, lit a pre-stacked pile

of kindling and waited for the flames to grow higher. Satisfied with the fire he turned to her.

Her mountain man.

"You probably want to shower. Give me a minute to check it out. There's a teapot in the kitchen if you want some tea."

"Tea and a hot shower sounds wonderful."

The first thing that sounded normal in twenty-four hours. After the long, hot shower, she felt human again. A flannel robe three sizes too big but smelling deliciously like Evan rested on the big bed. Wrapping the robe around her she felt right at home. She walked around the living room barefoot, checked out photos on a coffee table, enjoyed the crackling fire.

Evan walked in through another door with a large paper bag. "I ran out for supplies. Hungry?"

Fruits and vegetables poked out of the bag, and she smelled fresh-baked bread. Her stomach growled.

After they ate salad and sandwiches she phoned Heather to wish her sweet dreams. Several times she stopped to catch her breath. She'd come so close to losing her baby forever. Glancing across the room she found Evan seated in a large leather chair, staring into the fire. The toasty warm room smelled like wood smoke. The glow of flickering flames softened the angles of his cheeks and jaw.

She hung up the telephone and walked between him and the fire. "I haven't thanked you for coming to my apartment. As usual your timing saved my life." She swallowed hard around a pinch in her throat. Her gratitude sounded paltry compared to the feeling that washed over her. She sat down on an ottoman.

He leaned forward in the recliner. His hands clasped between bent knees and his smile faded. "Do you like it here?"

He'd changed into a tan chambray shirt and blue jeans. He'd kicked off his boots and framed against the rough wood logs looked as handsome as he was brave. She didn't answer right away, wanting to cling to the moment, imagining a different scenario where she wasn't a visitor. One where she walked up to him, kissed his lips and took her place on his lap as they watched the fire.

She nodded, and held back tears.

His gaze darkened.

Overcome with shyness she circled the room, looking at everything but the man setting her insides hotter. She pretended interest in a modern entertainment unit opposite the fireplace and ran her hand over the cool black glass. Funny, there were all kinds of electronic equipment, but no TV. "Don't you watch TV?"

"In my bedroom."

The air between them cracked with sparks that would shame a Roman candle. She remembered Evan's naked reflection in the hotel mirror and moisture collected between her thighs. She took another sip of tea and forced her eyes away from him.

If they made love tonight she'd tell him she loved him, but what if he didn't feel the same?

She'd be humiliated for years. No, life. One time Evan boasted he was a confirmed bachelor. Could she chance it? Then again, he might repeat her profession of love, not wanting to hurt her feelings or worse, out of some misplaced honor.

What she needed was a distraction. "Do you have any games we can play?"

He stood. Even from across the room his gaze made sweat trickle between her breasts. Wasn't there anything she could say without reminding them both of making love? She envisioned stripping off her robe and crossing the room to him. Instead, she secured the knot on her belt and dug her hands into its pockets.

He stoked the fire. "I bought dessert. I remembered you liked chocolate ice cream."

How could he speak so calmly?

Did he believe Dylan's tape was real? Was he trying to distance himself from her? Was taking care of her only part of his duty?

A bubble of dread rose up her throat.

She followed him into the kitchen, a generous room with cherry cabinets, granite countertops and stainless-steel appliances. A copper vent crowned the gas stove.

Evan lived well.

But alone.

No signs of a female touch.

The counter needed sunflowers, and the windows begged for curtains in warm-hued colors, like mustard or wine rather than drab white. She'd have pots of herbs on the windowsill, with a family of ceramic black bears frolicking around them. The sliding glass doors led down back steps to the docks. He needed a pair of Adirondack chairs facing the water to watch the ducks drift by.

The last colors of the sunset, now blue-green tapers in a deep violet sky, cast minimal light into the room. The sudden reflection of light in the window reminded her she wasn't alone. Evan had opened the freezer door. He removed a carton of ice cream, and then gathered two bowls from a cabinet.

"Two bowls?" she joked.

He returned a bowl to its shelf.

Scoops of dark chocolate ice cream dropped into the bowl. Her mouth watered. "Chocolate syrup on your ice cream, right?" His voice had cooled considerably since they'd entered the kitchen.

"I'd love some. Warmed."

The bottle disappeared into the microwave. He

studied her the entire minute but made no attempt to touch her. She chewed her lower lip until the timer went off. Fingers she knew could work magic squeezed the bottle and swirled the syrup over the contents. The ice cream softened immediately. "Just the way I like it," he said.

When he returned the syrup, she noticed a can of whipped cream on the door. *You can bring the whipped cream, Dawn's message had said.*

Cassie inched backward toward the living room, needing air. What made her ever think she was special?

He waved her closer. "Come here."

Despite her mounting misery, she obeyed. He held a spoon loaded with syrup. She opened her mouth and he placed a generous spoonful inside. Some of the syrup dribbled down her chin. "Oops!"

"Here, let me get that."

Rather than use his finger to wipe the smudge away he grabbed a dishtowel and ran it under water. Why tease her like this? Judging by all his politeness his desire for her changed. He must believe Dylan's accusations. How was it so easy for him to extinguish his desire? Had he ever cared as deeply as she?

"How's the head?" he inquired as he tilted her chin and moved the dishtowel closer.

Of course, he's still doing his job because they haven't caught her stalker. She fought back tears. "It doesn't hurt."

He paused to look deeply into her eyes and she thought she'd die of longing. She wouldn't beg. If only he'd given her another chance. "No headache?" he said, and focused on her forehead, then his gaze veered to her lips.

"No."

The towel hovered closer and she closed her eyes to hold back tears. She felt his warm breath bathe her face, and waited. But the rough surface of the towel never touched her chin. Tortured to the point of anger, she opened her eyes and then her mouth to tell him to give her the rag.

His lips came closer and licked her chin. Then his tongue slid inside her already-open mouth, entwining their tongues. He rocked his hips upward between hers legs and she nearly came.

Her fingers fisted in his hair to hold him closer. *Never let go,* her mind chanted. His lips grazed down her neck, branding her where they kissed. Before they went further, she needed to tell him the truth. "Wait...Dylan...the tape."

His lips never stalled on the journey to her breast. As his tongue began to lick between them, she lifted his head. He looked perturbed but there was no going back. "I have to tell you something," she said and she caressed his jaw. He might never make love to her again after she explained, but she had to confess. "I never intentionally made a pornographic video."

His eyes darkened with some emotion she couldn't name. She felt a stab of panic and the blood rushed from her head. He didn't believe her. *Please don't let him hate me.*

She began to tremble. "I can explain—"

Callused knuckles stroked her cheek, then his finger went to her mouth. "Shhh." Cold air breezed over her skin as he untied her robe and pulled it off. "You can tell me all about it later. This can't wait."

Before she breathed a sigh of relief, he surprised her by grabbing her waist and hoisting her onto the counter. One gentle tap pushed her back until she reclined with her legs dangling on either side of him. After flipping up his shirt sleeves he grabbed the syrup bottle. Warm syrup landed on one nipple. She sucked in a breath when he lowered his lip and curled his tongue around the nipple. She lay back on the cool counter as he rolled it around with his tongue. The combination of pressure and warmth of his mouth made her toes curl.

The refrigerator door kicked open, startling her. It spilled a wedge of white light upon her nakedness. Sprawled on the counter, she prepared to watch her undoing.

****

Evan couldn't wait another minute to make love to Cassie. Show her how much she meant to him. Worship her like no other.

At first he'd been hesitant, worried about her injuries, but the disappointment in her eyes tugged at his heart.

He wanted her then and there, coated in chocolate syrup. Like in his dreams.

Dripping syrup on the other nipple until it disappeared, he then sucked it harder, encouraged by her sexy moans, knowing the satin taste on his tongue was more Cassie than chocolate. His hands brushed down her sides, around her back, over her belly, recalling the feel of that soft skin. Skin that he'd didn't need nerve cells to remember.

He retrieved the bottle again and squeezed. A stream of the dark liquid detailed her breasts and trickled down to her belly like an artist's sketch. Stepping back, he viewed his handiwork. Lying there with half-closed eyelids, parted lips and ribbons of chocolate waiting to be licked, she looked better than any fantasy he'd conjured.

A breath punched out of him.

He didn't know where to start first.

She rose on her elbows and her eyes widened when she spied the trails of thick brown syrup. His head dipped and his tongue found the dainty dent of her navel. She arched into his touch. He lapped a chocolate ribbon trail to both breasts and didn't stop until every drop disappeared. Her gentle moans fueled his resolve to make love to her the way she'd never forget.

His ragged breathing matched hers as he tore his clothes off while she reclined like a goddess on his countertop. If Aphrodite did exist, Cassie must have been a descendent. There was no other explanation for the power she possessed to make him wild for her. He grabbed the bottle again. This time he chose a path from her navel to the juncture of her parted thighs. When the syrup puddled there, her soft cry of surprise made his cock throb. Anxious to taste her, he buried his face between her thighs, seeking the chocolate-drenched little nub. He licked and probed with his tongue, tasting both woman and chocolate. She writhed under his mouth as he lapped every dip and crevice and surrendered under his assault.

"Evan, please, no more."

"Can't take it?"

He raised the bottle above her navel. Should he tell her how often he'd imagined this? That he was addicted to the way she responded to his touch?

The indecision that wrinkled her brow a moment earlier morphed into the same competitive grin she gave when they played games. She lay back on the counter, spread her creamy thighs and watched as he coated her again.

Time to love her the way he'd always wanted.

His tongue showed no mercy, even when she bucked beneath his mouth. He held her to his face and deepened the licks, pushed harder with his tongue, deep into her core until he felt the first spasms.

"I want you inside me." Her words were choppy. "Evan!"

He pulled her to the edge of the counter and drove into her. He couldn't linger like he wanted and succumbed to the overwhelming urge to piston into her as she cried her release. Contractions pulled on his cock. Within moments he followed. Like a sudden shower of hot rain, his release deluged his body.

Never had he felt so wonderfully alive.

Gathering his wits, and regaining his strength after one hell of a release, he lifted off her. An arm fell over her closed eyes but a satisfied smile lit her face. No complaints about the awkward position, half on the counter, half falling off but goose bumps marred her skin.

He scooped her up. "Grab the bottle."

He carried her to the living room. The heat from the roaring fire erased her goose bumps and she parted her lips in another contented sigh. When she reopened her eyes, her green stare made the fire seem cool.

"My turn," she said when he tried to take the syrup. "Lie down."

Grateful that the past few days hadn't broken her spirit, he wished it could always be this way.

He pulled her arms behind her back and trapped her against him. Surprised by his action, she opened her mouth. He clamped her to his body and kissed the breath from her. He loved her for her innocence. Didn't she know by now he'd do anything she asked? Anything to make her feel safe and happy.

"Beware," he said. "Anything you do to me, I'll double to you." He growled and nipped her lips. Orange sparks glowed in her eyes. He let go and allowed her to push him down.

Settled on top of the blankets, she dripped syrup all over his still body. The smell of chocolate overpowered the room's outdoor scent. Her tongue traveled from his shoulders to his abs. He fought the demand to halt her lapping, turn her over and plunge inside her.

Sunshine strands of hair draped over his chest, bringing light to his darkness. Her lips drew on him and he journeyed into a new oblivion, one warm and loving. "Enough," he grated. He pulled out of her mouth and switched their positions. He paused to suckle her breasts, drawing more sexy little sounds until she squirmed. He lifted her hips and slowly thrust, dragging completely out before plunging back inside her warmth. His release pulled at the base of his spine. The fire crackled, reminding him that Cassie was in his home and he was loving her, something he'd only dreamed possible.

All thoughts left his head but one: wanting this fantasy most of all.

****

Later as she lay sated in Evan's bed she decided it was time to tell Evan the rest of her ordeal. "There's more you need to know," she began, rolling onto her belly to face him. "About the tape."

His hands relaxed behind his head but his jaw ticked. "All right."

She thought about it but her mind was made up. She wanted him to know everything. No lies between them. Her fingers fidgeted with the edge of the blue top sheet. "I went to Dylan's studio. For a screen test. He'd pestered me for months. Said I could make a lot of money doing commercials."

How stupid she'd been. Some men would say and do anything when they wanted something bad enough.

Evan tilted her chin. "What happened?"

"The worst that could happen." She swallowed. "All I remember... it started professionally, a cameraman and a white backdrop... me sitting on a stool. I remember laughing at something Dylan said. The lights were hot and he handed me a can of soda. Then... I couldn't see, like my eyelids were glued shut. I opened my mouth to call Dylan but my tongue felt like it was wound with cotton. When I opened my eyes I was lying on a bed without my

338

clothes." She pushed away the tears running down her cheek. "I was in a different room with a larger camera pointed at me, and then—"

Evan sat up. "Shhh. You don't have to talk about this."

"No, I want to—" She pressed her fingers to her lips. "—*have* to get this out."

He pushed her bangs from her eyes. "Okay, but know this. Nothing you can say will make me think any less of you."

His eyes mirrored his words.

"I believe that."

The knowledge gave her the courage to continue. "My head felt like a rock on my neck. My clothes were thrown on a chair. I was still having trouble focusing when the door opened. A man I'd never seen before walked in with a towel wrapped around his waist. Dylan followed. He went over to the camera, removed a tape, put it in his pocket and s-said, 'You did real good, baby.'" She took a huge breath. "The man...in the towel...laughed and nodded."

Evan reached for her, but she pushed him away, caught in the memory. "When I could stand, I grabbed my clothes and ran. My doctor confirmed I'd been drugged and—" She fought to keep from hyperventilating.

Evan's knuckles were white against the blue sheets. She heard fabric tearing. "Was he arrested?"

"My samples and test results got lost." She swallowed a scream that burned to be freed. "Dylan was furious with me for reporting the rape and swore I'd pay."

Evan squeezed her hand and tried to speak, but she had to finish.

"He knew Jake was coming for a visit the next weekend. My mom babysat that day and waited for Jake while I showed out-of-town property. I never told Mom what happened at the studio. She liked

Dylan so when he arrived at my apartment to take Heather for ice cream, Mom didn't think to check with me or object. He'd left an address for Jake."

Evan's face turned to stone but she pressed on.

Her stomach cramped. She pulled her knees to her chest. "Jake found Heather in that studio. Women and men were barely clothed. Heather looked scared and confused."

Evan rubbed a hand over his mustache and said something under his breath.

"Jake took her away that day. I went crazy. The judge awarded us joint custody and Jake said I'd blown it. Heather was allowed to leave the New York State only with his permission."

A sob escaped her throat and there'd be no stopping the rest. Her heart felt like it was ripping apart all over again but she needed to get the words out. "I rushed to Dylan's office to beg him to tell Jake it was all a mistake. Dylan was out. That's when I spied the tape marked *Cassie* and took it."

Evan threaded his fingers through his hair. His bicep twitched. "Does Dylan have a copy?" he asked in a barely controlled voice.

Evan's naked body pressed against hers, broiling hot, but her teeth still chattered. "I don't think so. The one he flaunted at court was a blank. He said something about his partners wanting mine. That's what he came for, that's why he tore my place apart—" She shook so hard she thought she would break. The tears that followed stung her eyes.

"It's okay. I'm here."

Evan's voice was calm and reassuring but she still felt like a cliff diver staring down at sharp rocks. She pursed her lips to keep the sobs back and breathed through her nostrils. If she let them out, she'd waste hours crying.

Evan stood and began to pace. "This doesn't add up. Dylan had a warrant for your arrest so he could get you back to L.A., all for a tape? One that his partners wanted? What else is on that tape?"

Unable to answer his question, she choked back a sob. The room swam before her. Her chest ached and ached, impaled on the sharp rocks of regret.

Chapter Twenty-Three

Evan cursed in three languages.

Death was too good for Dylan. Torture, Al Qaeda style, came to mind. He held Cassie's stiff, shaking body and worked to put aside his rage.

He handed her some tissues. "Let it out. Let it all out." Christ, he couldn't stand seeing her this broken but nothing short of Heather walking into his home would stop this. Before he left, he was calling Jake.

After a while, she calmed down. Her story made no sense, unless he'd missed some bit of information. He hated to ask again, but he needed to know. "Did you watch the entire tape?"

A red blush from her cheeks to her chest marked her embarrassment and her skin felt feverish. She wasn't the one who needed to be ashamed.

Black was a dead man.

She gestured with her arms and prattle. "I had to get back to Syracuse for a court date and barely remembered to pack it. I went to show it to the custody judge, but my lawyer advised against it. Without the rape evidence...it might have looked like I did the video willingly, and...well, he said to get my life back on track for now and then appeal later."

His arms dropped. "Then, your lawyer watched the tape?"

"No," sounded more like a yes, but she'd buried her face in her hands.

He knelt on the bed and turned her face upward. Her pupils dilated and her nostrils flared. "Tell me." It was on the tip of his tongue to say, *you can trust me*, but after Iraq, he'd grown to hate the expression.

Her entire body seemed to slump. "I tried once, got it into the VCR, pressed *Play*...There I was, sitting on the stool, looking so happy. The next minute I was naked, sprawled on a bed. I saw a man enter the room, his towel dropped...he started to climb on my body. I couldn't watch him—" Her finger pushed repeatedly at an imaginary button. She covered her mouth and turned deathly pale.

He took her icy hand in his. "Did it ever occur to you there might be something else on that tape?"

Her eyes looked impossibly hopeless.

He rose off the bed and reached for his jeans. "Where's the tape now?"

"In my garage. I wanted to burn it on my grill but my neighbor from across the street interrupted me. He said it would make a terrible odor and someone would call the cops. I was so paranoid I locked it in my tool box until I was certain I could get rid of it."

It sickened him that she'd carried this burden for so long. If he hadn't been wrapped in his own pity party he would have contacted her as soon as he'd returned from Iraq. Maybe he could have saved her all this trouble.

No, he definitely would have, starting with a jet ride to L.A.

He checked his watch. Past midnight. His jacket hung on the chair. He wanted to jump in the car and watch that tape this minute. Purple circles under her eyes made him reconsider. She couldn't take much more of this turmoil without rest and he didn't dare leave her.

He pulled on his jeans and got in bed with her. "I want to see that tape as soon as we get back." He stroked her cold cheek, wishing he could absorb her pain.

She turned in his arms and closed her eyes. Before long her breathing slowed and she slept. He held her, not wanting to let go. Eager to protect her from this new threat, his combat experience taught him things got worse before they got better. The real reason Dylan came back was on that tape.

As he listened to Cassie breathing he considered all the possible things that could be on that tape, from a murder to drug dealings, maybe a prostitution ring or a tape of a secret meeting. Each scenario was worse than the other.

First things first.

Keep Cassie safe.

Call proper authorities to deal with the evidence she'd recovered. He'd need assistance, especially if drugs were involved. The new job in Albany, although unwanted, might be her only hope since he'd have unlimited resources and connections and no questions asked.

What irony.

To keep her safe he'd have to accept a promotion that would take him hundred of miles from her.

****

The sounds of loons singing and water lapping on the shore woke Cassie. A dim light filled the room. After revealing her secret, she thought she'd have trouble sleeping. But knowing Evan believed her meant everything. Once during the night she stirred and reached for him. He was still there. Her confession hadn't changed his treatment, if anything, he was more tender and caring when he kissed her goodnight.

The evening had been the sweetest lovemaking of her life, almost perfect, except he hadn't mentioned love. *I love you,* nearly slipped from her lips several times. The part of her that feared his reaction to the tape held back the words. If he'd said he'd loved her and then took it back, it would destroy not only her heart but her soul.

She wriggled under the thick quilt. For the first time in years she felt safe. The smell of brewed coffee and smoked bacon forced her to rise. He'd made her breakfast. Starving, she got out of bed. She didn't have slippers but Evan's thick robe stopped the chill. His earthy smell enveloped her like his embrace.

Okay. Enough craziness. Time she laid her chips on the table, professed her love and prayed he'd feel the same.

How could he help her, treat her the way he did, stand by her, believe in her, without loving her? Every action, every word, every minute together resonated that he cared. The realization ignited a new warmth in her chest, inflating her heart until it felt like it would burst.

Relief brought a small smile to her lips. She loosely knotted the robe and combed her hair with her fingers. Evan loved her. She didn't need to hear the words. Fortified with that knowledge, she marched out of the room. By the door she bumped a chair. Evan's jacket fell to the floor. Something crinkled beneath her feet. Papers? She picked up several white sheets that fell from an envelope and skimmed the header of one:

Office of the Captain, New York State Police.

Evan met with his captain after court.

Curious, she read on.

I hereby resign my commission—

Evan resigned his job! Because of her? He'd lost so much helping her.

There was a second page. The words blurred as she began to read.

The Governor of the State of New York is happy to inform you of your promotion... Albany Team Commander... effective immediately—

She reread the last line.

He'd taken the Albany job.

When was he going to tell her? After they made love all day?

Unable to walk, she sat on the chair. Maybe he wouldn't have told her at all. Why tell her if he didn't think they'd be seeing each other much longer? What had Jake joked? Evan's *ponies* never lasted more than a Saratoga race season. She'd been such an idiot to confuse concern with love.

Pain knocked against the walls of her stomach. She folded her knees to her chest until it receded. Coldness followed like an icy artic blast blew through the window. She pulled the robe's collar up around her neck but it was futile. Nothing could warm her now.

She looked at the papers again.

How could he do this? Between running the sweet shop and fighting to get Heather back, moving to Albany was out of the question for her. Besides, this was Heather's home. Evan knew that but he'd already made arrangements to go.

Without her. Two hundred miles were more like a billion.

Time to get to the bottom of this.

Neatly refolded papers scooted back into the envelope and then disappeared into his jacket pocket. She repositioned the jacket on the chair and stormed into the living room. The smell of dying fire greeted her. A window was cracked open allowing cool, fresh air to circulate. At first she didn't see him, but heard talking. Seated on the large ottoman facing the dead fire, Evan held the cordless phone.

"Yeah. You heard right. I have to start the Albany job next week...I'm sure I'll have a lot of *fun*...I'll tell you later. So we're set for next week?"

Fun? She pedaled backward right into a twig-legged table. It wobbled and a picture frame cart wheeled to the carpet. Two proud young men displaying fish, with a beautiful little girl holding the tackle box, stared up at her through a crack in the glass. She bent to pick it up and heard the phone slam on the base. Holding the picture to her chest, she faced him.

Evan's grin reminded her of a young boy caught in the act of a wrongdoing. He rose from the ottoman and stretched then picked up a blue pillow from the floor and set it on the couch next to another blue pillow and crumbled up blanket. They weren't there last night.

His hair was wet and he was barefoot. His shirt was unbuttoned and his jeans slung low on his hips. Would he tell her about Albany now?

"Ready for some breakfast?"

How could he be so pleasant when she bled from every pore? Her face must have betrayed her pain because his mustache drooped and concealed his smile.

"I think I broke your picture." She fought to steady her hands as she handed the frame over.

"That crack's been there for years." He paused and stared at it, then put it on the seat of a chair rather than the small table. "Are you feeling okay? Does your head hurt?" Those quick hands managed to push aside her bangs before she backed into the wall.

"I'm fine."

His touch stung but she kept focus on him. Dark bruises circled his eyes. From fighting Dylan? Or from lack of sleep rethinking their relationship? Did he think she'd willingly do porn? Maybe she'd wrongly assumed he'd understand. No, in all fairness, he probably did understand what happened in L.A., all too well. Maybe he planned to leave her all along.

She tried to move away but tripped on the robe and fell forward. Her hands landed on his shoulders. Muscles bunched beneath her touch. She let him hold her tight, wanting to feel his arms band around her one last time.

"Let's start again. Good morning. Sleep well?" He tilted his head to the side and his lips merged with hers in a lengthy, heady kiss, full of promises his heart couldn't keep. She'd known all along he was a player. She'd followed her heart again but by the ache in her chest, this time she didn't think she'd survive.

She pulled back and halted the kiss. "Was that Tony?"

His face became unreadable. "No." He touched the tip of her nose. "You're cold. A hot shower before breakfast will warm you up."

His lips found her lips again, coaxing a tiny warmth through her body that she didn't want to feel, couldn't respond to any longer, knowing she was no different from the objects in his garage—a temporary play thing.

"I don't think we have time," she whispered.

He stroked her lips with his thumb and her chin rose. Dark, impenetrable eyes stared back at her.

She met his gaze. "I've thought about it and I better help Karen make the wedding delivery."

He looked surprised.

He's going to Albany.

"It's a large order and the bride's very nervous."

He untied her belt and his hands circled her waist. His thumbs fanned the underside of her breasts and her nipples puckered in response.

How could a man with such warm eyes have such a cold heart?

She turned her head away. "We don't have time." Her clipped tone echoed through the room.

His forehead leaned on hers. He slowly retied her robe. "Yeah. We should get going. I want to see that tape."

"Is that all you have to do?"

"That tape's the most important thing, besides keeping you safe." He said, turning from lover into cop mode.

Evan knew all about duty. Maybe it was all he was capable of knowing.

A sob that bubbled up her throat expanded and she turned and ran into the bedroom before he heard it. Unspoken words about Albany were all the affirmation she needed.

A few minutes and several tissues later she closed the bedroom door and entered the kitchen. She sipped some orange juice and ate some jellied-toast while he closed up the cabin. When he'd finished he waited for her by the back door, jacket in hand, no sign of the papers. She couldn't trust herself to speak about Albany without leaking like a damaged faucet. Wanting to be transported away at light speed, neither spoke as they got into the car.

Feigning sleep, her mind worked double time as he drove. He'd date her maybe for another week so she didn't think it had anything to do with the video and all the trouble she caused him. He'd go to Albany, call her the first few days and call less frequently, until he'd stop calling.

No, she couldn't bear to be treated so charitably. She'd never be able to run her business waiting for 'the break-up call.' She could barely think coherently now.

Tell him it's over, the voice in her head

demanded. *Thank him for all he's done but tell him it's time to move on.*

She nodded in agreement and dried her tears. Her head throbbed and her nose hurt from pinching it to hold back tears. Time to stop thinking. She'd made her decision although her heart pleaded to reconsider.

She wouldn't regret her days spent with Evan. She'd cherish them.

****

Evan didn't know what to make of Cassie's mood change but maybe it was better they left the cabin. He had to see that video. And he wasn't going to rest until Black paid for the pain he'd caused her. He'd charge Black with rape after he beat a confession out of him.

A few miles from the cabin he pulled into a gas station. Cell phone reception sucked in these mountains but by some cosmic phenomenon he could get reception at this spot. It was too risky to call Tony from the cabin on the chance that Cassie might overhear. He didn't know how long she'd listened to the call from Clay. A few yards from the car he placed the call, near enough to hear Cassie call if she needed him.

"Anything on Black?" he said to Tony, scanning the parking lot. One driver absently pumped gas.

"No. The guy's a pillar of the community," Tony snorted. "A lot of shit has happened since you left, though."

A cool morning breeze slapped Evan's head. "Go ahead."

"Forensics went through the apartment and found a handgun in Black's luggage. Black claimed it wasn't his gun and that his associate left it there. Same caliber as the slugs we pulled out of your car, though. Then again, Black couldn't have shot at you and Cassie. Airport records show he flew in two days

350

ago. And dozens of witnesses saw him at his studio all last week. Lunched with Spielberg that day. Lab's gonna run ballistics today to make sure."

Evan absorbed the information. *Black had a gun while in Cassie's apartment.* Fury rolled off him in heat waves. "Who's the gun registered to?"

Tony paused. "Unregistered."

"Any prints?"

"Yeah."

"Black's?"

"Nope," Tony replied. "Would you believe we got a match for Stone?"

"Shit." Evan paced around the parking lot but stayed in view of the car.

Tony continued. "We didn't know at the time Stone was his associate and we couldn't hold Black any longer. Black made bail on the assault charges. Came up with a lawyer and a lot of money real fast." Tony whistled low.

Evan rubbed his eyes as he neared the car. Fatigue tugged at his mind. He'd stayed awake most of the night watching Cassie sleep, listening to her breathing, comforting her when she stirred. When he'd decided to close his eyes, he slept on the couch. From the gas pumps he watched Cassie dab her cheeks with a tissue behind a veil of golden hair. That goddamn tape.

"Find Black. Arrest him for attempted murder." He shouted into the cell marching back to the car.

"Why?"

"Because he hired Stone to scare Cassie into running back to L.A. with that phony stolen money story. Probably promised Stone half the money. Stone panicked when he lost her at the cabin and tried to scare her further with the shots."

"And nearly killed you both. Okay, APB on Black. I'll check flights," Tony said.

Evan interjected. "Black won't skip town. He

still wants something." He'd be searching for Cassie and that tape. "He doesn't know we know about Stone. Keep a car on Cassie's place. We're heading there. Any leads on Stone?"

"Black's rental car was found abandoned by the Canadian border. Stone had picked it up at the impound a few hours earlier. He had the rental paperwork and everything. We blew it."

"Damn." Evan slapped a metal lamp pole when he wanted to punch something.

"In a big hurry to get out of the country after seeing his boss get arrested, I guess," Tony added.

"Stone planted the gun on Black to buy himself time to escape with the money."

"Except there is no money and he doesn't know that," Tony acknowledged.

They had to get these guys behind bars. "Keep Black locked up until I get there. I want to have a discussion with him."

Tony grunted. "Right. We'll keep him warm for you. Sure glad Cassie's innocent."

"I'll tell her."

Evan snapped the cell shut and hopped into the car. Cassie was asleep curled up against the door. He covered her with his jacket and didn't rouse her until he pulled into her driveway several hours later. Headlights of an unmarked police cruiser blinked across the street from the shop. Evan signaled to the driver and scanned the street looking for fast-moving traffic. He scoped the windows for moving curtains before he opened Cassie's car door. Her car had been returned and parked in her driveway.

She got out and mutely walked up the stairs to the porch. Then she handed over his jacket and held up both hands. Without meeting his eyes, she said, "I have just enough time to change and meet Karen at the reception."

"I'm not leaving you alone," he replied, and

unlocked the porch door with his set of keys.

She brushed past him. "I'll be about five minutes."

"I want that video."

She pirouetted and gave him a thousand mile stare. Her green eyes shimmered.

Yep, that's what's bugging her. He gestured and let her lead the way upstairs.

The door was back on its hinges and someone had picked up the apartment, probably Tony and some of the guys. The couch cushions were flat as pancakes but returned to the sofa. The magazines, paperbacks and games were stacked in neat columns. The broken television was missing.

She walked straight to her bedroom and returned in less than five, wearing a long skirt and matching blouse that reminded him of a fairy princess. Pale and exhausted looking, he should have insisted she stay home in bed. Usually people who'd gone through a trauma wanted to do something that was part of their normal routine. Hell, when he'd first returned from Iraq he'd reorganized his office files a dozen times and drove for hours on the Thruway, trying to soak up something other than the stench of death and powdered air. He'd felt detached and alone until the night he'd watched the full moon rise over Onondaga Lake, a sign he was truly home.

She took a raincoat from the closet and started down the stairs, ignoring him.

The officer in the unmarked car would take her to the wedding reception and stand watch. Karl said Karen left for the reception but he'd tell her to expect Cassie. She'd be safe there. If his men didn't have Black behind bars by now, they'd have him soon.

"The tape," he said, pointing to her garage.

She led the way past her car to the back of the

house. Outside the garage he stepped in front of her. "I'll watch the tape at the station. Officer Pope will take you to the reception. Call me when you're ready to leave."

Lifeless eyes stared back.

He went to kiss her to remove that desperate expression but she wrenched away from him. "No," she said between pursed lips. Her face was a lighter shade of pale, her eyes hooded.

"What's wrong?"

She shook her head and then spoke words he somehow knew in the depths of his soul were coming.

"Evan, I appreciate all you've done, but I think it's best if we don't see each other any more."

****

Cassie expected some type of reaction, vocal or body gesture or maybe a fist through the garage wall.

Nothing. Not even a flicker in those all-knowing eyes.

Maybe he didn't believe her. She tried again. "I need to concentrate on my business. To get my daughter back. I'm sure you understand."

His dark eyes bordered dangerous. The muscle on his jaw ticked furiously. "I see. And when did you decide this?" The sharp edge to his voice cut worse than the kitchen knife.

"I've been thinking about it for a while." She nodded, feeling lightheaded.

His cheeks darkened. "If this is about the video—" His chest heaved.

"No. Let me get it for you." She opened the garage door and slammed it behind her. To get away from him, before she weakened.

In the garage she found the key ring and began throwing tools out of a rusty metal box. Hiding on the bottom, still in its plastic sleeve, sat the tape

354

marked, *Cassie.*

Evan entered and she handed him the tape.

He took it, slapping it once on his palm and spoke through clenched teeth. "We'll talk later."

She stood frozen, swamped by her tools. Did it matter? She'd lost him either way.

He bent and picked up tools until all were boxed. He didn't try to touch her, but looked irate. "Don't go anywhere alone."

He had the nerve to point his finger like he could still boss her around. Then he stepped forward and surprised her with a wonderful kiss that she fought not to return. Her muscles ached from staying motionless. He stared into her eyes and touched her cheek with the pad of his thumb.

The garage door slammed. Dust fell from the ceiling and she sneezed. She leaned against the door. With all her heart she wished things could be different, that Evan loved her enough to stay and she wasn't his newest rescue.

But she knew Sergeant Jorgenson would finish his job. He'd solve the case, rescue the damsel in distress one final time, then move on to his next rescue.

In Albany. Where he'd keep millions safe.

Her heart knocked painfully against her ribs, but she gathered her strength. She still had a child to get back, a business to run.

She straightened, raised her chin and walked toward the unmarked car.

****

With the prospect of future customers, Cassie lingered at the wedding reception when she really wanted to go home and sleep for days. Several people complimented her confections and asked for her location. Karen had hugged her fiercely, and demanded all the details. Cassie summed what happened in court, Dylan's timely return, the subsequent attack in her apartment and Evan's rescue.

"Thank God Evan's no fool. And so brave." Karen sighed and hugged her again. "Lucky thing he didn't lose his job by disobeying the warrant."

"The judge and his captain reprimanded him."

She'd tell Karen about Albany later. Karen meant well but she didn't want to discuss her heartache at this beautiful wedding. The bride and groom waltzed a few feet away. He had the build of a warrior and in her flowing white gown, the bride would be mistaken for a princess in any century. The looks they gave each other left no doubt they were deeply in love.

Evan looked at her that way last night. His gaze promised passion and he'd delivered. Now, other plans took precedence. But she had plans of her own. She wasn't afraid of Dylan anymore. Hopefully he'd be in jail a long time for whatever was on the tape. She'd work day and night to get Heather back.

One last time, she'd have to face Evan. She didn't understand why he'd looked so upset that she wanted to stop seeing him. Hadn't she saved him the trouble of breaking up? What more did he want from her? If it weren't for the reception she'd have confronted him based on that look alone.

Karen insisted she stay the night at her house, but Cassie wanted her own bed. The bedroom was the one room Dylan avoided. She shivered, speculating why her bedroom remained spared.

Back home she took a long bath and put on her jeans and sweatshirt. Then she phoned Evan's apartment. "I'm back. No sign of Dylan. The alarm's set. I'll be—"

"I watched the tape. I'll tell you about it when I get there. We have a lot to discuss."

He didn't wait for her reply.

She dropped the phone.

An ominous chill flew up her spine.

****

Evan found Cassie curled up on the cushion-less couch, a pillow folded under her head, another clutched to her chest, and sleeping soundly. He set the pizza on the plastic cube in front of the couch. Then he sat on the rocking chair, wrestling with the right words to say to her.

The video was worse than he'd thought. He'd stopped it four times and once he'd left the room before he could resume watching it. He never wanted to see anything like it again. And he hated even more that he'd have to pass it on to the D.A. as admissible evidence for Black's trial. At least now he knew why they'd tried to kill her to get it back.

He stood up and crossed the room then crouched before her and kissed her lips.

"Evan?" She said, still in a dream-like state.

"Who else?" He returned for a deeper kiss, entwining his tongue with hers.

Her response was better than a hit of oxygen, waking up every cell in his body, helping to drive out the aftereffects of watching the video. On the bright side, he was grateful she'd never watched the entire video but wished like hell she'd shown the judge.

"I brought pizza," he said, when her eyelids slid half open and she sniffed. Steam escaped the cardboard box, warming his face. The smell of tomatoes and peppers and pepperoni made him ravenous.

She sat up and rubbed her eyes. "What's wrong? What was on the tape?" The peachy color in her cheeks washed away.

"Eat first. Then we'll talk."

She carried her slice to the kitchen table and nibbled at it. Her restless fingers made her napkin look like origami. When she finished, she sipped her tea and looked at him over her cup.

He started with the good news. "Stone was spotted entering Canada by the border patrol. I doubt he'll be back for a while."

Her gaze collided with his. "What does Stone have to do with the tape?"

"He's Dylan's partner, hired to scare you into returning to L.A., looking for the bogus money."

Her eyebrows rose. "I can't believe Dylan went that far to get me back."

"Dylan's been arrested on new charges. He'll be in prison for a long time." Evan couldn't hide his grimace.

Pieces of her napkin fluttered to the floor as she braced her hands on the edge of the table. "Evan, please. What was on the tape?" Her eyes roamed all over his face.

He sighed. "It wasn't all you."

She exhaled loudly, then sucked in the next breath. "What?"

"Shorts... child pornography."

Her hands flew to her face. Horrified eyes peeked over her steeped fingers. "My God! Dylan had Heather there." She swayed in her chair. Tears sprang from her eyes. "Tell me the truth, Evan. Was Heather on it?"

"No," he exhaled sharply. "But there were teenage girls. We figure some of the kids are probably missing and exploited children."

He wanted so badly to hold her and comfort her but she got up and rushed past him.

He followed her into her bedroom. "Cassie, that tape will make some parents happy to know their kids are still alive. The Orange County District Attorney wants the tape. And...he'd like you to testify against Dylan."

He found her sitting on her bed, holding a picture of Heather and blotting her face with a wad of tissues. It took her a minute to compose herself.

She nodded.

He looked down on her golden head, and wished she'd stop shaking. "It may take years to get to court."

Emotions cascaded one after another over her beautiful face, from awareness of how wrong she'd been about Black, to fear, to anger.

She cleared her throat. "I can't believe I dated that horrible man."

He joined her on the bed and handed her more tissues. "You couldn't have known what type of man he was. He had a lot of people fooled." He tried to put an arm around her.

Stiff arms pushed him away, and then she stood and hurried from the bedroom.

He found her pacing the perimeter of the living room like a trapped animal. She threw the window sash up and half of her disappeared through it. He heard her gasping for air, and then gagging. He tried to imagine how he'd feel if his child were in danger.

He sunk into the cushion-less couch. If it were one-hundredth of what he felt for Cassie, it would kill him. She pulled her head back inside. Still looking green, she said, "Evan, are you sure Heather's not—"

"Positive." He rubbed his mustache, then explained. "Child pornography's serious. You're a hero for recovering the tape." She'd done a brave thing whether she realized it or not. He tried to approach her again, but she stalked away. He gave up and sat back on the couch.

"A hero? My daughter was with a child pornographer!" Her chest heaved.

"He used her to get to you, but he didn't harm her. You know that. Dylan will tell the truth about what he did to you in L.A. to try to lessen the counts against him. You'll get Heather back with no problem now."

She pivoted around. Her mouth opened and pursed closed. She looked at him as if he'd grown fangs.

"Cassie, what's wrong?" Once again he reached for her, only to catch air. He stepped in front of her. "I thought you'd be more happy."

"And fall into your arms again!" She pushed past him on her way to the kitchen, nearly knocking him over with the force of her words. The teapot slammed on the stove.

What did she mean by that remark? He followed her into the kitchen and watched her select a teabag and a cup, then put water on to boil. She crossed her arms and seemed mesmerized by the blue gas flame.

He tensed. "I'll get a signed confession from Dylan about your rape if that's what you're angry about."

"Dylan will try every trick to get out of charges. He'll never confess," she spat, still engrossed in the flames.

He spun her to face him. "I'll get him to confess." Give him two minutes alone in the interrogation room.

The kettle hissed and she turned the burner off. She didn't brew the tea.

She moved to the living room and started pacing circles again. He'd hold her all night if necessary until she believed him. "You're tired. You need some rest. You'll feel better in the morning."

"You're right. I need rest." Her shoulders heaved. Her face was white, her eyes glistening emeralds. "Evan, I appreciate all you've done for me, but as I told you earlier, I think it's best if we didn't see each other anymore." Her lips trembled as she spoke.

A block of ice settled in his stomach. He'd missed something important.

"What's this really about?"

"I should think it's obvious."

"No, it's not," he growled, feeling the same sense of dread he'd felt five minutes before the IED went off.

"From the beginning——I have a business to run and a daughter to think about."

He understood and nodded.

"I have to focus all my energy on Heather. I appreciate all you've done and I owe you my life but I'd like to part on good terms."

"What the hell are you talking about?" Was this delayed shock from all she's been through? He gripped her arms and pulled her off the floor.

She winced. Tears spilled down her face. "Still not clear enough?" she whispered, her green eyes glaring.

"Clear? I have no idea what you're talking about."

She looked at his hands on her arms. He set her down, but wasn't about to let her go.

"You did a great job rescuing me, Evan. Everything is taken care of. It's time to part, as friends."

His jaws clamped so hard, his teeth ached. His hands fell by his sides, then fisted. "You're upset about the tape. You need to calm down."

"I am calm. This isn't—" Her voice faltered, and she put her face in her hands.

"Honey, whatever's bothering you—" He stepped toward her again.

She straight-armed him. "Don't. I mean it, Evan. I know I owe you a lot, but we both know this is over. Please don't make this any harder."

Her words made Dylan's right jab seem like a caress. His frown stretch to his jaw. If his arms hadn't locked, he'd have turned and punch a hole in a wall.

He still couldn't move a muscle while he

watched her walk to the front door and open it. Her face turned to alabaster, devoid of any warmth or love, only emptiness shone in her eyes.

He crossed the room and sat on the couch. "I'm not leaving. Something's been different since this morning. I'm not a mind reader. I'm not leaving until you tell me what I've done."

She glanced at his jacket, carelessly thrown over the back of the rocking chair. It was a quick glance, but long enough for him to understand. His letter about the Albany job was in the pocket. He exhaled, and his muscles uncoiled.

"Come over here. Tell me what's wrong."

Perplexed at his calm, she moved within reach. He snatched her by her cold fingers and pulled her onto his lap. Her feeble resistance was no match for his strength and he trapped her in his arms.

Twin red blotches brightened her cheeks. She heaved in anger, arms crossed over her breast, green eyes shooting daggers. "When were you going to tell me you're going to Albany?"

His fingers kneaded her tense back muscles. He wouldn't sleep tonight until he'd massaged her from head to toe. "Who told you I'm going to Albany?"

"No one." She pointed to his jacket. "I found your transfer papers on the floor. How could you take that job? How can you leave me when I love you."

He leaned back, searching the expression on her face.

He'd only fantasized about hearing her say those words. "*You* love me?"

"Of course I do. At least one of us has the guts to say it." She punched his chest.

He laughed and covered her fist. "You think I can't say it? Or, do you think I can't say it to *you*."

She looked about ready to lop off his head. Her chin quivered and her lips parted. He rubbed his thumb over her lower lip to stop her reply.

"When I was in Iraq, I never stopped thinking of you. I kissed your lips a million times. At night, I replayed every sexy sigh you made when you were in my arms. I made love to you more times than I can count. My battalion was blocked from communication with the outside world but every day I wrote you a letter in my mind. Thoughts of you kept me sane when I should have lost my mind. When I came back to the States, my mind still resided in a burned-out hole in the desert. I'm still messed up at times, but I'm getting better." He exhaled and pushed a strand of hair behind her ear.

She touched his hand to keep it there. "That explains the pillows on the couch."

He nodded, feeling his chest swell with the look of love in her eyes.

"Oh, Evan. I wrote you every day. All my letters were returned. I went insane worrying about you."

He picked up her hand. "We were so deep undercover that our orders prohibited mail. If you still have them, I'd like to read them."

"I saved them all." She turned her head and kissed his palm.

He continued. "Yesterday at the cabin, you looked like you belonged in my home. You'd always lived there in my mind. In my kitchen. In the living room. Lying in my arms before the fire or sleeping in my bed. And I felt like the luckiest guy alive."

He looked down, finding it hard to speak. "For a long time, I've thought about retiring from police work. Start that outdoor outfitter business Clay and I always talked about. Settle in one place and try to have some kids. A dream I thought I'd lost. As corny as this sounds, I fell in love with you the first moment I saw you, and I knew I'd love you the rest of my life. No other woman will do."

He reached inside his pocket and opened up his transfer papers. "I thought we'd burn these transfer papers in the fireplace tonight when I told you I wasn't taking the Albany job. But most of all, I thought I would make love to you and tell you how much I love you, how much I need you in my life, and now that I've got you, I'll never let you go."

She smiled and tilted her head. "All this time you've loved me?"

He nodded. "Believe me when I say there will never be a time I won't love you."

She took the papers from his hands. "I have a gas stove. We can still have that party."

He took them from her hand. "Right now, I've a better idea."

He kissed her with all the love that flowed through his body. No fire could match the one that kindled in his soul, fanned by his love... for Cassie.

Chapter Twenty-Four

The following Friday Cassie tallied her weekly sales and nearly cart-wheeled down the main aisle. More and more orders phoned in every day, not from police officers' wives, but from people who'd attended the wedding and friends of friends. She talked to a newspaper rep about an ad. At this rate, she'd be able to hire a few employees. Evan went to Albany to work for two weeks while they found a replacement. Butterflies in her tummy reminded her that he planned to visit her tonight. Thanks to a special court decree, Heather would join them for the weekend.

That creepy feeling she'd felt all week must have been nerves.

At five-thirty there was one chore to do before closing at six. A shadow loomed over her as she stood at the cash register. Odd, she didn't here the chimes. "Can I help you...You!"

"Hey, pretty lady. Glad you remember me. Your boyfriend made a mess of things. But you're gonna fix everything for Ole Stoney. Now, where's the money."

Anger surged through her body. "Listen carefully, *Ole Stoney*. There is no money. Dylan lied to you."

"Yeah, he never told me about the tape, too. It's worth more to his partners. Stupid dick thought I was working for him. But you're gonna get me both."

"The police have the tape."

"Nice try. You haven't moved from this place in days. Let's go."

Evan was due in about two hours. Heather, any minute. She had to get him out of there. "It's over. Dylan confessed about his partners to save his neck."

"You don't tell on these partners."

"The police are looking for you, so I suggest you leave because I'm expecting my boyfriend any minute."

"In that case, we'd better move." He pulled a gun from his pocket and pointed at her chest.

The gleeful look in his eyes told her he wasn't kidding. When her legs buckled, she grabbed the edge of the counter and managed to press the alarm button under the counter. She had no choice but to play along, or end up with a bullet.

"My cabin keys are in the drawer. I'll take you there on one condition. You have to promise you'll let me go. I have a young daughter." As she pulled open the counter drawer with one hand, she knocked over the bottle of hand lotion with the other. "Oops." The lotion spilled on the counter and into the drawer over her kisses. One lotion smeared hand shook her register keys in front of his face, while the other palmed some kisses and slipped them in her pocket. At least Evan would know where to find her body.

The phone rang.

"I saw you push the alarm. Let's get moving. Trust me, money's not worth dying over."

Stone drove. He was too agreeable and she feared what he'd do when he didn't find any money.

This time of year the sun set early, before five. If she could distract him she might be able to escape and lose him in the woods again. But last time she had Evan to help her survive. A cold sweat slicked her back. She had one chance.

At the cabin, the car rolled to a stop and she ran.

"I've used this gun on women before." To prove it, he fired. The shot split the night.

She skidded to a halt and turned with her hands up in the air. "It's not here." She shouted between hot gulps of air. "I buried it in the woods. Not too far from here."

"Sure you did. Come back here. There's no hurry to find it tonight. Let's go inside and have that talk we started last time, before your boyfriend busted in. I haven't seen him around your place. He leave you?"

She was too scared to answer.

"Ah, he did. Thanks to you, I haven't had me a girlfriend in some time. If you're really nice to me, I'll keep you around, rather than kill you."

The blood rushed to her feet. She'd rather die with a bullet in her back. Tears welled in her eyes and she thought of how much pain her death would cause Heather. Her poor baby. She'd miss her so much. And Evan...

She reached in her pocket and dropped some kisses to mark her direction. Then she pivoted and sprinted as fast as she could into the blackness.

****

Half way home, Evan got the dispatch from Tony that the silent alarm had been pushed at 5:41 PM, in Cassie's shop. He turned on the siren and cruised at ninety-five mph on the New York State Thruway, heading West. Within minutes he approached the Utica exit.

"Evan, she's not at the store," Tony said over the radio. The professional in Evan knew to keep his head, the first hours in a kidnapping meant life or death for the victim. The man in love was terrified.

"Any signs of a struggle?"

"Nothing.... except the counter drawer was found open and a bottle of hand lotion spilled inside."

"The register counter?"

"Yeah. Looks like some lotion on the counter spilled in the drawer all over some foil—no, it looks like Cassie stashed those chocolate kisses."

The burst of adrenaline pumped through Evan muscles so fast he fought to stay seated. "I know where she is. Get a helicopter out to that cabin at Snowflake Lake, Adirondack Park."

"Where we found you the last time?"

"Yeah. Contact the Remsen station to meet me on Mills road. Set up a road block on the turn off for 28 north. I'm nearing Utica. If traffic's light, I'll be at the lake in thirty minutes. How much time has passed since the alarm?"

Tony paused and talked to someone else. "About a half-hour, give or take ten minutes."

"Good. Snowflake Lake is about sixty minutes from Syracuse, but a half hour from Utica. I may beat them there. "

"You think Stone's got her?"

"Yep. That's why she took him there." Smart thinking on Cassie's part. She bought herself some time.

"It'll be dark by then," Tony added.

"Have Mobile Response prepare for a night rescue."

****

The sound of the helicopter made Stone look up. Cassie whirled around and then headed into the woods behind the cabin. A shot fired and whizzed past her, splintering the bark of the nearby pine tree. She ducked and moved her feet as fast and carefully as possible. The helicopter skimmed a light on the ground.

Another shot sprayed the ground next to her. Pieces of rock stabbed her leg. She heard Stone crashing through the brush behind her. Gaining? She thought she felt fingers touch her shoulder. A stitch tugged at her side but she kept her feet moving.

The helicopter light focused on a cluster of rocks up ahead. A place to hide? On either side, trees were too dense to navigate. She had no choice. *Run for the rocks*, she commanded her aching legs. She slipped and paused to catch her breath for a second. She smelled water. Yes, now she heard gurgling water.

More shots fired. Stone cursed. "I'll kill you for leading the cops here."

Pebbles exploded off the boulder in front of her. Shards hit her face and stung. She'd lost a shoe and her ankle throbbed but she stayed moving and focused on one of the largest boulders. The smell of fish and decaying leaves intensified. She was close to water. Maybe she could hide by the shore.

She thought she heard her name being called but didn't stop. The ground around the boulder was sandy but firm. She scampered behind the biggest boulder and took a calming breath.

The ground crunched beneath her feet and then it wiggled before it slid away from the boulder. She fell backward and reached up, but grabbed nothing but air. Her arms flapped wildly by her sides as she dove backward. Her stomach dropped, like going down a tall elevator. The rotten smell and sound of rushing water grew louder.

Her back hit first with a painful force that shocked her system, followed by the knife-edge cold that robbed her breath as she sank. Icy water filled her mouth before it closed. Her nostrils burned and she twisted as fingers pulled her downward into

blackness.
Coldness.
Heather...Evan.
Nothing.

****

Evan threw the car door open and raced to the cabin. Locked and no sign of footprints.

He searched around, squinting in the darkness. The helicopter's light found him and he signaled to open a bigger radius around the cabin. He saw a silver reflection on the ground. Kisses? He motioned to the pilot to follow him and he took off in a dead run through the woods toward the sounds of running water. Stone's broad back appeared in the distance. Evan's heart nearly stopped when he heard the gunshots. Evan fired a shot at the ground behind Stone. The giant stopped firing and raised his arms.

The helicopter lowered a rope and two MRT men dropped from the chopper and restrained Stone. Evan signaled the chopper to move ahead. Cassie was somewhere in the darkness.

Running for her life.

Relief washed over him when her form appeared nearing an outcrop of boulders. "Cassie, stop!" he shouted, but the whipping of the chopper blades drowned him out. He saw her, illuminated for a second in the chopper spotlight, but then her arms wind-milled and she disappeared. He reached the boulder in time to see her hit the black water and disappear.

In rescue dive position, he jumped in and braced for the cold water to suck him under. Although prepared, the water stung like a thousand razors cuts and stole his breath.

His head popped above the surface. Had she surfaced? He listened for splashing water. Nothing. No time to waste. He submerged and grabbed for the bottom. Lake weeds slipped through his fingers. He

370

came up with fist of silt.

Another breath. Stay down longer.

He came up for another breath. Splashes. He had help.

The chopper lights scanned the water, lighting it for several feet down, and he re-submerged. He surfaced for a third time, coughing water. His mouth felt like he swallowed pins. He couldn't feel his legs. More lights shone from the top of the cliff, more men jumped in.

"Cassie! Where are you?"

Panic seized him and threatened to make him useless in the rescue. He imagined he heard her voice. Then he thought he saw something and dove for it. It was pitch black and he knew he probably conjured seeing her and was on the verge of losing it, but he pulled at something soft and began to lift it up. Someone swam next to him and helped him with the bundle. He broke the surface. The bundle was removed from his hands.

"No!"

"Let her go, Evan. We've got her."

The voice of one of his MRT trainees registered in his brain and he loosened his grip. He felt a stabbing pain in his chest that doubled him over, but managed to swim to the shore. He staggered toward his men as they bent over Cassie's body. He needed to get to her, tried to push them aside, but his arms didn't work. He had to help her, to keep her warm. His teeth rattled together. He took several gulps of air, then collapsed to the ground at her side. "Cassie. Wake up!"

"Sergeant Jorgenson, you need to get in the ambulance. You're suffering from hypothermia."

His words slurred when he tried to object. "I w-ant to s-ee Cassie."

"She's being taken care of, sir. We need to help you now."

"S-she...o-kay?" It became harder to speak, to think about anything but resting.

"I'm not sure, sir."

Like preparing for the head on collision when he was younger, he froze. He heard his mother screaming, then the sting of glass as it rained on his hands. He felt the fire lick his hands as he pulled his men from the burning Humvee. The air in his lungs burned like gasoline on hot coals. In the background he heard his dad screaming, "No!"

Epilogue

The sun shone like a white marble in the center of an iris blue sky. A warm afternoon for early November. Many people drifted to Lake Placid again for one last hike before the snow came. Looking back, for years he hadn't noticed his surrounding, simply existed, until the day he saw Cassie on the summit of Mount Jo.

"I can touch the leaves," Heather said as she stretched up her arm. A few stubborn leaves flickered with her touch. The air filled with her musical giggles. So like her mother. Her laughter, her smile, her spirit.

"You sure can," Evan replied as he held his precious cargo on his shoulders. The twinge in his chest throbbed when he thought about his new responsibility, but it was one he welcomed. He'd never let anything or anyone hurt Heather.

"I want Mommy to see me."

"She can, sweetie."

"Where is she? Up there?" Heather pointed up the path to the summit.

"No, sweetie. You've got the wrong direction. Your mommy isn't as quick as us." He turned

Heather around so she could see the top of an identical blonde head coming up the trail.

"What's the rush? Can't I ever climb this mountain at a leisurely pace? First Karen, now you."

"And me, Mommy. I want Evan to hurry up and—"

"Shhhh." Evan said, and turned around. Their two heads met for a moment.

When Evan turned her back around, Heather crossed her hands over her mouth.

"You're lucky Evan insisted you come along, missy. But you were supposed to hike up, not get a ride." Cassie said with a laugh.

"She's no problem." And to prove it, he reached up for Heather and hoisted her by the legs higher, causing both mother and daughter's laughter to ring out.

Only one thing would make Evan happier than being on Mount Jo with Cassie and Heather today. The thought made him replace Heather and aim his shoulders up the trail. He needed to get to the summit, fast.

The sight of Heather with Evan swelled Cassie's heart. Thanks to Evan and an understanding judge, Heather was home at last. She'd bruised her arms from pinching herself.

Evan was hers, too. He told her he loved her so often that she accused him of being the most romantic man in the world. He had an occasional nightmare but was no longer afraid he might hurt her unconsciously and slept in peace.

They stopped again, not to let her catch up, but to point to a fat squirrel jumping from branch to branch. Good thing. She'd recovered fully from her fall but tired so easily lately. Heather clapped her hands when the squirrel jumped and held onto a branch upside down.

Evan turned and smiled. The big, beautiful,

golden man that stole her heart had given his in return. They'd have a good life together, one filled with love and trust and friendship.

The summit of Mount Jo was unchanged except for fewer visitors. She inhaled the smell of fresh sun-washed air, thick with the smell of earth and pine.

"Cassie, over here. Take a picture of Heather and me with Heart Lake in the background." Evan said.

"Okay."

After several adjustments, Cassie had the perfect shot.

"Ready, Mommy?"

"Say cheese."

Evan looked up at Heather as she clicked the picture.

"Evan, don't move. I'm taking another one." Cassie looked through the viewfinder to see Evan staring at the camera with a huge, loving smile. This time Heather said something to Evan before the picture clicked.

"Heather, don't look down. One more try, you two." She looked through the viewfinder and Heather's arms were extended. She held something in her little hands.

Cassie lowered the camera to look closer.

"Look what Evan bought, Mommy. It's a shiny ring. He says if we'll have him, he'd like to marry us. Can we?"

The breath whooshed out of her lungs but that didn't stop her from running up to Evan's open arms shouting, "Yes, yes."

Heather clapped her hands and Evan set Heather down in time to catch Cassie and twirl her around. Then he took the ring out of the box and got down on one knee.

"You're the love of my life. Marry me?"

The diamond ring slid on her finger before she

replied. She nodded, unable to speak past the catch on her throat. Sunlight reflected off his hair, the light of her life. They were going to be a family. Only one other thing would make her world more complete, and she suspected that miracle would happen, too.

"Took you long enough to get up here." Tony's voice bellowed from behind a group of saplings. Then he pointed behind him.

"But it was worth it. It was the most beautiful proposal I've ever heard." A package of tissues covered Karen's mouth. She hugged Cassie. "I'm so happy for you, sweetie." Her tears mingled with Cassie's.

Heather ran up to the boys, who broke free of Karl's grasp. "We're getting married," she shouted. They both frowned, and one said, "I'd rather eat worms."

"Hey, let's get a picture of the three of you by Heart Lake," a distinctly male, but unfamiliar voice shouted from behind Karl.

A tall, rakishly handsome man with a lock of hair over one eye walked up to Cassie. He looked her over before speaking. "You realize you have to put up with his mule-headedness. He never looses an argument. And he's a neat freak."

Cassie was immediately engulfed by Clay's long arms. "You have the better part of the deal, Evan. You're lucky you saw her first." Clay pulled her back and kissed her on the cheek. "I'm very happy to meet you."

Evan turned to Clay. "The store will be open by spring. I can't do the white water rafting and hiking trips all by myself."

"Yeah, yeah, yeah. I'm blind in one eye not deaf, Ev. I'm thinking about it."

While the group clustered together, Evan pulled Cassie aside. They walked over to the edge and Evan pointed in the distance. "I never saw that heart until today," he said.

"Me too."

Evan hugged her closer. "I guess you have to be in love to see it."

She nodded as his lips came down on hers for the sweetest kiss, sweeter than any chocolate in the world.

A word about the author...

After her fifth grade class made a mockery of her first dramatic play, Susan gave up writing in favor of painting and playing the guitar. Years later, the stressed scientist and mother of two bought her first romance novel on a whim, and was instantly hooked. She began writing for pleasure, until she discovered a local chapter of RWA and honed her craft. The scientist-turned-science-teacher spends her days teaching the laws of nature, and evenings penning modern day damsel-in-distress stories that will satisfy any romantic sweet tooth.

Visit Susan at www.susanstthomas.com

Or her Blog at:
www.susanstthomas.blogspot.com